THE EXPIRATION
of
JOEY AND MEGAN

A Tony Piza Novel

J.F. Pandolfi

L & A
Publications

For Mom

Judge R. Terrance Williams was on the verge of climbing onto his court bench and hurling himself at Seth Kaplowitz. A robed missile intent on relieving the aggressive young lawyer of his larynx.

That's how it looked to Tony Piza as he sat at the plaintiff's counsel table. He only remembered seeing the normally even-keeled judge this rankled once before, when a woman representing herself in the final hearing of her settled divorce donned a red clown's nose each time her husband's attorney got up to speak. When the jurist directed the court officer to confiscate the prop (after his second admonition went unheeded) the defiant litigant shoved it down her blouse, where it stayed put for the remainder of the hearing.

Judge Williams rapped his gavel. "Enough, Mr. Kaplowitz! If you object one more time I'm going to hold you in contempt. And you're not going to just pay a fine. You're going to take up residence in the county jail for the evening. Are we clear, sir?"

Kaplowitz blinked a few times, as if coming out of a trance.

He stood there, draped in an ill-fitting dark-blue suit, sporting mid-length black hair that appeared to be the victim of a self-administered haircut or a distracted barber. It seemed to Piza that the tall, slender man was someone who either wasn't concerned with his appearance, or couldn't afford to do anything about it.

"Take a seat, counsel," the judge said, his tone calmer. "How long have you been practicing?"

"I was admitted to the bar last November, Your Honor. And I got a job with Nadia Bruzek and Associates end of February."

"So you only have a little over two months under your belt. Well, let me explain something to you. Histrionics is never a good idea, whether in a trial or a short and sweet, client-free motion hearing, like today. Now——"

"Excuse me, Your Honor, but with all due respect, what you call histrionics I prefer to think of as passion. My people have been battling injustice for thousands of years, long before Moses led the Exodus from Egypt. So fighting for what I believe is right is ingrained in me. I think people who haven't had to deal with a history of oppression sometimes can't relate to that."

The judge nudged his half-rim reading glasses to the tip of his nose and peered over them. "Mr. Kaplowitz, you do realize I'm Black, right?"

"Um, yes, Judge, now that you mention it. And, you know, I wasn't necessarily referring to you just then."

"Ah. Okay. Thanks for clearing that up. Anyway, for future reference, when a judge is rendering a decision, there's really no reason to object. And tossing in adverbs doesn't make it any more acceptable. The fact that you 'strongly' objected, 'strenuously' objected, 'vehemently' objected . . . it doesn't matter. Okay? So please, no more objecting."

"But, Judge——"

The jurist put up a hand. "No more interruptions. Period.

Now, as I was attempting to say before, the defendant in this matter filed a motion to reduce his alimony payments because, as stated in his affidavit"—picking up the document—"'he had a run of bad luck in Atlantic City'. Apparently to the tune of around thirty thousand dollars. Be that as it may, I don't believe his ex-wife should have to bear the burden of his self-inflicted misfortune. So I'm denying the motion."

Up rose Kaplowitz. "But it's a legitimate loss of funds on his part, Your Honor. In effect, you're penalizing him for exercising his right to take advantage of casino gambling here in New Jersey, which is perfectly legal."

"It *is* perfectly legal. Unfortunately, so is stupidity. So you might want to suggest to your client that he stick to the beach if he decides to visit AC again. Mr. Piza, anything you want to add?"

"No, I'm good, Judge."

"Okay then. Good morning, gentlemen."

When the two lawyers exited the courtroom, Kaplowitz started to walk away. "Hey," Piza said. "Hold up a minute." The young attorney turned around. "It's Seth, right?"

"Right," he answered with a glower.

"Do you mind if I give you a little advice?" Kaplowitz was still glaring, but didn't make a move to leave. "If you're with Bruzek's office, you're gonna be doing a lot of divorce work here in Bergen County. Which means you'll be appearing before the same six judges over and over. And they talk to each other. Believe me, you don't want to get a reputation as a pain in the ass. So you might consider turning it down a notch."

"I'm not going to sacrifice my principles to placate a judge."

There was as much weariness as frustration in Piza's voice. "Well, working for Bruzek, let's see how long your principles last." Kaplowitz looked like he was about to respond, but Piza cut him off. "But as for sacrificing those principles, I'm not suggesting you do that. And that judge, who happens to be one of the most astute and decent people you'll ever meet, certainly wasn't asking you to."

"Could've fooled me."

"Why, because he indirectly told you to stop making a fool of yourself? Look, you're bright, notwithstanding your little 'oppressed people' speech. The arguments you first made inside were creative and well thought out, despite the fact you pretty much didn't have a leg to stand on. But you lost any chance of scoring points when your arms started flapping and you almost caused poor Judge Williams to stroke out on the bench."

The other attorney's mouth twisted into a grimace.

"If your performance in there *was* theatrics, then you'd be wise to heed what the judge said. But if it wasn't . . . if it really was passion, then that might be even worse, because it means you're letting it blur your objectivity. If you don't learn where to draw the line, you'll be hurting your clients. Not to mention that you'll be burned out before you know it. Lawyers aren't immune from the emotional toll divorce takes. Believe me. I've been doing this for nine years." He paused. "Anyway, that's my advice for the day."

Kaplowitz gave a slight, rigid nod and walked away.

"I'll be sure to give you a professional courtesy discount when I send you my bill," Piza called out.

The fledgling lawyer didn't bother to turn around.

Piza worked for the firm of Shapiro & Manetti, with offices in a converted nineteenth-century house in Hackensack, New Jersey. Its refurbished exterior—red brick, gray-shuttered windows, and pitched roof with two chimney stacks—remained true to the building's original design. The historically accurate facade belied a modern, practical interior that managed to be tasteful despite its heresy.

Sitting at his oak-colored desk made of the latest faux wood 1986 had to offer, a listless Piza thumbed through a stack of pink message slips.

He'd had one motion that day in addition to the one with Kaplowitz. Ordinarily, arguing a motion only took about fifteen minutes. So even if you had to appear before a couple of judges, you could usually get done early enough to spend a portion of those bi-weekly Friday mornings shooting the breeze in the courthouse coffee shop, returning to the office just in time to go to lunch.

But the lawyer on his other motion had gotten delayed at another courthouse, which resulted in him arriving barely in time for them to argue the motion before the twelve-thirty lunch break. The tedium of waiting—an ever-present malady associated with any kind of trial work—had drained Piza, and he'd decided to eat in.

The buzzing intercom jolted him from his quasi-stupor, and he jabbed at the blinking yellow button. "What's up, Cecilia?"

"You have a visitor, Tony," the receptionist replied.

Cecilia was the niece of one of the partners. Interacting with her was more a process than a simple exchange of information.

"Every time you say those words, Cecilia, it makes me feel like I'm either in prison or a hospital."

A giggle was the response.

"Does this visitor have an appointment?"

"Hold on. . . .No."

"Does he or she have a name?"

"Hold on. . . .He says his name is Joe Sabatini."

A chill ran through Piza as his grip on the phone tightened. Joey "Strikes" Sabatini. The author of one of the most painful moments in Piza's life.

The balls on this guy, showing up at my office. How'd he even know I was a lawyer? Through gritted teeth he said, "Tell him I'm unavailable. Now and in the future."

There was a brief pause. "Uh, he said he knows you probably hate him, but this is urgent. It's about his kids."

He has kids? Shit. "Fine, send him back."

CHAPTER 2

Joe Sabatini stood in the doorway of Piza's office.

The lawyer leaned back in his chair. Expressionless.

"So, can I come in?"

"That was kind of implied when I told Cecilia to send you back here. But if you'd like to stand there, that's fine with me."

The man entered the room and pulled out a chair in front of Piza's desk. Wearing a cautious smile as he sat down, he said, "I see you still have that nice full head of hair. Couple of grays mixed in with the brown, but it looks good. How are you, Tony?"

"I don't think that's any of your concern. And how did you know I was a lawyer?"

"Word gets around." He couldn't seem to get comfortable in his seat. "Look, I realize this is awkward for both of us, but I wouldn't be here if it wasn't important."

"It's not awkward for me," Piza lied. "But let's get something straight. If you hadn't said this has to do with your kids, we wouldn't be talking right now. How many do you have?"

Sabatini reached into his back pocket and extracted his

wallet. "Two," he said, opening it and taking out a picture. "Lisa and Amy."

Piza took the photo from the man's extended hand. "Beautiful girls." There was a trace of warmth. "How old?"

"Lisa's nine and Amy's six. They're my joy." With a terse, pathetic laugh he added, "About the only joy I have left."

"Meaning?" Piza said, irked by what he saw as a veiled plea for pity.

"Megan and I are separated, Tony." No reaction from the lawyer. Clearing his throat, Sabatini continued. "Uh, about six months now. You've read about the savings-and-loan problems, I assume."

"Of course. A lot of them are going under."

"Well, the banks knew the writing was on the wall long before now. My bank laid me off last June. I couldn't find work. And Megan hadn't been working since Lisa was born. She wanted to be a stay-at-home mom, which I was okay with. We were making ends meet. I don't know how much you know about the banking industry, but mid-level management doesn't pay a ton of money. I mean, I was moving up the ladder slowly but surely but. . . Anyway, after the bottom fell out all I had coming in was unemployment benefits, which was a joke."

He hesitated, eyeing his former friend. But if he was anticipating even a whiff of sympathy, he'd miscalculated the degree of Piza's bitterness.

Looking increasingly uncomfortable, he said, "Um, truth be told, Megan and I had been drifting apart for a while before all this other stuff happened. But when I got laid off, and the money problems started piling up, it was like everything came to a head, ya know?" Melancholy and puzzlement swept across his face. "I never would've imagined indifference could turn to hate so quickly." A brief silence segued to, "Anyway, she threw me out."

With a sardonic smile Piza said, "Not very Christian of her."

Sabatini smirked and shook his head. "How long you been waiting to unleash that one?"

"Don't flatter yourself, Strikes. I haven't spent a whole lot of time thinking about you."

"'Strikes'. Nobody's called me that since . . . well, the last time we were all together, back when."

"April ninth, 1974."

"Jesus. You remember the exact date."

Piza's eyes narrowed and his cheeks flushed. "You're damn right I remember the date. It's not every day someone destroys a lifelong friendship. And for what? Because Frankie had the courage to come out? Trusted us to accept it? And don't forget what you—"

"Wait a minute! You know damn well why I walked away. I believed homosexuality was a sin, just like I told all of you that night. And did you ever think that maybe I was the one who felt let down? By Frankie? And you, Jeff, and Sal? No one even trying to see my side? It was—"

"Oh bullshit. Cut the act. I know you were always more religious than the rest of us, but for as long as we knew each other you never said a word about feeling like that. And the more I thought about that epically shitty night, the more I realized you made a conscious choice in that bar. You didn't wanna have to deal with your holy-roller wife about this. So you bailed. Face it, Strikes, you're a spineless prick."

Sabatini gulped and looked away. A few moments later, his voice tremulous and barely above a whisper, he said, "We— We should have talked about this a long time ago. All of us."

"Why? You made your position clear. What good would—"

"No. Listen to me. You're right. What you just said." He ran a hand through thinning blond hair. "I've turned it over in my mind again and again, Ton. I think that in that moment, I knew how fiercely Megan would react when she heard. I mean, even if

I didn't say anything, it would only be a matter of time before word got out. Do you realize the bind that would've put me in?"

Piza understood what he meant. But he wasn't about to let him off the hook. "What 'bind'? What're you talking about?"

"C'mon, Tony. You guys never liked Megan. That bothered me, sure, but it never got in the way of our friendship. But this? How she'd feel about Frankie? You'd never forgive her for that. So what was I supposed to do, never mention her name again? Walk on eggshells every time I was with you guys? And what about my relationship with *her*? Was I supposed to lie to her every time I wanted to hang out with you guys? Because I knew she'd be upset if she thought Frankie was gonna be there, as irrational as that might be? I was in a hopeless position. I knew it as soon as the words came out of Frankie's mouth."

The man went silent and pressed his palms to his forehead, kneading the flesh with an intensity that exposed the depth of his distress. But Piza remained dispassionate. He possessed a capacity for analytical detachment that could sometimes graze the edge of cold-heartedness. When he first recognized it, in his mid-teens, it had unsettled him. It was a trait he believed betrayed his Catholic upbringing. But for the past nine years he'd come to see it as an asset; a tool of the trade, to be used as he deemed appropriate.

Sabatini's hands dropped to his lap. "You see it, Ton, right? How it was a no-win situation for me? I made the choice to keep the peace at home. And I used religion as a cop-out." He paused. "By the time I realized it was the *wrong* choice, too much time had passed to make things right with you guys. In *my* mind at least. You gotta believe that." The desperation in his eyes morphed into sadness, and his body sagged in the chair. "I wrecked a friendship that was one of the best things in my life."

After a few moments, a skeptical Piza asked, "So when did you experience this come-to-Jesus epiphany? Irony fully intended."

The banker shrugged and looked past him. "I'm not sure,

exactly. All I know is that for a long time I felt something was off in my life . . . besides my relationship with Megan."

Breaking the resulting silence, Piza said, "It is what it is. But if you're looking for absolution, your conversation needs to be with Frankie."

"If he'll even talk to me."

"Well, I'll leave that to you to work out. Now, what is it about your daughters you came to see me about?"

"I told Megan I want a divorce. You know, a clean break. Well, you can imagine how that went over. Catholic Church says no. End of discussion. But—"

The lawyer lifted a hand. "Not to cut you off, but have you considered marriage counseling?"

"Yeah. We tried that. Couple of sessions. But things were too far gone. Anyway, I kept pushing the divorce issue, and now Megan's threatening not to let me see the girls if I pursue it."

"Well, if that happens you'll have to get her into court right away. I know you guys moved out of Carteret in '75. To Avenel? Iselin?"

"Iselin. But—"

"I can ask around about lawyers down there to refer—"

"No, you don't understand. I'm up here now. Bergen County. I landed a job with a bank in Paramus in January. Friend of my father knew a guy. Tough going back to managing a dinky branch office but, ya know. . . I got a studio apartment in Lodi. Size of a closet, but the rent was right. I moved there when I got the new job. So can't we do something up here?"

"You can. I can recommend several good lawyers around here. Give me your phone number and I'll have my secretary—"

"Can't you represent me?"

"Are you kidding?" Piza said, his face contorted in disbelief. "Despite your alleged conversion, we're not friends. I don't wish you any harm, but there's no way in hell I'd represent you."

Fists clenched, Sabatini replied, "You think this is easy for me? To come here practically begging for help?" He closed his eyes for a few seconds in an apparent attempt to calm himself. "No matter what you may think of *me*, I trust you, Tony. And I know I'd never have that with another lawyer, especially after the way my sister got hosed in her divorce. You remember, right? When we were in college? That piece of shit shyster bled Gina dry, then sold her down the river."

"Do you honestly think I'd refer you to someone like that?"

The chastened-looking man said, "No. Not really. But Tony, it's my kids. I can handle a war, if that's what it comes down to. But I'm scared to death of what it might do to *them*. And I know in my heart you'd do anything you could to protect a child. So please, won't you at least sleep on it?"

A ten-minute conversation wasn't about to erase twelve years of resentment for Piza. Plus he couldn't help but feel that taking Sabatini's case would betray Frankie Falco, his closest friend since grammar school.

Yet, he knew that no child—whatever the age—walks away from a divorce completely unscathed. But a lawyer's approach to the case can make all the difference in the amount of damage inflicted. The image of those two innocent girls weighed on him. "Fine. I'll think about it. For your children's sake. And no promises."

"I understand. And I really appreciate it. And look, if you wanna talk to Frankie about this, it's fine. I get it." He heaved a sigh. "Honestly, I really don't care who knows."

"Okay. Jot down your phone number, and I'll get back to you at some point next week."

I definitely need to run this by Frankie.

CHAPTER 3

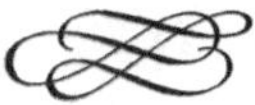

"On behalf of the residents of beautiful Carteret, New Jersey, I'm delighted to welcome you home," Frankie Falco said as he stood and hugged his friend of twenty-four years.

"Were you elected mayor since I saw you two months ago?" Piza responded with a smirk.

"No, just being my charming self. Besides, I don't have the stomach for politics." Casting a wary eye, he said, "Speaking of stomachs, how come you never seem to gain any weight?"

"Easy. Exercise, clean living and, unlike you, I don't put butter on every morsel that crosses my lips."

"Well, if that's your secret, you can keep it. And, just for the record, I don't put butter on *everything* I eat."

"Frankie, you spread it on hotdogs."

"Well, yeah, but that's for, ya know, like for lubrication. So I don't choke like I almost did when we were kids, if you recall. Besides, plumbers' union regs say we have to maintain a full-bodied appearance. Apparently, people trust you more if you're moderately overweight." He grinned and, catching the waitress's attention, held up two fingers.

Piza returned the grin and slid onto the cracked, red-vinyl bench seat. For him, sitting in a booth at Murp's held the comfort of slipping into an old coat, whose warmth is derived more from the memories it evoked than its worn-out material. The hometown bar's actual name was Murph's Pub. But Piza and his friends had long ago dubbed it Murp's, the result of the "h" in the neon sign only sporadically mustering the energy to glow. The fact that the tavern was the site of Joey Sabatini's ultimate act of betrayal hadn't diminished its status as the place to go for intense discussions, celebrations, or seeking solace.

"You been home yet?" Frankie said as the waitress set down two Heinekens.

"You guys want something to eat?" the woman asked.

Frankie looked at his friend, who shook his head. "Not for me, thanks. I'm having dinner at my parents."

"We're good, Vera. Thanks," Frankie replied.

The two men clinked bottlenecks. "In answer to your question," Piza said, "no, I haven't seen my parents yet. I came straight here. I'm sleeping over there tonight anyway."

Frankie drew back in exaggerated shock. "What? A Saturday evening without the oh-so-lovely Mandy? Am I sniffing trouble in paradise?"

"Well, clearly you've been sniffing something, wiseass, if you think there's a problem with our relationship. If you must know, she's got a bridal shower tonight."

Wincing, Frankie said, "Oh, that's not good. Starts giving them ideas. Next thing you know you'll be finding bride magazines and stuff strategically placed around her apartment."

"First of all, Mandy's not like that. She's not big on subtlety. Second, we've only been going out seven months."

"Well, that may be. But she's only two years younger than you, right? Thirty-two? That old biological clock's gotta be ticking just a little louder." Piza shook his head and rolled his eyes. "Make all the faces you want, Ton. Just don't say I didn't warn ya. Anyhow, you said in your mysterious phone call you had some news you wanted to talk about in person. So what gives?"

After a quick, furtive scan of the room, Piza lowered his voice and said, "You'll never guess who I saw yesterday."

Frankie checked the room as well and leaned in. "Bigfoot? Is that why you're kind of whispering?"

Piza's burst of laughter was followed by, "I don't know why I just did that." Taking a sip of beer, he said, "Strikes."

Frankie straightened in his seat. "Strikes? Where'd you see him?"

"He came to my office."

The plumber looked incredulous. "Holy crap! What'd he want?"

"Did you know he and Megan were separated?"

"No. Not a clue."

"Yeah, about six months. He got laid off from that bank he was at, and he couldn't find work for a while. Apparently things weren't that great between them before that, and when the money problems hit, everything went south. She booted him out of the house. He finally got a job in a bank in Paramus, and he's living in some dinky apartment in Lodi."

"Oh, geez, that's not far from Hackensack, right?"

"Next town over. Also borders Hasbrouck Heights."

With a grin Frankie said, "So he's close to your apartment too. Lucky you."

"Thanks. Not that I told him where I live."

"So did he want some legal advice? That why he came to see you? I didn't think he'd have the balls."

Piza arched his eyebrows. "It's more than that. He wants to file for divorce, and he wants me to represent him."

"*What?* I assume you told him no freakin' way. Not after some of the shit he said to you that night."

"Well, it's not that simple. He's got two kids."

"Really? I had no idea."

"Me either but, yeah, little girls. He showed me a picture. Beautiful kids. Anyway, he claims that if he goes through with filing for divorce, Megan's threatening to keep them away from him. Not that she legally could, but it could get ugly fast if she tries. He said he doesn't wanna go to any other lawyer, because of what happened to his sister. You remember that fiasco. So apparently he only trusts *me*. Or so he says."

"Well, he's right about trusting you. You wouldn't let what happened get in the way of doing your job. But even so. . ."

"No, I hear ya. And believe me, I'm not sure I wanna take this on. But I definitely wasn't gonna do anything until I spoke to you. I just said I'd think about it. And if you don't want me to do it, that's the end of that."

With a warm smile Frankie said, "I appreciate that, Ton. But it's not my place to weigh in on this. What happened sucked, but it was a long time ago. Don't get me wrong, I sure as hell haven't forgotten. But I've got a good thing going with Roger now. I'm happy. At this point, I kinda wanna leave the past in the past. So whatever you decide to do, I'm fine with it."

"You're a good man, Falco. Next round's on me." He signaled the waitress.

"Not gonna say no to that. So, how's he look?"

"Pretty good. Little bit of a paunch, but he's tall enough so it's not the first thing you notice. Hair's thinning. And he grew a mustache. Probably to compensate for the hair loss."

That drew a laugh. "Does he still bowl?"

Through a shrug Piza said, "Got me. But he said nobody's called him 'Strikes' since that night."

"Guess the name got buried with the friendship."

Piza was ten minutes late as he pulled into the driveway of his parents' house. Seeing his mother, Mary, peeking through the living room curtains, only to vanish as he extinguished the headlights, he laughed under his breath. *Some things never change.*

As he crossed the threshold into the entry hall, he was met by the aroma of broiling sirloin, followed immediately by a body blow from a charging Patty Piza, his younger sister.

"Tony, you're home," she gushed as she wrapped her arms around his waist. Her speech was slightly distorted by Down syndrome, her condition severe enough to leave her with the intelligence of a seven-year-old.

He kissed the top of her head. "Are you trying to knock me back into the driveway?"

"You're funny, Tony." Unsuccessfully trying to stifle a grin, she said, "You better not call me Peppermint Patty."

"Okay, I won't call you Peppermint Patty . . . Peppermint Patty."

The twenty-nine-year-old laughed and slapped her thighs. "I knew you were gonna do that. You're sneaky, Tony."

He ruffled her short, graying hair. Yet again he noted that she looked years older than she was, an observation that always induced a conflicting blend of heartache and clinical fascination. Turning her forward and standing behind her, he placed his hands on her shoulders, and they marched to the kitchen. A parade of two.

He greeted his mother and kissed her on the cheek as she poured olive oil into a salad. He decided not to call her on the curtain spying, knowing she'd deny it and dismiss any implication that she'd been worried.

"Anthony. You finally decided to show up. After all these years I still don't understand how someone so smart can't tell time. If these steaks are tough, it's your fault. *And* your father's. He only got in five minutes before you. No doubt about who you take after. You lose weight since whenever the last time I saw you was?"

"No, Ma. And it was only three weeks ago. I thought Pop was gonna start closing the store an hour or so earlier on Saturdays."

"He says he changed the time on the sign, but people keep showin' up last minute, with that pitiful look in their eyes. 'Oh please, Angelo, I just need a pound of prosciutto. And maybe a half-pound of provolone. Only take a minute, I swear.' And you know him. Mr. I-can't-say-no-to-nobody."

"That's true. But that's what makes him so lovable." He smiled. "Just ask him. He'll tell you."

"You guys talkin' about me again?" Angelo Piza entered the kitchen and hugged his son. "You look good, Anthony. Keepin' in shape."

"Trying to, Pop. Not that easy though. How're you doing? You look tired. I don't know how you keep schlepping back and forth to the Bronx six days a week."

"I look tired 'cause I'm old. When you're old, even when you're *not* tired you look tired."

"What 'old'?" Mary said. "You're only sixty-eight."

"Sixty-nine in a couple'a months," the man replied. "Old."

"Well, I'm sixty-seven. So I'm old too?"

"'Course not. Women don't age like men do. Totally different." He winked at his son.

"Wink all ya want, you're still in trouble."

"No, Pop's right, Ma. I remember reading something about that in a scientific journal. Last year I think it was."

"And what scientific journal was that, may I ask?"

"I believe it was the *Sports Illustrated Swimsuit Edition*."

Angelo laughed out loud, and Mary gave her son a snide smile. "Very funny, wiseguy. Carry these mashed potatoes into the dinin' room before everythin' gets cold."

Over dinner, Piza filled them in on his meeting with Sabatini, and his discussion with Frankie. He hadn't gone into great detail twelve years earlier, when telling them about the falling-out. They'd learned that Frankie was gay, and Strikes couldn't deal with it. They didn't know that Sabatini had goaded their son that night, implying that Angelo and Mary wouldn't let Frankie back into their house once they found out. That moment was the closest Piza had ever come to hitting a friend, choosing instead to tell him to "get the fuck out" of Murp's. He hadn't been sure how deeply Sabatini's sentiment would hurt his parents, and he'd had no intention of finding out.

"Such a shame," Angelo said. "See a marriage break up like that. Especially with little kids. But hey, these days it's happenin' everywhere you look."

His son nodded. "You got that right, Pop. Probably around fifty percent. And never mind the people who stay together even though they're miserable. Lot of unhappiness out there."

"Sometimes I think young people today don't try hard enough," Mary observed. "They think everythin' is gonna be all lovey-dovey, and when they realize it ain't, they give up. You gotta work at it. I guess a lotta people don't wanna do that. I dunno." After a few silent moments, she said, "Okay, enough with the gloom and doom. Who's ready for dessert?"

As she and Patty went to retrieve the coffee, coconut custard pie, and eclairs, Angelo and Piza cleared the table.

"What I said before, Pop, about you looking tired? Have you considered slowing down a little? Maybe close the store on Mondays, so you have a couple of days rest."

"Stop worryin', Anthony. I'm in great shape for an old guy." He flexed his muscles. "You should look this good at my age."

"I hope I do. But still. . ."

"I'll be fine. So, anyways, whaddya think you're gonna do? You gonna take Joey's case?"

"You think I should?"

"I ain't sayin' one way or the other." The fingers of his right hand got lost in thick white hair as he scratched his head. "I dunno. It's just that this thing between you guys and Joey happened a long time ago. And from what you said, it don't seem Frankie would mind. Maybe it's time to make peace."

"I dunno, Pop. I hear what you're saying, but there just might be too much baggage here to deal with." He followed up a sigh with, "To tell you the truth, these divorce cases are starting to wear me down. I think I'd like to concentrate more on regular trial work. Less emotionally draining."

"How would your bosses feel about that?"

"Not sure. There's only two of us in the office who do matrimonial work, so they'd have to hire another associate. As much as they like me, I don't know if that's a viable option." He shrugged. "But, I'll cross that bridge when I come to it. As far as this thing with Strikes, I'll give it more thought. I told him I'd get back to him sometime next week. So I've got time to mull it over."

Actually, he'd only have until Monday.

CHAPTER 4

The double-tap on the car horn was Joe Sabatini's third attempt to have his wife send out their two children. That was the deal. Sunday at ten forty-five he'd pull up in front of their house, beep, and the kids would bolt out the front door to spend the day with him. He'd have liked to pick them up earlier, but Megan insisted they attend nine o'clock mass with her. Up until that morning, the weekly transition had gone smoothly.

"What the hell is going on here?" he muttered as he exited the car and slammed the door. Making his way up the decaying driveway, he bent down, picked up an abandoned hula hoop, and tossed it onto the lawn. He could hear the doorbell ring as he thumbed the plastic white button, but he didn't detect any movement in the house. A thirty-second wait led to another attempt, again without success.

Her car's here. I hope to hell nothing...

He fumbled to isolate the front door key on his key ring and was about to insert it in the lock, when the door opened half-way and a grim-faced Megan stood there. "What are you doing here, Joey?"

Taken aback, he said, "What are you talking about? It's Sunday. Why *wouldn't* I be here?"

"Because the girls don't feel well. I left you a message."

"When?"

"This morning, after mass. They looked a little flushed when we left church, and I didn't wanna take any chances. There's a bug going around."

"You called after mass? Mass doesn't end until ten, and I'm already on the road by then. You know it takes me at least forty minutes to get here. Did you take their temperature?"

"Of course I did."

What minimal patience he had was quickly evaporating. "And?"

"And they were normal. But like I said, I didn't wanna take any chances. Maybe you should consider getting a beeper, so I can—"

"I want to see them," he said as he pushed open the door and strode past her into the living room.

"Hey! You're not supposed to be in here."

"Girls," he called out, making his way toward the staircase leading upstairs. "Girls. Daddy's here."

The petite woman caught up and planted herself in front of him. "You're not supposed to be in here, Joey. You don't live here anymore, remember?"

"I may not live here, but it's still my damned house as much as yours. And I can come back any time I want. I only left to keep the peace, and you know it. So don't tell me what I can or can't—" He stopped as his daughters appeared at the top of the stairs, holding hands. Six-year-old Amy gave a timid wave. "Hey, you guys." A broad grin swept away the darkness that had clouded his face seconds before. "Come on down and give me a hug."

Amy looked at her sister, as if seeking direction. The older girl's uneasy expression held no answers.

"What's going on, Megan? What have you—" He looked up at the girls. "You don't have to be afraid to come down. Lisa. Amy. It's me."

Lisa moved down one step, and Amy followed. Their father's smile must have alerted Megan, who turned toward them with a faltering shake of her head; just enough to stop them in place. "I — I told you, Joey. They don't feel well. And you need to leave. Please."

The man eyed his daughters and said, "Do you guys really feel sick?" His tone was harsher than he'd intended. Lisa's eyes welled up, and Amy was now whimpering.

"Oh my God, Joey. Is this what you want? To traumatize our kids?"

"I'm sorry, you guys. Daddy didn't mean to yell like that," he said, extending his right arm toward them. An entreaty for forgiveness. "Tell you what, you stay there and I'll come up to you. We'll sit on the stairs and talk." He locked eyes with his wife and murmured, "Please get out of the way, Megan."

"No. I, I won't. I—"

She gasped as he gripped both her arms enough to lift her and set her to the side. "Stay right there, girls," he said with a forced grin. "Here I come, and I've got"—in a high-pitched voice —"Tootsie Pops." As anxious as he was to reach his daughters, who looked confused by what they'd just witnessed, he took pains not to bound up the stairs, afraid it would startle them. As he reached them, they wiped their eyes and hugged him. Smiles appeared as he plucked the candy from his pocket.

He peered down the staircase. His wife hadn't moved, and seemed to be staring into space. Then she gazed in his direction, her expression more revelation than fury. It knocked him off-kilter. He'd been girding himself for an attack. For all of Megan's demonstrable piety, she'd been known to fling the occasional inanimate object if angry enough. Instead, she headed toward the kitchen. Measured steps; no evidence of urgency. He wasn't sure what was going on, but he used the unexpected reprieve to coax the girls off the stairs and into their room.

He was desperate to learn what their mother may have told them to cause their reluctance to come downstairs. But he wasn't about to resort to interrogating his children. He sat cross-legged on the faded purple carpet. They immediately joined him, all of them sucking on Tootsie Pops and laughing at their garbled speech. After a couple of minutes, Amy retrieved Candy Land from the toy chest. Lisa reacted with a dramatic huff and her "I'm too big for this" face, but Sabatini knew she enjoyed the game as much as her sister did.

As the girls set up the board, he debated checking on Megan, but decided not to tempt fate.

Then he heard the first police siren.

CHAPTER 5

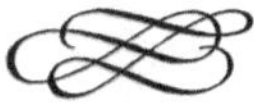

"What the hell is he doing here?" an irritated Piza snapped. He'd just gotten back to his office after an early-morning conference at the courthouse, and was looking forward to a quiet Monday. Having come into the building from the private entry in the rear, it wasn't until he went to collect his messages from the receptionist that he discovered Sabatini was in the waiting room.

"He got here a little before nine," Cecilia said. "I told him you were in court, but he insisted on waiting."

Through the sliding-glass divider in front of her desk, Piza could see Sabatini sitting in one of the light-brown cloth chairs, eyes red and puffy, right leg pumping like a manic piston. He bordered on disheveled in his slightly wrinkled suit and loosened tie.

There was no one else in the waiting room, so the lawyer opened the door and approached his one-time friend. "Jesus, Strikes, what part of 'I'll get back to you next week' didn't you understand?"

Sabatini vaulted out of his chair. "I'm really sorry for

showing up like this, Tony, but she called the cops on me. I've gotta go to court on Thursday and I'm a goddamn wreck."

"Shit. When did this happen?"

"Yesterday, when I went to pick up the kids. Outta the blue she—"

"Is there a restraining order?"

"Uh, yeah." He reached into his inside jacket pocket, pulled out the paperwork, and handed it to Piza, who scanned it with the eye of someone who'd seen the form many times before.

"All right. Let's go into my office."

When they sat, Sabatini told him everything that had happened before the police arrived. Continuing, he said, "So I'm upstairs with the kids, and the next thing I know I hear sirens and then there's two police cars outside. I couldn't believe she did that. I ran downstairs, and she's got this panicked look on her face, like she was scared they were banging on the door. I mean, what the hell did she think was gonna happen?"

"Stay focused here, okay? What happened when you let them in?"

"Turns out one of them, Bill Anderson, is Lisa's softball coach. Really good guy. But he was all business. I mean, he acknowledged me and all but, ya know. . ."

"He was just doing his job. Domestic violence isn't something the police tend to screw around with."

"Makes sense, I guess. How were they supposed to know what happened? Although there was a little less tension when they saw Megan wasn't hurt or anything."

"Any marks on her arms? From where you picked her up?"

Shaking his head, Sabatini said, "No. Nothing. I wasn't rough, Ton, I swear. I picked her up just enough to get her out of the way."

"Well, they're listing harassment as the basis for the complaint, rather than assault. So that's good. And they opted not to sign a criminal complaint. So there's just the domestic violence issue, and that's taken care of in Family Court."

"Yeah, I saw harassment checked off on the form, but I didn't understand it. How the hell did I harass her? If anyone was harassed it was me. Not letting me see my own kids? What about that bullshit?"

"Well, under the statute, harassment includes an 'offensive touching'. So—"

"So when I picked her up I was screwed?"

"Not necessarily," Piza replied. "There are certain things she has to prove. But I'm not gonna lie to you, the possibility of a violation exists."

"So can't I sign something against her? For what she did?"

"There's no court order about visitation. It's just an oral agreement between the two of you. So, technically, she didn't do anything illegal."

"God, this sucks. You had to see the girls, Ton, when the cops banged on the door and all. Crying like you can't believe. Thank God both of them knew Bill. He managed to calm them a little. But they were still scared shitless. You could see it." He stood and began pacing; a sullen, brewing storm. "This is exactly the shit I was afraid of when you and I spoke on Friday! What the fuck is wrong with her?" A few more steps, then he dropped back into his chair, as if he'd expended all his energy on that fleeting eruption.

Waiting until he was sure Sabatini was composed, Piza said, "That's actually a very good question. What *is* wrong with her? The thing that always turned me off about Megan was her self-righteousness. But even with that, I never saw her as the vindictive type. Unless that's changed over the past twelve years, this thing with the kids doesn't make sense."

"As far as being vindictive, no, that hasn't changed. I'm not sure what you're getting at though."

"My point is that what happened Sunday seems pre-planned.

And if that's not in her nature, then someone else is stoking the flames. Think about it. All of a sudden she uses some bullshit excuse about the kids being sick. And she waits to call you until she knows you're already on the road and won't get the message. It's like she was provoking you. Why?"

Sabatini extended his hands, palms up. "Not sure. Maybe me pushing the divorce sent her over the edge."

"I'm not buying that. And what about her calling the police? I mean, granted you shouldn't have laid a hand on her, but you weren't violent. You didn't threaten her. At least according to your story."

Sabatini's eyes widened. "I didn't. Jesus, do you think I'm lying to you?"

Piza motioned for him to calm down. "I didn't say that. What I'm getting at is that, under those circumstances, why would she even think about calling the cops? Did she ever threaten to do that before?"

"No. Of course not. As pissed off as we've been at each other, nothing's ever happened where that subject would've even come up."

"Well, there you go. I think someone's been coaching her."

The banker massaged his forehead with his right hand. "I can't believe this is happening. I have no idea who she's been talking to."

"Well, whoever it may be seems to have an awful lot of influence, for her to break out of character like this. Is it possible she's seeing someone? Although considering her feelings about divorce, I don't know where that would be going."

Sabatini issued a lethargic shrug. "I don't know. Doubt it though. Lisa probably would've let it slip if she was." After a momentary pause, a look of new-found resolve formed, and he straightened in his chair. "Okay, whatever's going on, the bottom line is I've gotta go to court on Thursday. Can you go with me?"

Their years of past friendship, abetted by Frankie's tacit blessing, was beginning to erode Piza's reluctance. So there was a hint of apology in his answer. "Look, Strikes, this thing happened in Iselin, so the hearing is gonna be at the courthouse in New Brunswick. That's a hike from up here. I really think you'd be better off getting someone down there."

"How am I gonna get another lawyer fully up to speed between now and then? By the time I get an appointment and all? You already know our history. And I told you, I don't really trust—"

"I just don't think it's a good idea. Plus, I'd have to charge you more considering the travel time. So why don't I—"

"I don't care. How much are we talking about? Total."

Piza puffed out a breath of surrender. "I could probably do it for seven-fifty."

"Done. So tell me what's involved with this hearing."

CHAPTER 6

As Piza approached the entrance to the county courthouse in New Brunswick, his oversized black umbrella fought to maintain its dignity in the face of volatile wind gusts and pummeling rain.

I knew I shouldn't have taken this case. Driving fifty miles in this monsoon.

Entering the lobby, he saw Sabatini pacing—head down, gray raincoat draped over his right arm. The lower half of his tan suit pants looked waterlogged.

"Strikes," Piza called out.

Sabatini whipped around, his startled expression shifting to relief. "Tony. Thank God. I was afraid you weren't coming. We were supposed to be here for eight thirty."

"Yeah, sorry I'm late. The few times I've been down here it took me around an hour. But people seem to forget how to drive in the rain. Plus there was a little ponding on the stupid turnpike."

"I know, right? Moderate showers my ass. Idiot weatherman. Weather person?"

"Go with meteorologist. It's safer. You didn't hit traffic?"

"A little. But I left at six thirty, so. . ."

Piza was one of those inherently conflicted souls who insist on their wristwatch being perfectly calibrated, but fail to be on time for anything; a disharmony he was aware of, but attributed to fate. The thought of Sabatini leaving two hours early for a one-hour drive generated something akin to awe. "Six thirty. Wow." It passed. "Well, let's get upstairs."

One of the elevators was out of service, and too many people were waiting for the others.

"Let's take the stairs," Piza ordered. As they walked toward the stairway door, he noticed the soaked trousers again. "Nice pants, by the way."

Blushing, Sabatini said, "When I left the apartment, I thought my umbrella was in the back of my car. Didn't look until I got down here. Needless to say, it wasn't. Opted to sacrifice the pants and use the raincoat to protect my hair." He shrugged.

Piza glanced at the top of his client's head. "Well, from the look of things, that's a choice you won't have to worry about making much longer." Bygones weren't bygones quite yet.

"Hey, it's not *that* bad up there," the man responded with a strained smile.

After an awkward pause, Piza said, "You remember everything we went over on Monday?"

"Yeah. I've gone over it in my head every day."

"Okay. You'll be fine. When did you start smoking, by the way?"

Sabatini's head snapped back. "Couple of years ago. How'd you know I smoked?"

"Cigarette breath."

"Oh," his client said as his hand went to his mouth. "Shit. Sorry about that. You have a mint or gum or something?"

"No. I'll just breathe through my mouth until the hearing is over."

Three flights up they exited the stairwell landing, rounded a corner, and encountered a noisy, skittish crowd. Piza checked the time. *Court was supposed to start thirteen minutes ago.* Reaching the courtroom door, he was about to grasp the handle when someone said, "Don't bother. It's locked."

"So much for worrying about being late," Piza muttered. He snaked around a few bodies and made his way to a list of cases posted on the wall to the left of the door. *Crap.* "We're number twelve," he told Sabatini as he led him away from the nucleus of the crowd. "We'll probably be here all morning, if not later."

"Damn, I'm sorry, Tony. I didn't want you to have to kill most of your day here. I mean between this and then the ride back and all. If you need more money, I can—"

"I don't need more money, Strikes. This happens all the time. Luck of the draw."

"Oh, speaking of money." Sabatini reached into his pants pocket and retrieved a check. "Little damp. Sorry."

"Don't worry. I'll stick it under a dryer in the men's room. You see Megan anywhere?"

"Not so far." He scoured the area. "Wait. There," he said, pointing. "Sitting on the bench on the right, down the hall. Tough to see, with all these people."

"Okay, got her. The woman next to her . . . neon-green pantsuit. Do you know if that's her lawyer?"

"I have no idea. I don't even know if she has one." He squinted. "Fuck me! That's Candy . . . Janicek. The realtor who sold us our house. Jesus, she lost a ton of weight from back then. I hardly recognized her."

"Your realtor? How long have they been friends?"

"I didn't know they were. We only met her when we went house hunting. And the two of them didn't hang out while I was living at home, at least as far as I know. So this has gotta be something fairly recent."

"Well, they must be close. She seems to be holding Megan's hand in her lap."

With a scowl Sabatini said, "She was always all over Megan. Constantly touching her arm, her shoulder. Hardly ever acknowledged *me*. I didn't think anything of it, but I bet she was looking to get in her pants. Goddamn dyke."

"Dyke? Really? And you were worried about 'weatherman'?"

"I know, I know. I'm just pissed. I remember she had an opinion about everything. And she was always going on about her ex-husband. How shitty he was. How he abandoned her and their daughter. Wouldn't shut up about him." His eyes turned fierce as his fists clenched. "Bitch! I guarantee she's behind this crap. Goddammit!" He smashed his right fist into his left palm, then shook off the sting as he stepped away from Piza.

"Hey, hey, calm down," the lawyer said, grabbing his arm and looking around to see if anyone had noticed. A few people were staring, but their interest appeared to quickly dissolve. "What the hell is wrong with you? You really think this is the right time and place for that shit?"

"Sorry, Ton," he replied, the crimson complexion fading. "I know I've gotta keep it together."

"I sure as hell hope you know. You need to stay as close to saintly as you can get. And not just here. No matter what happens today, you've gotta toe the line from now on. No more incidents."

"No, you're right. I'm just so damned frustrated is all. I just wanna see my kids. What scares me though is that sometimes Megan can be really naive, and if this woman is manipulating her. . ."

"I get it. But one thing at a time, okay?"

"Okay. Hey, the fact that she doesn't seem to have a lawyer is good for us, right?"

A slight grimace from Piza. "Not necessarily. Sometimes if one party has a lawyer and the other doesn't, judges bend over backwards to accommodate the people representing themselves. Kind of see them as the underdog. It's not really fair but—"

Movement down the hall drew his attention. "Ah, good. They opened the courtroom."

CHAPTER 7

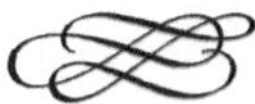

The dank odor of wet clothing and an air of apprehension flooded the small courtroom before most of the assemblage settled into the rows of oak-colored, pew-like benches. A three-foot-high wood divider of similar color set the gallery apart from the counsel tables and judge's bench.

A drone of muted conversations vanished when the court clerk emerged from a door at the front of the room. The matronly, silver-haired woman took a seat at a partially enclosed desk appended to the judge's bench. "Good morning, everyone. I apologize for the delay, but Judge Diaz got held up in traffic because of this horrible weather. She's here now, and we're ready to go. Are there any attorneys here who haven't already sent in a letter of representation?"

Piza and two other lawyers stood up. The clerk pointed to Piza and said, "Which case are you on, sir?"

"Number twelve. My name is Anthony Piza. P-I-Z-A. Representing Mr. Sabatini."

"Great. Thank you."

She took the information from the other two attorneys, then announced, "Okay. We have six cases with attorneys, which we'll get to first." That met with grumblings from the unrepresented. "Those of you who don't have attorneys, this doesn't mean your case is less important. It's just that attorneys often have other courts to get to, so we try to accommodate them and the judges who may be waiting for them. Now, I'm going to go down the list of cases, and when you hear your name, let me know you're here."

Piza leaned in toward his client. "Lucked out with that."

When the clerk reached Sabatini's case, Piza stood and once again gave his name and indicated he represented the defendant. Up to that point, he'd avoided making eye contact with Megan. But now he looked at the ashen-faced woman two rows behind him, as she stood and said her name. She looked well enough, although even thinner than she used to be. Satiny dark brown hair rested on her shoulders. No obvious signs of wear on her plain, wholesome face. When the clerk asked if she had a lawyer, she shook her head, then sat. She briefly returned Piza's gaze, gold-flecked hazel eyes asking what he was doing back in their lives.

After breaking off eye contact with Megan, he shifted to Candy, who appeared to be in her mid-fifties. *Good grief. The woman's wearing enough makeup to face-paint the entire cast of "Cats".* Candy was doing double duty—gently rubbing Megan's back, and boring into Piza with a stare so absurdly malevolent he had to bite his lower lip to stop from laughing.

"I don't think Candy likes me," he murmured to Sabatini.

"Welcome to the club."

Of the cases listed before Sabatini's, three involved attorneys. The clerk marked one to be called again later, because the plaintiff hadn't yet appeared. The other two had attorneys representing both sides. In a way, Piza was glad there were cases ahead of his. It would give his client a chance to see the process in action, and hopefully ease his anxiety to some extent.

When the clerk finished the list, she told the gallery to rise, and announced Judge Maria Diaz. The judge entered from a door directly behind the bench, took her seat, and instructed the assembly to do likewise. She looked to be fortyish, with straight black hair pulled back tightly, and large, smiling brown eyes that countered the no-nonsense hairstyle.

While watching her handle the first case, Piza concluded she was a good fit for the highly charged environment of domestic violence hearings. Pleasant and calming, she tamped down occasional runaway emotions without raising her voice, and kept the lawyers on point and civil.

As the second case started, Piza noticed Sabatini's right leg start vibrating. Clearly, watching the proceedings had done nothing to diminish the man's angst.

When the clerk called their case, Piza and his client navigated to the opening in the divider, and stood behind the counsel table with the "Defendant" nameplate. Megan approached the "Plaintiff" table, with Candy right behind her.

Piza hadn't realized how tall Candy was, standing about even with his 5' 10". He was about to object to her being there, but the judge spoke before he could say anything. "Which of you ladies is Ms. Sabatini?" Megan half-lifted her hand. The judge shifted her gaze to Candy. "I have only one attorney listed here. Are you an attorney, madam?"

Candy replied, "No, Your Honor, but I'm Megan's friend. She's kind of nervous, so I'd like to sit with her. For moral support. I'm a realtor, by the way."

A few people in the gallery laughed.

The judge's lips formed a scant, wry smile. "And your name is. . ."

"Candy Janicek."

"Well, Ms. Janicek, I applaud your loyalty to your friend. And while I don't doubt you're a fine realtor, you're not an attorney. So you're not permitted to be up here. And Ms. Sabatini, don't be nervous. I can assure—"

"I won't say anything," Candy interrupted. "I'm just concerned for my friend's well-being. As I think *you* should be."

The gallery came alive with nervous murmurings and a few gasps. An armed court officer standing in a corner shook off a slouch and squared his shoulders.

Judge Diaz, however, looked unruffled, although there was now a slight edge to her voice. "Ms. Janicek, I can assure you that I care about the well-being of *every* individual who appears before me in this courtroom. Now please get back behind the divider and take your seat."

The realtor complied, but not before huffing a breath while facing the judge, then whispering something to her friend.

"Okay, counsel, can I have your appearance for the record?"

"Yes, Your Honor. Anthony Piza for the defendant."

"Ah. Long 'i'. I would've gone short. Good thing you pronounced it before I butchered it."

"It's my curse, Judge," he replied, his delivery almost flirtatious.

"Well, I've seen people burdened with worse, counsel," she said, looking amused. "Okay, take your seats, and let's have our first witness."

The court clerk directed Megan to take the witness stand and state her full name. Then she administered the oath. At that point, the judge took over.

"Okay, Ms. Sabatini, I want you to tell me, in your own words, what occurred." There was a gentleness to the instruction. "What happened that led you to seek a temporary restraining order?"

Megan related the events of Sunday morning. As Piza took

notes, it seemed to him the facts she laid out basically mirrored what his client had told him.

"Let me ask you something," the judge said. "When Mr. Sabatini picked you up and moved you aside, did he hurt you?"

"You mean— You mean physically?"

Diaz nodded. "Yes. Physically."

"Um, no, not really."

"Did you have any bruising on your arms, where his hands had been?"

"I don't think so. One of the police officers . . . the younger one, I don't know his name, he checked and he said he didn't see anything. And I didn't see anything after that."

"Were you scared when your husband picked you up like that?"

Megan's uncertain eyes targeted Candy. Piza looked back to see the woman nodding, and he shot to his feet. "Your Honor, I'd appreciate it if you'd instruct the witness not to look to Ms. Janicek for cues as to how she should testify."

"I noticed that myself, counsel. Ms. Sabatini, this is your testimony, not your friend's. So please refrain from looking at her for help in how to answer. If you can't, then I'll have to ask her to leave the courtroom. Okay?"

With a contrite nod Megan answered, "Yes, Your Honor. I'm sorry."

"So, were you scared?"

"Well . . . maybe, I guess? Joey . . . I mean the defendant had never done anything like that before."

"Okay," the judge said. She added a comforting, "And it isn't necessary for you to call him 'the defendant'. We're not that formal here."

Megan blushed and nodded.

"So, is there anything you'd like to add?" Diaz asked.

Megan tilted her head to the right and homed in on Candy

before catching herself and turning away. "Um, no. I don't think so."

"Okay. Thank you, Ms. Sabatini." Looking at Piza, she said, "Any questions, counsel?"

Megan, who was halfway out of her seat, twisted her head toward the judge. "He— He gets to ask me questions?"

CHAPTER 8

Megan's apparent shock at learning that Piza could question her seemed to take Judge Diaz by surprise. "He has the right to cross-examine you. Didn't you notice that in the two cases before this?"

"Well, uh, sure. But I thought that was because the people both had lawyers."

"No, that's not how it works. Each party or their attorney has the right to ask questions. You'll have the opportunity to ask Mr. Sabatini questions if he decides to testify."

Megan was visibly distraught, and Diaz asked her if she wanted some water. She declined with a slight shake of the head. "You sure you're okay, Ms. Sabatini?" The response was a vigorous nod that seemed more rooted in panic than conviction. "Okay, Mr. Piza."

The lawyer opted to question her while he remained seated at the counsel table. It was a tactic he often used when dealing with an emotionally vulnerable witness. There was nothing to be gained by hovering and potentially skewing the sympathy factor. "Good morning, Ms. Sabatini."

"Tony." An obvious attempt at a brave face fell short.

The judge's brow furrowed. "Counsel, you know Ms. Sabatini?"

"Yes, Your Honor. *Mr.* Sabatini and I were old friends. That's how I know her. Although I haven't seen her in several years."

"I see. Mr. Sabatini, you have no issue with Mr. Piza representing you, despite the fact he knows your wife?"

"No, Your Honor. Not at all."

"Mr. Piza, have you ever represented Mr. or Ms. Sabatini in any legal matters?"

"No, Your Honor. In fact, before this matter came up, the last time I saw either of them was before I was in law school."

The judge nodded at him. "Okay. Just checking off the possible conflict of interest box. You understand."

"Absolutely, Judge."

"All right. Proceed."

"Thank you, Judge. Ms. Sabatini, before last Sunday there'd never been an incident like this in your marriage, correct?" The beauty of cross-examination is that you pretty much get to lead the witness as much as you like.

"No. Never."

"And prior to Sunday, there'd never been a problem with your husband picking up the children, right?"

She nodded.

"Ms. Sabatini," the judge said, "you have to verbalize your answer, okay? A tape recording is being made of this hearing, and it obviously can't pick up a nod or a gesture of any sort."

"Okay, sorry. Um, right. There's never been a problem with Joey picking the kids up or dropping them back off."

"It's fair to say Mr. Sabatini loves his children very much, wouldn't you agree?"

Tears welled up. "Yes. That's fair."

The judge asked her again if she'd like some water. This time she accepted. The clerk poured some into a paper cup and brought it to her.

Piza could have gone on questioning her for an hour, burying her in detail, mining for inconsistencies. But she was visibly upset, and he didn't want to risk having her break down completely. Plus, there was a courtroom full of people whose cases needed to be heard. As patient as Judge Diaz seemed, getting through the rest of the docket had to be on her mind. He decided to limit his questioning to the essentials.

He stood up, went to the front of the counsel table, and leaned back against it, almost sitting. "You okay?"

She nodded as she wiped her eyes. "Yes. Thanks."

"Megan, the girls weren't really sick on Sunday, were they? I mean, you took their temperature and it was normal. And they weren't complaining about feeling ill."

She shifted in her seat. "Well, um, like I said, it was more precautionary. I mean, if he took them to some fast-food place or whatever, they'd be exposed to a lot of people. And I heard there's a bug going around."

He maintained a gentle tone through an impish smile. "So earlier that morning, you'd anticipated that the three of you would be the only ones at nine o'clock mass?"

"Well, no. But . . . I don't know. It's not the same. Germs can spread more in those other kinds of places. And the kids are always touching things there."

"So people don't cough or sneeze in church? You don't touch the pews and prayer books? You don't shake hands with the people near you when the priest calls for 'the sign of peace'?"

After a brief hesitation, she answered with a deflated, "I just don't think it's the same, that's all."

Having made his point, he moved on. "Have you discussed your marital situation with Ms. Janicek?"

"Well, yeah. She's my friend and, you know, she's gone through this before."

"She's the one who suggested you keep the children away from Mr. Sabatini, isn't she?"

"I never did that," a shrill voice objected.

Judge Diaz glared at Candy. "I'm trying to be patient with you, ma'am. But one more outburst and you can wait in the hall. Clear?"

The woman turned away without answering.

"Was it her idea?" Piza repeated.

Megan's face shaded deep red. "Uh, not in so many words. Look, she had a bad marriage. Her husband was rotten, okay? And, and she told me I was being too nice to Joey, and that if I didn't toughen up, he'd walk all over me. And so when I thought the girls looked a little flushed . . ." She broke eye contact with him.

"She's also the one who told you about calling the police?"

"She said if he ever did anything to me or threatened me or whatever, that's what I should do."

"But he didn't threaten you. Or shove you or curse at you or anything like that."

A look of tentative confidence appeared. "No, but he picked me up."

Piza bumped up the aggression meter a notch. "Because you were blocking him from seeing his children." He went back behind the counsel table. "When Judge Diaz asked you if you were scared, the first thing you said was"—checking his notes—"'maybe, I guess?'. So you weren't really sure. In fact, it's more likely you were surprised rather than scared, wouldn't you agree? Considering, as you also said, that he'd never done anything like that before? That's certainly possible, isn't it?"

The woman looked drained. Throughout the last round of questioning, her shoulders had gradually elevated and rounded to a point where her body appeared to be collapsing in on itself.

"Ms. Sabatini?" Piza coaxed. "More surprised than scared, correct?"

She produced a listless shrug and weary nod. "Probably, yes."

"Thank you. No more questions, Your Honor." He took his seat.

Megan slowly rose from the witness chair. Almost as an afterthought, she turned toward the judge. "Am I done? Is it okay for me to get down?"

"Absolutely."

After she made her way back to the counsel table, Piza stood up. "Your Honor, I move for a dismissal. Even considering the inferences the plaintiff is entitled to at this juncture, it's clear that she hasn't presented enough to ultimately prove her case under the statute. If you look at—"

The judge signaled for him to stop. "*At this point*, counsel, I don't feel a dismissal is warranted. So how do you want to proceed?"

It's unusual for a court to dismiss a case after the plaintiff's portion of the trial, but it was standard procedure for a lawyer to at least make the effort. Now, he had to make a decision. He believed his cross-examination had been strong enough to justify a dismissal of the complaint at the end of the case. And for the case to end, all he had to do was "rest".

In denying his motion to dismiss, Judge Diaz had emphasized the words "at this point". Piza wondered if that was her discreet way of signaling that if he rested his case, he'd win. He'd seen judges do it before. But this was his first time appearing before her, and it wasn't a chance he wanted to take.

"Your Honor, I'd ask that Mr. Sabatini take the stand."

The judge didn't register surprise, which made him feel better about his decision.

"All right, Mr. Sabatini," she said. "Come up and the clerk will swear you in."

As the clerk administered the oath, Piza took his seat. He'd decided to do something he'd never done before. He was going to ask only one question. When his client was settled in, the lawyer stayed seated. Motionless. It only took seconds for a suspenseful silence to drape the room. "Mr. Sabatini, when you picked up your wife last Sunday in your home, was it your intention to harm her?"

The heartrending passion in the man's answer intensified the rapt attention evident throughout the courtroom. "God, no. I just wanted to see my kids. I'd never hurt her. I asked her to move out of the way. I think I even said 'please'. When she wouldn't, I did the only thing I could think of for me to be able to get upstairs and see them." He turned to the judge with a look so pitiful, his words were probably redundant. "I just want to see my kids, Your Honor. That's all."

Diaz gave him a barely perceptible nod.

"No more questions, Your Honor."

The judge asked Megan if she had any questions, and when she said no, Sabatini was instructed to step down.

"Mr. Piza, anything else?"

"No, Judge, we rest."

"All right. Do you wish to make a closing statement?"

Most lawyers who do trial work would sooner have an impacted molar extracted than pass up a chance to talk. But Piza knew the judge had all the information she needed to make her decision, and sometimes you just need to keep your mouth shut. "I don't believe it's necessary, Your Honor. Thank you."

"Do you wish to say anything else, Ms. Sabatini?"

With a tentative shake of her head she responded, "I don't think so."

Judge Diaz clasped her hands and leaned forward, resting her elbows on the bench. It almost looked like she was praying. "Okay. As you've heard me say in the previous two cases, the burden of proof is on the plaintiff to prove her case by a preponderance of the evidence. In non-legalese, that means I have to be convinced that it's more likely than not that an act of domestic violence occurred.

"The basis of the complaint in this case is 'harassment'.

There are several aspects of harassment under the New Jersey statute, but the only one that seems relevant here is 'offensive touching'. It's clear, based on the testimony of both Ms. and Mr. Sabatini, that he touched her by picking her up and moving her out of his way. There's also no doubt in my mind that she found that offensive. She certainly didn't *want* him to do that."

Piza's peripheral vision picked up Sabatini's panicked gaze at him. But the lawyer wouldn't acknowledge it, keeping his eyes on Diaz, looking for some sign that would quell the sense of impending defeat that had invaded his nervous system and turned his skin cold. She'd ruled against the defendants in the two prior cases, but that hadn't bothered him, as the facts had left no doubt about the outcome. But he'd believed she'd see his case differently. Now he was anything but sure, and the judge's expression revealed nothing.

"There's another element involved here, and that's 'intent'. Was it Mr. Sabatini's intention to harass Ms. Sabatini by picking her up? I think it's fair to conclude that he was angry when he did what he did, despite his testimony that he believes he said 'please' when he asked her to move out of the way."

Piza was straining to contain a look of disgust.

"So the issue is whether it was that anger that motivated him to touch her." She looked at Megan, then at Sabatini. "Domestic violence is abhorrent, and it's more pervasive in our society than most people might be aware of. That said, a judge's job is to determine in each particular case whether a confrontation crossed the line into domestic violence. Sometimes it's obvious; sometimes it's not. This case falls into the latter category.

"I acknowledge that Mr. Sabatini had good reason to be upset. Ms. Sabatini's contentions notwithstanding, her reason for attempting to keep him from seeing the children was flimsy at best. However, even a legitimate reason for being upset doesn't justify violating the law. And it goes without question that Mr. Sabatini shouldn't have put his hands on his wife.

"But it seems to me that if anger had been the motivating factor in what he did, the way he did it wouldn't have been as . . . for lack of a better word, 'gentle'. He didn't shove her out of the way. Didn't viciously squeeze her arms. On the contrary, it seems he took pains not to hurt her. And I believe him when he says that all he was trying to do was simply move her to clear a path to his children. In light of that, I find that the intent necessary to prove harassment is lacking here. So I'm dismissing the case and lifting the temporary restraining order. But let me—"

"This is a joke" came rocketing out of the gallery.

Heads snapped around toward Candy.

Judge Diaz's inherently soft features instantly hardened. "Madam, I warned you before." She turned to the court officer. "Please escort that woman into the hall."

As the man started walking to the opening in the divider, Candy squirmed past the people sitting between her and the aisle. "I don't need any help," she declared as she tossed a scowl at the judge and waved off the approaching officer. He ignored the gesture and followed her into the hall.

When the gallery settled down, the judge smiled and said, "Sorry about that, folks. Usually the excitement is on this side of the divider." That met with a collective laugh. "Now, as I started to say, Ms. and Mr. Sabatini, you have two young children. You both seem like decent people, and I have no doubt whatsoever you love your kids. So I think you'll agree that they should never again have to be exposed to what they saw last Sunday."

The two somber litigants nodded in unison.

"Mr. Sabatini, from what I've seen today you have a very competent attorney. If there's a problem with visitation, don't force the issue with your wife. Contact your attorney and let him take the necessary steps to address the problem. Mr. Piza, are any efforts being made to put together a written separation agreement that could formalize visitation rights?"

"Not that I'm aware of, Judge, unless Ms. Sabatini has

consulted a lawyer about it. I only got involved this past week."

The judge addressed Megan. "Have you met with a lawyer to discuss your marital situation?"

"No, Your Honor."

"Okay. Obviously, I can't order the two of you to settle your differences. But I'm strongly suggesting that you attempt to get an agreement drawn up that will address visitation, as well as the usual other marital issues. Financial matters and such. And, Ms. Sabatini, you'd be wise to get any future advice from an attorney, not a realtor . . . as well-intentioned as your friend might be. Good luck to both of you."

Megan started crying before they made it out of the courtroom. Piza wasn't sure whether it was because she'd lost, or the experience had been too overwhelming. Once in the hall, Candy hurried her away, speaking to her while a consoling arm drew her close.

Sabatini couldn't stop shaking Piza's hand. "Holy crap, Ton, you did it. The way the judge was talking, I thought for sure I was screwed. I can't freakin' believe we won."

"Well, for what it's worth, I thought you were screwed too. A lot of judges are reluctant to dismiss a DV complaint. They're worried about what might happen if they end up making a mistake. And I get that. It's a hell of a responsibility. But, fortunately, this judge did her job."

"Well, I owe you big time. So look, what about this agreement the judge was talking about? Can we do that?"

Piza had no desire to discuss the future. "Look, Strikes, I only agreed to handle this hearing for you because it was an emergency. I'm still not sure I wanna get involved with anything else."

A forlorn-looking Sabatini said, "Oh. I, uh, kind of thought we were okay. You and me. I mean, maybe not completely, but you know. . ."

"It's got nothing to do with that. I don't think I wanna keep doing divorce work."

"Why? You're obviously good at it. Jesus, look at what you just pulled off."

"This was a hearing. One and done. It's nothing like a divorce. A divorce is an endless emotional slog. And I've got enough of them in the pipeline already to last me another year. Probably longer."

Sabatini made no effort to hide his dejection. "I understand, Tony, I do. And I've already told you how I'd feel about having to work with someone else. So I'm not gonna beat that dead horse. But after what we saw today, I'm convinced there's no way Candy is gonna let go. And if Megan has to eventually get a lawyer, and that woman has a hand in that, God only knows what's gonna happen. So if you could at least think about it, I'd really, really appreciate it."

"Listen, I'm wiped out right now. Between the miserable drive down here, and the hearing and all. Let me give it some thought, okay?"

A resigned nod. "That's all I'm asking for." After a moment's pause, "You got time for a coffee? They must have a cafeteria in this place."

"No, thanks. I've gotta get going."

"Sure. Of course. Well, I'm gonna try to grab something." The lawyer took a few steps, but Sabatini said, "Hey, one last thing, Ton." Piza stopped and turned around. "And I should've said this to you the first time I saw you, but I was too embarrassed. What I said about your parents that night at Murp's, I—"

Piza put up a hand. "Not now, Strikes. I don't—"

"Please, Tony. Considering I may not see you again. What I said that night was inexcusable. Your parents always treated me and the rest of the guys in our little group like we were their own kids. I'm ashamed of what I said, and I'm sorry. And I know an apology . . . the timing and all, may seem a little suspect. But I mean it."

Piza stared at him, nodded, and walked off.

CHAPTER 9

He might as well have been staring at a blank screen. Despite appearing totally absorbed in the game between the Yankees and White Sox, the broadcast had become background noise as Piza replayed the details of the Sabatini hearing that morning.

He recalled what Strikes had grumbled about at their first meeting in his office—how none of the members of their circle had ever really accepted Megan. He was right. So much about her had been off-putting. She'd worn her religious fervor like a garish cloak, while challenging you with a look to comment on it. And there was a rigidness to her, an arid aloofness her husband's closest friends had always assumed emanated from an innate sense of superiority.

That wasn't the woman he'd seen in court. That person was vulnerable. Unsure. Possibly even lost. Piza had been doing this work long enough to know that what he'd observed was real. He wondered if she and her husband's struggles over the past few years had been so punishing they had eroded her old persona, exposing insecurities holed up below. Or maybe this was who she'd been all along, and fault lay with him and the rest of their group for not making a better effort to understand her.

When previously weighing whether to represent Sabatini in his divorce, he'd thought this could be one of those rare cases where a lawyer truly believes the opposing party is undeserving of sympathy or mercy. Sometimes that made the job easier. But the hearing had gutted that illusion. The question now was whether the nagging tug of an old friendship, and the possible emotional fate of two little girls, was enough to warrant once again signing on to play a role he longed to escape from.

An hour later, Mandy Sheppard opened the door to Piza's apartment and set down her briefcase. Tucking her shortish black hair behind her ears, she made her way to the couch where he was sitting.

"Well, hi there," he said, instantly entranced by grey eyes that were so radiant they dared you to look away.

Without answering, she hiked up her skirt a bit, straddled his lap, then leaned in and gave him a lingering, open-mouthed kiss. Glancing down, she said, "Oh my. I see Tony Junior is wide awake."

"How could he not be? You've got a tongue like a Komodo dragon, God bless you."

She laughed. "You do have a way of making a girl feel special. Any other admirable qualities you'd like to pay tribute to?"

Piza twisted his mouth. "Um, let's see. Ah! Your beauty and brains. They are so staggering, they usually block out any thoughts of Barry Manilow when I say your name."

She landed a punch on his left arm.

"Ow. What was that for?"

"First of all, 'usually block out' implies that *occasionally* you do conjure up thoughts of Barry Manilow when saying my name. Tell me that's not a little disturbing. Secondly, you said his name like you were on the verge of gagging, which leads me to believe you don't like his music. Which means you don't like 'Mandy', which I happen to think is a pretty song, regardless of the fact that it's my name."

"Wow, talk about an intended compliment nose-diving into oblivion. I'm not saying 'Mandy' isn't a pretty song. Little soppy for my taste, but I do admit to humming along when I hear it. And I don't have anything against Barry Manilow."

"Fine. But enough about Barry. More about me."

Piza sighed. "You're pushing your luck here, lady."

Arching a brow, she said, "It's *your* luck you should be concerned about, my dear. You know how obsequious flattery gets me"—slowly rocking back and forth—"going."

"Holy shit. Think, man! Uh. Um. Wait! I've got it! You're the only girl I've ever dated who seems incapable of emitting body odor. Even after exercising."

She arched her back and cried out, "Oh God! That was the one. I won't make it to the bedroom. Do me on the cocktail table!"

Piza laughed so hard he almost bucked her off his lap. She grinned, gave him a peck on the cheek, and stood up, saying, "I haven't eaten since breakfast. Got anything lying around?"

Coughing out the remnants of his laughter, he said, "There's a little penne vodka in the fridge."

"Great."

"You know, you really shouldn't be going from breakfast to eight thirty at night without eating," he called out as she headed to the kitchen.

"I know. But we just picked up a new client, and we were brainstorming a possible game plan." She removed the aluminum foil from the dish of pasta, grabbed a fork, and walked back into the living room. Kicking off her shoes, she stretched out on the couch, resting her long legs on Piza's lap.

He scrunched his face. "Aren't you gonna heat that up?"

"Nah. I'm good." She held out a forkful. "Want some?"

"No. Thanks. Anyway, I know you advertising creative types can get into a zone, but at some point during the day you need to clear your head, no? And stick something in your stomach?"

With a conceding nod she said, "I'll have to work on that. So, how did your friend's case go today?"

"Well, I haven't re-elevated him to the status of friend quite yet. But it went well. We won."

"Terrific. How'd his wife take your being there?"

"Surprised. Upset. I thought she was gonna implode when she realized I was gonna cross-examine her. She didn't have a lawyer though, so I didn't push too hard. Weird thing was she had this older woman glued to her hip. The realtor who sold them their house. She wanted to sit at the counsel table with her."

"Is that allowed?"

"Definitely not. But the lady got pissed when the judge told her no. Even sitting in the gallery she was making comments. The judge ended up tossing her out. Strikes is worried about the influence she might have on Megan. He's afraid she's gonna steer her to some shark if this whole thing moves forward."

"Is it? Gonna move forward?"

Tossing a shrug, he said, "I dunno. He really wants me to represent him. And I told you how Pop thinks maybe it's time to make peace. But you know how I feel about taking on more divorce work."

"No, I get it. But you did say you were worried about what might happen to his kids."

"I know. I'll give it some more thought." He started massaging her feet. "So what's on tap for tonight? You staying over?"

She smiled. "If you promise to keep the foot massage going for the next couple of hours. Actually, I've got a presentation first thing in the morning, and some of the material is back at my place."

"Hmm. So the whole cocktail table thing. . ."

"It's a nice little cocktail table. We wouldn't wanna break it." She placed the plate on the table and, like a prowling cat, inched her way on top of him. "This couch, however, is *very* sturdy."

CHAPTER 10

"Hey, Tony. Which one you on?" asked prosecutor Michael Feldman, ten minutes before the Bogota municipal court was scheduled to begin.

"Thirty-seven, Mike. Bruno Bosco," Piza answered.

Bruno was a private investigator. He was also a first cousin of Piza's "Uncle" Nunzio. (Nunzio wasn't a blood relative, but he and Angelo had been close friends forever. He was also Piza's godfather.)

There are certain people whose strong points always seem to fall prey to their shortcomings. So it was with Bruno: taller than average at 6'1" - but weighing in at 350 pounds; handsome - but sweat glands that would require a potential girlfriend to invest in scuba gear; making good money - but never met a bet that wasn't "a sure thing". Thus, at age 42, was he living in the semi-finished basement of his brother and sister-in-law's house. They'd installed a stove, refrigerator, and bathroom with a super-sized stall shower for him. In return for their benevolence, he bought cold-cuts every Saturday.

Bruno was also an accomplished collector of traffic tickets.

And he was happy to take advantage of Piza's broad interpretation of his law firm's generous policy on not billing family members for small matters. Piza often said that if he actually charged his virtual cousin for municipal court appearances, he could leave his firm, put Bruno on retainer, and live quite comfortably. Today's violation—which carried dreaded motor vehicle commission points against his license—was "making a right turn on red" at an intersection where a clearly visible sign prohibited the maneuver. It was an offense of which Bruno was unquestionably guilty.

Feldman flipped through his sheets of case listings. "Okay, here we go. 'No right on red'. Shawn McMurray's the cop. Good guy. I can knock it down to a no-points ticket. Usual fine, court costs, your client's insurance premium doesn't take a hit, and you're out of here nice and early."

"You don't have to sell me, Mike. I know the drill. And ordinarily, I'd take the deal and run." He winced an apology. "But I think you've got a problem with your case."

Most municipal court prosecutors are part-timers, and don't get paid enough to warrant staying in court any longer than absolutely necessary—one of the reasons they push for plea bargains. The Bogota municipal court met one evening, every other week. The town had a tiny courtroom and, tonight, defendants were overflowing into the hall. No wonder then that Feldman's face fell when Piza delivered his answer.

"What problem? It's cut-and-dried. Sign says no turn on red; the light was red and your guy turned. End of story."

"Well, the ticket was *mailed* to my client. Maybe your cop was on foot at the time, but whatever he was doing, all he got was a license plate. He didn't pursue the car. And it was nine thirty at night."

With a smirk the prosecutor said, "You're saying McMurray can't identify the driver."

"Exactly. I don't think you can prove operation."

"You really wanna take that chance? Once we start the trial, the deal's off the table."

"I know. And I don't like putting you in this position. But it is what it is, Mike. Oh, and by way of a heads-up, when the case is called I'm not bringing anyone up to the defendant's table with me. So your cop is gonna have to pick out the driver from the mob of people in the courtroom."

"Yeah, but if he does identify him, Judge Donetti might be pissed you wasted his time."

Piza smiled. "Well, first of all, I didn't say the driver was a 'him'. And second, you know I've been here before. Donetti's a laid back guy, so I don't see him penalizing me for doing my job. He might actually enjoy the drama."

Feldman huffed and said, "Let me talk to McMurray. He'll level with me if he can't make the ID."

"Okay, great."

Piza had instructed Bruno to mingle with the crowd and stay away from him. No reason to invent another meaning for "guilt by association".

Feldman was back in a few minutes. "He couldn't tell who was driving."

And that was that. Case dismissed. Once they were outside the building, Bruno administered a now all-too-familiar bear hug of gratitude.

"Okay, big guy, you can put me down now," Piza wheezed.

"Tony, you're my freakin' hero. I mean that from deep down in here," he said, patting the general area of his amorphous upper body where his overworked heart was probably lamenting its fate.

Piza nodded as he discreetly checked the front of his suit jacket for dampness. "I know you mean it. But if you wanna show your appreciation, stop getting tickets. Nobody'll be happier about that than me."

Bruno raised his right hand. "I swear. Super swear, even. Um

. . . but in the one-in-a-million . . . make that *trillion* chance I screw up again. . .”

A headshake merged with a sigh. “Call me.”

“I owe ya, Ton. Anytime you ever need anythin’, day or night. I’m super serious.”

Piza had no idea that one day he’d collect on that debt.

Elizabeth Agostini re-tied her light brown ponytail as she approached Piza’s booth in the Heritage Diner, a classic eatery about a block from the Bergen County courthouse. Elizabeth was Nunzio’s daughter from his first marriage. Although she was three years younger than Piza, they had been close since they were kids, and she was as much a little sister to him as Patty. Her friends called her Beth, but to him, she’d always been Lizzie. She’d long ago given up telling him not to call her that; now, it was a term of endearment. Bright, funny, and effortlessly compassionate, her job as a medical social worker at a local hospital fit her perfectly.

They exchanged cheek kisses.

“Well this is nice,” Piza said as they sat. “We haven’t done lunch in a while. I’m glad you called. Are we just catching up, or is there a specific reason why we’re here? I only ask because I’m bored, so I could really use something deliciously sinister.”

A grin lit her face, only to have her expression regress into despondency moments later. “Who am I kidding? Like you wouldn’t see right through my trying to fake being happy.”

Looking alarmed, he said, “Hey. What’s wrong? Tell me what’s going on.”

“I— I’m sorry, Tony. I don’t think I can do this. Calling you was a mistake.”

“Don’t say that. You know you can tell me anything. So, c’mon. What is it?”

She gulped. "Look, I'm not proud of this, okay? But. . . Crap, let me just get it out. I've been impregnated by a being from another plane of existence. There, I said it."

Piza bent forward, and with his forehead an inch from the tabletop, let it drop, rattling the silverware. "How?" he mumbled into the table. "How is it that I never see it coming?" He lifted his head. "I concede defeat. If I wasn't afraid people would mock me, or think I was proposing to you, I'd genuflect in the presence of your sadistic genius."

A throaty laugh preceded, "Hey, you said you wanted something 'deliciously sinister'. Don't blame me for making your wish come true, pal."

He flung an overblown sneer.

"If it makes you feel any better, the alien and I would like you to be the baby's godfather."

"Oh. Well, in that case, congratulations!"

The waitress brought over menus and took their drink order.

"So," he said, "how've you been? Other than the extraterrestrial pregnancy thing."

"Good. Work is great."

"Any love interest I need to do a background check on?"

A fleeting smile. "Well, now that you mention it, there *is* something I wanted to run by you."

"Of course. What's going on?"

"So there's this guy at work. Pediatrician. He seems to be interested in me."

"Seems to be?"

"I know. Sounds weird, right? It started out with the usual. Smiles passing in the hall. Brief chats by the water cooler. Then he started occasionally confiding in me. But over the last couple of months, the dynamic's been shifting. We've kind of been dancing around this— Whatever it is we've been doing."

Piza nodded. "Okay. Sounds like you're interested in him as well."

"I am. A lot."

"So why the coy two-step? Not that it isn't adorable . . . if you guys were fifteen."

"Funny, wiseass. The problem is he's married. And before you give me the look— Ah, too late. He's separated. About six months."

"How long has he been married? Any kids?"

"Ten years. She helped put him through med school, actually. And no kids. He just became an attending. Fortunately, they agreed to hold off on children until he got established. But—"

"Sorry to interrupt, Lizzie, but has either of them filed for divorce?"

"No. And, as usual, you've instantly cut through the fog. What if they reconcile? Six months isn't all that long. I mean he says it's over, but if he's so sure, why hasn't he started a divorce? I don't wanna toss my heart in the ring only to find out he's forfeited the match."

"No, I hear ya." He gave her a warm smile. "Just as an aside, that was a pretty cool metaphor you just came up with."

She returned the smile. "Kind of impressed *myself* with that one. So, whaddya think?"

The waitress returned with his coffee and her lemonade, took their orders, and left at lunch-hour speed.

Opening a minuscule, plastic half-and-half container, Piza said, "I know you hate answering a question with a question, but what's your gut telling you?"

She sighed. "You know how much alike you and I are. Always a battle between head and heart. My heart's telling me 'take a shot', but my brain's flashing giant red strobe lights."

"Have you ever met his wife?"

"Not formally. Saw her once by chance when she stopped by to give him mail. I guess it had bypassed the forwarding address instructions."

"How did they interact?"

"Seemed civil enough. No gestures of affection, but no hostility either, that I could see. Actually, a couple of light smiles, now that I'm thinking back on it."

He shifted in his seat. "Look, there's no easy answer to this. You know that, right?"

"Of course I do. That's why I'm bouncing it off you."

After a few moments in which he looked lost in thought, he said, "You remember my old college roommate?"

"Sure. Jack. *He's* a doctor, right?"

"He is. Jack got involved in a relationship in his second year of med school. Wound up falling in love with this girl. And it was mutual. But med school and residency? It's a merciless grind. And they didn't survive it."

"I'm not sure I'm getting your point. Are you saying that since Rob . . . that's his name . . . and his wife somehow made it through the worst of times, this crack in their relationship can be fixed? There's still hope for them?"

Piza rested clasped hands on the table. "Listen. No relationship's a sure thing. But you'd at least like the scales to be balanced at the beginning. I don't think that's the case here. I'm not saying give up on the guy if you feel that strongly about him. But I'd give it a little more time before committing to anything."

They sat looking at each other. Then, she nodded. "Thanks. Deep down I suspect I knew that was the right answer. I think I just needed it confirmed. I'm usually on firmer ground, but with this one. . ."

"Believe me, I get it. But you'll be fine, whichever way this goes."

As she smiled a 'thank you', the waitress brought their food.

Elizabeth laughed as she watched Piza drown his Belgian waffle in syrup.

"Laugh all you want," he said, "but this is solely for my mental health. I need the syrup to offset my cynicism."

"Uh-huh. Whatever gets you through the night, buddy."

Wrestling with a burger that looked like it could have fed two of her, she asked, "So how're things with you and Mandy?"

"Good, actually. We're keeping it loose. You know, see each other a couple of nights a week. Weekends together, usually. Sometimes her place, sometimes mine."

"What's it been? Seven months or so?"

"Yeah, little over seven."

She tilted her head. "And neither of you wants more than that?"

He shrugged through a sip of coffee. "I'm fine with it. And she seems content. If you're asking is there something there, the answer is 'sure'. We're taking it slow, that's all."

"Can I ask you something?"

"Of course. As long as it doesn't kill my sugar high."

"Do you still think of Theresa at all?"

He hadn't seen that coming although, knowing Elizabeth, perhaps he should have. "Not really," he answered, instantly remembering to make eye contact. He had a habit of averting his eyes when he was uncomfortable. Forcing a smile, he said, "And why exactly are you dredging up ancient history?"

She scrunched her face in mock puzzlement and rubbed her chin. "Oh, gee, I don't know. Maybe because she broke your heart that year you taught after college? And maybe because Mandy is the longest relationship you've had since then, and I'm still not sure how serious it is?"

"Well, I am." He waved out the window they were seated by.

"See someone you know?" she asked.

"No. That was me bidding 'bon voyage' to that sugar high."

Looking penitent, she said, "I'm sorry. But I worry about you. I worry that you're not over her. I just want you to be happy."

His expression softened. "I know. But trust me, I'm okay. There's no emotional residue. Although I used to occasionally kick myself for being an idiot. Who falls in love with a nun? Not that I'm saying I deserved the hurt as payback for my stupidity. I'm not *that* big a masochist."

"You're not that big an idiot either. She loved you too."

"I guess. Neither of us ever said the words. But the bottom line is she bailed rather than deal with it."

"I know. Transferred to Philly."

"Yep. New parish. New school. New life."

"True. But Philadelphia's only a two-hour drive down the turnpike. I still think you should've gone down there, if only to get some closure."

"She didn't want me to contact her. That was the message I got. You know that." It came out louder than he'd meant it to. Calming himself, he said, "Look, Lizzie. I know you worry about me. And I love you for it. But it's in the past. Believe me, okay? I'm fine."

A grudging "okay" was the response. Then, with the broadest of grins, she said, "But if you ever want to discuss it. . ."

He tossed an empty half-and-half container at her.

CHAPTER 11

As Piza stood outside Nia Bradley's open door, there were so many files on her desk it looked like she was erecting a barricade. Nia was a senior partner and, as the only other attorney in the firm to practice family law, was also Piza's immediate supervisor. The two of them had hit it off from the get-go.

Nia had started her career handling family matters at a Legal Aid office, a job she'd been happy with for ten years. But even with her husband's salary from teaching science and coaching wrestling at a local high school, the reality of raising three children in the New York metropolitan area had yanked her out the door of Legal Aid and escorted her into the offices of Shapiro & Manetti. She'd made partner in three years; one of a mere handful of Black female partners in the county.

He wasn't surprised to see her in on a Saturday. She had an uncompromising work ethic. That quality, her savvy, and her innate intelligence made her one of the most respected family law practitioners in the state.

Piza had come in to catch up on the mail and take care of a few other housekeeping chores. He didn't mind coming in on

Saturday mornings. You could dress down, and an answering service fielded the phone calls. Maybe not nirvana, but about as close to it as a law office could get.

He rapped on the doorframe, and her head snapped up. "Geez, Tony, you scared the hell out of me," she said as her eyes returned to normal size.

"Sorry. I seem to have a habit of doing that to people. A psychic once told me I was a ninja in a previous life. Probably accounts for my stealth . . . and my ability to carve a turkey in forty-five seconds."

She replied with a crooked smile. "Uh-huh. So, what's up?"

He took a seat in front of her desk. "How is it that you're wearing jeans and a sweatshirt, and you still manage to look elegant?"

"It's probably the cat-eye-shaped glasses. They add a touch of panache no matter what you're wearing. And no, you can't have a raise. Or Bill O'Leary's parking spot. He'll be back from disability leave next month."

Piza slowly raised his right hand and slapped his chest, wearing a look of tortured hurt. "I can't believe you'd think there was an ulterior motive to my compliment. I'm not looking for a raise. Although I wouldn't mind one, truth be told. And I would never try to take advantage of poor Bill's unfortunate encounter with his electric garage door. In the three years I've been here, have I ever given you a reason to doubt my sincerity?"

"No, Tony, you haven't. In fact, you're goodness personified."

"All right then. I'm assuming that's your idea of an apology, which I accept. I was gonna talk to you Monday, but as long as you're here, can I run something by you? Actually, two things."

"Of course. Shoot."

"Okay. First, I've decided to represent an old friend for his divorce. What I need to know——"

"Is this the guy you went to New Brunswick with for the DV hearing?"

"It is. But he lives in Lodi, so I can start the suit up here. The thing is, he's hurting money-wise, and I was wondering if I can bill him at a discounted rate."

Having worked for Legal Aid, Nia had an ingrained soft spot for people in financial straits. "What'd you have in mind?"

"I was thinking a buck seventy-five an hour?"

"Fifty an hour below your normal billing rate. How far back do you go with this guy?"

"Grammar school."

A slight chuckle. "Doesn't get much further back than that, I guess. Okay. Do it."

"Thanks. I appreciate it."

"You're welcome. And the second thing?"

Piza adjusted himself in his chair. "This divorce work is starting to wear on me, Nia. As you know, I've been doing it for nine years, between my old firm and here." He paused. "It's— It's kind of gotten to the point where everybody's stories are starting to sound the same. One narrative, just change the names and faces."

Nia sat back. "That's not unusual. As long as it doesn't affect the quality of your work. And I haven't seen it impacting yours. Your clients seem very pleased as far as I can tell. I mean there's always those few who'll never be satisfied, but that goes with the territory. But you work hard for them, and there's no shortage of empathy on your part."

He managed a smile. "Well, I appreciate the sentiment. But at this juncture, I'm not sure how much of that empathy is sincere and how much is muscle memory."

With interlaced fingers touching her lower lip, she said, "So how do we handle this? Because if you're looking for a clean break from matrimonial, I don't see how that's possible. Not if you're looking to do it immediately."

There had been nothing antagonistic in her tone. But knowing that the firm had hired him specifically for his family law experience, he couldn't shake a sense of guilt. And, outside his circle of immediate family and closest friends, he often fought off guilt with defensiveness. So there was a hint of pique when he responded, "God, Nia, don't you think I know that? I wouldn't just waltz in here and make that kind of demand."

He couldn't read her, and he wondered if he'd crossed a line. She removed her glasses. "Did I say it was a demand?"

He broke out the disarming grin that had gotten him out of trouble since he was old enough to *get* in trouble. "No, you didn't. Sorry about that. I guess I'm a little on edge about this."

"It's fine. What would you rather be doing?"

"Honestly, I'd like to do straight-up litigation."

She nodded and returned the glasses to the bridge of her nose. "The excitement of trial work without the emotional turmoil of divorce. I get it." A few moments of evident contemplation led to, "There are variables at play here, but as long as we're talking about a transition *down the road*, it might be doable."

"Great. And I hope I didn't blindside you with this. That wasn't my intention."

"I know that," she said. "And you didn't blindside me. I'll bring it up at the next partners' meeting, and we'll see where it goes from there."

"Terrific. Thanks, Nia."

As he left her office, he debated calling Sabatini to give him the news, but decided to hold off until Monday. He wasn't sure whether it was because he wanted him to twist in the wind a bit longer, or because he didn't feel like dealing with what he knew would be Sabatini's gushing gratitude and a desire to immediately strategize a game plan. He determined it was probably both.

Monday'll be just fine.

CHAPTER 12

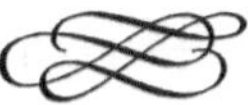

On his way to pick up his children the second Sunday after the domestic violence hearing, Sabatini's body felt like a giant Gordian knot. He'd missed the previous week's visitation due to a stomach bug that had him spending the weekend bonding with his toilet. He'd managed to call the kids, though, and was relieved there was no indication of lingering anxiety from the prior Sunday's trauma, or an inkling they knew about the hearing. He had enough faith in Megan's maternal instinct to assume she hadn't said anything. But he wondered whether their angst—so painfully evident that terrible day—would resurface with his presence.

His fears were allayed when they came bounding out of the house, all smiles, honey-blond braids bouncing off their shoulders with each step. Their buoyancy skyrocketed when he laid out his agenda for the day: a visit to the Turtle Back Zoo, lunch at McDonald's, and the remainder of the afternoon at their favorite park.

As they sat in a booth at McDonald's, the kids were still engaged in the animated chatter that had begun as soon as they left the zoo. They'd been to Turtle Back a couple of years before, but today they'd reacted to each exhibit with the joy and awe of a new revelation. Moments like that invariably provided Sabatini with a much-needed dose of self-worth.

Amy tugged on her father's scarlet Rutgers sweatshirt. "Can I have another Happy Meal, Daddy?"

Before he could answer, Lisa huffed the condescending breath of a seasoned older sister. "How many times has Daddy said 'only one Happy Meal'? I don't understand why—"

"Thanks, Lis, but I can take it from here," their father said. He picked up Amy and planted her on his lap, trying not to laugh as the child's expression teetered between a scowl and a frown. "You know the rule, peanut. One Happy Meal. Are you really still hungry, or is this about the prize inside again?"

The child lowered her eyes. "The prize. I really wanted the spinny thing this time, not the stupid eraser."

"It's called a 'top', not a 'spinny thing', silly," Lisa said.

"Fine!" her sister shot back, looking like she would have stomped her feet if they weren't dangling two feet above the floor. Her eyes suddenly brightened. "How about this, Daddy? We'll give this Happy Meal back, and ask them for a new one."

He smiled and kissed the top of her head. "Good idea, sweetheart, except all that's left of this one is three french-fries. So I don't think Mr. McDonald will go for that. Plus, even if you got a new one, you couldn't be sure it would have a top inside."

The child's face showed the strain of deep thought. Then, with a resigned nod, "I think you're right. Okay, maybe next time."

"That's my girl. Okay, so let's clean up, and then we're off to the park."

Lisa pulled a face and said, "Do we have to clean up?"

"Yes. You know the rules."

"Well, sometimes it's good to be messy. And rules are no fun. That's what Aunt Candy says."

Sabatini froze. *Aunt Candy? What the hell.* Doing his best to keep a light-hearted tone, he said, "Well, there *are* times when it's okay to be messy. But being in a restaurant isn't one of them. And rules may not be fun, but they're necessary. So clean up and let's get this show on the road."

———

As his children navigated the playground at the park, Sabatini sat on a weathered wooden bench, pondering the potential damage "Aunt Candy" could wreak on his family. Telling the kids it's okay to be messy? Rules are no fun? And how was she getting away with this with Megan, who was borderline obsessive-compulsive about neatness and regimentation?

He needed information on this bizarre and troubling relationship his wife had formed with Candy; had to uncover the basis of the Svengali-like hold the older woman seemed to have on her. He certainly wasn't going to get it from Megan. She'd sent the kids out to him that morning without showing her face. And after the domestic violence debacle, he had no intention of interacting with her, short of an emergency. The only other source he could think of was his precocious older daughter, and that realization set off alarm bells.

When he and Megan separated, he'd vowed never to become one of those parents who—inadvertently or otherwise—used their children as instruments of war. But now, he reasoned that a benign interrogation wouldn't breach that commitment. The purpose wasn't to poison her mind; he wouldn't utter one disparaging word about her mom.

And that was that. Necessity may be the mother of invention, but she also gave birth to rationalization—a distinctly less noble offspring.

All Sabatini needed was an opportune moment to speak with Lisa. The ride home provided that.

With Amy asleep in her car seat, and a wide-awake Lisa buckled in on the passenger seat, Sabatini decided to forge ahead with his investigation. "So, Lis, is Aunt Candy at the house a lot?"

The girl gave a non-committal shrug. "I guess. She has dinner with us a lot."

"Does she, um, sleep over at all?" He wondered if he'd crossed a self-imposed boundary, but immediately determined he hadn't. He believed it to be a legitimate question, and the need for an answer had been gnawing at him since that day at court.

"No, she goes home at night." After a reflective pause, "But a couple of times, when Mommy was really sad, she asked Mommy if she wanted her to stay over. But Mommy always said no, she was okay."

"Is Mommy sad a lot?"

"Kind of. She doesn't smile much anymore. Sometimes she cries. Especially when she and Aunt Candy drink wine. It's weird. First she seems happy and then she gets sad. Aunt Candy always puts her arm around her and tells Mommy that she reminds her of her daughter, and then Aunt Candy cries too."

Jesus, what the hell is that about? "So then—"

"I don't know why Mommy likes wine," she interjected. "It's yucky."

Her father's eyes went cold as he stared straight ahead. "How do you know it's yucky?"

The girl responded with an innocent, "Aunt Candy let me try it once."

Sabatini was fuming. "Was Mommy there when Aunt Candy let you taste the wine?"

"Uh-huh." She giggled. "She was laughing and said I made a face like I had sucked on a lemon." She replicated the look, and frowned when it didn't garner a laugh from her father.

Picking up on his miscue, he reached over, tapped her nose,

and said, "That's the best suck-on-a-lemon expression I've ever seen, Lis. You definitely have a gift for making weird faces."

She grinned. "Thank you, Daddy. It's nice to know I have talent."

"Never a doubt, kiddo." A brief lull preceded his next line of questioning. "I agree with you, by the way, that sometimes wine can taste yucky. Do, uh, Mommy and Aunt Candy drink wine with dinner?"

The girl nodded. "Uh-huh. And sometimes they drink it when we're watching TV, like when Mommy puts out this smelly cheese and some crackers. And I saw Mommy drinking it in bed once too. I got up to go to the bathroom, and her door was, you know, like a little open? She was sitting on her bed with her pajamas on, reading a book, and she had a glass of wine in her hand."

He hoped his daughter hadn't noticed his face become a pale, stone mask. Megan's father had been an alcoholic, before cirrhosis took him at 58. She'd often lamented how the man's addiction had reduced her once sprightly mother to the sullen woman Sabatini knew. Megan rarely spoke about her own relationship with him, but he knew she'd been scarred. And he sensed it was the cause of her immersing herself in religion. He'd never known his wife to drink anything stronger than a glass of wine, and that was restricted to one small glass at Easter, Thanksgiving, and Christmas.

"Did Mommy see you out in the hall that night?"

"I don't think so. Why?"

He gave a cursory headshake. "Just wondering, that's all." If she *had* seen Lisa, he would have liked to know if she'd made any effort to hide the drink. He waited a few moments, then decided to change topics. "So, when I drop you guys off on Sunday, does Mommy ever ask you what we talked about during the day?"

"Um, not really. Usually she just asks us if we had a good time. Sometimes we tell her what we did, especially if we did something cool like the zoo today." A quizzical look crossed her face. "Daddy, how come you're asking so many questions about Mommy?"

Shit. One question too many. "Uh, no reason. Since I'm not in the house anymore, I just wanted to see what was going on with you guys. Ya know, how Mom is doing and all." That answer seemed to satisfy the girl. But he felt the need to cover himself. "You know, Lis, you're getting to be a big girl. You're very mature for your age."

She beamed. "Thanks, Daddy."

"I mean it. I'm very proud of how responsible you've become. And I've gotta tell ya, I really feel like I can confide in you about certain things. You know what that means, right?"

An emphatic nod accompanied, "Of course I do. It means you can tell me stuff that maybe you won't tell anyone else."

"Exactly. And I want you to know that you can confide in me too. About anything. And so 'confidential' will become our magic word. If you tell me something's confidential, I won't tell anyone. Not even your mom. And if I tell *you* that something's confidential. . ."

His daughter mimed locking her lips. "Not a word to anyone."

He smiled and said, "Not Mom or Aunt Candy or anyone. And we'll seal it with a pinky swear, okay?" He extended the pinky of his right hand.

"Deal," she answered as they locked fingers.

"Great. And to start things off, everything we just talked about here in the car is confidential. Okay?"

"Okay. Thanks for trusting me, Daddy."

He almost choked on the guilt.

CHAPTER 13

Piza pressed the intercom button on his office phone. "Gloria, do you happen to have Joe Sabatini's number handy?"

"Give me a sec. I'll get it for you."

"Great. Thanks."

A minute later the woman came into his office, a slip of paper in hand. "Here you go. Home and work."

"Thanks. You're the best."

"Finally. Validation of what I've been saying for years."

Gloria was what Piza referred to as an "old school" legal secretary. Neatly attired in a dress, or skirt and blouse, every day; earrings and a necklace of some sort; not a gray hair to be found ("Over my dead body," she'd once told him), or a chestnut-dyed strand out of place. He surmised she was in her early sixties. Still married to her high school sweetheart. She was clever without ever being impolite, and so familiar with family law that he was certain she could adequately represent half his clients.

"You've decided to handle his divorce," she said.

"Did I say that? I could be calling to tell him I'm *not* handling his divorce."

"Haven't you figured out by now that I can read your mind? It's a gift."

"Gift indeed, devil woman. Anyhow, I spoke with Nia on Saturday. And yes, I'm gonna take his case. Reduced fee. He's hurting for money right now."

"So, what's in the past is in the past?" she asked through a gentle smile.

"For the most part. Still stings a bit. Truth is I'm mostly concerned for his kids. Especially after what I saw at court. That woman. Candy."

"Well, hopefully she doesn't have her hooks too deep into his wife. Otherwise, this could be a rough one."

"I know. We'll see, I guess."

When she left, he released a prolonged exhale and dialed.

"You have no idea how happy I am you're gonna do this, Ton," Sabatini said as he settled into his seat. "And thanks for seeing me after five."

"Not a problem. But before we start discussing the process, I need to know you're going to be able to pay for this, Strikes. I spoke with—"

"Whatever it takes. I'll get the money."

"Well, hear me out. I normally bill at two twenty-five an hour." Sabatini blanched. "But I've been given the okay to bill you at one seventy-five." Piza offered a weak smile. "Family-and-friends discount."

Sabatini's face took on the comically contorted expression of someone trying to look grateful, but clearly unable to interpret what he'd heard as good news. "Um, uh, geez, Tony. Wow. Uh, thanks." A nervous laugh. "Boy, am, uh, am I in the wrong profession. Um, do you have . . . like, can you tell me how many hours a case like this usually takes? Just, ya know, so I have an idea?"

Piza fought the urge to stand up and escort the stammering man to the exit. But he'd seen this reaction to a fee discussion with virtually every unwealthy client he'd ever represented, and he determined that being upset at Sabatini's "wrong profession" remark was probably more residual resentment than anything else.

"This is why I wanted to discuss the fee with you first. I can't tell you what the bottom line is here. It depends on any number of factors. What issues are contested? Is she gonna be willing to compromise? And that goes hand-in-hand with who ends up representing her. A sleazebag can blow up any chance of an early settlement. They drag cases out to build up their fees. Sucks, but there's really no way to stop it."

Sabatini had been nodding like his head was on autopilot. He looked like he couldn't wait for Piza to stop, so he could speak again. "I get all that, Ton. But maybe just like a ballpark." Palms out, he held his hands out in front of him. "Trust me, I won't hold you to it or anything like that."

Piza noticeably exhaled. "Okay. You're probably looking at something in the area of ten thousand. Could be less, could be more. But with your particular circumstances . . . fairly long marriage, kids involved and all . . . that's about average. And I'm going to need a retainer. Standard is twenty-five hundred, but I'll reduce it to fifteen. I'll take the fees out of that as they accrue. But when the retainer runs out, you'll have to replenish it. Can you handle that?"

With a look bordering on panic Sabatini said, "Uh, honestly, I don't have that kind of money lying around. I'm not sure what I can— I mean my parents don't have a pot to piss in, and my sister's barely getting by." He massaged his forehead.

"What about your brother? He's loaded, if I recall."

Scowling, Sabatini said, "The dry-cleaning king of Middlesex County? Forget that cheap bastard."

Piza grimaced. "Look, if I dispense with the retainer, can you promise me you'll pay the bills as they come due? I'm breaching protocol here for you. So I need to know——"

"You have my word, Ton. Man, you have no idea how much I appreciate this. I can't thank you enough."

"All right. But I'm just telling you, if you fall behind I'll have to file a motion with the court to let me out of the case. Let's be clear on that."

"I understand completely. I do."

"Okay." He buzzed his secretary. "Gloria, can you prepare a fee agreement for Mr. Sabatini. No retainer, and a hundred seventy-five an hour."

"Sure thing" came from the phone speaker.

"So, any visitation issues last couple of weeks?"

"No. I missed last week. I was sick. Yesterday she just sent the kids out. Didn't even see her. Same when I dropped them off."

"Just as well."

"Yeah. But here's the thing. I found out 'Aunt' Candy . . . *Aunt*, you believe it? Apparently, she spends a lot of time at the house. Dinner and such. But I don't think there's any hanky-panky going on between her and Megan. According to Lisa, she's always telling Megan how much she reminds her of her daughter. I don't know what the story is, but seems like that's the connection."

A look of concern materialized as Piza said, "Crap. If this is a maternal thing, that could be even worse. Makes her that much more protective."

Sabatini leaned in, like he was about to disclose a confidence and didn't want to be overheard. "Yeah, but there's more. You remember Megan's father?"

The lawyer raised his hands slightly. "The only time I met him was when you got married."

"Well, he died a few years ago. Miserable bastard. Only good thing he ever did was take out a hefty life insurance policy. Left Megan's mom set for life. Anyway, he was an alcoholic. Did you know that?"

"No. You never really talked about her side of the family."

"Well, he was. Kind of a well-kept secret. You'd never know it to look at him. Great job. Active in the community. But it's what killed him. And as I learned yesterday, the apple doesn't fall far from the tree."

"What are you talking about?"

"Megan. Seems she's been drinking like a proverbial fish. Wine. Dinner; watching TV." He paused, apparently for dramatic effect. "Even in bed."

"Are you sure? Any time we all went out, she always looked at us like reprobates if we had more than one drink. And I don't ever remember her having even one."

Sabatini nodded in agreement. "Because she didn't. I'm guessing her genes finally caught up with her."

"That's a little cold, don't you think?" Piza said. "I don't think the fact her father was an alcoholic necessarily preordained—"

"I know, I know. It's just that with all the stress we've been under. . ."

The lawyer leaned back in his chair. "How do you know about this?"

"Lisa. It was completely innocent, of course. We were talking about Candy and all, and this stuff about her and Megan drinking just came out. Do you believe that woman even let the kid taste some wine? And all Megan did was laugh. Something's seriously off here, Ton."

"Well, it's something to think about."

Shaking his head, Sabatini said, "I don't think there's *anything* to think about. I wanna sue her for custody."

CHAPTER 14

When Piza and Sabatini met on Monday, they agreed that Piza would start the divorce rather than follow his usual practice, which was to first send a letter to see if the other spouse had an attorney and wished to discuss settling the case. Considering Candy's disturbing influence on Megan, they both doubted that settlement talks would go anywhere. Plus, although it was unlikely Megan would initiate the divorce—what with her strong feelings on the subject—by filing first they'd assure the case was heard in Hackensack, thus avoiding Piza having to continually trek down to New Brunswick.

But not everything had gone smoothly at the meeting. Although he understood Sabatini's knee-jerk reaction to what he'd learned from Lisa, Piza felt his demands were unrealistic. He wanted the children to live with him. He wanted the final word on the important decisions affecting their lives. In effect, he wanted Megan out of the picture. As things stood, the lawyer explained, the chance of that happening was virtually non-existent.

At that point Sabatini had pushed back, leading Piza to agree that proof of an alcohol problem might enhance their chance of success. But he also said there would be a lot of variables at play, not the least of which was whether they could back up their contention with hard evidence. The only information they had so far was based on what Lisa had seen. And if they included the alcohol issue in the divorce complaint, wouldn't Megan peg her daughter as the source? Or suspect it at least? Did Sabatini want to put the child in that position? And did he really expect her to testify against her mother down the road?

That had elicited a marginal acknowledgement of the problem, which was immediately offset by: "But isn't that something we have to risk, if it's best for her and Amy?"

Using Lisa to prove an allegation—albeit a potentially crucial one—was incompatible with Piza's mission to shield the children as much as possible from the divorce's inevitable fallout. But in the end, he agreed to go along with his client's wishes. If Megan was drinking excessively, even if only in the evening, at some point it could affect her ability to care for the children. There was no evidence of that as yet, but the possibility existed. And if something happened to those kids, he'd never forgive himself.

In the course of the office conference, Piza had spelled out the pitfalls of a custody battle by delivering an often recited but sincere monologue. Living with unrelenting anxiety for a year or more. The probable emotional impact on the children. If court-mandated mediation didn't work, then psychological evaluations of everyone involved, as well as assessments of living conditions. And, the likely rapid buildup of legal fees. That last one produced Sabatini's first and only visible reaction to the warnings —a flicker of alarm.

Piza asked his client if he understood the implications of everything he'd just told him, particularly the possible effect on the children and the fact that he'd undoubtedly have to get a bigger apartment. Sabatini assured him that he did. The lawyer's push for details on how he planned to deal with the issues met with a hazy and unsatisfying: "Don't worry, Tony, I'll handle it." Concluding there was no point in pressing him more, Piza let it go and said the divorce complaint would be ready by the following week.

When he arrived at the office Friday morning, a manila envelope with his name hand-printed on the front was sitting on his desk. A memo from Gloria read: *Mr. Sabatini dropped this off earlier.* Inside were pictures of a blue plastic bin abutting what appeared to be the exterior foundation of a house. Close-ups of the container revealed a minimum of five wine bottles lying among crushed cans and empty jars.

A note was paper-clipped to one of the photos:

Megan takes this recycling stuff really seriously, I guess! And don't worry, I didn't take the pictures. Gina did, while Megan and the kids were at Amy's tee-ball practice. Hope this helps.

Would it help? It was a lot of bottles, assuming they weren't accumulated over a long period. The optics alone were pretty compelling. Disturbing too. And while he wasn't thrilled with the idea of Sabatini's sister sneaking on to the property to play amateur gumshoe, at least the pictures gave him something concrete to work with. It also helped shore up his belief that he was doing the right thing. And now he could couch the alcohol abuse allegations in the complaint in terms of "objective third-party evidence", hopefully routing suspicion away from Lisa.

That afternoon, he was finishing the final edit of a draft of the complaint. Tie loosened, sleeves rolled up, chair tilted back almost to the point of tipping over—to accommodate resting his feet on his desk. He removed the pockmarked, yellow No. 2 pencil clenched in his teeth, and made a note in the margin of the typewritten page pressed against the legal pad in his left hand. Returning the pencil to its dental perch freed his right hand to wipe sweat from his forehead, condensation directly related to an air-conditioning system more in need of euthanasia than repair.

Great way to be spending the Friday before Memorial Day.

As he removed his feet from his desk, Gloria appeared in the doorway. "It's three thirty. Why are you still here? Just about everyone else has gotten a jump on the weekend."

"I live for my work. You know that."

"Uh-huh. You're a model of dedication. You finish reviewing the Sabatini complaint? I can type it up if you have. That way we can get him in to sign on Tuesday, and get it filed Wednesday."

"I *have* finished. But I'll tell you what. Since the temperature in this place is rapidly approaching nuclear meltdown levels, why don't we *both* bolt. There's nothing here that can't wait."

"Well, nuclear meltdown may be a bit much, but it's definitely uncomfortable in here. So I think I'll take you up on your offer . . . assuming you don't dock my pay for the remainder of the day, of course."

Piza shook his head in mock dismay. "Boy. Talk about having your cake and eating it too. Fine, you'll get paid for the whole day."

Holding her hands to her heart, she said, "Oh, thank you, Mr. Scrooge." She took a step to leave, but then turned around. "Enjoy your parents' barbecue extravaganza Sunday, by the way."

"Thanks. You and Bob doing anything exciting this weekend?"

She shrugged. "Not really. Board games, probably. Grill some burgers. Ring people's doorbells then run and hide. The usual."

He laughed as she flashed a teasing smile and walked away.

CHAPTER 15

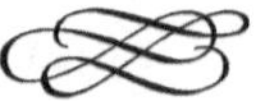

"I have to tell you, Mrs. Piza, I may start eating this pasta before I get it to the patio. I've never been to a barbecue that had baked ziti and sausage and peppers on the menu. This is fantastic." Mandy made the observation while accompanying Mary in the kitchen.

"Well," the beaming woman replied, "that's because you never been to an *Italian* barbecue before. Oh, and just so ya know, Italians never call it 'pasta'. It's 'macaroni'." A wink put the finishing touch on the point.

"Macaroni it is," the girl said as she used her backside to hold the door open for Mary, who was carrying the tin of sausage and peppers.

As they set the food on a folding table adorned end-to-end with a paper American flag table cloth, Piza wandered over, bent his head over the food, and made a show of sniffing. "God, I'm salivating like one of Pavlov's dogs. So, anything else you need to bring out, Ma?"

"Now you ask? After me and Mandy lugged the heavy stuff out here? In this heat?"

"How was I supposed to know you were bringing it out? Why didn't you say something?"

Wiping her hands on her apron, Mary answered, "You're the son. I'm the mother. I shouldn't *have* to say somethin'." She shifted her gaze to Mandy. "Am I right, dear?"

"One hundred percent, Mrs. Piza." She cast a disapproving look at her boyfriend. "This has been very enlightening. I may have to re-think our relationship."

With an animated nod Mary said, "See that, Anthony. You could scare Mandy away if ya don't shape up."

Piza's exhale through tightened lips sounded like a snorting horse. "Let me try this again. Hey, Mom! First of all, you look fantastic. That new reddish-brown hair color? The shorter cut? Stunning. Second, I was wondering if there's anything you'd like me to help you with, because I want to be the best son I possibly can. Now and forever."

Mandy grinned, drawing a wagging finger from Mary. "Don't encourage him, sweetheart." Looking at her son, she said, "You can bring the bread out, mister comedian, if you remember where the kitchen is."

He took a deep bow. "I live to obey."

"Hmm. *That's* good to know," his girlfriend said, wiggling her eyebrows.

Mary chuckled. "Maybe you should go with him, Mandy, so he don't get lost."

As he and Mandy walked to the kitchen, Piza said, "This isn't good."

"What isn't good?"

"She likes you."

"And that's a bad thing because. . ."

"The only other girlfriend I had who my mother actually liked was when I was in high school. And a month after she told me she liked her, we broke up."

Through a smirk Mandy said, "I'm gonna take your mom's

advice and not encourage you. So for today, go weave your tall tales somewhere else, pal."

Piza stopped short. "I swear I'm not lying. We broke up. And *she* broke up with *me*. The only girl ever to do that. The one girl Mother Mary liked. So you can understand my concern."

Her face a snapshot of cynicism, she said, "Well, my initial reaction is that you're full of shit, and trying to goad me into reacting. For your amusement, of course. But it's a beautiful day and I'm in a great mood, so I'm going to play along. So here's the deal. I swear on the pan of baked macaroni I just brought out that I won't break up with you because your mom likes me. In fact, I'll up the ante. I promise not to break up with you, period. Unless, of course, you do something so monumentally unforgivable I'd have no choice."

"Which I'd never do."

"There you go. So, do we have a deal?"

Eyes narrowed, Piza said, "Before I answer that, I need to know you're fully cognizant of the profound sanctity of a baked-ziti oath."

"Being with you and your family these past seven-plus months, rest assured I do. So, deal or not?"

"Deal."

"Great."

"But just to avoid tempting fate, stay as far away from my mother as possible for the rest of the day."

Rolling her eyes, she said, "Such a jerk."

The Memorial Day Weekend Piza Lawn-bocce Tournament was an annual event that could be thwarted only by rain heavy enough to require calling on Noah for assistance. Earlier in the day, Piza and his father had reminisced about tournaments past; how participants had come and gone over the years. Piza had been particularly nostalgic. A few years before, two of his oldest friends, Jeff Jennings and Sal Amico, had moved to Florida and California, respectively. He still missed them. And since Sabatini had been declared persona non grata, Frankie was the only one of his childhood buddies who was still a fixture. Reacting to his son's wistfulness, Angelo had said: "Life is change, Anthony. Just be thankful for all your good memories, 'cause there's plenty of people out there who ain't got nearly as many." A kiss on the cheek was Piza's response.

After the main course, Angelo announced the start of the match. "Okay, who's in?"

Uncle Nunzio was already retrieving the bocce balls from the shed, so there was no doubt about *his* intentions. Piza and Frankie volunteered as well. Frankie's father, Lou, was there, and was normally a mainstay. But he had to beg off because his sciatica had flared up.

"How about you, Roger?" Angelo asked Frankie's boyfriend. "Wanna give it a shot?"

Through a wince the man said, "Unfortunately, Mr. Piza, I've never played. I have no idea what's involved."

Angelo instantly assumed the role of mentor. "You're a psychologist, Roger. You'll get it." He hollered to his friend. "Nunzio, bring over the pallino and one of the big balls."

Nunzio hurried over. "Here," the man said, his voice gravelly and so strained you'd swear that even a medium-length sentence would end in a convulsion. He handed Angelo a white hard-plastic ball about the size of a large walnut, and a solid red plastic ball that might have been a grapefruit in a former life. "What's goin' on?"

"Roger never played bocce before, so I'm gonna explain it to 'im."

Nunzio looked at Roger as one might regard an animal carcass on the side of the road—with a mix of pity and revulsion. "Really, kid? You never played?"

The man answered with a good-natured shrug.

"Okay," Angelo said, holding up the small white ball. "You see this little guy? He's the 'pallino'. At the start of the game, someone throws 'im onto the lawn, as far as they want. This big red ball? There's four of these and four green ones. Each player throws a big one, and tries to get it as close to the pallino as they can. Whoever ends up closest gets a point. If two greens are closer than any of the reds, green gets two points. And so on. Capisce?"

Nodding, Roger said, "I see. Okay. But let's say, for example, one of the green balls happens to hit one of the red ones that's in the way? Is that allowed?"

Nunzio jumped in before Angelo could speak. "Allowed? You kiddin'? If one'a them other balls is in the way, you smash the shit out of it!"

The three younger men broke out laughing, while the two older ones wore expressions that asked what possibly could have been amusing about Nunzio's statement. To their generation, the solemnity of bocce was on a par with soccer and electing a pope.

"Okay," Angelo said. "Me and Nunzio against you three. We'll get two balls each. You guys get one each and take turns throwin' the fourth ball. Fair?"

"Probably not," his son answered with a skepticism seeded in history. Then, lowering his voice, "Uh, Pop. Don't you think it's about time to break with tradition and ask the women if any of them wanna play?"

Angelo had the look of a child who had raided the cookie jar and gotten nabbed one step shy of a clean getaway. He turned to Nunzio, whose raised-hands "It's your house" couldn't disguise his disenchantment.

Huffing a breath and donning a cheery look so obviously forced it was probably painful, Angelo called out, "Hey, any of you ladies wanna play?"

Mary and Nunzio's wife, Cheryl, begged off. But Elizabeth,

who'd arrived only a few minutes before (having covered for a co-worker at the hospital), said, "Let me get some food in my stomach, and then Mandy and I will play the winners." She glanced at Mandy, who nodded approval.

"Hey, what about me?" Patty asked, briefly breaking away from the ravaged ear of corn ensnared in her grip.

"And Patty too," Mandy said, garnering a yellow-dotted grin from the girl.

"Oh, okay. That sounds good," Nunzio said with unmistakable insincerity. "Oh, but wait a minute. We usually play best two outta three. Game goes up to eleven so, ya know, it could be a while."

"That's fine, Dad," Elizabeth responded with an inflated smile. "We're not going anywhere."

When the game started, it took Roger all of five minutes to get the hang of it, after which he had Angelo and Nunzio exchanging scowls and cursing under their breath every time it was his turn to throw.

An agitated Nunzio took his godson aside during a break after the first game, which the older men had lost by three points. "What's the story with this Roger guy, Anthony?"

"Whaddya mean?"

"I never seen nobody be this good first time playin'. I think he's some sort'a ringer. You sure he's gay?"

Piza's face twisted in disbelief. "Geez, Uncle Nunz. Really?" Shaking his head, "Yes, I'm sure. And what does that have to do with anything? What, gay people can't be athletic? Look at Frankie. He's great at sports."

"Yeah, but he stinks at bocce!" After a pause, his face ablush with repentance, Nunzio said, "Look, I'm sorry. You know how I get when it comes to bocce. I didn't mean nothin' by it. You know that."

"I know." He gently nudged his godfather. "Your verbal filter just needs a little servicing, that's all."

"Yeah, you're right. I was never known for thinkin' before speakin'. Got a few scars to prove it." A deep sigh. "So. Mandy. I ain't never seen 'er in shorts before. Some pair'a legs she's got. You and her, are ya . . . ya know?"

"God. Seriously? Weren't we talking about filters like ten seconds ago?"

"What? What'd I say?" The man truly looked confounded. "Oh! No, no. I wasn't thinkin' what I think you think I was thinkin'. I meant is it gettin' serious. Like talkin' about gettin' engaged maybe."

Piza let out a laugh. "Okay, my turn to apologize. I completely misunderstood where you were coming from with that. Anyway, have you been talking to your daughter? She seems to have my love life in her sights as well."

"We talk about you once in a while. Face it, kid, you ain't gettin' no younger. And Mandy's a nice girl. Plus, your parents are crazy about 'er."

"I've noticed," Piza replied. "And you're right, she's a great girl. We're taking it slow, but I'd say that, yeah, someday."

"Well, get a move on, 'specially if you want kids. I read somewheres that around your age your sperm ain't exactly takin' home swimmin' trophies."

"I can assure you, Uncle Nunz, that my sperm's in tip-top shape. But thank you for your concern."

"Just tellin' ya what I read," Nunzio said with a nonchalant shrug.

"Duly noted. Look, while I've got you alone, let me ask you something. I'm a little concerned about Pop putting in so many hours at the store. And that schlep back and forth to the Bronx six days a week. Does he talk to you about it at all?"

"We do every once in a while. And I tell 'im the same thing you're sayin'. Ya know, it's time to start takin' it easy. I think what he was hopin' was that one day Manny would buy the store from him and your mother. Ya know, the same way they bought it from old man Pescatore when *they* was workin' there. He figured maybe then he could go in one or two days a week. Help out. Keep himself busy. But since Manny moved his family to California last year. . . Now the only help he's got is that high school kid a couple'a afternoons a week and on Saturday."

"Well, that's what worries me. I mean, I talk to him. Ma talks to him. But he's such a thick-headed Sicilian. I think in his mind he's still twenty-five. I dunno. But do me a favor and see if you can maybe try to push him a little. I think he may listen to you more than he does to us when it comes to this stuff."

"I'll lean on 'im a little more, Anthony. See what I can do."

"Great. Thanks."

"Eh, looks like we're ready for round two. No more feelin' sorry for you's guys. Me and your father are gonna kick your asses this game."

<hr>

As Piza and Mandy lay on the queen-size bed in her apartment Sunday night, they were enjoying a replay of some of the barbecue's notable moments. The recollection that produced side-clenching laughter was Angelo and Nunzio's petulantly inconsolable reaction when Roger led his team to victory in the match's deciding game, by following Nunzio's advice and "smashing the shit" out of the ball that would have won it for the elders. Fortunately, their distress had been relatively short-lived, eventually snuffed out by the healing power of pastries and espresso.

Lying on his back, staring at the ceiling, Piza mused, "You know what would be the perfect ending to this delightful day?"

Similarly positioned on her side of the bed, Mandy replied, "Eating vanilla fudge ice cream out of the container while beating you at Trivial Pursuit?"

"Oooo, so close," Piza said as he turned on his side, slipped his right hand under her tee-shirt, and ran his fingers across her taut stomach.

A muted moan led to, "Eating ice cream out of the container and beating you at Trivial Pursuit while you stroke my stomach?"

"Not quite there yet," he said, pulling her close. As they held each other, a soft kiss was enough to unleash the raw desire that had drawn them together from day one. A smoldering longing bursting yet again into the fevered venting of passion.

After they both climaxed, Piza remained on top of her, the two of them allowing the pace of their breathing to return to normal. Cupping her face, he kissed her forehead and the tip of her nose, then used his thumbs to gently wipe away the tiny beads of sweat resting on her upper lip.

They gazed at each other, serenely adrift in the depth and tenderness of the silence. Mandy brought them back, her voice hushed but steady. "I love you, Tony."

Neither of them had professed love for the other before, although he'd long known how she felt. Just as he'd known he wasn't in the same place, but hoped he would be when the inevitable arrived. Now he was out of time; unsure how to respond. He saw his hesitation register in her eyes, and in the anguish of indecision he whispered, "Me too."

And with those words, their relationship ended.

CHAPTER 16

Elizabeth shoved the shifter into park and yanked the emergency brake lever. Exiting, she slammed the driver-side door shut, only to re-open it, reach in, and grab her pocketbook off the passenger seat. She ran up the walkway, took the six front steps two at a time, and pressed long and hard on the doorbell to Piza's second-floor apartment in the two-family house where he lived.

Not easily flustered, she was about as close to unglued as she could conceive of. She'd never heard him as distraught as he'd been on the phone twenty minutes before. In the course of the ten-second call, all she could make out was that something had happened with him and Mandy, and he needed to see her. His despair had been so primal and clutching, she'd felt it rush through her, like being possessed by a besieged specter.

When he answered the door, she unwittingly grimaced. The torment she'd heard on the phone appeared to have morphed into a sadness so abject he looked pathetic—a word she'd never have imagined associating with him. Normally vibrant eyes were sunken and lifeless, the olive-green irises overwhelmed by a bloodshot background. His loosely hanging left arm had a tenuous grip on a quarter-full beer bottle, the latest in a line of predecessors, she surmised.

"Thanks for comin' over, Lizzie" was the slightly slurred greeting.

"Of course."

"C'mon up."

She followed him up the stairs, watching as he polished off the rest of the beer with one swig. When they entered the living room, he placed the bottle on the cocktail table, adding it to a soldierly row of four other empties.

Navigating the three-foot gap between the couch and the table with a caution apparently warranted by his condition, he ultimately flopped backwards onto the middle of the seat. Elizabeth took the recliner, a few feet away. After a moment, he tapped his forehead. "Shit, where's my manners? Wanna beer?"

She declined with a shake of the head.

"Hmm, 'kay. I think maybe I'll indulge if you don't mind."

"I really wish you wouldn't. You asked me to come over to talk, and I think that'd be easier if you stopped drinking."

He looked perplexed. "Really? Not so sure about that. But if you want."

"I want. What happened, Tony? I could barely make out what you were saying on the phone. Did you guys have a blowout?"

A condescending laugh. "Blowout? That's a fight, Lizzie. Two-sided. When someone shoves you out of their life without you getting a chance to . . . ya know, like *defend* yourself? That sound like a fight, Lizzie?"

Elizabeth sat there, mouthing the words 'shoves you out of their life'. She was too dazed to reply.

With glaring sarcasm he said, "What's a matter, cuz? Cat got that glib tongue a yours?"

That jarred her. She stood up. "You asked me to come over. I'm here. And I'm worried about you. But if you need a whipping boy, call someone else." She picked up her pocketbook and started toward the door.

He struggled to his feet and, making his way to her, reached for her shoulder. She pulled away before he could grab it, almost causing him to fall.

"Don't go, Lizzie. I'm sorry. I really am. I'm just upset is all. I didn't mean to take it out on you, okay?" He extended his right arm. "C'mon."

The gesture was all she needed. She grasped his arm and led him back to the couch, depositing him on one end, then taking a seat at the other end. "Tell me what happened. Are you saying Mandy broke it off with you?"

Elbows resting on his knees, head in his hands, he nodded.

"I don't get it. The two of you were fine at the barbecue today. Happy. I'm at a loss here, Tony. I know her. She loves you. What could possibly— Did— Did you do something? Something that could make her hurt you like this?"

"She didn't hurt me," he mumbled.

Elizabeth gazed at him in disbelief. "What're you talking about? My God, look at yourself. You're tortured. You're not making any sense."

Sitting up, he clenched his fists and turned toward her. "It was me!" He repeatedly jammed his index finger into his chest with the speed of a jackhammer. "*Me*, Lizzie. I hurt *her*."

"I don't— How? Why?"

Unsteady, he stood and began pacing, never straying far from the couch. "All she needed to hear was four words. Four words and everything would'a been fine." He raked his hair with both hands. "But no. Not me. The best *I* could fucking muster was two." He stopped and met her stare, tears now streaking his cheeks. "She looked into my eyes and told me she loved me. The first time that ever happened. And you know what I said, Lizzie?" He looked away. "'Me too'."

"Oh God. You couldn't say it back," she muttered under her breath.

He turned toward her again. "I was lying on top of her"—looking at his palms—"her face in my hands. And, and she looked so beautiful. And vulnerable. I've never seen her look vulnerable. Not once. She's so damn strong and self-assured. And the one time . . . the one time she lets me see her like that. . ." His face contorted with disgust. "There was absolute trust in her eyes. And Christ Almighty, I say 'me too'? What kind'a piece a shit am I? All I had to say was 'I love you too'." He took a few steps and dropped back onto the couch. "Was that so fucking hard to say?"

As he peered straight ahead, Elizabeth slid over until she was a foot away from him. "It was more than hard to say, Tony. It was impossible." He turned his head only enough to barely make eye contact. "Don't you see? The reason you couldn't say it is because you're not in love with her. If you were, the words would've been there. But you're too decent to lie about something as meaningful . . . as heartfelt as that. Especially to someone you care about. You think saying 'me too' was a cop-out. Maybe it was. But what were you supposed to say? 'Sorry, but I don't love you back, Mandy'?"

He wiped his eyes. "Right then, I'm not sure I knew if I loved her or not. I think I felt more confused than anything."

"You know that's not true. You're too self-aware to—"

"I know, I know," he said, waving her off with a listless flick of the wrist. He remained silent for a few seconds. "I tried to explain, ya know? With some pleading, bullshit rationalization that I can barely remember now. But she wasn't buying it." He leaned back, resting the back of his head on the top of the couch, so he was staring at the ceiling. "What the hell did I think I'd accomplish by saying something as pathetic as 'me too'?"

"You were trying not to be cruel. It was a kinder way of telling her you didn't love her. Somewhere in the recesses of your brain you knew that saying those words would convey that message. Especially with someone like Mandy, who's too sharp not to see it for what it was."

He started to choke up again. "You had to see her face when I said it. My God, the shock. And pain. She was devastated. I took a moment so beautiful and, and pure and I poisoned it. How could I do that to her? She's the last person in the world who deserved that." A frantic, haunting desperation shoved aside the dejection. "Why? Why don't I love her? What the fuck is wrong with me?"

Sobbing now, he lay his head on her shoulder. Her eyes welled. His suffering broke her heart.

CHAPTER 17

Megan wasn't quite sure what she expected, but it certainly wasn't the pale, unadorned woman standing behind a mahogany desk that looked Lilliputian against her gangly height. A semblance of a smile and a "Hello, Ms. Sabatini" greeted her as she entered the office.

"Hello. And, Megan is fine."

A nod. "I'm Nadia Bruzek. And"—pointing to her left—"this gentleman is Seth Kaplowitz, an associate who'll be assisting with your case, should you choose to retain me." The young lawyer nodded. "And you must be Ms. Janicek," she said, turning her gaze to Candy, who was standing next to Megan and seemed so anxious to be recognized it looked like she was on the verge of doing a pirouette.

"Please, call me Candy," the exuberant woman said. "That's what my real estate clients do."

Motioning for them to sit, Bruzek said, "Yes. When Bill Barlow called to let me know he was referring Ms. Sabatini to me at your request, he said you send quite a bit of real estate work to his firm. He made me promise to take good care of Ms. Sabatini, which I most certainly will." She glanced at Megan. "Again, if she decides—"

"Oh, it's already decided," Candy interrupted, waving away the possibility of an alternate outcome. "When I asked Bill for a referral, he said you were a— Um, ya know, that you were very aggressive." She wagged her finger. "And that's what we need to fight these ridiculous, uh, terrible, horrible, um . . . *despicable* things her husband's saying about drinking and all. Lies, lies, and more lies." She folded her arms and huffed with suitable disgust.

"Yes, I've reviewed the divorce complaint and the client interview questionnaire Ms. Sabatini sent in."

Megan cleared her throat. "I appreciate you seeing me. I'm sure you're a very good lawyer, and I'm very upset about those things Joey put in the divorce papers. But I'm Catholic. I don't believe in divorce. So what I—"

"God, Megan, we talked about this," a visibly exasperated Candy interjected. "You can't just—"

"Let me finish, Candy," Megan said, placing a conciliatory hand on her friend's arm. "What I need to know is if there's any way we can get Joey to drop this whole thing. Some legal thing you can do to get him to stop?"

Bruzek leaned back in her seat. Eyes so intensely blue they looked eerie latched on to Megan's gaze. "You love your children," the lawyer stated, a flat declaration unaccompanied by the slightest facial expression.

Megan wasn't sure if she was supposed to respond. After a few seconds, she said, "Of course. Of course I love my children. But that's not the point. What I'm—"

"Forgive me for cutting you off, Megan, but that *is* the point. And it's the only point that matters. Believe me, I'm not dismissing your religion or its importance to you. But you need to understand something. One way or another, this divorce is going to go through. The alleged alcohol abuse is only one of the allegations your husband is making. The rest are much less significant, but in a state like New Jersey, where we don't yet allow divorce based on incompatibility or irreconcilable differences, judges are ruling that run-of-the-mill marital problems meet the requirements for a divorce based on extreme cruelty. That's not the way the law was intended, but it's today's reality.

"And that's because attitudes have changed. Society is more accepting of divorce. So things like 'she never listened when I talked' or 'I had to beg her to have sex', and the myriad of other gripes in your husband's complaint, are enough to get him his divorce. So you have a decision to make. Either you fight him, or you do nothing and let a judge who doesn't know the first thing about you decide the fate of your daughters . . . without your input. Your call, Megan."

Exiting the ladies' room, Megan turned the corner and met Candy at the elevators. As they rode down to the parking garage, Candy said, "You made the right choice, sweetheart. Don't doubt it for a second." Her attempt at comfort fell short, as evidenced by the younger woman's white-knuckle grip on her pocketbook.

Megan didn't need to be told she'd made the right decision. What alternative did she have? When she asked Nadia for a detailed explanation of what could happen if she did nothing, the lawyer's recitation of possible consequences was terrifying. Not having the children live with her? Not having a say in where they went to school, or if they attended church? The possibility of not being able to see them without someone supervising the visits, because of her alleged alcohol abuse?

No, she had to fight—and pray that God understood.

Kaplowitz transitioned from the couch to the seat vacated by Megan. Bruzek put down her pen and leaned back. "So," she said, "any thoughts?"

"Seems to have gone well," he responded. "Not sure she'd have signed on with us if that pushy realtor wasn't here, though. It almost felt like *she* wanted the divorce more than the client did."

"Well, Ms. Sabatini has religious issues. I've seen it before. Be thankful Ms. Janicek was here and holds some sway."

"I don't get their relationship. Apparently they're not family, so why would Janicek agree to guarantee payment of Sabatini's legal fees if she runs into a money problem?"

With a tepid shrug Bruzek said, "I don't know. Might've been a hollow gesture, considering Ms. Sabatini said she's getting money from her mother."

"True, but still. . ."

"Well, I really don't care. But whatever the reason, apparently Ms. Janicek can afford it. When Barlow called to say he was referring her and her friend, he told me it seems her whole reason for being revolves around making money."

Kaplowitz wasn't sure if his boss's slight twist of the lips was a smirk in condemnation of Candy, or a flicker of admiration. After three months, he still couldn't read her. He'd never met anyone whose face and body language conveyed so little information. It was unsettling, and he found that his customary brashness evaporated in her presence. He'd already learned to refrain from saying anything that could be construed as criticism.

"You concerned about this drinking issue at all?" he asked, attempting to guide the conversation toward something more substantive.

"It could be a problem for her. We'll know better when we find out what this 'objective third-party evidence' is that they referenced in the complaint. She said she's never had anything other than an occasional glass of wine, and never outside the house. So I have no idea what they're talking about. But we'll see soon enough. They have to provide it to us. Plus, we'll do our own digging into her history. Driving records and such."

"Is that standard operating procedure? She said she's never had a problem."

"You have an objection to more billable hours?"

"Uh, no. Not at all."

She started going through mail. Kaplowitz assumed that was a signal for him to leave, and ordinarily he'd have liked nothing better. But something about the interview puzzled him, and he needed an answer.

"Can I ask you something? You told Ms. Sabatini that if she didn't respond to the divorce complaint, her husband could get custody and she wouldn't even know about it. I thought that even if you didn't file an answer, the plaintiff still had to notify you in writing of any requests like that before the final hearing."

Bruzek stared at him long enough for him to squirm in his seat. Then, "What I told her wasn't true. Just like it wasn't true when I said that in order to make her case for custody she *had* to countersue him, laying out her own list of cruelty allegations. Is that a problem for you?"

Kaplowitz wished he could take back the last minute of his life. "Um, you've been doing this a long time, so I imagine— Rather, I *know* you know what you're doing. It's just that, well, this is all still new to me, so I was just wondering. That's all."

She let out a sigh that oozed condescension. "Let me explain something to you. Divorce clients come to see us, and invariably they're a mess. Emotionally. Even if they don't realize it. Their minds are cluttered to the brink of overflowing. They're scared or mad or both. Do you think someone in that state is competent to make a rational decision? About anything? Of course they're not. They may think they know what they want . . . or need. They don't. So I set the goals for them, give them marching orders in the guise of suggestions, and pretend to let them steer the ship.

But *I'm* really the captain. Because I know what's in their best interest." She slowly folded her arms. "So, did I lie to Megan Sabatini? I did. For her own good."

"I understand," he said. It was a tentative response.

"Good. And. . ." Her eyes bore into him.

"And I'm okay with that."

He wasn't though. But he really needed this job.

CHAPTER 18

Like trying to swim through a pool of sludge. That was Piza's assessment of his ability to function since the breakup with Mandy. He couldn't get past the guilt. And he missed her company.

He'd had to briefly feign signs of life when fulfilling his perceived duty to let the most interested parties in his life know what had happened. His deeply distressed parents got a sanitized version of the event; Frankie a more fulsome accounting; and, a bare-bones report for Gloria, who'd noticed something was wrong the minute he arrived at work the Tuesday after Memorial Day.

But now, two weeks later, something happened that breached the shroud of apathy and yanked him out: receipt of Megan's written response to the divorce complaint. Even before reading it, he knew it was trouble. The look on Gloria's face when she handed it to him—a squinting, tight-lipped expression of dismay and condolences—told him instantly. The only remaining question was: how bad?

A glimpse at the text in the upper left corner of the first page answered that question. Megan had hired Nadia Bruzek, known in the local divorce-lawyer community as the Duchess of Death, because she sucked the life out of everyone who dealt with her. She was obnoxious on the best of days, and there were far too few of *them.*

It was common knowledge that she determined up-front how much money she wanted to make on a case, and wouldn't consider settlement until she reached that number. As her firm grew, she'd stopped going to court, leaving that to a few associates who were more energetic and quicker on their feet. She paid them well, but made it clear that they would never get a piece of the action. Take it or leave it.

She was also one of the first to take advantage of recently permitted attorney advertising in New Jersey, portraying herself as a relentless advocate for justice. The reality was that once a prospective client came through the door, her sole role was to seduce them with unattainable promises of success, and reinforce the ruse along the way if a client's commitment seemed to be flagging. Those who bought into the hype thought her "take no prisoners" approach translated into her fighting hard for them. What she was really doing was taking their money by inventing problems; manipulating a plodding and outdated divorce process that unwittingly allowed a few unscrupulous attorneys to run up legal fees with impunity.

In addition to being dejected by Megan's choice of lawyers, Piza was taken aback by the fact that she had filed a counterclaim as well. He could understand her answering the complaint, to protect her interests. But taking the affirmative step of counter-suing flew in the face of her strongly held beliefs opposing divorce. She had opted to base the counterclaim on extreme cruelty, matching her husband's move. He saw Bruzek's hand in this; Candy's as well.

As he read through her list of cruelty allegations, he abruptly stopped, his face purged of color. He let go of the document and reached for the phone.

———

"When you said you'd get here as soon as you could, I figured you meant after work," Piza said as Sabatini planted himself in a chair.

"Well, that was my plan, until I realized I couldn't concentrate on anything. I mean, when you tell me you need to see me, and you don't want to discuss it over the phone. . . Told my staff I wasn't feeling well. Which was the truth. My stomach's in knots. What the hell's going on?"

Piza pushed Megan's response papers toward his client. "She's filed a counterclaim against you. Based on cruelty, just like our complaint. Go to the fifth page. That's where the allegations are listed. Mostly bullshit, again like ours. But check out letter D."

Hands shaking, Sabatini started flipping through the pages then abruptly dropped the papers, rushed his right index finger to his lips, and sucked on it. "Son of a bitch! Paper cut, goddammit. You got tissues around here?"

A smirking Piza reached into a drawer and pulled out a box. "I'm a divorce lawyer. I get a fresh supply of these things every month," he said as he slid it across his desk.

Sabatini snatched a handful of white fluff and wrapped his finger. "What the hell are you smiling at, Tony? It hurts."

The smile morphed into a grin. "I figured they were looking to draw blood with this counterclaim, but I doubt even they took it this literally."

"You've got a messed up sense of humor, and now I'm even more worried," his dour-faced erstwhile friend responded as he used his left hand to make his way through the document. He was half-way down page five when his breath caught and his body turned into a sculpture. "That bitch," he finally got out, the tone muted, an apparent victim of shock. It was a momentary reaction. His breathing quickly ratcheted up to the brink of hyperventilation as his face shed its pallor in favor of a scarlet that blazed as bright as the bloodstain marring the tissue on his wounded finger. "Can— Can they say this? This . . . this unadulterated crap?"

"Unfortunately, yes. Whether they can prove it is another matter."

"'Whether they can prove it?' Holy shit, do you honestly believe there's an ounce of truth to this? Christ, Tony, please don't tell me you think there's a fucking snowball's chance in hell that I'm mentally impaired."

"Of course I don't. I didn't mean it like that," Piza said. "But you do have a history of depression."

"Which has been under control for years, for God's sake!"

"Look, I'm sure this whole thing is bullshit. But unfortunately, Megan's choice of attorneys couldn't be worse for us. Nadia Bruzek. She has a 'scorched earth' mentality. So this doesn't surprise me."

Sabatini's anger visibly plummeted, as he slumped in his seat and stared at his lap. "I can't believe Megan would stoop to this. I don't care who her lawyer is."

"Listen, if they were really serious about this, Bruzek probably would've filed a motion to restrict your visitation."

Sabatini's head snapped up. "Can they do that?"

"They could, but they wouldn't win. There's been no problem with your behavior over the past few years, right?"

"Of course not," he said, dejection seeming to take hold again.

"Okay, so we should be fine. Plus they probably wouldn't want to risk us filing the same kind of motion against her, based on the drinking. But you've gotta realize that this issue is out there, and we might have to deal with it down the road. You still taking meds?"

"Yeah. But the doc only has me on a maintenance dose." His expression hardened. "I've lived with this condition since high school, and I've functioned just fine since therapy and with the meds. She knows that. Now, all of a sudden, I'm too fucked up to take care of my kids?"

"Calm down. All they're doing is fighting fire with fire. Don't forget, you all but accused her of being an alcoholic."

"Because she's drinking like she never has before! That's real. This"—holding up the papers—"is total horseshit." He swatted the air in disgust.

Piza waited a few moments to let things settle. Then, "Any idea what the alcohol situation is now? I figured after the complaint she'd lay off . . . or at least slow down."

With a shrug Sabatini said, "I dunno. If she's still drinking, she's probably hiding it. Gina snuck on to the property a couple more times, but nothing in the recycling bin. I pressed Lisa a bit for information, but she's been close-mouthed about Megan. Actually, she's been withdrawn in general. Not sure what that's about." Another shrug, more sullen than the last. "This whole thing sucks."

Piza understood his client's frustration. Although he hadn't seen him in twelve years, he'd never known the man's battle with mental illness to be an impediment to dealing with day-to-day living. And he hadn't seen any evidence of it in their recent meetings. But in the world of divorce law, it was easy to weaponize presumably benign elements of someone's life. And in those situations where you weren't able to prove an allegation, at times merely planting the seed could be an effective tactic.

Sabatini finally stood up to leave after fifteen minutes of reassurances. They'd respond to the counterclaim by denying all the allegations. Eventually they'd get a medical report confirming his stability, if need be.

As a parting gift, Piza gave him a manila envelope stuffed with a stack of papers received from Bruzek's office. Interrogatories, he explained. A seemingly infinite number of questions, all part of the "discovery" process through which divorce lawyers gather information about every aspect of the other spouse's life. The man balked at the sheer volume, but seemed somewhat pacified when Piza told him he'd be sending Megan's lawyer an equally massive package shortly.

The Sabatini case was becoming every bit the nightmare Piza had hoped to avoid. He contemplated that fact while sitting at his desk after his client left. He wasn't prone to self-pity, but between the unrelenting angst of the Mandy aftermath, and the pitched battle he now knew awaited him with this lawsuit (at a reduced fee, no less) he couldn't help but feel he was a victim of cosmic sadism.

His mood did an about-face though when he remembered that relief was only a couple of days away. He was heading down the Jersey shore for a week. His vacation spot of choice for as long as he could recall. Seven days of sun-and-sand solitude that would allow him to decompress and regain his emotional footing.

Little did he know.

CHAPTER 19

Damn, the ocean's amazing. Not exactly a memorable observation, but about the best Piza could muster as he gazed out over the Atlantic from the balcony of his motel room in Wildwood Crest. A copy of Philip Roth's *Zuckerman Unbound*—untouched for the last twenty minutes—rested on the small, white wrought iron table to his right. The abandonment of one of his favorite authors was about as clear a sign as imaginable of the malaise that continued to dog him five days into his vacation.

The second day down there he'd begun to question whether traveling alone had been a good idea. The seclusion did deliver a welcome disconnect from the people and places that could remind him of the disarray he'd left behind. But it also cultivated a climate for him to get even deeper into his head. It was like getting a respite from a grueling march by inadvertently stepping in quicksand.

Ultimately, he'd determined that his inability to ignore problems until he figured out a solution would have made him a miserable companion. Even Frankie and Elizabeth, the two people who knew him best and were most tolerant of his moodiness, would likely have raised a white flag in short order.

With only two days of vacation left, he'd made some progress. He'd resolved not to agonize over the Sabatini case. It was what it was. Plus, before he left work on Friday, Nia had told him that the partners were willing to discuss moving him to litigation from family law at the end of the year. So there was some light on that front.

But the Mandy situation remained a stumbling block. Although thoughts of their time together lingered, the guilt had ebbed. What troubled him was more deep-seated; existential even. He was worried about his capacity for romantic love.

He'd always had an interest in psychology. Not enough to major in it, but he'd taken a couple of courses as electives while at Fordham. He'd read an article once about love; more precisely, why people fall in love. There was a litany of factors: physical attributes, brain chemistry, societal influences, and on and on.

That article had come to mind during his talk with Elizabeth, on the night of his breakup with Mandy—after he'd sobered up and regained control of his emotions. He couldn't comprehend how he wasn't in love with Mandy, when so many of the elements in that article had been present in their relationship. Elizabeth had listened patiently, as always. And when he finished, she'd said: "I think you're so anxious to find an answer, your thought process is out-of-whack. You're looking for logic where there's none to be found. I know you well enough to know there's no way you believe you fall in love by checking off items on a list."

She was right, of course. But while their eventual conclusion that "it's either there or it's not" may have settled the general issue, in his mind it didn't explain his twelve-year hitless streak.

Elizabeth had suggested various theories. One was that he simply hadn't met the right girl during that time. He parried by stating that, as she well knew, he'd dated a good number of women since he was twenty-two, several of whom he'd been quite compatible with and whose company he'd enjoyed. What were the odds that not one of them could light the flame?

She'd also reminded him that he'd been in love twice in his life, and had his heart broken both times. (He'd protested that high school didn't count, but her pointed response that he was "full of it" quashed that objection.) Maybe he'd erected a barrier to shield himself from potential pain, she offered. Not letting anyone get truly close enough to give the relationship a chance to cross the finish line. His counter-argument was that he'd opened himself up completely to Mandy: sharing the highs and lows of his life, present and past, including lost loves; allowing her to see him at his best and worst, the silly and the sullen, the gracious and the selfish. In his opinion, a wall would never have allowed for that.

So here he was. Wearing a deep tan, and the beneficiary of a pristine sky and temperate Atlantic breeze that carried the briny scent of treasured memories.

And he was miserable.

Saturday—Piza's last day at the beach—began with him waking, checking his watch, and spitting out an obscenity. He'd slept later than he wanted to, the result of an apparent overnight glitch in his usually reliable internal clock. You'd have thought over-sleeping while on vacation was a trifling misfire, especially for someone whose chronic tardiness was probably worthy of psychoanalysis. But there were certain situations that temporarily transformed him into a paragon of punctuality. His Jersey shore routine was one of them: awaken, address hygiene needs, and head over to a local convenience store for a sesame bagel, coffee, and *The New York Times*.

The obscenity he'd uttered had nothing to do with the bagel and coffee; there was always an abundance of that fare. The

Times was a different story. As far back as he could remember, the daily south-Jersey supply of the paper was glaringly limited for some reason. Thus, a late arrival was the kiss of death.

Next time I set the damn alarm.

He splashed water on his face, gargled, finger-combed his hair, slipped into a tee shirt, shorts, and sneakers, and headed out. He knew his window of opportunity was rapidly closing at best, but he hesitated for precious seconds when he reached the lobby. Although the urge to rocket up the street couldn't have been stronger had he sat on a cattle prod, it was colliding with the need to preserve his image. A frantic dash could result in his possibly being perceived as an arm-flailing madman. The compromise: a respectable jog. But in the end, it didn't make a difference.

"It's after ten," the owner said in answer to Piza's desperate inquiry about the existence of more copies. "The *Times* was gone before nine. What you were just lookin' at is all I got."

A dejected Piza turned, took a few steps, and surveyed the newspaper rack. The only remaining legitimate paper (in his opinion) was the *Philadelphia Inquirer*. Two copies left. He brought one to the counter, ordered his bagel and coffee, paid, and trudged off.

As he sat on his balcony, the hot coffee was a comforting offset to the slight chill that resulted from occasional gusts off the ocean crossing paths with fair-weather clouds that dimmed the sun. As the last piece of his bagel became history, he picked up the *Inquirer*. He read the sports section first, then the national news. After that, he started skimming the paper, more out of a sense of obligation than anything else. (He had paid for it, after all.) He was about to turn a page when his mind skidded to a stop, his face blanched, and a queasiness-inducing anxiety overwhelmed him. The headline of the article tucked away in the lower left of the page meant nothing to him:

Nursery School Owner Appointed to City Board of Ed.

But the photo below it. A grainy, black-and-white thumbnail. He began to read:

Theresa Brennan, owner of the Sonas Nursery School, has been appointed to the Board of Education by the Mayor. Brennan's appointment was approved by the City Council yesterday. She will take the seat left open by the resignation of long-time board member Letitia Santomarco, who is relocating to North Carolina.

Brennan, a former nun, has been an outspoken advocate for increased early education opportunities for the poor. She stated that she opened Sonas five years ago and that the facility, which has no affiliation with the city, is funded primarily through donations.

The paper fell to his lap. Thoughts flung themselves at him at a disorienting pace. He forced himself to take deep breaths, closing his eyes in an attempt to sort through the flurry.

She'd left the sisterhood. At least five years before. But when exactly . . . and why? How come she hadn't tried to contact him? Could he possibly have misread her feelings all those years ago? Or, affection notwithstanding, perhaps she'd opted to tuck his memory away and move on. And he had no idea her name was Brennan. He'd only known her as Sister Theresa. But what if Brennan wasn't her *maiden* name? What if she had married?

Purely mental analysis of the cascading "what-ifs" wasn't working. Maybe if he put pen to paper he could more easily sort through the havoc. Then, devise a rational plan to obtain the information he needed; something short of going down there, which he doubted he was emotionally equipped for.

Barely into the writing task, it became apparent that, no matter the medium, objectivity and clear-minded strategy in his current state were out of reach. He was drowning in maddening uncertainty. Desperate to find a lifeline.

Then he remembered Bruno.

In the parking lot of the Meadowlands Diner in Carlstadt, Piza sat in his new Mustang GT, left hand resting on the bottom of the steering wheel, right index and middle fingers channeling his edginess by drumming a random beat on the gear-shift knob. He checked his watch for the third time in the last minute. Given his own deplorable track record, he was relatively forgiving of others with promptness issues. But as of fifteen seconds ago, Bruno Bosco was officially seventeen minutes late. Unacceptable even by Piza's standards.

Straining to look as far as he could up Route 17 South, which abutted the diner, there was no sign of Bruno's '76 Cadillac Fleetwood. (Probably one of the few cars that could accommodate his girth.) A minute later he puffed out a testy breath and was about to head to the diner's payphone, when the silver tank pulled into the lot, windows open and radio blaring. Bruno exited, his shirt already soaked with perspiration. Walking like a tipsy sumo wrestler as he attempted to keep his feet from fleeing his flip-flops, he extended his arms for a hug. "I am like super sorry, Tony." Piza deftly avoided the potentially drenching encounter by throwing his hands up to emphasize his annoyance. "No hug, cuz?" Bruno whined.

"Not when you're almost twenty minutes late."

"Shit, I'm really sorry. I ran into traffic. You know what this damn road is like. Super busy."

"It's nine o'clock Sunday morning, Bruno. One of the rare times it actually *isn't* busy. Let's just go inside, okay?"

As they sat in a booth, Bruno said, "Boy are you super tan. I didn't even know you'd been down the shore till you called me last night."

"I didn't know I had to run my travel plans by you."

"You don't. 'Course not. I'm just sayin'."

The waitress brought menus and asked if they wanted coffee. They both said yes.

"So how come you picked here to meet, Ton?"

"Because it's near my house and I like the food."

Bruno nodded more enthusiastically than you'd have thought necessary. "Yeah, me too. A lot. I had a gig workin' security near here when I was younger. Before I started doin' the P.I. stuff. Came here every morning for breakfast." He chuckled. "Man, those were the days. Used to pack away two breakfast specials at a time. Three sometimes, if I was *super* hungry. Seems like yesterday."

Piza arched a brow. "From the look of you, it probably *was* yesterday."

"Ohhh! Seriously, Tony? Fat jokes? When you ask me here to do you a favor?"

"Excuse me? Do me a favor?"

Bruno squirmed in his seat. "Yeah. You know. You do for me and I do for you. Like it's always been."

Clucking his tongue, Piza said, "Let me jog your memory. Before today, I never asked you for a thing. You could rescue me from a pack of wolves . . . ten times, and you wouldn't be close to squaring your debt."

Appearing duly chastised, the big man said, "No. You're right. I was super off-base with that one.—"

If he says 'super' one more time, I'm gonna stab him with a fork.

"—So, tell me what's goin' on."

Bruno was aware of Piza's teaching job in Staten Island after college, but hadn't been privy to the details. Piza wanted to keep it that way as much as possible, so in relating the story he characterized his relationship with Theresa as "really good friends" who had lost touch. He told him about the *Philadelphia Inquirer* article, and how he was worried about her on learning she'd left the sisterhood.

Bruno asked why he didn't go talk to her himself. "Ya know, more direct kinda." Piza had anticipated this, and said that since she hadn't contacted him to let him know what was happening, it might mean she was embarrassed about it. He didn't want to put her in an awkward position, so better to find out what her situation was first.

On its face, it was a reasonable explanation, but Piza's delivery had been a little tentative, as evidenced by a glint of skepticism in Bruno's expression. He looked like he was about to respond, but perhaps the recent, stinging reminder of his indebtedness prompted him to keep his mouth shut.

Piza told him the main things he wanted to know: when she left the order, where she was living, and—more out of curiosity than anything, he said—whether she was married. He had no expectation of Bruno discovering why she'd left, but if he could, that would be great, as would anything else he could find. When Piza asked about a timetable, Bruno said he could get down to Philly Wednesday afternoon, but it might take a couple of days to get the information.

When they finished breakfast, Piza took the check and turned down Bruno's mumbled offer to leave a tip. They hugged good-bye in the parking lot, the hour spent in the diner's air-conditioning making for a relatively dry embrace.

As he drove home, Piza anguished over getting through the coming days. Before leaving for vacation, he'd told Gloria to schedule as little as possible for him his first week back (not that she needed reminding), since it usually took him a while to transition back to office mind-set and slog through the accumulated mail and phone messages. But now he wished he had something interesting on tap to divert his attention from watching the clock as he waited to hear from Bruno.

Sabatini took care of that.

CHAPTER 20

Sabatini hadn't been sure whether he should even take the call. But he figured Megan wouldn't be contacting him at work (or at all for that matter) if it wasn't urgent.

As he drove down to Iselin later that afternoon, on the last Monday of the school year, he couldn't fathom why his good-natured older daughter would have pushed a classmate. Seeking clues, he did a quick assessment of the past few Sundays they'd been together. She'd been quieter than usual. And, as he'd mentioned to Piza when they last met, she was reluctant to engage him on anything involving her mother. But nothing in her behavior had flashed a warning sign.

The more he thought about it, the more he was convinced this was an anomaly. Even a child as sweet as Lisa was entitled to a bad day. An occasional burst of anger. And maybe this other girl had provoked her. Were her parents being called in too? They'd better be if their kid was the instigator.

By the time he pulled into the school parking lot, he was seething. As he saw it, some hyper-cautious, ass-covering bureaucrat had forced him to leave work early and waste time driving to Iselin over nothing.

Like I don't have enough shit to deal with. Goddammit!

He slammed the steering wheel and stubbed out his cigarette.

As he walked through the halls on his way to the principal's office, Sabatini's ill-humor spiked, fueled by vivid memories of how upbeat he used to feel when visiting here for parents' night and teacher conferences. The exhilarating aura of hope; the vibrant hand-drawn posters that lined the walls and celebrated the seasons; starred book reports and essays pinned to corkboards in classrooms, waiting to be discovered by proud parents; the invariable praise for Lisa by teachers who confided they wished all their students could be like her. Now, navigating those cheery corridors was like running a gauntlet lined with barbed reminders of a happier time.

He hadn't gone to any school events since the separation, using work as an excuse when explaining to his disappointed daughters why he wasn't able to attend. The reality was he didn't want to deal with the sober handshakes, reassuring shoulder pats, and awkward conversations he was sure awaited him from well-intentioned friends he didn't really miss.

Entering the waiting area of the main office, he saw Megan seated in a blue plastic chair, fingering rosary beads. He startled her when he said, "You still think those things are gonna help?"

"Oh! You're here."

"Yeah, I'm here. Did I really have a choice? And where's Amy?"

"I picked her up and dropped her off at my mother's, then came right back here."

"Where are this other kid's parents? The one Lisa supposedly pushed."

"It's just us, Joey. Lisa admitted what she did."

His simmering temper wasn't content to let her simple statement go. "You spoke to Lisa already? Without me?"

"Calm down, okay? I haven't spoken to her. Ms. Kim told me, when she called."

"Well, where's Lisa now? Why isn't she here?"

"She's in her classroom. Her teacher agreed to stay after class to keep an eye on her. Ms. Kim didn't feel it would be productive if Lisa—"

An opening office door cut her off, and a svelte, well-dressed woman smiled and motioned for them to come in. In Sabatini's estimation, she looked too young to be a principal. She shook hands with them and said, "Hi. I'm Janice Kim. It's nice to meet you both." She motioned for them to sit.

As she took her seat behind her desk, Sabatini tossed out an edgy, "Circumstances aren't exactly ideal though, I think you'd agree. Look, I know my daughter, and I know she'd never push someone unless she was provoked."

The woman appeared slightly ruffled, but recovered quickly. "You're right about the circumstances, Mr. Sabatini. But, unfortunately, it's clear to me that Lisa pushed this other child for no reason other than wanting to go ahead of her in a game of hopscotch. One of the lunch aides saw it and, frankly, Lisa admitted it when I spoke with her. I think—"

"Well, *I* think we should get her in here and hear it for ourselves," he said, making no effort to hide his hostility.

"We're not going to do that, Mr. Sabatini. She shouldn't be present for what I need to discuss with you."

It was his turn to be elbowed off-center. "What are you— Don't you think you're blowing this out of proportion? It's a lousy schoolyard spat."

"It's not the first time this happened, Joey," Megan said before Kim could answer him. She averted her eyes, like someone guilty of an indefensible non-disclosure. "She got into a fight two weeks ago too. And she's been acting up a little in class."

"Whaddya mean? Why didn't you tell me?"

"It didn't seem like, ya know, like a big deal. Lisa and I discussed it. She said she was sorry. I figured that was the end of it."

The principal jumped in. "Her grades are starting to slip a little, as well. Nothing terrible, but still. . . Any of these things on their own, I'd say chalk it up to a little bump in the road. But taking them all together? I believe it might indicate a bigger problem."

With an expression marginally shy of a sneer, Sabatini responded, "All due respect, but are you qualified to make that call? You look kind of young. No offense."

A red-faced Megan managed to squeak out, "Joey!"

Kim's lips curved in a smile that wasn't entirely reflected in her eyes. "I've only been principal here a year, Mr. Sabatini, but I've been an educator for seventeen."

"Fine," he replied. "So what's this revelation you have in store for us?"

"Well, we normally attribute behavior like Lisa's been exhibiting to ongoing stress. And, assuming there's no evidence of bullying here at school . . . and we're not aware of any . . . the cause typically lies at home. So let me ask you, are there difficulties in the household?"

"I wouldn't know," he snapped. "I don't live there."

The woman's eyes widened. "Oh. I had no idea."

"We're separated," Megan offered, her tone almost apologetic. "About nine months now."

"Actually, we're in the process of getting divorced," he corrected.

With a grimace Kim said, "I wish we'd known that. Usually parents inform us if something like that is going on. This can explain a lot. Is Lisa aware of the divorce?"

Sabatini glared at his wife. "Have you said anything? I certainly haven't."

"No! I figured we'd tell her in due time. You know, when she and Amy were ready to hear it, I guess." She turned toward the principal. "Honestly, I don't really believe in divorce, so this isn't something I ever wanted or am comfortable with. But—"

Her husband shot out of his chair. "What, so whatever's going on here is my fault? Is that what you're trying to say?"

"Mr. Sabatini, please sit. I don't think that was—"

"If our daughter's screwed up, it's on me?" he shouted.

Megan, ashen and discernibly frightened, was all but cowering in her chair.

"Mr. Sabatini! Enough!" Now Kim was on her feet.

He looked like she'd slapped him out of an altered state. Eyes that moments before reflected rage, now radiated fear. "My God, have we hurt Lisa? Damaged her somehow?" He glanced at Megan, then focused on Kim. "I— I don't get it. The only reason I agreed to leave the house was to avoid the kids seeing us fight all the time. Was that a mistake?"

The principal shook her head. "No, I don't think so. By all accounts, continued exposure to hostility is normally more harmful to a child than the parents separating."

Sabatini sat back down. "She doesn't even know about the divorce so . . . so why is this happening? She seemed fine. Maybe a little off her game the last couple of Sundays but, ya know, she's nine. Kids get moody. It happens, right?" There was anything but certainty in his voice.

Kim sat as well. "Mr. and Ms. Sabatini, I can't tell you exactly what caused this change in Lisa. You've been separated for a while now, and you haven't told her about the divorce. So, barring a more recent triggering event, it seems kind of strange that this should be cropping up all of a sudden. Has something else happened recently?"

He managed a half-shrug. "Not that I'm aware of."

"Me either," from Megan.

Eyebrows raised, Kim said, "Well, then I'm not sure why this is happening. Who knows, maybe it's been building up and suddenly came to a head. But something's clearly wrong." She leaned back. "Would you have an objection to Lisa speaking with the school counselor? She's around all the time, so the children know her. And Lisa might be more willing to disclose something to her she'd rather not discuss with either of you."

"If— If it could help her," Megan answered, eyes welling up.

Her husband appeared on the verge of tears himself, but then he set his shoulders and coughed into a stern expression of concern. "Before I agree to something like that, I need to know a couple of things. First, what are her qualifications? And second, I want a guarantee that Lisa's not gonna get labeled because of this . . . either in her school records or socially. Ya know, by this leaking out to other kids."

Kim's head had started bobbing before he finished. "I get your concerns, Mr. Sabatini. Donna Capalbo, our counselor, is state-certified, obviously. She has her MSW and is on her way to a Ph.D. She's great with the kids, and I have the utmost confidence in her."

Sabatini acknowledged the answer with a nod.

"As for Lisa getting labeled, I can assure you that, barring something truly dark going on here, like Lisa wanting to hurt herself or others, nothing—"

"Do you think that's possible?" a terrified-looking Megan blurted out.

Shaking her head and motioning for Megan to calm down, the principal answered, "I'm not aware of anything that would suggest that. The two recent incidents she had were relatively minor. And frankly, if it were something more, you'd probably already have seen evidence of it at home"—looking at Sabatini—"or when you're with her. But as I was saying, short of anything dangerous manifesting itself, nothing she discusses with Ms.

Capalbo will negatively affect her status. And we're very careful to make sure none of the other children know what's going on in situations like this."

"Can you guarantee it?" Sabatini reiterated.

"Assuming Lisa doesn't tell anyone, it's highly unlikely anything would get out."

"But 'highly unlikely' isn't a guarantee," Megan observed. "The possibility of Lisa being stigmatized worries me too."

Her husband glanced at her, surprised but gratified by her support.

"Listen," Kim said, "none of us has control over every possible contingency. So if I used the word 'guarantee', it wouldn't be honest. But we take every precaution, and I don't know of any problems in the past. Realistically, there's virtually no time for anything to leak anyway, considering school ends Wednesday. So I can have Lisa sit down with Donna tomorrow, just to see if she feels there's anything going on."

"And if she thinks there is?" Megan asked.

"Then obviously we'll let you both know immediately. But short of that, it's probably a matter of waiting to see how Lisa does over the summer. If Donna sees something, or if you're concerned, you could always look into private counseling."

"Well, let's not jump the gun," Sabatini said, attempting a measured response to disguise his alarm at the prospect of adding another bill to the pile. (Even the health insurance *deductible* was a heavy lift at this point.)

Megan nodded. "Yes, let's take it a step at a time. Let's see what happens tomorrow before we make any decisions, okay?"

"I agree," Kim replied. "I'll make arrangements for her to sit down with Ms. Capalbo. I'd like to do it after class, so it doesn't interfere with Lisa's schedule or raise any suspicions. And you can certainly speak with Lisa about the incident, but I don't know that I'd mention the meeting tomorrow. We don't want her getting anxious. Are you both okay with handling it this way?"

"Yes," they answered together.

"Okay, great. And Mr. Sabatini, why don't you leave your contact information with me. I'll make sure they have it in the front office."

———

I already said I'm sorry. It was only a stupid little push. I don't know why they're making such a big deal about it.

"Lisa, are you listening to me?" Sabatini asked, as he, Megan, and Lisa stood in the school parking lot. His face was twisted with frustration. He looked at Megan, who seemed baffled as well as she shook her head and turned her palms up. "Saying you're sorry isn't enough," he continued. "And I refuse to believe you pushed that girl just to go ahead of her in a game. I want— Your mother and I want to know the real reason you did it. This isn't like you, Lis."

Lisa hadn't volunteered a word from the moment they left the principal's office. "Did you really push that other girl?" her father had asked as they made their way to the exit. An unrepentant nod was the answer. "Why?" from her mother. A shrug in response. "Did you push her because you wanted to get ahead of her in line to play hopscotch?" was Megan's follow-up. Another nod.

As they stood in the lot, Sabatini and Megan looked completely at sea. He ran his fingers through his hair, then squatted so he was eye level with his daughter. "Lis, something's going on. Mom and I are both worried about you. Two fights in two weeks? I don't remember you ever having had even *one* before? Please, sweetie. Talk to us. What's bothering you?"

She didn't want to talk to them about why she was angry. And even if she did, she couldn't. She'd promised Aunt Candy. And everyone knows you never break a promise.

CHAPTER 21

Piza pulled into a parking spot in the expansive strip mall where Sabatini's bank was located. Scanning the storefronts, he missed it at first, then found it sandwiched between a pizzeria and a deli. As he entered, he scrunched his face. *Geez, I had piggy banks bigger than this.*

Ordinarily, he might have been annoyed by Sabatini's request to meet there. But he'd said it was important, that it related to Lisa, and that they were short-handed that day, so he really couldn't get away. Besides, Piza was moderately interested in seeing where he worked.

From a glass-enclosed cubicle, Sabatini waved him over. "Thanks for meeting me here, Tony," the banker said, standing and extending his hand. "My assistant manager's out and so is one of the tellers, so it's just me and the other teller. And she's kinda new."

"No problem." He looked around. "From the size of this place, I'm surprised there's enough oxygen in here to sustain four people anyway." He hadn't meant it maliciously, but from Sabatini's expression he could see it had stung him. He considered letting it hang there, but then said, "I didn't mean that as a diss. It's just that compared to your old job. . ."

With a flick of the wrist that couldn't escape looking contrived, Sabatini said, "Nah, don't worry about it." He followed that with an equally feeble chuckle. "How the mighty have fallen, huh?"

Piza had no desire to travel that road. "Hey, you'll bounce back. So, tell me what's going on with Lisa."

Sabatini related everything that had happened at school, and reiterated the fact that she seemed withdrawn when she was with him—a status he said had become more worrisome the more he thought about it. He mentioned that Lisa had met with the school counselor the day before, and the woman had concluded that something was clearly bothering her. But the child's refusal to engage—other than flatly stating nothing was wrong—hadn't allowed for even an educated guess as to the cause.

"I'm at a loss here, Tony," he said as he slouched in his seat. "The principal suggested we might wanna get some private counseling for her, and the school counselor seconded that. But the cost. . . My coverage through work sucks, so I'm assuming there'd be a pretty hefty out-of-pocket layout. And—"

"Yeah, but if she needs it she needs it. Plus, there are resources available out there. But whatever money may be involved, that shouldn't be all on you. Megan should kick in something. Has she thought about getting a job, even part-time? Help out a little, at least? Lisa and Amy are both in school all day. So maybe starting in September."

"We haven't discussed it. I mean, when would we? We don't talk. When she called me about Lisa, that was the first time I talked to her since the domestic violence thing."

"Well, assuming you guys can be civil toward each other, maybe that's a discussion you should be having. And now that I'm thinking about it, who's paying her legal fees? Are you giving her—"

"Are you kidding? It's not coming from me, believe me. I assume her mother's helping her. You know, with the money from her old man's insurance policy."

"Okay. Then maybe her mother would be willing to help with therapy for Lisa."

Sabatini responded with an animated, "But that's just it. We don't know if she actually needs therapy. Maybe this'll just pass. Maybe therapy would do her more harm than good."

Looking askance at him, Piza said, "Well I seriously doubt that's the case. Everybody seems to agree something's wrong."

"I get that. But do we know for sure that therapy's the answer? What if she shuts down even more if we force her to sit down with some stranger? I— I feel like I'm in no man's land here."

They sat silently for a few moments. Then, Piza cleared his throat. "Look, I may know someone who could help. At least as far as making a decision on this. But—"

"Great! How soon can we—"

"Hang on a minute. It's not that simple."

"Why?"

"Because the person I'm thinking of is Frankie's boyfriend. Roger. He's a psychologist. But I can't say whether he could . . . or would do this."

The desperation on Sabatini's face seeped into his voice. "Listen, Tony. If getting Frankie's boyfriend to help me with this means going to Frankie and begging forgiveness, I'll do it in a heartbeat. Besides—"

"No, that's not the point. What I'm—"

"I need to make things right with him regardless of this thing with Lisa. So just tell me what I need to do, and I'll do it."

Piza puffed out a breath. "You're missing my point. This has nothing to do with you apologizing to Frankie. What I'm trying to say is I'm not sure if there's some potential ethical problem here. I know Roger's never met you, but with the history between you and Frankie . . . I dunno. Maybe there could be objectivity issues or some such thing. I have no idea. I just don't want you getting your hopes up."

Sabatini nodded. "I get it. But you'll try, right?"

"I'll talk to him, and let him decide what he's comfortable doing. I'll call him when I get back to my office."

"And you'll let me—"

"As soon as I find out, I'll call you."

Roger said yes, and indicated he could see Sabatini the following day. It would be a courtesy consultation. No charge. He wouldn't treat Lisa or any family member. He'd discuss the situation generally, nothing more.

Sabatini insisted that Piza go with him, despite the lawyer's advising him that he'd have to bill him for his time, especially since Roger's office was in New Brunswick. They drove down in Sabatini's car.

As they pulled into the parking garage of the sleek, glass-clad office building, the banker was still kicking himself for something he'd said while they were on the road. He'd asked how Frankie had managed to "snag" a psychologist. Piza had become so agitated, Sabatini thought he was going to tell him to turn the car around. "Are you shitting me? A professional can't be attracted to a plumber? Frankie's a great guy, in case you've forgotten. And maybe he only had a year of college, but he's smart as hell." Sabatini's effort to get a word in had gone nowhere, so he decided it would be wiser to let Piza say his piece. "Plus, Frankie's got more common sense than most of the college grads I know. And I'll take that any day of the week. And do me a favor and lose the 'that's not what I meant' look, okay? Because you've already dipped into that well way too often."

Piza had cooled off a while later, but not enough to talk

beyond monosyllables. Sabatini was anxious. He'd been counting on Piza to be a comforting presence. *Screwed the pooch on that one, I did.*

When they entered the lobby, the lawyer scanned the directory. "Pretty sure he said suite 304. Let me double-check. Yeah, 304."

His client had been peeking over his shoulder. "Latham? That's his name? What nationality is that?"

"It's Outer Mongolian. How the hell should I know?"

"Geez, calm down. As long as I've known you, you've kinda always known everything. Sorry I asked."

Through a smirk Piza said, "If I knew *everything*, I'd have gone on every quiz show on TV and been blissfully retired by now." His right hand shot out and his index finger pointed to an elevator a few feet away. "See if you can grab that before it closes."

When they reached Roger's office, they'd barely sat down in the waiting area before he came out to get them. Taller than I expected, Sabatini thought. Thin too. I guess maybe opposites do attract.

"Tony," Roger said as he and Piza shook hands. "Great to see you again."

"You too," Piza responded. He gestured toward Sabatini. "This is Joe Sabatini."

Roger shook his hand, and with an earnest smile said, "Hi, Mr. Sabatini. Nice to meet you."

The psychologist's gracious manner quelled Sabatini's anxiety —to some degree, at least. "Really nice to meet you too. You have no idea how much I appreciate you seeing me like this."

"My pleasure."

"Oh. And please, call me Joe."

Roger's office was spacious and tastefully decorated. Pastels ruled the room, and serene prints adorned the walls. Partially open vertical blinds behind his teak desk sliced the sunlight from the high window into dust-strewn shafts. Roger bypassed the couch abutting one of the walls, and the two cushioned chairs that faced each other in the middle of the room, leading them instead to the two leather office chairs in front of his desk. "Grab a chair and we can talk." They obliged as he took his seat behind the desk.

"Okay," he said. "Just to take care of some housekeeping, Joe, I want to make sure you understand that this isn't a therapy session. No doctor-patient relationship. I'm doing this as a favor to Tony."

"Got it," from Sabatini.

"Good. And, even though this technically isn't a consultation, you have no objection to Tony sitting in on our discussion?"

"None at all. In fact, I asked him to come."

"Great. So, I got some skeletal information from Tony. But why don't you tell me what's been going on with your daughter."

Sabatini related the recent history, adding his concerns about Candy's influence and Megan's alcohol use. He also mentioned his uneasiness with the suggestion that Lisa go into therapy, taking care to tiptoe across the subject so as not to insult his host. He said nothing about the financial component that played a role in his therapy misgivings.

Roger listened intently, letting Sabatini talk without interruption until "So, whaddya think" signaled the man was finished.

"Well, there seems to be little doubt that Lisa is acting out. The real challenge, as is usually the case, is figuring out why. There are some things that stand out. The question is how significant they are, if at all. The separation is certainly one. And, realistically, I don't see how that could not be playing a role in all this. As far as your wife's drinking, that could be having an impact. But that's not easily discernible without a lot more information. The same with this other woman's influence. The things Lisa indicated the woman told her and . . . I'm sorry, your other daughter's name was. . ."

"Amy," Sabatini responded.

"Right. Amy. What she said about not needing to obey rules and such is concerning. As is the fact she let Lisa try some wine. I don't know that a one-time sip of wine is such a terrible thing. What troubles me is that this Candy person is the one who initiated it. If she's that presumptuous, is she saying or doing anything else that might be harmful?" He turned to Piza. "I don't know exactly what you can do in that regard, Tony, from a legal standpoint."

Concern was etched on Piza's face. "Honestly, I'm not sure there's much we can do at this point without revealing that Lisa was the source of the information. I mean we're talking about remarks made directly to her. Doesn't leave much to the imagination."

"Whatever we have to do, Ton," Sabatini said. "You know I don't trust this woman. And if there's even a remote possibility she's got something to do with what's going on with Lisa. . ."

"I know, Strikes. Let me see what we can do."

"All that said," Roger continued, "there could be other factors at play here. Maybe she's having some anxiety at school. Perhaps she's feeling guilty about her grades dropping off, but she's unable to stop the decline because whatever's eating at her is causing it. A vicious cycle, so to speak. It's also possible she's having issues with friends. And I'm not talking about bullying, which you indicated the principal addressed. Just a normal falling out among kids. Present circumstances might magnify the impact of something like that on Lisa."

Sabatini's body had slowly coiled during Roger's remarks; his legs tightly crossed, his folded arms pressed against his chest. "God, there's so damn many possibilities here. How do we figure all this out?"

"Well," Roger replied, "I know you have your concerns about therapy, but I think it's probably the right way to go."

"And you don't think it could hurt her?" Sabatini asked,

feeling like he should pose the question despite knowing the answer.

Roger shook his head. "I don't," he said, his voice conveying a compassionate patience. "And look, I'm not saying that what Lisa's going through won't pass on its own. That's certainly a possibility. But in all honesty, as far as I'm concerned there's no downside to therapy. It could help Lisa unburden herself, and maybe aid her in learning some life skills as well."

Piza cocked his head. "When you say 'life skills', what are we talking about?"

"Well, things like organizing your thoughts and learning to communicate, for example. Dealing with emotions. Building strong relationships. Basically, enhancing social-emotional competencies in general."

Sabatini was now tilted so far to the right in his seat, the arm of the chair was the only thing preventing him from falling off. "Um, okay. I see what you're saying. I imagine we could wait to see where this goes but, ya know, then if she only gets worse. . . If you think therapy could really help, then maybe we should give it a shot. Megan seemed in favor of it after the school counselor suggested it. Ya know, after meeting with Lisa." He offered an empty smile. "Looks like you professionals are all in agreement."

Roger flashed a more genuine smile in return. "So it seems." He glanced at a wall clock. "I've got someone in about ten minutes. Do you have any questions before we wrap up?"

Sabatini nodded. "Um, yes, if you don't mind. Do you have anybody you could recommend? You know, in Iselin, where we live. I mean, Megan and the kids live." Blushing, he mumbled, "And also, do you know what this might cost?"

"Well, I'm not familiar with anyone in Iselin per se. Which is not to say there aren't good psychologists there. But I can give you some names in that general area. And as to cost, do you have insurance?"

Making a face, he said, "Yeah, but in all honesty, it's not the best. Especially with this kind of stuff."

Roger replied, "Okay. But there are also county and state resources available. And a few non-profits you might look into. I can fax you the names of some therapists, Joe. Or I can send them to Tony if you'd prefer."

"Better to Tony," Sabatini responded. "I don't have a personal fax machine at work, so . . ."

"Sure, no problem. And we have a list of those other resources I was talking about. Just ask my secretary for one on the way out."

He stood, and Piza and Sabatini followed suit. "Oh, one last thing, real quick," Sabatini said. "Do I get to participate in this at all?"

Roger gave a resolute nod. "Of course you do. You're her father. Whomever you end up seeing will undoubtedly want to talk to you *and* your wife, individually and together with Lisa."

"Oh, okay. Great. I, ya know, I wasn't sure." A deep exhale preceded, "So, thanks so much."

"You're very welcome. I hope our discussion helped a little," Roger said as he made his way around the desk.

"Are you kidding?" Sabatini answered, shaking his hand. "You've been great. I mean all your input, and not charging me. You have no idea how much I appreciate this."

"My pleasure. And I hope this works out for Lisa, and the rest of you as well," he offered as he escorted them to the door.

After Sabatini exited, Piza turned to Roger, shook hands, and said, "I owe you one, buddy."

"Forget it, Tony. I was happy to do it."

On the ride home, Sabatini said he'd call Megan that evening to let her know he was okay with Lisa seeing a therapist, and that he'd look into it through his health insurance carrier. He wouldn't mention seeing Roger.

Piza promised to give more thought to what they could do

about Candy. But he made it clear they really didn't have much to go on if they wanted to avoid implicating Lisa. Realistically, they'd probably have to wait for Candy to do something independent of talking to the kids. Something serious enough to warrant going to court if need be.

They wouldn't have to wait long.

CHAPTER 22

As he hung up the phone with Megan (slammed down the receiver would be more accurate) on the evening of his meeting with Roger, Sabatini was a smorgasbord of emotions. Anger. Confusion. Fear.

Megan had changed her mind about therapy. Didn't think it was a good idea anymore. Why? Because Candy had concerns. Sabatini had tried to remain composed, despite the fierce indignation that instantly surfaced at the thought of the insolent realtor. Rather than initially ranting about her disturbing impact on his family, he'd asked what Candy's objections were. The answer was both demoralizing and edifying. Demoralizing because it seemed to have instilled in Megan an acute dread regarding therapy. Edifying because it filled in gaps about Candy's near- obsession with her.

Candy's daughter had been a troubled child, Megan had said. (Not the least bit surprising to Sabatini.) She blamed it on her ex-husband, who'd abandoned Candy and their daughter when the girl was fourteen. By the time she was sixteen, a school counselor recommended therapy. Candy was initially against it, but ultimately gave in as the girl's behavior problems worsened. One evening, after a few months in therapy, the daughter—who Megan said bore a resemblance to herself at sixteen, based on an eroded picture living in Candy's wallet—said she was going to a friend's house for a sleepover. She never went. And never returned home. A phone call received after two frantic days of searching went like this: "I just wanted to let you know I'm alive, but I'm never coming home again, so don't try to find me." Click. That was more than twenty years ago.

Sabatini had asked his wife what any of that had to do with Lisa. How could Candy possibly be certain that therapy was the force behind her child's desertion? More likely, it had something to do with the malevolent father. Or maybe it was Candy's overbearing personality. (He'd kept talking before she could protest his vilification of her friend.) Conceivably, a million other reasons. Plus, he and Megan were nothing like Candy and her husband he repeated several times, in minced phrases—his galloping mind causing him to stammer.

It was after her fourth (he'd been counting) "I just don't think we should take the chance" that the underlying heat of his frustration melted the patina of patience he'd been able to project.

"What the hell is wrong with you, Megan? You're gonna let Candy overrule the school psychologist? She's a freakin' realtor! No matter what happened to her daughter!"

"That's not the point, Joey. She's been through this. Seen it firsthand. She—"

"No, it's exactly the point. She's not a shrink. I feel bad for what you said she's been through, but clearly it screwed up her head. Big time. My God, don't you think this . . . this fixation she has with you is—"

"She's not fixated. She cares about me. And she cares about the kids. More than you do sometimes I think. So—"

"Excuse me? Where the hell do you get off making a statement like that? You know damn well those kids mean everything to me. And I'm a good father. And you should be the last one to talk. You used to be smart, Megan. And strong. But ever since that woman attached herself to you like . . . like some kinda leech, you've turned into this . . . I dunno, this squishy . . . whatever. Afraid of your own shadow. No mind of your own. Letting that obnoxious bitch influence the girls with her crazy ideas. What kinda mother does that?"

"What are you talking about, Joey? What crazy ideas? That's ridiculous."

"Yeah, right! 'Rules are no fun'? 'It's okay to be messy'? Letting 'em sip wine? You think—"

Oh shit. What'd I just do?

Piza held the phone a couple of inches from his ear. "Jesus, calm down, Strikes. You're shouting. She won't agree to what?"

"Therapy. She changed her mind because of that piece of shit Candy."

"But I thought you said she was okay with it, once the school counselor suggested it. What does Candy have to do with—"

"Candy's daughter was in therapy a million years ago, and the kid wound up running away. Forever. She blames the therapy. Megan saw a picture of the kid, by the way, and apparently she looks like Megan when *she* was sixteen."

Piza clucked his tongue. "Well, that clarifies the attachment even more. Did you try to change her mind?"

"Of course I did. But she won't budge. Candy is basically preventing Lisa from getting help. That's what this amounts to. *Now* can we do something about this bitch?"

"Possibly. We can't bring Roger into this, but the fact that the school psychologist recommended therapy gives us something to work with. I can give her attorney a call this morning to see if we can come to some agreement on getting Lisa some help, and maybe even cut into Candy's exposure to the kids. But we probably won't get an answer today. And, knowing Nadia Bruzek, I wouldn't hold out too much hope for cooperation."

"So what's the alternative? Can we go to court?"

"Yeah, I can file a motion and try to get a judge to weigh in on this."

"Motion. Is that like what we did in court on the domestic violence thing?"

Piza said, "No. That was a 'hearing'. In a 'motion' the lawyers appear before a judge and make an argument for whatever relief they're seeking. There's no testimony from witnesses. We'd submit an affidavit from you, telling your side of the story. They'll do the same. And then the judge will make a decision."

"Okay. I see."

"It's likely, at this point, that this case is gonna go to mediation, to see if a court-appointed mediator can get you guys to resolve the custody issue. Under normal circumstances, I'd say we could wait until then. But I'm concerned that Lisa may need help right now. Plus, mediation would probably still leave Candy's presence up in the air." He scratched the back of his neck. "Let me make the phone call to Bruzck and see where that goes. Maybe we'll luck out. But if she refuses outright . . . or she ends up stonewalling me, then we'll file the motion. I'll let you know one way or the other, after I talk to her."

"Okay, great. Thanks."

"You got it. Talk to you—"

"Ton, there's one other thing."

"What's that?"

"I think I fucked up."

Piza's body tensed and his tone took on an edge. "Whaddya mean? What'd you do?" No response. "Strikes, what—"

"When I was talking to Megan, she pissed me off so much I started lacing into her about Candy and her, ya know, her obsession with Megan. She shot back that Candy cared about her and the kids more than I did. So I told her that was bullshit because Candy was filling the kids' heads with crazy ideas."

"Okay. That doesn't sound so— Oh, shit. You didn't."

"Yeah. I mentioned the crap Candy told them about rules and making a mess and all. And . . . I said something about sipping the wine."

Piza felt like he'd been gut-punched. "Oh Christ. What'd she say?"

Sabatini's words gushed out. "Well she, she asked me how I knew about that and, and I said something like— I think I said I could just tell from the way the kids were acting when they were with me and, and from the evidence we have that she was obviously drinking around them and, ya know, Candy was such an asshole that it seemed logical that she probably made them taste it."

"You expected her to buy that? Jesus, she's gonna head straight for Lisa and—"

"Well wait a second. After I said that, she didn't say anything. Maybe she was trying to process what I'd said. I dunno. But suddenly I realized that she hadn't denied any of it. All she wanted to know was how I knew. So before she said anything else I told her she'd basically admitted what I'd said was true. Kind of turned the tables on her. Accused her of being a bad mother. Ya know, letting this shit happen and all. It shook her up. She started crying and she said she couldn't do this anymore, and the next thing I know I'm standing there listening to a dial tone. I dunno, Tony, maybe she'll feel guilty and let it go and not talk to Lisa about it. Or Candy."

Following a snicker, Piza said, "Yeah, good luck with that. I hope to hell this kid's gonna be all right. But there's nothing we can do about it now. Like I said, I'll call the other attorney, and I'll let you know."

"Hey, maybe she'll surprise you and agree to it."

"Don't bet on it."

Bruzek wasn't in her office, but her secretary transferred Piza's call to Seth Kaplowitz. It seemed to Piza that the chip on the young lawyer's shoulder had only grown larger from when he'd first met him in court back in early May. After telling Piza he was assisting Bruzek on the case, he said they had no knowledge of the therapy issue. And as to Ms. Janicek, he didn't think it was anyone's place to tell their client who she could or couldn't associate with.

It was evident to Piza after about thirty seconds of making his counter-argument (and being interrupted twice in that limited space) that continuing the discussion was useless, so—using his best "Listen to me, sonny" voice—he instructed Kaplowitz to pass the information to Bruzek, and let him know her position as soon as possible. He also made it clear that he'd be taking the issue into court if he didn't get a timely, positive response.

Sabatini was understandably disappointed at the news, having held out hope for an immediate resolution despite his lawyer's warning against pie-eyed optimism. Piza told him he'd touch base with him again the following week.

That afternoon, Piza was sleep-walking through reviewing the terms of a proposed settlement agreement in another case. He realized he'd have to start from scratch when he was more alert, but holding the document gave him a sense (albeit a dubious one) of fulfilling the purpose of his employment.

The intercom jarred him with its disquieting ability to convert Cecilia's almost child-like voice into a grating squawk. "Tony, it's that Mr. Bosco on line two. Want me to tell him you're busy, like usual?" (Cecilia had the once-annoying-but-now-endearing habit of putting "that" in front of the name of anyone she was announcing.)

"No, it's fine, Cecilia. I'm actually expecting his call this time." Picking up the receiver, he felt like a vise was squeezing his chest. "Hey, Bruno."

"Hey, cuz. I'm back from the City of Brotherly Love. I got some info. Wanna do this on the phone?"

Piza was desperately trying to regulate his breathing. "Um, no. No. Think you could come over to my apartment around six or so?"

"You providin' dinner?"

"Uh, sure. Of course. Pizza okay?"

"More than okay. Meatball and pepperoni on top?"

"Sure. One large pie's enough, right?"

"Yeah, that's what I *usually* have."

"No, I meant enough for— Never mind. See you at six."

CHAPTER 23

Bruno's beet-red face and heaving chest greeted Piza as he opened his front door. A tiny spiral notepad looked lost in the investigator's baseball mitt of a hand. "Geez, cuz, if you ever move, you should think about gettin' a place with no front steps."

"There's only six of them, Bruno. And"—motioning to the interior staircase—"how are you gonna make it up those? I don't remember this being that big an issue last time you were here."

The visibly flustered man said, "I was probably younger then. I dunno." He gazed up the staircase. "I'll just take 'em one at a time. Elevator in your next place would be nice too."

Piza considered walking behind him to buffer a potential fall, but quickly surmised that if the man succumbed to gravity, his act of kindness would likely result in two fatalities instead of one. So he walked ahead of him up the stairs, but in reverse, ready to extend a supportive hand as long as it didn't jeopardize his existence.

When Bruno finally made it to the upstairs landing, he headed straight for the kitchen, crumpling onto a wooden chair with such force Piza was astounded it hadn't splintered.

"Man, that was some workout," Bruno said as he fruitlessly attempted to dry his sweaty brow with his sweaty forearm. "I was like super hungry before, but now. . ."

Piza took the cue, retrieved the pizza box from the counter, and placed it on the table. You'd think the phrase "manic contentment" would be an oxymoron, but Piza couldn't imagine a more appropriate description of Bruno's expression. It made him smile.

He considered holding off until after eating to get to the point of Bruno's visit but, even though he was aware of the man's effortless (one could say ruthless) speed and precision in consuming every manner of food, the thought of an eight-slice delay in learning what he'd found out was untenable.

He cooled his heels as his obviously ravenous quasi-cousin eradicated three pieces and a bottle of Mountain Dew. While waiting, Piza picked at one of the two slices of Sicilian pie he'd ordered for himself. When Bruno eventually paused to wipe his mouth (applying the napkin with an almost comical daintiness), Piza said, "So, let's talk while we eat. How'd you make out?"

Bruno pinched a wayward piece of mozzarella with his right thumb and forefinger, tilted his head back and, with the proficiency of a skilled bombardier, dropped it into his mouth from a foot above. Rubbing his hands together, he said, "Okay. So, first of all, super pretty lady."

Piza's heart rate spiked. "You saw her?"

The investigator looked at him like he was demented. "Of course I saw her. It's kinda why I was down there, no?"

"Sorry about that," the sheepish-looking Piza replied. "So anyway. . ."

"So, like I said, good lookin' woman. Decent rack too. Little more on the hips than I like personally, but—"

"Jesus, did I ask for an anatomy lesson? What else did you find out?"

"Okay, calm down. Sheesh. So, like you told me, she runs this nursery school. Sonas . . . weird name by the way . . . on Kensington Ave. Not the nicest area, if you get my drift."

Piza uttered a disdainful, "Meaning what, Bruno? It's a 'Black' neighborhood?"

Bruno's discomfort was on full display. "Well . . . ya know. I mean not just Blacks. You got a mix of— Um, the neighborhood's kinda run down is all I'm sayin'. I didn't mean anythin' by it."

"Yeah. Right. Keep telling yourself that. Just tell me what else you found."

Bruno mumbled a peevish, "No reason to go gettin' all high and mighty." He turned his focus to the pizza. Without looking at Piza, he folded another slice and dispatched it in five bites, conspicuously ignoring Piza's rat-a-tat fingernail table-tapping. Finally, he resumed eye contact with the satisfied look of someone who'd delivered a dose of comeuppance. A squelched belch segued into, "'Scuse me. So, anyways, she lives upstairs from the school." He checked the notepad. "Apartment 3B. Think I could get another soda?"

"Sure," Piza said. Bruno didn't move. Sighing deeply enough to almost generate a breeze, Piza stood up. "Please, allow me to get that for you." As he made his way to the refrigerator he asked, "So how'd you find that out? The apartment number."

"I saw her leave work and go into the door right next to it. I checked out the mailboxes in the lobby, and I saw the name you gave me. Brennan. 3B."

"Okay, so then—"

"I talked to her too."

"*What?*" Piza practically shouted as his head jerked around.

A sly smile. "Yeah. Yesterday I went into the school and asked for directions. She was super sweet. Runs a nice place too. Super cheerful. Kids looked like they were havin' fun. There was a . . . a Black girl in there helpin' her. Looked around twenty I'd say, give or take."

I can't believe he talked to her. "Did you—"

"Oh, not to cut ya off, but you wanted to know if she was married. I didn't have enough time to go searchin' through records, but she wasn't wearin' a wedding ring. She had a ring on her right hand though. Two hands around some kinda heart."

Piza nodded as he handed Bruno the soda. "Yeah, it's called a Claddagh ring. Two hands holding a crowned heart. It's kind of like an Irish friendship ring. A girl I took out a couple of times in college had one. Gift from her parents."

"Huh. Learn somethin' new every day."

Piza tried to picture what Theresa might look like now. She'd be around forty-one. (He wasn't sure of her birth date.) When he first met her, he thought she might be younger than him. He'd been shocked to learn she was twenty-nine. But now he wondered how much of a toll life had taken. "How does she— Does she look forty-one?"

"She's forty-one? You're shittin' me, right?"

"I shit you not."

"Holy crap. I pegged her being a lot younger. Like maybe late twenties? Thirty at the outside? Although now that I'm thinkin' about it, that makes no sense, 'cause you were right outta college when you taught. Yeah, so she couldn't be younger than you. Or not by much anyways. Sometimes I'm an idiot."

Everything after Bruno's "late twenties" observation might as well have been gibberish. Although he knew that how Theresa looked wouldn't diminish the intensity of his feelings for her (feelings that broke free the second he saw her picture in the paper), the fact that she apparently hadn't changed much catapulted him back to their year of teaching together. A flashback that produced a physical sensation of excitement, warmth, and joy so overwhelming it made him shiver.

Bruno intruded on the nostalgic interlude. "Um, I was kinda hopin' you'd tell me I wasn't an idiot, Tony. That's kinda the normal response when someone says 'I'm an idiot'."

"Huh? Oh. Right. No, you're not an idiot."

Pursing his lips, Bruno leaned back in his seat, but immediately bolted upright in response to the chair's creaking scream for help. "Lemme ask ya somethin'. You got a thing for this chick?"

Piza's look of disbelief arrived a second too late. "What? Thing for her? No way. Like I said, she's an old friend and I was worried about her." A forced chuckle. "You're good at your job, Bruno, but you're way off-base with that one, pal. Um, so is that it? Ya know, everything you got?"

As his wary look slowly dissolved he replied, "If that's all I got for the time I was down there, I'd have to give you some money back." A contemplative expression dawned. "Oh, wait. You're not payin' me." He broke into a boundless, self-congratulatory grin, and pointed at Piza. "Got ya with that one, right? Anh? I'm just bustin' your balls."

"That's all it better be," Piza said with a concocted stony stare. "So, now that you've had your little laugh, is there really more you found out?"

"Yep. She stopped bein' a nun seven years ago."

"How did—"

"I went to the library and checked the phonebook for Catholic schools in north Philly. *She's* in the phonebook too, by the way. Figured I'd check as long as I had the book right there. So anyways, I figured if that's where she's livin' now, odds are she taught at a school around there. Good place to start, at least. Got a hit at the second school I tried. I went to the convent and . . . ready for this? I told some nun that this Sister Theresa taught one of my kids when she was in Staten Island, and that she really helped him a lot, and we really liked her and all. I said we found out she transferred to this school, and I was here on business and thought I'd stop by to say hi."

"She bought that?"

A pouting Bruno said, "Gimme a little credit, Ton. I can really turn on the charm when I have to. So the nun told me she wasn't there anymore, and that she left seven years before, like I just said. She even told me where to find her, not that I needed the info at that point. Very trustful, these nuns."

Piza smirked. "Some, maybe. So, that it? I assume the nun didn't give you a reason why she left."

"No. I asked, kinda like off the cuff? I didn't wanna make her suspicious. She just said 'personal reasons', and looked a little uncomfortable, so I didn't push it. And that's pretty much it." He took a swig of soda. "I gotta tell ya, cuz, doesn't seem like she's got much of a life. I mean, I was only down there a couple'a days, but aside from the school, she didn't do much. Didn't go out at all at night, 'cept to this little restaurant around the corner." He checked his notes again. "Shorty's. Not that I blame her. I don't even think I'd go out if I lived—" Piza's scowl cut him off. "Never mind. So she went to the restaurant around five thirty both nights. Then straight home. I felt a little bad for her. Good lookin' woman like that? I dunno."

Through a nod Piza said, "I always figured she had simple tastes. I mean being a nun and all I guess she kind of had to but, even so, you just got that feeling about her. Very genuine person."

"Well, simple tastes is one thing, but that doesn't mean you gotta spend your life alone. Makes no sense to me, ya know? But she seemed happy when I saw her in the school. So, bottom line, I really don't think you gotta worry about her."

"You're probably right. Sounds like she's okay."

"Now that you know there's nothin' terrible goin' on . . . best as I can tell, at least . . . maybe you oughta go see her. Seems like she could use the company."

Piza hoped his attempt at nonchalance was convincing. "Yeah. Maybe I will at some point."

"Okay. Good. Uh, I got a little agita right now, Ton. Think I can take the rest of this pie home for later?"

"Sure. I bought some cannolis, but if you're not up for dessert. . ."

Bruno's eyes took on new life. "Cannolis? Um, well, as long as you went to the trouble and all. Plus, the cream might calm down the heartburn."

When Bruno left, Piza settled into his lounge chair. He removed Bruno's notes from his shirt pocket, and glided his index finger over Theresa's address on the first page. He needed to process what he'd learned. But not in desolate silence. He got up and put a Miles Davis album on the turntable.

What Bruno had shared was a mixed blessing. He was heartened by the news that she was apparently unattached. But that consoling revelation was eclipsed by the numbing fact that she'd been free of her vows for seven years. Seven years. Without the faintest effort to contact him. To explain why she'd left before the end of school back in '74. He understood she'd been troubled, as the school principal, Mother John, reluctantly revealed to him when he all but begged for information. She wouldn't give him details, other than finally acknowledging that Theresa's admitted feelings for him was *one* factor in her transferring to Philadelphia. It was a frustrating conversation, but at least it confirmed that their emotional bond was real.

Still, she'd left with no warning. No goodbye. How could someone as astute as her, someone so inherently kind, not realize —or care?—that, one way or the other, he needed some semblance of closure?

It didn't take long for him to accept that sitting in that recliner and endlessly speculating would accomplish nothing.

Whatever the consequences, he had to see her.

CHAPTER 24

In the summer of '86 (or any other summer for that matter), driving south on the New Jersey Turnpike on a Saturday morning was a beast. At least until you reached Exit 11, which entices the majority of cars over to the Garden State Parkway, the road of choice to the endless row of shore towns.

Piza had hopes of escaping the pre-Exit 11 mayhem by leaving at seven thirty—hopes that were dashed within minutes. Eastern spur. Western spur. Express lanes. Local lanes. Made no difference. Just an inharmonious assemblage of motor vehicles, most crammed with coolers, beach blankets, inflated plastic floats, antsy children, and sagging hope of hitting the beach any time soon.

Beating traffic was one reason for his leaving early on the hundred-mile journey to Philadelphia. (Stop-and-go driving wasn't fun when you drove a stick shift.) He also wanted to be sure he left himself more than ample time to complete his objective. Find Theresa, say his piece, take in her response (whatever it might be), and blow town one way or the other—likely never to return if she didn't exactly fall to her knees and praise Jesus when the vision of Saint Anthony of Hasbrouck Heights appeared to her.

The excursion wasn't just marred by traffic. His mission was leaking some of the certainty of early last evening, when he was sitting in his recliner and Miles Davis helped smooth the edges of a jagged decision. The doubt that reared up later that night had prompted a call to Elizabeth. After filling her in on Bruno's findings, he asked if his plan was delusional. Wasn't an impromptu visit probably the worst idea imaginable? She reminded him of their lunch a few months before. How she felt all along this was something he had to do. "Just take the damn plunge, Tony. No preliminary contact. No intellectual foreplay. You and her, one-on-one, out of the blue. It's your best bet for unvarnished answers. And call me as soon as you get back."

Elizabeth's pep talks usually worked, but this one had done nothing to ease his anxiety. As he inched down the turnpike, it occurred to him that this was like visiting the dentist after years of neglecting your teeth. Sitting in the padded chair and praying for good news, but knowing full well you were playing Russian roulette with five of the six chambers loaded.

God. I'm more messed up than I thought. I'm mixing metaphors.

As he turned onto Kensington Avenue, Piza pulled over to the side of the street to allow himself to calm down. Not because of nerves about seeing Theresa, but because he'd reached his landing spot two hours after his worst-case-scenario arrival time of eleven, thanks to general traffic volume and two road-narrowing accidents.

It's been said that the adventure lies in the journey more so than the destination. Piza didn't necessarily disagree, as long as that theorem was confined to philosophical concepts—like "life". But when it came to physically getting from Point A to Point B, he shunned excitement and demanded boring, comforting surety. And as someone with a deficient sense of direction and no knowledge of Philadelphia's geography, a road map he'd picked up with his coffee and bagel that morning didn't come close to meeting his need for a stress-free expedition.

If there was an upside, it was that his travel anxiety had tucked his Theresa anxiety into his subconscious. But now, after a few normal inhales and exhales, his original goal burst out of the shadows.

Oh boy. I feel a little queasy.

He opened the remaining bag of pretzels he'd bought at a turnpike rest stop and nibbled on a few of the knot-shaped acid sponges, mindlessly wiping crumbs off his navy blue polo shirt and beige chinos as he contemplated what lay ahead.

When he finally pulled out of his parking spot, he concentrated on finding the numbers on the stretches of row houses that populated the street. It wasn't easy. Many of the buildings were in some stage of decay. Some had no visible address. Others had numbers, but it appeared one or more of the digits had abandoned their post. At least he was able to determine, from the address Bruno had given him, that Theresa's building would be on his left.

As focused as he was, it was impossible to ignore the hopelessness that coated the area. Acrid-smelling air that seeped in through the car vents; colorful graffiti art that was losing its luster but still managed to accentuate the dreariness of its canvas; clusters of young people milling around by stoops or on street corners that appeared to be their final destination for the day; glazed-eyed souls sitting on sidewalks, propped up by battered chain-link fences and whatever elixir was hidden in the brown paper bags they clutched.

Creeping down Kensington, under the rusted, sinister-looking elevated train tracks that loomed over the landscape, Piza was grateful the woman driving behind him didn't seem to care about his lack of speed. If he'd been following someone moving at his pace, he'd have been close enough to the car to read the radio dial. It was fortunate for him that she didn't share his mind-set, because a collision would have been inescapable as he slammed on the brakes when the vibrant SONAS sign jumped out from behind an awning on an adjoining building. (His move did garner one pithy beep as the other driver cautiously maneuvered past him on his left.)

He pulled to the side, abreast of the weather-beaten cars that lined the curb like a stagnant caravan. He knew he couldn't stay there, but he wanted to position himself across from her building if possible, for easier surveillance. Circling the block a few times in the hope that a space would open up proved to be a dead end. He finally settled for a vacated spot on the same side of the street as Sonas, about thirty feet down.

When he cruised past the place the first time, he could see through the plate-glass window that the lights were out. He'd expected as much for a Saturday, not that he would have walked in anyway, what with kids, or anyone else, around. He was also reluctant to ring the lobby doorbell for her apartment, mentioned in the notes Bruno had turned over to him. Bzzzz! "Yes, who is it?" "Hi there. Tony Piza here. You used to call me Anthony. Remember? Just wanted to say I'm still in love with you from twelve years ago, and I was hoping you'd have a minute or two to chat about that?" Not exactly ideal. Although if Plan A didn't work, the doorbell was his fallback position.

Plan A. Based exclusively on Bruno's report that she went to the same restaurant at five thirty both evenings he'd been watching her. Shorty's. Piza had spotted it on his block-circling stint. So: watch her as she exited her building; follow her at a safe distance to be sure that Shorty's was actually her destination; wait a few minutes for her to settle in; then, casually join her. "Surprise! Guess who?" Less likely she'd freak out in a public place. Too reserved for that. And she probably wouldn't just pick up and walk out. Okay . . . that one he wasn't so sure about.

When he was first devising his plan (in the course of a sleepless night), his lawyer brain had shifted into overdrive. What if she wasn't around? Maybe visiting her father in the retirement complex she'd once told him about. Or what if she left her building at some point before going to dinner? He'd have to be there early enough to account for that possibility. And should he intercept her then, when—with no walls to confine her—it would likely be easier for her to ditch him? But then again, what if that turned out to be his only shot, short of the doorbell gamble? And what if she decided not to eat at Shorty's that evening? What if she did go to Shorty's and wasn't dining alone? Maybe meeting her coworker. Or (gulp) some guy. Those were but a few of the demoralizing scenarios that had washed over him like an interminable onslaught of shrieking Huns—to the point that he did something monumentally out of character. He said: "Screw it. Whatever happens, I'll figure it out then."

He sat back against the driver's side door, stretched his legs over the center console, and started reading Margaret Atwood's *The Handmaid's Tale*. All he could do now was glance up the block after every few sentences.

And wait.

5:20. No sign of her yet, although her building had seen some activity. From what Piza had observed so far, the place housed a mixed bag of residents. A young woman who appeared to be on the brink of adulthood had exited while struggling to contain a free-spirited little girl who called her "Mommy". A mustachioed man wearing a neatly pressed security guard uniform and a well-meaning toupee followed about a half-hour later. An elderly couple leaning shoulder to shoulder—evidently to protect themselves from the peril of the earth's pull—entered around four thirty.

During his curbside hiatus, Piza also noticed an assortment of visitors whose twitchy hyper-vigilance and record-breaking entry-to-exit time left little to the imagination. Bruno's assessment of Theresa's status was that there was probably nothing to worry about. Maybe that was true of her mental state but, based on what Piza had witnessed, her safety was another matter.

Ten minutes to go. Ten minutes until the irresistible siren call of Shorty's lured her into the open for dinner and a date with destiny. Piza's reaction to the final countdown to this keenly anticipated, twelve-years-in-the-making encounter? Melt into his seat and look as despondent as a politician diagnosed with a case of moral accountability. Perhaps it was a subliminal mechanism to tamp down his expectations. Maybe it was the fact that she hadn't stepped foot outside her building since he arrived, which struck him as odd for a lovely Saturday and intimated that, in fact, she might not be around.

Then she stepped into his peripheral vision.

She's here.

Jeans. A white SONAS tee-shirt, the letters askew and brightly colored like the sign above the nursery's door. Shoulder length, wavy blond hair brushed away from her face in no apparent style. A book and something he couldn't quite make out clutched in her right hand.

After he made his decision to head to Philadelphia, he'd previewed this moment more than once, each vignette featuring a different possible reaction on his part. None of them prepared him for the wave of euphoria and terror that surged through him and left his skin tingling.

She started walking up the street.

Okay, good. Right direction for Shorty's. He exited his car for the second time since he arrived, the first time being an angst-laden visit to a McDonald's across from Shorty's, to heed nature's call.

That bout of anxiety wasn't just rooted in losing sight of her building for a few minutes. The pit stop also meant abandoning his vehicle. Despite his sincere display of indignation when Bruno made his disparaging comment about the neighborhood's population, when the first passing group of kids stopped and stared at his nifty new sports car, he'd locked the doors and wished he'd taken his father's '69 Plymouth wagon.

He followed at a safe distance, picking up the pace when she turned the corner. Shorty's was the second door on the left. Peeking around the corner, his chest tightened when she passed the restaurant, until he realized she'd gone to help a woman pick up some groceries that had fallen from a ripped bag. Then, she did an about-face and crossed Shorty's threshold.

He made it to the restaurant's generous front window, which allowed for a view of almost the entire interior. The place looked like a page from a 1950s home decor magazine, with a linoleum floor of alternating black and white tile squares, and tables topped with light-pink laminate and bordered with stainless steel.

A stocky, freckle-faced Black woman who appeared to be late-middle-aged waved to Theresa from behind the counter and flashed a contagious smile. Theresa waved back and made her way to a small corner table. She rested the bottom of the book's spine on the table, angled the book, put on black horn-rimmed glasses—*So that's what she was holding*—and began reading. A few moments later, a trim young waitress with curly, blazing-red hair brought a cup to her table without any interaction between the two women before that.

Probably tea. Her favorite. Yeah, she's definitely a regular here. Okay, this is it. Surreal as it seems, the moment of reckoning is at hand, pal. All well and good, except he felt like his feet were cemented to the sidewalk and his teeth were glued together. And his rehearsed opening line suddenly seemed as coherent as a group discussion in the Tower of Babel. *C'mon, man. You're Tony Piza. Quick-witted. Charming. Self-assured . . . usually. Shit. What the hell do I say to her?*

A memory darted into his consciousness. Back of the school library. Beginning of '74. She was alone at a table, reading. Their combined classes were sitting cross-legged on the floor in the front of the spacious room, enduring hard-of-hearing Mrs. Fitzsimmons blaring a narrative on something or other. He'd approached and tapped the chair next to hers. Absent the library and kids and Mrs. Fitzsimmons and twelve-year gap, this was that all over again.

He confirmed his fly was closed, executed the cupped-hand breath test, and opened the door.

CHAPTER 25

The woman Piza had seen wave to Theresa acknowledged him with a nod and pointed toward a small cluster of tables on the other side of the room from where Theresa was sitting, implying he had his choice. He waved and made his way in that direction, veering toward Theresa as soon as the woman turned away. If he could have seen himself maneuvering across the room, he probably would have laughed out loud. His normally lithe body looked mummified; his strained attempt at stealth drew stares—some nervous, some amused—from other patrons. Had the woman behind the counter been paying attention, she undoubtedly would have dialed the mental health hotline.

He'd been keeping an eye on Theresa, who appeared so absorbed in her reading that she hadn't lifted her head. *Okay. Remember what you said that day in the library: "Pardon me, madam, but is this chair spoken for?"* Four yards away from her now. Ready to dust off one of the classic lines of their relationship.

And then she looked up. You'd have been hard-pressed to find a historical event (other than perhaps the "big bang") that devolved from order to chaos with such velocity. Theresa's mouth dropped open, her book fell from her hands, the book hit the teacup saucer, the teacup unleashed a geyser, the geyser sloshed onto Theresa's spotlessly clean Sonas tee-shirt, and Piza screamed like a terrified three-year-old.

The counter lady hurried over with the look of a woman on a mission. "Good Lord, Theresa, what the heck happened?" (She may have been in Philadelphia, but there was no mistaking her Southern roots.) "Oh my Lord, that hot tea splashed up right on your titties! You burned or somethin', honey? You want me to call the police, get you to the emergency room?"

Theresa was blotting the tee-shirt with a cloth napkin. "No, no, I'm fine, Jasmine. It's okay. Book slipped out of my hands. Sorry for the mess."

"You got nothin' to be sorry for, sugar. We'll clean it right up. You sure you're okay?"

"Yep. Positive."

Jasmine glared at Piza. "What're you doin' over here, mister? Didn't I give you the high-sign to sit across the room?" Piza started to answer, but the visibly concerned woman brushed him off and turned back to Theresa. "This guy botherin' you, honey?"

"Uh, no. No. I know him. He's— He's a friend from my teaching days in New York. Guess he wanted to surprise me." Her mouth reshaped itself into something resembling a smile.

"Oh, okay then. Maureen'll clean this up for you in a jiff. Get you some seltzer water to put on that stain. So big I'm not sure it's gonna work though." Without looking at Piza she added, "He gonna be joinin' you?"

Piza felt like every muscle in his body was cramping.

Theresa's glance at him was barely momentary. "I— I guess so, yes."

"You wanna see a menu, mister?"

"Um, sure. Yeah, menu would be great." He sat in the chair across from Theresa.

In the few seconds it took the waitress to come over to the table, Theresa didn't return Piza's gaze. The young girl put a glass of seltzer and a dry cloth on the clean portion of the table, then wiped away the spill. "Not sure if you wanna try the seltzer trick, Theresa," she said with a pronounced brogue. "But I'll leave it here if you do. And I'll bring you another cup of tea." She turned to Piza. "You a tea drinker too, sir, or can I get you something else?"

"Never touch the stuff. Strictly a coffee guy. Better suits my virility." His awkward chuckle dissipated almost as soon as it hit the air. "Um, but for now I'll take a lemonade, if you've got it."

"Do indeed. Be right back."

If the left side of your brain has logically assessed the possible outcomes of an intended act, that doesn't mean the right side won't register disappointment or worse when the outcome isn't the one you'd hoped for. Piza's brave face notwithstanding, Theresa's near-appalled reaction to his presence had leveled him. *Christ, it's like she couldn't bring herself to even look at me.* Panic setting in, he summoned the foolproof coping mechanism he hadn't had to use in a long time: virtual deep breath; will the mind and body to calm down.

It hadn't aged as well as he might have hoped.

This is ridiculous. Just be yourself—minus the torment. He smiled and tossed out, "Despite the fact you were here first, I'm tempted to conclude that you're stalking me."

She turned to him. "Why are you here, Anthony?" Wistful eyes belied a chilly delivery. Piza picked up on it, and that glint of emotion gave him hope.

"Well, that seems like a highly intrusive question, but seeing it's you. . . So here's the thing. I was down the shore and—"

"Here you go," Maureen said as she set down the tea, lemonade, and a menu. "I'll give you a few minutes. Be back in a bit."

As she walked away, he opened the menu. "So what's good here, Sist— Sorry about that. I meant Theresa."

"Everything. Why are you here?"

"Well, like I was saying, I was, um, down the shore, and this deli I go to in the morning ran out of the *Times*. So I picked up a copy of the *Inquirer.* And lo and behold, whose picture should I see? The newest member of the Philadelphia Board of Ed. Congrats on the appointment, by the way."

She didn't respond.

For some reason, that lack of acknowledgment was what it took to rip the scab off the ancient wound that refused to fully heal. "Okay. Enough, Theresa. Enough. You wanna know why I'm here? Why the hell do you think I'm here?" He was fighting to keep his voice down. "You left the order. And not once did you make even the most minuscule"—he held his left thumb and index finger millimeters apart—". . . microscopic effort to let me know. Like everything that happened twelve—"

"Beef stew, Theresa?" Maureen asked with a lilt in her voice on her way to the table.

"If it's Saturday," Theresa replied, mimicking the brogue in what Piza perceived to be an attempt to cordon off the tension before the waitress slammed into it.

She needn't have bothered, as Maureen's chipper demeanor dissolved when she saw Piza's face, although he wasn't looking directly at her. "Did you, um, get a chance to look at the menu, sir?"

He turned to her, his features softening. "Uh, you know what? Stew sounds good."

"Okay, then. Two stews comin' up."

The interlude had disrupted the flow of Piza's rant. Now he and Theresa sat there, he staring at her, she not making eye contact. Then she met his gaze.

"When I left in May of that year—"

"Without a word," he interjected, his ire springing back to life.

"When I left, I was as lost as I'd ever remembered being in my life. Even more than when my mother died."

His nod signaled recollection of their conversation about her mother's death from cancer when Theresa was in college.

"But back when she died, at least I knew why I was floundering. As close as I was with Dad, she'd always been my guiding force. So how could I not be lost?" Piza could see her sorrow revisiting her, and wondered if he should intercede. She made the decision for him, as she moved on with her narrative. "When I left Our Lady of Perpetual Tears, it was different than with Mom. With her, even though I knew losing her was inevitable, when it actually happened there was this . . . this stunning suddenness to it. One second she was there, then she wasn't. 1974 was nothing like that. There was a myriad of things that had been troubling me for a long time. Even before I got to OLPT. Always lurking in the shadows, taking turns pecking at me in some fashion."

"Death by a thousand cuts," Piza said.

That elicited a sad smile. "You always *were* good with analogies." He could see the pleasant nostalgia seep away as she continued. "When I first started at the novitiate . . . you know, training for the sisterhood, it was exciting. The newness of it. The feeling I was doing something special with my life. Special beyond just teaching."

"God's work."

"Yes. God's work."

Maureen arrived with their food, her approach more discreet than before. "Okay. Here. We. Are. And, of course, some cornbread fresh from the oven."

"Thanks, Maureen," from Theresa.

"Yes, thank you," Piza said. "This cornbread smells amazing."

"'Tis," Maureen confirmed as she smiled and left.

Neither of them touched their stew. Piza nudged the conversation. "So, you were saying."

After taking a sip of tea, Theresa said, "I don't need a lot to make me happy. But the one thing I do need, the thing that's indispensable to me, is freedom. And I didn't have that as a nun. It's a funny thing, you know? When you're on a path you believe is the one you need to follow, you find ways to reconcile your doubts. Toward the end of my time at the novitiate, when I started having misgivings, I convinced myself that once I got out of there and into the classroom I'd be fine. And the teaching did help. It's what I love doing. But outside of the classroom, the restrictions on what we could do became stifling. Do you remember that outing in April of '74? The Sunday we took our students to the park?"

"How could I not? For so many reasons, but mostly because it was the last time I saw you."

"I know. Of course you'd remember. But my point is that I had to lie to Mother John and sneak out to attend. A day in the park, with our students. Who was that possibly hurting?"

Piza knew it was a rhetorical question, but he answered anyway. "No one."

"But ultimately that was neither here nor there, was it? I was told not to do it. I had an obligation not to do it. And I did it anyway. And that's when I knew I had to pull back. From everything. Take time to try to make sense of things." Talking about that time of reflection seemed to prompt a similar reaction in the present, as she appeared to withdraw from the moment.

Piza wasn't sure whether she was done or merely pensive. But there was no way he was letting the conversation stall out. "From the look of things, moving to the parish here in Philly wasn't the answer either."

"Nooo, certainly wasn't. It was just like I said before, about concocting ways to reconcile your doubts. I thought that moving here, just ten minutes away from where my dad was living, might make things better. Give me a chance to see him more often. Kind of a counterweight to the strain of the rules and regulations. And the loneliness.—"

But you didn't have to be lonely, dammit. You had me.

"—And again, it made things a little better. But how long can you keep skirting the real issue? Keep deceiving yourself? And then when Dad died, I—"

"Oh God. I had no idea. I'm so sorry. When?"

"November, 1979. Three days after Thanksgiving."

He felt like a fool. He'd been so intent on solving the puzzle that had bedeviled him from the day she vanished from his life, that he'd neglected to calculate the toll his pursuit of answers might take on her. He needed to make this right, even though the consequences might be crippling for him. "Theresa, I need to apologize. Coming down here. Practically forcing you to rehash those painful moments in your life. You don't have to say anything else. I wasn't—"

She put her hand on his, stopping his words and eradicating rational thought as his love for her overwhelmed him. He fought the urge to take her in his arms and hold her until everything he was feeling became as much a part of her as it was of him. He fought it as fiercely as he could ever remember fighting any impulse in his life, because he knew that giving in would likely frighten her and end any hope of venturing past this point.

"You haven't done anything wrong, Anthony. This conversation was a long time coming. I owed it to you. I could give you a million reasons why I haven't done it, but I guess that doesn't really matter now."

Matters to me.

She removed her hand from his, ostensibly for no other reason than to straighten herself in her seat. Despite that, he wondered whether touching his hand had held more meaning for him than for her.

"Not surprisingly, when Dad passed I did a lot of soul-searching. And one day it struck me. How, with his death, he'd blessed me with an unobstructed view of my life. For the first time in ages. It was like he was telling me I'd run out of excuses. And I finally became aware that I'd based my decision to become a nun on terribly flawed reasoning. That day in the library, I told you that I joined the order because I wanted to somehow be like those amazing, compassionate nuns who'd cared for my mother in the hospital in her final days."

"You said you knew you couldn't do the kind of work they did . . . you know, nursing . . . but maybe you could honor them by joining an order where you could use your teaching skills."

"Good memory," she said. "I also felt that, in some way, it would be honoring Mom's memory too." A sudden bleakness twisted her demeanor and dulled her eyes. "But the reality was that I wound up doing the exact opposite. When I realized in the novitiate that I wasn't happy, that being there was so contrary to my nature, I should have left. If my mother wished anything for me, it was my happiness. In my work. In life in general. But by blindly following the path I was on . . . the wrong path, I wound up *dis*honoring her." She appeared on the verge of tears.

His brain churned to find the words to comfort her. "Look. It may have been the wrong path, Theresa, but you can't beat yourself up over that. If you made a mistake, so be it. But there's no way that qualifies as dishonoring your mom. And she sounds like the type of person who would love you all the more for changing course when you realized you were going in the wrong direction. And she'd certainly understand that your intentions were good."

With a dubious smile she said, "You know what they say about the road to hell."

His sigh reflected an awareness that—no matter what he said —he wasn't going to dislodge a conclusion that had undoubtedly embedded itself in her psyche over the past few years. So he shifted the conversation. "Well, I hope that time heals that wound. I really do. And I appreciate your trusting me enough to share what you've been through. But the more I hear about it, the more I don't understand why you cut yourself off from your friends. People who'd have had your back through this. Especially Colleen. I mean, you taught together for five years. You were so close. I speak to her occasionally. There are two little O'Briens now, by the way. Girl and a boy. I should say 'Sullivans'. She married a detective in her brother's precinct."

"I'm happy for her. She'll be a great mother."

"I agree. But anyway, she didn't want to reach out to you because she felt it would be intrusive. Leaving the way you did, with no goodbyes, she figured you needed space. She chose to respect that but— Listen, I certainly don't want to make you feel worse, but I can tell you, she was hurt."

"I think a lot of people were," she said, her voice subdued as she momentarily broke eye contact. "You have to understand something. The way I looked at it, I didn't want to burden anyone with my problems. And as time passed, even when I left the order, I felt it might be better for everyone from my old life if I left the past in place. Let go of it. Let everyone get on with their lives."

He leaned back in his chair. "Was that really your decision to make? To unilaterally assume you knew what was best for everyone?" He was trying to maintain an even disposition. But when he said, "Did you think *I'd* let go of it?", the tartness of his tone appeared to unsettle her. "The only reason I didn't make this trip sooner was because I didn't know you'd left the order. And truth be told, it took everything I had not to come down here even when I thought you were still a nun. My God, Theresa, I loved you."

This time her eyes did well up. Her regular pale complexion briefly turned crimson, then plummeted through a spectrum, bypassing its original hue and landing on ashen.

Jasmine's appearance at the table startled both of them. "Everything okay here, honey?" she said, her voice weighted with concern. "I couldn't help noticin' things from over by the counter."

"No, it's fine, Jasmine," Theresa answered, dabbing her eyes with a napkin. "Just a lot of memories. I'm good. But thank you."

"Okay, if you say so," the woman responded, tossing a look at Piza that promised a most unpleasant retribution if he did anything to hurt his dinner companion.

"She's very protective of you," Piza said after the woman walked away.

"Everyone around the neighborhood is. When you care for people's children. . ."

Another interlude.

Piza wasn't sure how to get the conversation back on track. Jasmine's intentions may have been pure, but her timing was abysmal. But then Theresa's expression changed. It wasn't a dramatic shift, more like a speck of determination that surfaced in her eyes.

"I think you're braver than I am, Anthony. Finally broaching the issue that's been hanging over this entire discussion."

"I don't know that it's bravery. Maybe if I was revealing something you didn't already know, it might be."

"I guess. And you're right. Of course I knew. If I didn't, I wouldn't have said I owed you this conversation."

Battling to mask his apprehension, he said, "So now that I've laid my proverbial cards on the table, I think fairness dictates that it's your turn. Mother John told me you had feelings for me. I sensed it too. But you were always much more circumspect than me. So tell me . . . was it true?"

"Yes." The tension that was constricting every molecule in his body instantly dissipated. It was a short-lived reprieve. "But I think it was a mistake."

"Why?" was the dispirited response.

"Because I was twenty-nine and you were twenty-two. You

were just out of college. As fresh-faced as could be. Guileless, in your way."

Piza contorted his face. "Are you sure you're not confusing me with someone else? Twenty-two? Yes. Just out of college? Yes. But fresh-faced? Guileless? Have you somehow blocked out the memory of my propensity for sarcasm? My penchant for convenient deception?"

The slightest smile appeared. "No. I wasn't blind to those traits. But, unlike you apparently, I didn't view them as the markings of a seasoned scoundrel. Far from it."

"So what then? You're saying you saw me as a boy? Seriously?"

"No, no. Not exactly a boy. Just—Just someone too young."

"Good God. You're making it sound like we were reenacting *The Graduate*. You weren't Mrs. Robinson, Theresa. I mean, other than shaking hands, we never even touched each other. Relationships don't get much more innocent than that." He turned his hands, palms facing up, to emphasize a look that said "Am I right?" She didn't respond. "Was it really my age that upset you? Or the fact that you had feelings you didn't think were appropriate for a nun?"

Through a faint shrug she said, "I don't know. Probably both. There was so much negativity hurling itself at me back then. I don't know."

He clasped his hands and touched them to his chin. Any trepidation he may have had about addressing the present had given way to his need to end the waiting. Today. Wherever it led. "All right. Let's move off phase one and on to phase two." He thought that might warrant further explanation, but she shifted in her seat and her face became taut, signaling she knew exactly what he was talking about. "So here we are. I'm thirty-four . . . thirty-five in a week, and you're . . . forty-one?"

"Forty-two last month." She looked like she wanted to escape.

"Okay, forty-two. Happy birthday. And I think it's fair to say that the age difference is a moot point now that I'm all grown up." He grimaced. "I didn't mean for it to come out quite like that." She didn't respond, other than looking even more uncomfortable. Tension seized control of him again. "I can't read that pained look on your face. Is it because I've just not too subtly revealed I'm still in love with you, and maybe you don't feel the same? Or because you're in love with someone else? Or is this just too much to take in? I need you to talk to me, Theresa."

She caught Maureen's eye and held up her teacup. "You want more lemonade?"

"Are you kidding right now?" He saw Maureen signaling to him and, completely flummoxed, he nodded. She quickly brought their drinks and glided away.

"Tea calms me." Then, after a pause, "Remember, you had time to prepare for this." She took a sip. But if the hot drink instilled a sense of tranquility, it must have lodged itself well below the surface. The only effect Piza noticed was a sudden coolness in her tone and an expression that was now blank. "There's been no one else in my life."

"Okay. And?" She said nothing, although she'd begun running her thumb gently along the handle of the teacup. He sat statue-like as he awaited the winner of the battle between anger and desperation raging inside him. "And?" he repeated matter-of-factly, anger and desperation having fought to a draw.

"Yes, I have feelings for you."

"Feelings. God. Could you be any more ambiguous?"

Weariness in her voice, she said, "Love. Okay? Are you satisfied now?"

He forced himself to unclench his teeth. "Only if it's true."

"You think I'd lie about something like that?" was her bristling response.

"I dunno, Theresa. The admission seemed to ring a little hollow."

Palms on the edge of the table, she shoved her chair back and stood up. "I have to use the ladies' room. Excuse me."

He couldn't get a grip on what was happening. Love. She'd said it. But the anemic declaration made him feel worse than when he walked into the place. This was hardly a glorious end to his quest. He'd taken delivery of his Holy Grail, only to discover it had been dented in transit. And a conversation he'd hoped would be worthy of enshrinement in the ethereal annals of resurrected romances had degenerated into a street-level pissing contest.

Half an hour later, he was back on the turnpike.

CHAPTER 26

"You realize you're a complete asshole," Frankie Falco said, in the way close friends can talk to each other.

"I think I'll be hanging up now," Piza answered. "Well, maybe not. Lizzie said the same thing to me last night when I got back from Philly, and I didn't hang up on her."

"Always liked that girl."

"Actually, she called me a brooding, narcissistic asshole." He manufactured a laugh. "She was infinitely more pissed at me than you seem to be."

"That's because she cares about you more than I do." Piza could almost see the grin through the phone. "So anyways, I hope you know what a jerk you must've sounded like. She admits she loves you and you basically say 'I don't believe you'?"

"I realize what a schmuck I was. But you know how I get. A speck of paranoia crops up and I instantly shift into lawyer mode. Even if it's not warranted."

"Like yesterday."

"Yeah. I don't know what I was thinking. My common-sense neurons short-circuited on me."

"And then some."

"I dunno, Frankie. I was so desperate to know for sure that she felt as strongly as I did, I think anything short of convulsive rapture on her part wasn't gonna cut it."

"Kind of like she was a groupie and you were all four of the Beatles rolled into one."

This time Piza's laugh was genuine. "Not exactly the first analogy that would've popped into my head but, maybe, yeah."

"So in the end, just how bad did you screw this up? Beyond repair you think?"

"Honestly, I'm not sure. When she excused herself to go to the ladies' room, she was really angry. But when she came out, she looked more determined than upset. She told me she needed time to process all this, which gave me some hope. But the next thing out of her mouth was that we lived in two totally different worlds. *My* response was that we were only two hours away, not on opposite ends of the planet."

"I think you may've been missing her point."

"Yeah, I kinda knew that when I said it. I was trying to put my own spin on it. But she didn't waste any time clearing it up. She told me there was no way she could give up her work there. And she loved where she lived. Then she said it wasn't a lifestyle I'd be suited for. So two hours or ten hours, it didn't make a difference."

Piza could hear Frankie cluck his tongue. "And you said. . ."

"I said that whether or not I could handle it should be my determination, not hers."

"Okay. So what did—"

"But I messed up. I hesitated for a second before saying it."

"Probably because you knew she was right. I mean, you really see yourself living like that?"

"Under any other circumstances, I'd say probably not. But to be with her. . . Anyway, she picked up on the hesitation right away. Called me on it straight out. I think I knew at that point that even if I said I *could* live there, my credibility was pretty much shot to hell."

"Tell you the truth, Ton, it sounds like she was just being honest."

"That may be. But if you love someone, and that person makes it plain as day that he loves you too, wouldn't you do whatever you could to be together? I mean, would it be that big a deal to move to a part of town less. . .."

"Seedy?"

"Well, I was thinking more in terms of run-down, but that might be a meaningless distinction. But I mean she'd still run the nursery. And I could get a job with some firm in Philly. Or in Jersey, right across the border."

"And you didn't tell her any of that."

Piza puffed out a breath. "No. My head was swimming at that point. It was almost like our conversation had turned into a purely intellectual exercise, and love had no place in the equation. I don't get it. I don't get *her*. It's as if she was purposely setting up roadblocks to happiness. Why would someone do that?" Dead air. "Frankie?"

"I guess it all depends on what your idea of happiness is."

"What're you talking about?"

Frankie's sigh was loud and long. "Listen, she made it very clear that she's happy the way she is. So—"

"But Jesus, there's degrees of happiness. We love each other. I admitted it. She admitted it. So it stands to reason that if we were together she'd be even happier."

"You don't know that. How old did you say she was? Forty-two? Maybe she just doesn't wanna complicate her life at this point. So who knows if being with you would make her happier? I don't mean to sound cold, but she lived without you for the last twelve years. And she never reached out to you, even though she could have. At least for the last seven anyways. It sounds like she knows what she needs to make her happy. And what she doesn't."

"I'm sorry, Frankie, but I can't accept that."

"Then I don't know what the answer is." Another pause. "So, how'd you leave it with her?"

"Well, like I said, with my credibility down the tubes and my being off-kilter with her reasons why it wouldn't work, I kind of ran out of things to say."

"That's a first."

"Yeah, tell me about it. The best I could muster was an apology for blindsiding her, which I did feel bad about. And don't think I didn't let Lizzie know what a crappy idea that was, by the way, since she encouraged it. So anyhow, after apologizing, I asked her if she'd object to my calling her occasionally, just to see how she's doing. At that point, I figured what the hell."

"How'd she feel about that?"

"Well, she didn't exactly jump up and down and clap her hands, but she said it'd be okay." His voice became more animated. "But here's the thing. She blushed a little and didn't make eye contact when she said it. Maybe I'm making too much of it, but I think that may have been a little crack in the armor. I have no idea what's going on in her head, but I swear, Frankie, I'm not convinced this is over."

"Well, time will tell, I guess. Oh! By the way. Did she ask you how you knew where to find her? Ya know, where she lived? The restaurant?"

"Actually, no. Either it didn't occur to her right then . . . too shocked maybe, or that's just not the way her mind works. But I had an answer ready if she did. Bruno told me her home address is in the phonebook. So my line was gonna be that I found her address, went to see her, and happened to get there just in time to see her walking up the street and around the corner. When I turned the corner and didn't see her still walking, I assumed she went into the restaurant. Case closed."

Piza wasn't sure if it was humor or cynicism he heard in Frankie's muted laugh. "Little thin there, pal. Glad you didn't have to use it though. Lying to her probably wouldn't have been the best way to jump-start the relationship."

CHAPTER 27

Sabatini was bristling as he pulled up in front of his former residence for Sunday visitation. He had no doubt who owned the white Jaguar sitting in the driveway. A light but persistent mist didn't help his mood, torpedoing plans for a day spent outdoors with the kids.

He immediately knew something was wrong. Instead of his children walking out the front door unaccompanied—the norm since the domestic violence incident—Megan stepped out. Only Amy was with her, looking fidgety as she tugged on the hood of her daffodil-dotted pink rain jacket.

He exited his car, jammed his hands into his windbreaker's pockets, and made his way up the driveway, taking care not to move so fast as to appear threatening. He stopped a few feet from his wife. "What's going on?" Returning Amy's broad, welcoming grin, he said, "Hi, peanut." Back to Megan. "Where's Lis? Is she sick?"

There was apology in Megan's voice. "No. At least I don't think so. But she said she doesn't wanna go. She sprung it on me literally fifteen minutes ago, or I would've let you know. I honestly don't know what's going on, Joey. She won't even come out of her room, and—"

"Well then, I'll talk to her. I was looking forward to celebrating her birthday with her, since I won't be seeing her tomorrow." He moved toward the door.

"Joey, please don't go in there." He stopped short, history still fresh in his mind. "She's obviously upset about something, and she was adamant about not going. I mean, to the point of being defiant. If you go in, I really think it's just gonna upset her more. And we don't need another commotion."

"Well then what am I supposed to do, Megan? What are *we* supposed to do? I mean, we're the parents. Are we just supposed to let her call the shots? And this is all the more reason for her to"—glancing at Amy—"ya know, do what the people at school suggested. I think this overrides your concerns, no matter what garbage what's-her-face has filled your head with."

The screen door flew open and Candy burst out, glaring at the instantly fuming Sabatini. "Yeah, that's right, I was listening. And I'm not filling Megan's head with 'garbage'. I'm trying to protect her from making a mistake that'll break her heart. *Someone's* gotta look out for her."

It was the smirk more than the words that got to him. "Who the hell do you think you are?" he spat out, aiming an index finger at the woman.

The realtor lobbed a retort, he countered by talking even louder, and Amy looked petrified as her father and Candy began yelling over each other.

"Stop it!" Megan shouted. "Just stop! This is insane! Candy, go back in the house." It was a testy command, and the realtor's stunned expression made it evident she wasn't used to that tone from her friend.

"I'm just trying to help," Candy said, managing to look both hurt and indignant.

"I realize that," Megan answered, her voice softer. "But you're not. So please go inside. You too, Amy."

The child's eyes welled. "But I wanna go with Daddy."

"Listen, Megan," Sabatini said as his eyes narrowed to slits. But she held up a hand that gently asked him to stop.

"You *are* gonna go, sweetheart. I just need to talk to Daddy for a minute. Grownup talk. Really quick. Promise, okay? And close the front door."

The frowning child nodded, then followed Candy into the house.

"Why is she even here, Megan?" Sabatini demanded. "Can't you see what she's doing to this family, for God's sake?"

"She's here because she's a friend. I know she can go a little overboard, but she means well. So don't blow this out of proportion. Plus, she's gonna help me get my real estate license. I was gonna go to a few house showings with her today, so I can get a feel for what's involved. But with Lisa home, I guess I'll go some other time. I think it'll be good, ya know? You can pretty much make your own hours, and I don't have to tell you we could use the money. If it wasn't for my mom, I wouldn't be able to make ends meet."

Ordinarily, he would have been doing handstands at the news of his wife's potential employment. But he was too worried about Lisa—and furious with the meddlesome Candy—to savor the moment. He fought the impulse to say "It's about time", and simply replied, "I'm glad to hear it. But what are we gonna do about Lis? She's been kind of sullen with me these past few weeks. And she won't discuss it. But now not wanting to see me at all?"

"I know. And I tried talking to her before. She kept saying there's nothing wrong but she just didn't feel like going." She paused, squinting like she often did when mulling over something. "She *has* been a little more subdued around the house, now that I'm thinking about it. Little testy sometimes too. But I mean nothing really dramatic. I dunno. Maybe it's just a phase."

Sabatini had no desire to repeat the mammoth mistake he'd made in revealing what Lisa had told him about Candy's rules-be-damned remarks, and the wine-tasting episode. But he had no choice. If Megan had spoken to Lisa about it, and the child felt her father had betrayed her trust, that could account for her not wanting to see him. He also realized it wouldn't help to use the confrontational approach he'd resorted to on the phone when he first divulged the child's comments.

"Let me ask you something, Megan. The other day, on the phone, the stuff I mentioned about Candy and the kids, ya know, about sipping the wine and all. Did you say anything about that?" Averting his eyes, he said, "Uh, like I told you, it was just conjecture on my part, but I was just wondering if you maybe said something to the kids."

His wife met his fumbling statement with a sarcastic smile. "Save the song-and-dance, Joey. I didn't mention it. I didn't want Lisa to think she couldn't talk to you about things. And I didn't say anything to Candy either, in case you're wondering. Because, frankly, it was all harmless. Not the end of the world like you seem to think. Just like I'm not the bad mother you told me I am." Her eyes turned cold. "Just like I'm not an alcoholic like my father."

Through a sneer he shot back, "Just like I'm not mentally impaired."

They stood there, locked in their stances. A duel of visceral emotions that had chosen an inopportune time to materialize.

He needed to move past this. Amy was waiting for him. He compensated for blinking first by prefacing his thought with a dollop of snark. "Well, assuming you actually *didn't* say anything, then I have no clue why Lisa's acting like this. But whatever's eating at her, it's obviously getting worse. And I don't think either of us is equipped to deal with it. She needs a professional."

As Megan's demeanor thawed, the contemplative squint reappeared. After a few seconds, with a slight shake of the head she said, "But what if Candy's right? Could you live with yourself if Lisa goes to a therapist and it messes her up the way it did Candy's daughter? I know I couldn't."

Sabatini fought to remain calm, despite his soaring frustration. "Look at what happened in school, Megan. And now how she's acting with me. Our daughter's already messed up. Why can't you see that?"

Located only a block away from the county courthouse, it hadn't taken long for General Poor's Tavern to become a fixture on lower Main Street in Hackensack. It was a popular destination for attorneys who sought to unwind from a stressful day by reliving it, unburdening themselves to fellow members of the legal community—pretty much the only other people on earth who had the capacity to feel sorry for lawyers.

Piza entered the restaurant at four forty-five on Wednesday, the fourth day after the Philadelphia excursion that still had him anxious and confounded. Fortunately, he'd been at the Passaic County courthouse in Paterson from Monday until Wednesday afternoon. His focus on the case he was handling had relegated the Theresa situation to a foggy disquiet.

Sabatini had called Piza's office on Monday and Tuesday, leaving urgent messages (apparently, the only kind he was capable of) about the need to meet as soon as possible. After determining that his situation wasn't life-or-death, Gloria had done her usual masterful job of holding him at bay, as she so informed her weary and grateful boss.

The intensity of the three-day divorce hearing—which had ultimately ended in a settlement—had left the lawyer needing to decompress. So he'd asked Gloria to call Sabatini and set up a meeting at Poor's, while he responded to a few "absolute must" phone messages.

When Piza got to the restaurant, he saw the banker sitting at a small table, his lackluster khaki suit conspicuous against the rich, dark wood of his surroundings. A glass of beer appeared to be untouched. Piza joined him and ordered a beer for himself.

"Hey, Tony. Good to see ya. Just got here myself. Rough couple of days I take it. I called your office a few times and—"

"Yeah, I know. That's why we're here. So tell me what's going on."

Sabatini filled him in on Lisa's status. "So, bottom line, despite whatever it is this kid's going through, Megan still won't agree to therapy. At least not immediately. She said she wanted to pray about it. I swear I almost lost it."

"What'd you say?"

"I said if God didn't contact her by the end of the week, then maybe that meant nobody was actually listening, so *I'd* handle it. She gave me this look that was part pity and part like I made her wanna puke. She didn't say anything else. Just went inside and sent Amy out."

"Speaking of Amy, how's she dealing with all this?" Piza asked.

"She's only six, so how much she actually understands, who knows? She never brings anything up, and I certainly don't think I should. I dunno. I haven't seen any lingering effects from when the cops were at the house that day. And when the drama this past Sunday morning finally subsided, she seemed fine. Truth is, I think she really enjoyed the one-on-one time with me. No annoying older sibling around. Reminds me of me and Gina at that age." The nostalgic smile that surfaced quickly succumbed to the here and now. "So, nothing from Megan's lawyer I take it?"

"Not as of today. And like I told you, I'm not optimistic about getting a positive response."

"So where does that leave us then? Do we give her more time

to get back to you? Or do we file that motion you were telling me about? 'Cause we've gotta do something. Lisa turned ten on Monday. Bad enough I couldn't see her on Sunday to celebrate, but when I called to wish her a happy birthday Monday, she wouldn't get on the phone with me. Megan said she wouldn't even open the card and gift I left when I dropped Amy back off Sunday. It's really making me nuts. I can't figure out why this is happening."

Piza responded with, "Well, something triggered it. Are you sure you didn't do something? Maybe say something? Something she could've misinterpreted somehow?"

"What're you implying?" Sabatini snapped.

"Nothing" was the equally edgy reply. "It was just a suggestion that you search your memory." He was tired and in no mood to be challenged.

"Sorry. Just frustrated, ya know? I've gone over this in my head a million times. I'm positive I didn't screw up." He rotated his beer glass as it sat on the table. "It's been kind of like a progression. One day she was fine. Then she got a little gloomy and withdrawn a couple of times. Not hostile, but certainly not herself. She said nothing was wrong, so I chalked it up to moodiness. But now she won't even see me?" He looked like he lost focus for a few moments, then came back. "And I'm not sure why Megan doesn't seem more concerned. I mean, as much as we've been at each other's throats since the separation, she's been really good about visitation."

Piza sipped his beer. "Yeah, she was really aces when she filed that domestic violence complaint."

"No, no. I know. I'll never forget that, believe me. But that was Candy's doing more than— Shit. Do you think she's somehow involved in this situation with Lisa?"

"No idea. What're you thinking?"

"I dunno. Maybe convincing Megan not to intervene? You know, not pressure Lisa?"

With a shrug Piza said, "Got me. But all the more reason to push forward on our end. In all honesty, at this point, I don't think it pays to dick around with Bruzek any more. I don't think she's gonna call me. And I'm concerned about this latest episode with Lisa. They hear motions every other Friday. But with the current motion day schedule and the mandatory time frame for serving papers and all, the soonest we could get into court would be about four weeks."

Sabatini's shoulders sagged. "Four weeks? Jesus."

"I know. So I think we should go in on an order to show cause. It's like a motion, but it's geared to getting you into court faster where the circumstances are urgent. I think it's worth a shot here. The worst that happens is the court doesn't see this as an emergency and puts it on the regular motion calendar."

"Okay, Ton. Whatever you think is best."

"All right. I'll get things started and Gloria'll call you when we need you to come in and sign paperwork. Friday's Fourth of July, so figure maybe Tuesday or Wednesday of next week. Oh, I've been meaning to ask you, where are you on finding a bigger apartment? Like I told you, if we want a shot at custody—"

Sabatini cut him off by raising a hand that said 'not to worry'. "I'm moving into a two-family in Lodi. August first. Two bedrooms. Decent size."

"Great. How big a hit did you take on the rent?"

"Only another hundred fifty a month. The woman who owns the place lives downstairs. She's pretty old, so she agreed to reduce the rent if I took care of routine maintenance. Lawn. Snow. That kind of stuff."

"Okay. But considering you're giving Megan roughly sixty-five percent of your take- home, which I still maintain is too much by the way, can you—"

"Oh, not to interrupt you again, but Megan's thinking about getting a realtor's license. Something positive in all this."

"Well, hopefully that happens," Piza responded. "Anyhow, I

know a buck-fifty rent increase isn't astronomical, but in your case. . . You sure you're able to handle it? We already have your expenses as low as plausible on the paperwork we've submitted to the court, and even then it slightly exceeds your income. Although that's not uncommon, because people usually still find a way to scrape by."

With a grin that labored to appear genuine Sabatini said, "I can make it work. It's not so bad when you have no social life and don't eat three meals a day. And store-brand cereal is just as good at dinner as it is at breakfast."

Piza winced. "Any chance of maybe getting a promotion? Or something better with a different bank?"

"Nah. With all these savings-and-loans on the skids, there's a glut of people like me looking for work. But I'll make do. Been paying *your* bills, right?"

"Well, I don't do the actual billing, but I'd have heard if you weren't. But that's not my point."

The banker stared at his beer glass. "Is what it is, Tony. Most important thing to me is my girls." Locking eyes with Piza, his expression took on a steely conviction. "I'll do whatever it takes to make sure they're okay."

Piza detected an almost ominous undertone to those last words. It unsettled him.

CHAPTER 28

"So thanks for letting me bend your ear," Elizabeth said. "And sorry about calling so late."

"Are you kidding?" Piza replied. "How many times have I called *you* around midnight?"

"That's true." A soft laugh. "Okay, I hereby retract my apology."

Through a smile he said, "Retraction noted. And again, I'm really sorry things didn't work out with Dr. Bob."

"'Rob', Tony."

He could visualize her smirk. "Sorry. Couldn't resist. But if he didn't see what a gem he could've had in you, he's getting off easy with me just screwing around with his name. And I hope that bimbo wife he's decided to reconcile with gains six hundred pounds and farts effusively in bed."

Elizabeth laughed so hard she couldn't catch her breath. Finally she said, "You are one sick bastard. And she's not a bimbo."

"Well, maybe. So you sure you're okay?"

"Yeah. And like I said before, I'm just really glad I didn't go all-in on this relationship. Keeping a bit of a distance, like you and I talked about at lunch that day, was the smartest thing I could've done. In all honesty, the longer he didn't make a move to get divorced, the more I realized this probably wasn't in the cards. It still stings, but I'll survive."

"I know you will. And I have absolutely no doubt you're gonna meet someone who actually deserves you."

"Thanks. And while we're on the subject of people deserving each other, have you decided when you're gonna call Theresa? Or whether?"

Piza felt his body tense up. "Uh, no not really."

"'No not really' when? Or 'no not really' whether?"

"Both, I guess. Dunno."

Her breathing and the delay in her response indicated a change in her disposition. "Okay. Listen, pal. When you got back from Philadelphia, you specifically told me you felt she'd left the door open a little. You asked if you could call her, and she said yes. So what's the hitch? Or is this just plain and simple procrastination?"

"Listen, Lizzie, this isn't as easy as you seem to think it is. I mean, what are we gonna talk about? I'm certainly not gonna call just to make small-talk. And if we got into a substantive conversation, how would it not lapse into me blurting out some form of 'I love you and I wanna be with you and it's killing me'? That's face-to-face dialogue, not phone conversation stuff. Besides, if I said that, it might scare the shit out of her."

"Hmm. If you ask me, the one scared here is you."

"What the hell does that mean?"

"Calm down. Just hear me out. Right now you have hope that this could still go somewhere. And I'm wondering if, at some level, you're worried that if you take the next step you might find that she doesn't want to pursue it. And then your hope would be gone. So maybe, rather than face that possibility. . ."

Piza heaved a sigh. "Ya know, Lizzie, as much as I appreciate your brain . . . and your psych background, you are totally off on this one. What you're basically saying is that I'd be satisfied living in a state of . . . I dunno, 'safe inertia' I guess, rather than deal with potential disappointment. You know me better than just about anyone. You know I can't let go of a problem until I find a solution. So your analysis doesn't make sense."

"It does if 'safe inertia', as you put it, *becomes* the solution. Not every answer to a problem is necessarily satisfying. But that said, I agree with you. This isn't you. At least not up to this point. But you're facing a situation that's possibly more important to you . . . more vital to your well-being . . . than anything you've faced before. And I'm not being hyperbolic here. I mean we're talking about your prospect for happiness."

Piza's response was tinged with weariness. "Wasn't this conversation supposed to be about you?"

She answered with a genial, "Too late to turn back now. Listen, you need to reach out to her, Tony. Trying to guess what she's thinking is only gonna make you crazy."

"So what're you thinkin' about, sugar?" Jasmine asked with a look of maternal concern. "You been starin' into space for the last ten minutes. Mind if I sit a bit? Things are slow today."

Theresa smiled and said, "No, of course not."

"I know it's none of my business,"—breaking into a grin— "not that that ever stopped me before. But it seems like you ain't been yourself for a while. And I can't help thinkin' it's got some- thin' to do with that guy that came to visit you. You know, from your old teachin' job? I never seen nobody make you that angry before."

"Come on, Jasmine. You know I've got a bit of a temper."

"Well, yeah. But only when it comes to politicians and people like that. Never with your friends."

"That's true, I guess. But, anyway, I'm fine. Just a little tired maybe."

"Honey, I been around a while. Lot longer than you. And I think you and me both know there's somethin' goin' on. So talk to me. You care for this guy?"

Surrender. "I do, yes."

"You love him?"

She gave the older woman another smile, more grudging this time. "Unfortunately, yes."

Jasmine drew back. "Why're you sayin' 'unfortunately'? Last I heard, love was a *good* thing. Wait a minute. Don't he love you back, the fool?"

Theresa almost choked on the tea she'd just sipped. "Don't make me laugh with tea in my mouth. Yes, he does. That's not it."

"Then what exactly's the problem?"

Theresa paused to collect herself. "The problem is that it wouldn't work."

"Why?"

"Lots of reasons. Look at where I work. Where I live. Other people may look at this neighborhood and see a place they'd want nothing to do with. But I love it here and have zero desire to leave. He's a lawyer. Living in the cushy suburbs of New Jersey. He could never settle here."

"He tell you that?"

With a shrug Theresa said, "Not in so many words. But I could sense it."

Jasmine's eyebrows dipped and she pursed her lips. After a few moments she said, "When did this guy— What's his name?"

"Anthony."

"When did Anthony find out you wasn't a nun no more?"

"Just recently. Week or so?"

"And how long's it been since you last seen him before he was in here that day?"

"Um, about twelve years?"

Jasmine shook her head as her expression morphed from inquisitiveness to bewilderment. "Twelve years. Now he finds out you ain't a nun and what's the first thing he does? Hustles his backside down here to find you. How're you not gonna give it a shot with a guy who loves you that much? 'Specially since you love him too. A lot from what I can tell. Only time I ever seen people argue as much as you two was doin' in here is when one of 'em owes the other one money, or they're crazy about each other."

Theresa responded with a light-hearted, "See, Jasmine? That's why I practically live in this place since you bought it. Great food and pearls of wisdom like that."

"Uh-huh. Anyways, whatever reasons you come up with for you and him not to work out, how'll you know without even talkin' to him about it. Seems to me the two of you need to start communicatin' better."

"You may be right about that."

"So how'd you leave it? You gonna see him again?"

"Don't know. He asked if he could call me, and I told him yes. But, honestly, I'm not sure that's a good idea. If this isn't gonna amount to anything, why prolong the agony? For both of us."

Jasmine's eyes narrowed. "Theresa, I love ya, but right now you're makin' me nuts. Why're you so damn sure this ain't gonna work? Pardon my French. You're usually so positive about things. But you seem set on endin' this before it even starts."

Theresa picked up her teacup and lightly rotated it, staring at the swirling liquid. Without lifting her eyes she said, "Truth is, I think that after a certain age people are incapable of changing. I think once you're in . . . I dunno, maybe when you hit thirty or so, with rare exception you are who you're gonna be. Like your essence is set. Your values. Your habits. Everything that *looks* like change after that is probably just window dressing."

Jasmine sat up straight, never taking her eyes off her friend. "You're probably the smartest person I know. But I think you're dead wrong on what you just said. I don't believe it's ever too late for people to change." She paused, then cocked her head. "Look at *you*. You stopped bein' a nun. When you was what? Around thirty-five or so? Change don't get much bigger than that."

Theresa answered with a vigorous shake of the head. "No. All I did was free myself to be me. I changed *what* I was, not *who* I was."

Through a leery look Jasmine said, "I dunno, honey. Seems to me that brain of yours is workin' overtime lookin' for a way to overpower your heart. And I still think you're wrong about people not bein' able to change."

"I'm not though. And this isn't a contest between my brain and my heart. It's just that there are times when the brain needs to step in and stop the heart from doing something stupid."

"Stupid? I'm sorry, sugar, but I refuse to believe you think love is stupid."

"I don't think love is stupid. But sometimes acting on it is." Impatience laced with despondency crept into her tone. "Don't you see? I waited too long. I should've done something twelve years ago. I should've left the order when I realized I was in love with him. And when I did leave, when *maybe* there was still an outside shot of salvaging the relationship, I still did nothing. I assumed he'd moved on by then. And I thought it would be selfish of me to intrude on that." She dramatically swept her right arm in front of her while she tossed out a self-mocking, "Wonderful accommodating me. So very, very considerate." A humorless chuckle. "If I'm the smartest person you know, Jasmine, I feel sorry for you. Truly smart people don't let an assumption dictate their future."

The consoling response Theresa was expecting didn't come. Rather, her friend offered an unembellished, "Let me ask you this. Would you be happier with him in your life?"

Theresa paused for a moment, then said, "Under certain circumstances, yes. I think so."

"What circumstances would that be?"

"If we could live *here* and I was positive he was really okay with that. Positive that someday he wouldn't wake up and think he'd made a mistake. One he couldn't live with. A mistake he'd resent me for."

Jasmine's expression was kindly. "You realize what you're sayin', honey? You're askin' for a guarantee on how life's gonna turn out. That ain't never gonna happen. Not for you, or me, or nobody. And I ain't tellin' you nothin' you don't already know." No response from Theresa other than a look that conceded defeat. "Ya know somethin', I seen you fight for the poor people of this neighborhood . . . hell, of this whole city. Fightin' politicians and anyone else that stood in the way of you tryin' to make life better for these folks. So I know you got it in you. That's why I can't understand how it is you won't fight for your own happiness. Makes no sense to me."

Theresa pushed her teacup aside and placed clasped hands on the table. "Jasmine, I've managed to screw up so much of my life. So many bad decisions. If I take the plunge on this relationship, and it turns out to be another gigantic error in judgment? I honestly don't know if I'd have enough fight left in me for anything."

Jasmine leaned across the table and took Theresa's hands in hers. "Sugar, if that's the way you're gonna choose to live your life, scared of maybe makin' another mistake, that'll be the most gigantic error in judgment you'll *ever* make."

CHAPTER 29

Where Memorial Day was always celebrated at the Pizas, the Falcos were the annual Fourth of July hosts. Angelo and Mary Piza had become friendly with Lou and Chickie Falco when their sons were in grammar school, and the friendship endured.

Chickie's concept of a barbecue was virtually a carbon copy of Mary's, the only difference being that Chickie favored manicotti over baked macaroni. But the sausage and peppers and the more traditional fare were present in abundance. On the "activities" side, the Piza bocce matches were replaced by the Falco horseshoes tournament.

The Falcos had an extensive backyard, with a large patio that accommodated three good-sized tables with umbrellas and some card tables for makeshift seating, with plenty of room left for the serving tables and an area where guests could dance if so inclined. Lou had installed four outdoor speakers, and every backyard event was graced with music from the early-to-mid 50s, especially Sinatra, Perry Como, and Tony Bennett, as well as a bevy of Italian instrumentals and selected cuts from *The Godfather* soundtrack.

Piza was sitting at a table with Frankie, Roger, and Frankie's unmarried older brother, Jimmy. Three of Frankie and Jimmy's friends from the plumbers' union were also there, with their spouses.

During a break between courses, Roger took Piza aside. "How are things going with your friend?"

"Honestly? Not great. Lisa's refusing to even see Joe at this point. And his wife changed her mind about therapy, based on some nonsensical theory spun by that other woman we were telling you about. Candy Janicek? She claims that therapy caused her daughter to run away from home years ago. She has Joe's wife terrified that the same thing could happen to Lisa."

"What? Unless whatever therapist the girl was seeing was a complete quack or a child molester, the probability of that happening is about as close to nil as I could imagine. Is there anything you can do about it?"

"Actually, I'm gonna be filing papers requesting that the court order therapy. Truth be told though, I'm not sure that's gonna fly. We may not have enough to back it up at this juncture."

With a scant headshake Roger said, "It seems like things have deteriorated since we talked. I fccl bad for Joe . . . and his daughter."

"I know. But at the very least, asking the court to intervene will put Joe's wife and her attorney on notice that we're not gonna just sit back and do nothing."

"Well, I wish you luck with it."

"Thanks. Ah, my mother seems to be trying to get my attention. I'd better go see what she wants before she starts yelling for me like I'm five again."

Through a grin Roger said, "Go. Talk to you later."

Piza sauntered over to a canopied lawn swing where Mary and Patty were sitting. "You summoned me, Mother?"

That prompted an eye-roll. "I swear, Anthony, you and your fancy words. It's a miracle you got any friends."

"Was there a reason you wanted to see me, Mommy dearest, other than to mock my enviable vocabulary?"

"Yes. There was. You ain't been around for a couple'a weeks, and you must'a lost our phone number, so I wanted to see how you're doin'. That a crime?"

He replied with a timid, "No, it's not." Instinctively, he reverted to form. "Although, the phone works both ways, you know." She answered the sarcasm with a firm stare. *I swear to God, it's like I can't help myself.* "Sorry about that, Ma. And about not checking in. Things have been kind of crazy at work, but that's no excuse. So, how are you guys doing? Pop still looks kind of drawn."

"What can I say? The commute every day into the city. The store . . . you know, not havin' Manny around no more. I don't think your father realized what a load Manny took off his shoulders." She sighed. "It's a lot. I worry about 'im. But at least he finally agreed to close on Mondays, startin' September."

"Oh, that's great. At long last."

A faint flip of the hand. "I guess. But honestly, I wish he'd just sell it. Nunzio told 'im the same thing, about maybe sellin'. We got some money put away, and with whatever we got from the sale, we'd be okay. I dunno."

"Well, the next time I come over I'll talk to him about it again. He's still got a lot of customers, despite the supermarket competition and all. You guys could probably get a decent price for it."

"Okay. That'll be good."

"And how about you? How're you doing?"

Her face scrunched into a "neither here nor there" expression. "I'm all right. Cholesterol's still a little high, so the doctor bumped up my medication a little. I'm not great with stickin' to a diet, but what else is new."

"Well, try harder."

"Yeah, yeah. So anyways, what's goin' on with you, besides

bein' busy at work?"

He gave her a wry smile. "No, Ma, I'm not dating anyone."

Mary's attempt at virtuous bewilderment was so over-the-top that her son broke out laughing, which prompted Patty to do the same.

"What're *you* laughin' at?" Mary asked as she eyed her daughter.

The girl shrugged. "I dunno. Tony made me do it."

"Thanks for throwing me under the bus, Sis."

Patty's eyes bulged. "I didn't do that. You're lying, Tony." She turned to her mother as panic swept across her face. "I didn't throw Tony under a bus, Ma. I promise."

It was Mary's turn to laugh. "I know. I know. It's just an expression. It don't mean you really threw 'im under a bus."

Still looking confused, Patty said, "Oh. Okay. 'Cause I didn't." She then fixed her brother with a perfectly executed stink eye.

"So anyways," Mary said, "I didn't say nothin' about you datin' someone, Mr. Wiseguy."

"You didn't have to. You had that 'am I ever gonna have any grandchildren' look in your eye. Again."

"No I didn't, 'cause that's not what I was thinkin'." A pause. "But since you brought it up, any chance of you and Mandy gettin' back together? She was such a sweetheart, Anthony. She would'a been good for you."

"I like Mandy," Patty chimed in.

"You're not helping, Patty," her brother said with a teasing scowl.

If it's possible to blindside yourself, that might be the best way to describe what happened next. Piza's brain fired off an impulse to tell his mother about Theresa, an urge he felt helpless to repel despite the instant awareness that this wasn't the right time or place.

"Actually, Ma, what I just said isn't exactly true. Although it isn't exactly false either."

Mary's eyes lit up. "Ya mean about you and Mandy? Ya think it's possible that—"

He waved his hands to dispel any hope. "No, Ma. Not that."

Mary's face clouded, a portrait of confusion and dismay. "What then? What the hell is true and not true at the same time? Is this one'a those riddles you used to like as a kid?"

"Calm down, Ma. I'm talking about my seeing someone. It's complicated."

"How complicated can it be? Either you are or you ain't." She stood up and yelled, "Angelo! Get over here!"

"We're startin' horseshoes in a little bit," the man yelled back. "Can't it wait?"

"No!"

Angelo threw his hands up and speed-walked (as best he could) to join them.

As Mary sat back down, and his father made his way across the lawn, Piza let out a sigh that embodied a swarm of emotions, not the least of which was concern that by spilling his guts he might propel his parents into an irreversible catatonic state.

"Okay, I'm here," Angelo said through labored breathing. "Woo. Ain't as young as I used to be. Anyways, what's so important?"

With undisguised sarcasm Mary answered, "Well, it seems Anthony may be seein' someone or not seein' someone. He ain't exactly sure."

"Whaa? I don't— Wait a sec. Is Mandy back in the picture? I sure hope so because—"

"Forget Mandy, Ang. I already tried that."

"I like Mandy," Patty said again.

"Then who're we talkin' about?" Angelo continued. "I don't get it."

Piza let loose an even deeper sigh than before. "Okay. Here's the thing. And look, I never told you guys about this because I didn't think you'd understand at the time. Remember when I taught, that year after college?"

"No, Anthony, we're both senile," Mary tossed out.

"Mary, enough with the mouth. Please. Let 'im talk."

Piza was too apprehensive to care about his mother's dig. "Anyway, while I was there, the other sixth-grade teacher was a nun. Sister Theresa. I'm sure I mentioned her. We, uh, spent a lot of time together and . . . um——"

"Jesus, Mary, and Joseph," Mary blurted out while executing a speed-of-light sign-of-the-cross.

Panic setting in, her son stammered, "It uh I— Look, we didn't mean for it to happen."

Mary's face contorted into a mask so grotesque you'd have sworn she was about to start speaking in tongues. "Didn't mean for it to happen! Oh my God, what'd you do to 'er?"

"Jesus Christ, Anthony," Angelo managed to squeeze out. "Did you knock 'er up? Holy crap!"

Visibly awash in horror, Piza practically screeched, "Are you both insane? I meant we didn't mean to develop feelings for each other! Fall in love!"

"Oh. Thank God," Angelo uttered, his starkly arched shoulders drooping to their normal position. "What a relief."

"A relief?" Mary yelped. "Your son was in love with a nun! How's that a relief? God help us and save us."

"Oh. Sure. He does somethin' stupid and now he's *my* son," an indignant-looking Angelo shot back.

"Okay, that's it," Piza said as he glared at his parents. "This was a huge mistake. So now I'm gonna go play some horseshoes and make believe this never happened."

He made it three steps before he heard, "Anthony Angelo Piza, you take one more step and I swear it'll be the last one you take on this earth."

This was serious. His mother only played the middle-name card when she was truly upset with him. He wasn't exactly over-the-moon with her either, or his father for that matter, but the values they'd taught him were deeply embedded. He turned around, endured a communal stare for a few moments, then told them the story.

Silence prevailed when he finished, as if they were all cemented in place. Patty broke the lull. "Daddy said a bad word before and he has to put a quarter in my jar when we go home so I can buy more records for my record player."

"I will, sweetie," Angelo said. Arching his eyebrows, he looked at his son. "So, where do you go from here?"

"Well, that's the question, Pop. I'm not sure. I don't exactly feel like having my heart broken, but I think if I don't follow up on this . . . see where it leads, one way or the other . . . I'll be second-guessing that decision for the rest of my life."

His father responded with an understanding nod.

"Nothing to say about any of this, Ma?" He'd rarely seen her look so sad.

Mary flipped her hands. "Whaddya want me to say, Anthony? The only thing your father and I ever wanted was for you to be happy. But you don't seem happy. This relationship, it's just, I dunno. Weird, I guess. I don't understand it."

Her concern touched him, and he loved her for it. "I get it, Ma. I do. For what it's worth, I'm not sure I understand it either."

A few seconds passed. Enough time for Mary's spunk to resurface. "Leave it to you to find an ex-nun to fall in love with. Although God knows there's plenty of 'em around these days. Nuns marryin' priests. What a world we live in. But it don't bother me as much as maybe when I was younger. I guess you get used to things as you get older."

"Amen to that," Angelo piped in. "You have to, or you'll make yourself crazy."

"So, you want my advice?" his mother asked.

"Of course. That's partly why I told you guys."

"Call her. Or go see her again. Whatever it takes to figure this out. 'Cause you're right. Unless you do, you'll never have a clear head."

"I agree," Angelo said. "I think this is somethin' you gotta see through. One way or the other."

He acknowledged them with a nod. Then he turned to Patty and grinned. "And what do you think about all this, Sis?"

She wore the innocent hesitation of an uncertain child. "I dunno," she finally said, and returned his grin, eliciting a laugh from her family.

Angelo exhaled a breath that signaled resolution. "Okay. Now that that's settled, can I go play horseshoes?"

"Both of you go," Mary said, "now that we solved all the world's problems."

When the matches were over, Piza went to find Frankie to tell him what had happened. He had just reached him when their attention was drawn to the dance area, as the now pumped up volume of the speakers (thanks to Lou) blared the tarantella, a traditional and lively Italian folk dance. It was one of Patty's favorites, and she'd never been shy about getting up and commandeering the dance floor for the tarantella or any other dance that was there for the taking. She had the floor to herself until she grabbed Frankie's brother's hand and yanked him from the fringe of the area, where he and most of the other guests had been clapping with gusto.

It was quite a sight. Jimmy was 5'7" and thin as a hair strand; Patty was 4'7" and bottom-heavy. Always a good sport, Jimmy locked arms with her and they pranced around the patio with the speed (if not the grace) of well-conditioned athletes. As the song ended, Patty topped off the crowd-pleasing spectacle by hip-checking Jimmy into the side-dishes table and onto the floor. A collective gasp went up, immediately followed by howls of laughter as Jimmy sat up and raised a cellophane-covered bowl of potato salad. "Saved it!" Applause by all.

"That alone was worth the price of admission," Piza said, wiping his eyes.

At the tail end of catching his breath, Frankie answered, "Oh, man. How freakin' funny was that? Good Lord. You up for another beer?"

"Sounds good. Thanks."

When Frankie returned with the bottles, a few moments passed before he said, "So what was with the family meeting by the lawn swing, if you don't mind me asking?"

"I don't mind at all. In fact, that was what I came over to tell you. I told them about Theresa."

Frankie's face registered stratospheric shock. "Say what? Holy shit! What the hell possessed you to do it here? Not that I'm not happy you finally told them. They deserved to know."

"You're right. They did. And I have no idea why I did it here. The thought just flashed in my brain, and then my mouth took over."

"Wow. On behalf of Family Falco, thank you for choosing our humble home for this truly momentous occasion. So, how'd they take it?"

"You mean *after* I quashed their knee-jerk notion that I'd gotten her pregnant?"

"What? How the—"

"Don't ask," Piza said with a head-shake eye-roll combination. "Anyhow, bottom line is they told me to go for it, if I felt it's what I needed to do. Could've knocked me over with a proverbial feather. Especially Mom. You know how religious she is. I mean, the ex-nun revelation and all."

Frankie shook his head. "Parental love, man. Never ceases to amaze me."

"Agreed," Piza said as they clinked bottles.

"So, now that that aspect of the adventure's out of the way, what's your next move?"

"I wish I knew, pal."

CHAPTER 30

Piza had filed his papers on the Wednesday after his tavern meeting with Sabatini. The court had scheduled oral argument for the second Friday after that, at 1:30. That was the motion day they wouldn't have been in time for had Piza not gone the "order to show cause" route. He'd requested that the court: order therapy for Lisa; bar Candy from interacting with the children; and, order expedited custody mediation. As he saw it, his best shot at success was the expedited mediation.

The case was assigned to Judge Williams, much to Piza's delight. He was his favorite family court judge—a compelling fusion of expertise, compassion, and wit. Also, knowing that Nadia Bruzek never went to court unless she had no choice, he assumed Seth Kaplowitz would be handling the hearing. He didn't know whether Kaplowitz had appeared before Judge Williams since their first encounter back in early May, when the young attorney's melodramatic performance led to his putting his foot in his mouth. But observing the dynamic between the two of them would be interesting.

Sabatini wanted to attend the hearing, despite the fact that only the lawyers would be participating. But a mandatory meeting at his bank's main branch made it a moot point. (Piza would have liked him to be there to see first-hand what transpired, rather than having to explain it in a phone call, which invariably diluted the zing of live action.)

Judge Williams's courtroom was in the oldest structure in the courthouse complex—the rotunda, a relic from a more reverential era. An elegant architectural creation crowned by a dome adorned with now cloudy stained-glass, and featuring tarnished brass railings that bordered the circular opening in the middle of each of the upper-level floors. Veined-marble pillars managed to look stately despite the yellowish hue of neglect. Piza (a traditionalist in some aspects of his life) often said he felt most like a lawyer when in that building.

The courthouse environment on Friday afternoons in the summer was usually laid-back, particularly on motion days, when most business was completed before lunch. Coming off the staircase on the third floor, Piza (remarkably, a few minutes early) exchanged greetings with some administrative staff who were meandering back to their offices from their lunch break. But other than that listless few, there were no signs of life.

The courtroom was open, and he peeked in. Nothing. That surprised him. He'd anticipated that the ultra-eager Kaplowitz would have already arrived and set up shop at the counsel table, pacing the floor in anticipation of battle.

Judge Williams's staff was housed in an office adjacent to the courtroom. Piza knocked and entered. The judge's secretary wasn't at her desk, but his law clerk—working in a small room a few yards away—motioned to him to come in.

"Hey, Tony," she said. "You're here on the Sabatini order to show cause, right?"

"I am indeed, Connie. Just checking in. Cut your hair, huh? Looks good short."

"Why thank you," the young woman responded through a

blush. "So, you're the only case we have on this afternoon. Is the wife's attorney here yet?"

"Not that I've seen. Want me to pop in when he shows up?"

"That would be great. The judge is already back from lunch, so we're ready to go whenever you guys are."

He saluted a goodbye on his way out. As he closed the door, he saw a grim-faced Kaplowitz exit the elevator about thirty feet away. He was holding a briefcase with his right hand, and had a bulging red folder pinned to his body with his left arm. He didn't seem to notice Piza, who was positive the man was talking to himself.

Doesn't surprise me, working for Bruzek. I sincerely hope that humongous arsenal he's lugging isn't all for this case.

"Ah, Seth. You're here."

"Yeah. Did you think I wouldn't be?"

Cuddly as ever. "Here, let me get the door for you." He thrust his chin toward the red folder. "Looks like you came loaded for bear."

"Huh? Oh. Nah. Different case. Just got back from a motion in Morris County. Lot of sensitive information in the file, so I didn't wanna leave it in my car."

Not even in the trunk? And I thought I was paranoid. "Yeah, can't be too careful these days. Your client gonna be here?"

"No. I think one of her kids is sick."

"Oh, sorry to hear that. You know which one?"

"No idea. My boss talked to her."

Piza decided to test the waters. "Speaking of the kids, isn't there some way we can work out an agreement on Lisa getting therapy? From what I understand, the school psychologist suggested it. So I would think that—"

"Look," the young lawyer said as he lay the red folder on a chair at the counsel table, "my client's against it. That's the bottom line. So there's nothing to discuss." He placed his briefcase on the counsel table and started removing papers.

Shaking his head, Piza said, "If that's the way you want it. I'll let the judge's law clerk know we're ready."

As he sat at the counsel table, waiting for Judge Williams, Piza marveled (as always) at the courtroom's entrancing character. A vast vaulted ceiling presented the illusion of boundlessness. Luminous sconces, affixed to gold columns that lay flat against the off-white walls, cast light on murals depicting Roman law. The rich walnut of the judge's bench, the counsel tables, and the swiveling juror chairs enhanced the room's air of dignity. Even the gallery was populated with individual wooden seats, rather than the pew-like benches favored in more current design schemes.

One of the courtroom's double doors creaked, and a tall, silver-haired court officer entered and made his way toward the front right. He flashed a wide grin when he saw Piza. "Hey! Tony! How's it goin'?"

"Hangin' in there, Bill. How 'bout you?"

"Same. Hangin' in. Five months till retirement. Countin' the days."

"I bet, ya lucky stiff."

A door to the front left opened. A slightly hunched over older man, with thick glasses and a head of hair that must have been bequeathed to him in Einstein's will, came out and took his seat at the court clerk's station, a waist-high enclosure attached to the judge's bench. Looking up, he pushed his glasses up to the bridge of his nose. "Well, hello there, Tony. Happy Friday."

"Same to you, Mike."

The clerk looked at Kaplowitz. "Afraid I don't know your name, young man."

"Seth Kaplowitz. From the office of Nadia Bruzek."

"Ah," the clerk said, looking like he'd suddenly had an acid reflux attack. "Judge should be out in a jiff."

The words had barely left his lips, when the door to the right of the bench opened, and Judge Williams emerged.

Everyone stood as Mike intoned, "All rise. The Superior Court of Bergen County is now in session, the Honorable R. Terrance Williams presiding."

"Okay, please be seated," the judge said. "Can I have your appearances for the record."

"Anthony Piza for the plaintiff, Joseph Sabatini."

"Seth Kaplowitz for the defendant, Megan Sabatini."

Judge Williams's eyebrows arched as he nodded. "Ah yes. Mr. Kaplowitz. I remember you. Your 'Moses leading his people out of Egypt' speech still rings in my ears. How are you finding the practice of law?"

"It's going pretty well, Your Honor. Thank you for asking."

"Well, I'm glad to hear it. Now, I've read everything you both submitted. Mr. Piza, I know you brought this as an order to show cause. I scheduled it for today even though, in all honesty, I wasn't a hundred percent convinced of the actual urgency. I don't know for a fact that Lisa Sabatini's behavior is all that different from how any child her age might react to the upheaval of a divorce. But I'd—"

Kaplowitz was on his feet. "That's exactly our position, Judge. So I have to wonder why we're even here."

Piza winced as he saw the jurist purse his lips. "Mr. Kaplowitz. The 'Moses' recitation isn't the only thing I remember from your last appearance before me. And I don't want a repeat performance. So, as much as I appreciate your enthusiasm, don't interrupt me when I'm speaking."

The rookie lawyer took his seat. "Yes, Your Honor."

"Okay, good. As I was about to say, since the child's behavior is directly impacting Mr. Sabatini's visitation rights, and her refusal to see him seems to have come out of the blue, I felt it better to err on the side of caution, and address the issue sooner than later. Mr. Piza, is your client adamant in his position that he wants residential custody of the children?"

"He is, Judge."

"Okay. I'm going to order expedited custody mediation. Hopefully, participating in that process can help these people resolve this and save everyone involved a lot of heartache. Now, Mr. Kaplowitz, I see from your client's affidavit she's dead set against therapy for this child. What's the harm in having her talk to someone?"

"Well, Your Honor, my client has reason to believe that therapy could significantly harm her daughter."

Looking skeptical, the judge asked, "Based on what?"

"Um, a friend of hers had a daughter who was in therapy, and the child ended up running away from home. My client is terrified that the same could happen here as well."

Piza got to his feet. "Judge, this involves the woman we referenced in our papers. Candy Janicek. As far as we can tell, there's nothing to indicate her daughter's problems had anything to do with therapy. And—"

Kaplowitz shot out of his chair. "Judge, unless Mr. Piza is a licensed psychologist, he shouldn't be rendering an opinion on this issue."

"I'm not rendering an opinion, Your Honor," Piza answered. "What I'm saying is that whatever precipitated Ms. Janicek's daughter's leaving home is an unknown, as opposed to what we know for a fact, which is that Lisa's school counselor recommended therapy. So if we have to weigh—"

"Oh, give me a break," Kaplowitz interjected. "The school counselor saw her one time."

"And obviously saw enough to feel the child needed help," Piza hurled back.

Judge Williams motioned for both attorneys to sit. "Let's tone it down, gentlemen. I'm not going to order therapy for this child today. I simply don't have enough in front of me to justify it. A psychologist's written report . . . even a preliminary one . . . might remedy that, at least as to whether Lisa needs ongoing counseling."

"With all due respect, Your Honor," Piza said, "that kind of puts my client behind the proverbial eight-ball, unless you're willing to order that initial examination. Since Lisa refuses to see her father, he can't take her to speak with someone. So short of a court order, the only way we can get a report is if Ms. Sabatini agrees to Lisa seeing a psychologist. And Mr. Kaplowitz has made it clear that's not going to happen."

"I understand the predicament, counsel. But I'm reluctant to force an exam at this point. Maybe Ms. Sabatini will change her mind with the aid of the mediator. And the mediator may request that the child be included in the mediation process, which could be helpful."

An animated Kaplowitz was on his feet again. "Your Honor, I really, really don't think having the child participate in mediation is a good idea. It could have the same effect as her seeing a psychologist. What if it traumatizes her? How do we undo that?"

Piza rose as well. "That's ridiculous, Judge. I don't see how sitting down in an informal, non-threatening setting with a trained mediator could 'traumatize' Lisa."

"How do you know?" was Kaplowitz's retort. He was close to yelling. "You seem to have a lot to say about things you're not qualified for."

Piza glared at his adversary as Judge Williams interceded. "All right, enough," the judge said, his tone stern. "Both of you sit. And Mr. Kaplowitz, calm down, before you spontaneously combust. Whether Lisa participates in the mediation will be determined by her parents and the mediator. And I'm certainly not going to order that the child *not* participate."

Up rose Kaplowitz. "Your Honor, with all due respect, I think that's a big mistake."

It was evident the judge was laboring to exercise patience. "Counsel, my duty as a family court judge in matters like this is to prioritize the best interests of the child. And that's exactly what I'm doing." He paused. "I'm going to assume that this child's well-being is important to you as well?"

Piza was surprised that the combative Kaplowitz looked hurt by the judge's remark.

"Of course it's important to me, Judge."

"Good. These mediators are highly skilled. So I don't foresee a problem."

"Yes, Your Honor" was the young lawyer's subdued reply.

"Now, on the issue of restricting the children's exposure to this other woman"—the judge shuffled through some papers—"Janicek. Mr. Piza, I've read what your client had to say in his affidavit, and I've read the wife's response. There doesn't really seem to be much disagreement about the things this woman did. It's really a question of whether those things were harmful to the children. Granted, the sip of wine and some of the things this woman said might not sit well with some people. But apparently Ms. Sabatini was there when they happened, and she didn't feel they were problematic."

He looked at the papers again. "And the remark Janicek apparently made a couple of Sundays ago, about 'someone' having to protect Ms. Sabatini may have been . . . 'snarky' I guess is as good a word as any. But it seemed to have been made in the heat of the moment, and I really don't see it as resoundingly disparaging Mr. Sabatini. So under these circumstances, I'm going to give her the benefit of the doubt. I'm not prepared to take the highly unusual step of telling Ms. Sabatini who she can associate with."

Piza considered countering the judge's reasoning on Megan's judgment by bringing up her alleged alcohol problem. But he still didn't have enough proof and, for that matter, wasn't even sure she was still drinking. So best not to muddy the waters.

He'd expected Judge Williams's ruling on Candy's involvement with the family, and knew it would be a wasted effort to object to it. However, he felt the need to make an additional point, more to keep Kaplowitz off-balance than anything else. "So, just to be clear, Judge, you're saying you don't feel it's appropriate to limit Ms. Janicek's exposure to the children *at this time,* correct?"

"Correct. Anything involving the children is always subject to judicial review. So if more information comes to light, we'll address it then."

"There won't be anything, Your Honor," Kaplowitz said. "I can absolutely assure you of that."

"Well, we'll see, Mr. Kaplowitz," the judge responded. "After sixteen years on the bench, I'm a little wary of guarantees. And let me add something. If this divorce is as contentious as it seems it's shaping up to be, I may find it necessary to appoint a guardian ad litem to represent the children's interests. I'd like to avoid that, but if I'm convinced they need an independent lawyer advocating solely for them, I won't hesitate to take that step. I hope that won't be the case, but I'm putting you both on notice. I'm sure both these parents are decent people, but—"

"At least *my* client is, Your Honor" was Kaplowitz's unmistakably snide comment.

A fiery-eyed Piza turned to him. "I beg your pardon? Ya know, I've had about enough of your sniping, so why don't you learn to keep your mouth shut."

Judge Williams hammered his gavel on the bench. "Stop it, both of you! Immediately. Mr. Kaplowitz, I wasn't soliciting your opinion. And I told you before I didn't want a repeat of your last appearance in my courtroom. Conduct yourself with the proper decorum or get someone else in your firm to handle this case. Understood?"

"Yes, Judge. I apologize." It was a superficial reply.

"Fine. We'll send a copy of the written order to both of you.

And you'll be hearing shortly regarding instructions for the mediation. We're adjourned." He left the bench.

As Piza finished packing up his papers, the court officer caught his eye. The lawyer buckled his leather satchel and strode to the corner of the courtroom where the officer was standing.

"Tony, what the hell is that kid's story? What a freakin' wiseass."

"I don't know, Bill. But I've gotta figure out a way to rein him in. Because this is bullshit."

CHAPTER 31

The TV news show wasn't holding Piza's attention as he sat on his couch, hands cradling a cup of coffee, hair uncombed, still in the boxer shorts and tee shirt that were his standard bedtime attire.

He'd awakened still tired, enervated by the seemingly unrelenting weight of the Sabatini case, and the frustration of dealing with Seth Kaplowitz at yesterday's hearing. A couple of years ago he'd have brushed aside the young lawyer's intractable aggression as a mere annoyance, lasting no longer than it took him to get back to his office. The fact that this battle (and similar ones in other cases) wore on him so much reinforced his conclusion that he needed to move on from family law.

He'd already decided to forgo his usual Saturday morning visit to the office, and was contemplating doing nothing for the rest of the day but renting some movies and testing the stamina of his VCR. The ringing phone forced him to relinquish his comfortable slouch and head to the kitchen.

"Hello." . . . "Hey, Ma. What's goin'—" . . . "What? Oh,

God. How bad?" . . . "Jesus, no. Which hospital?" . . . "Yes, yes. I'm on my way."

Tears were spilling onto his cheeks before the receiver made it back to the hook.

Piza burst through the hospital's front doors and ran to the information desk.

"Patient's name?" the smiling receptionist asked, her expression changing when she looked at his reddened eyes.

"Piza. P-I-Z-A."

"Okay. Let's see. Um, yes. Intensive care. Room 211. Are you family?"

"Yes, yes."

"Okay, follow the signs to the East Wing. Down that hall"—she pointed—"and to your right. Take the elevator to the second floor. Here's your visitor's badge."

He flicked a "thank you" as he yanked the badge from her hand.

Exiting the elevator, he spotted his mother in the hallway, leaning against the wall adjacent to the room's entrance, rosary beads in hand. He strode the thirty feet and engulfed her in an embrace as the tears came again. "Are you okay, Ma?"

She kissed him on the cheek and said, "Go inside. See your father."

In every mental picture Piza had of his father, the man was immaculately clean-shaven. And if he wasn't smiling outright, you knew there was one lurking at the corners of his mouth. That was why he almost gasped when he entered the room and saw a face that was a stubbled mask of abject suffering.

Angelo looked up as his son approached him. "Look at 'er, Anthony. She looks like she's sleepin' right?"

"She does, Pop," he answered, standing behind his seated

father and gently wrapping his arms around him. The man's right hand grabbed his son's forearm.

Piza took a step to his sister's bedside and kissed her on the forehead. Patty did look like she was sleeping. Except, of course, for the tube protruding from her mouth, a translucent snake that looked horrifying despite its simplicity. A flexible piece of plastic that was breathing for her. When Piza had asked his mother "how bad" in their phone conversation, she'd said the doctors had told them that Patty's brain was dead. She'd had a stroke in her sleep.

Mary came into the room, and Piza pulled up a chair for her. She waved him off. "I'm okay standin'."

"Has Doctor Iannello been in to see her?" Piza asked. (August Iannello had been the family physician forever.)

She shook her head. "Not yet. He knows though. The other doctor, the one who deals with strokes. I don't. . ."

"Neurologist," her son offered.

"Yes. Neurologist. She said she'd call 'im."

An hour later Dr. Iannello arrived. It had been a while since Piza had seen him, and he was taken aback by how much the man had aged. But he still had a full head of silver hair and, in Piza's estimation, had taken on the visage of someone you might find in a Norman Rockwell painting. And after a few minutes of talking, it was clear the passage of time hadn't affected his characteristic empathy.

He explained in detail how and why this had likely happened. What it boiled down to was that Patty's underlying heart condition (not uncommon in people with Down syndrome, and something the family was aware of) made her more susceptible to a stroke.

The Pizas listened intently, but their disconsolate expression made it clear that a clinical analysis—although appreciated—was no consolation for the sight of the girl lying motionless in that hospital bed.

The doctor's voice was soft and steady, but left no doubt about the somber weight of the conversation. "So. Right now, the ventilator is breathing for Patty. Her heartbeat, the rise and fall of her chest that you see, the machine is doing that, because she no longer can."

Angelo heaved an agonized breath, and his son quickly took his hand. "But Doctor Iannello," Angelo said, his voice brittle, "if the machine keeps 'er breathin' long enough, there's a chance she can come around, right? Ya know, if we give 'er brain a chance to heal?"

Piza felt his chest being ripped open. His mother moved toward her husband and lay a hand on his shoulder.

The doctor's response was seeped in compassion. "Angelo. Patty died the moment her brain stopped functioning. I wish to God there was a way to bring her back, but there's not. I'm so sorry."

Through tears, Angelo looked at his wife and son. "She's gone," he whispered, as if they hadn't heard the doctor's last words. He turned and gazed at his daughter. "My little girl is gone."

It was Mary who officially gave the authorization to remove Patty from the ventilator Saturday evening. Angelo concurred in the decision, but couldn't bring himself to participate in delivering it.

They could have given permission as soon as Dr. Iannello told them Patty was dead. But the visual evidence of her breathing, the beating of her heart (which they could still feel), and the numbness that settles in when the initial turbulence of shock is sapped of its energy, clouded reality enough to require some time to transition to lucid thought. Piza offered what soothing counsel he could, and then his parents parted ways, each going in the direction best suited to helping them come to grips with the merciless futility of their situation: Mary—to the hospital chapel; Angelo—outside to sit on a bench in a small, lush garden.

Piza called a couple of members of the immediate family (he included Elizabeth in that category) to let them know what had happened. He also asked them not to come to the hospital. There was nothing they could do, and his parents needed solitude more than comfort as they weighed a decision that was a foregone conclusion. He said he'd call them with any new information.

After the ventilator was turned off, the deceitful signs of life took their leave. A perfunctory departure befitting their limited role. It occurred to Piza that he'd be haunted forever by the chorus line of blipping heartbeats collapsing and ushering in the sterile hum of death.

He left his parents alone in the room, so they could lean on each other in saying goodbye; joined together in a grief that only a parent can know. Angelo looked pale and unsteady as they came out, and Piza assisted Mary in getting him to a chair in the hall. When he was sure his father was all right, he entered the room. He held his sister's hand for a few minutes, then kissed it and tucked it under her blanket.

When they got home, a couple of phone calls started the chain of notification. Angelo's sister, Rose, and her husband, Filippo, the only immediate family who was local, came to the house bearing dishes of hot food. Nunzio, Cheryl, and Elizabeth drove down as well, their arms laden with sandwiches and side dishes. (Cheryl had called Rose to coordinate their offerings.) Other friends and family members phoned to offer condolences. Mary handled most of the calls, handing the phone to the reluctant Angelo only when someone specifically asked to speak with him.

Filippo and Nunzio offered to assist in making the funeral arrangements. Piza graciously declined. Not that he would have accepted anyway, but it was his hope that the frenzy of planning her funeral—picking a casket, choosing flowers, booking the church, buying a cemetery plot—would perhaps blunt the sense of loss for them for the two days it took to accomplish everything.

The three of them went to the funeral home to select the casket and discuss the details of the wake. They scheduled it for Tuesday, with visitation from two to four and seven to nine. The funeral mass and burial would be on Wednesday. Piza and Angelo went to the local Catholic cemetery to purchase a plot for Patty. Angelo bought one for himself and Mary, adjacent to hers. He said he didn't want to take any chances they wouldn't be together.

He wanted to get one for his son as well, but Piza said no. "Don't you remember, Pop? I wanna be cremated, and in the dark of night have my ashes sprinkled in the end zone at Giants Stadium." He was gratified to draw a grin from the profoundly sad man.

Mary chose Patty's favorite dress to bury her in—short-sleeve yellow chiffon, with an oversized bow at the waist. Her favorite doll would join her, although Piza facetiously suggested it would be more fitting to have her boxy, battle-worn portable record player accompany her. "I think she liked that thing better than she liked me," he said with a warm smile.

"You may be right," Mary replied, her eyes twinkling at her son's comment. "That little machine was 'er best friend. When was it we got that for 'er, Angelo? Christmas '62?"

"Um, lemme think. Yeah. '62." He chuckled. "She played that "Jingle Bell Rock" record so many times Christmas Day she was drivin' us crazy. Remember?" That brought a laugh from his wife and son. "Anyways, Anthony, we'll keep the record player in her room. Somethin' special to remember her by."

Tuesday morning Piza woke up early, after a fitful night. When he got to the kitchen he found Mary with a spatula in hand, working a mixing bowl. "It's six o'clock, Ma. Whaddya doing?"

"Makin' a couple'a pies. For tonight. Anyone who's gonna go

to the wake both times are probably gonna come over in between. They gotta eat."

"I realize that. But people have brought over enough food for an army, and I can run to the bakery and get some cake. You don't have to do this."

"I know that, Anthony. And if you wanna pick up cake later, that's fine. But the bakery don't make chocolate cream pie like I do, do they?"

Piza realized this was something she needed. "No, Ma, they don't. Not even close."

She gave him a self-satisfied nod. "Now that we got that settled, have some coffee. I'm gonna make eggs in a little bit."

"Tell you what. You do what you're doing and I'll go pick up some bagels. Deal?"

"Okay. But I'm still makin' eggs. And make sure you get an onion one for your father."

* * *

Wakes have a certain commonality. A particular dynamic. Patty's was no different. The sight of her lying in the coffin assaulted the immediate family when they entered the room ten minutes before it was opened to the public. Secondary relatives, friends, and acquaintances appeared at random times during the cumulative four hours of visitation, their reactions ranging from tear-drenched hugs to handshakes and awkward condolences, depending on the number of layers separating them from the top tier of family members.

Nia Bradley came down for the evening session, representing the law firm (which had sent a large bouquet of roses and lilies), and stayed for about an hour. Piza's secretary, Gloria, and her husband also were there at night, not leaving until the viewing ended.

Even at the wake Mary assumed the role of dutiful hostess,

making sure to acknowledge everyone and spend time with some of the friends who hadn't integrated into any of the small packs that tend to form at these events. She continued while at their house in the period between funeral home sessions, overseeing food and drink distribution, grudgingly accepting Cheryl and Elizabeth's assistance when it became clear they weren't going to back down. (In Mary's mind, unless you were her husband or child, when you were a guest in her house you shouldn't have to lift a finger, never mind the circumstances.)

The funeral mass the next day was as touching as it was solemn, due in large part to the fact that the priest who presided over the ceremony, Father Martino, was very close with the Pizas. Mary was thankful that those in attendance wouldn't be subjected to a generic eulogy delivered by some cleric whose only knowledge of her daughter was information garnered at the last minute.

You don't often hear people laughing at a funeral mass, but some of Father Martino's "Patty stories" upended the cart on that front. As it turned out, that was just the warm-up to a tour de force engineered by Piza. As the family learned after the fact, on one of his store runs he'd visited the parish rectory and obtained Father Martino's blessing to do something off the menu.

At the end of his eulogy, the priest said, "I've asked our organist to prepare something special to honor Patty's love of music." But rather than play the organ, the woman put on a cassette tape (supplied by Piza) of Patty's favorite song, "Big Girls Don't Cry", by the Four Seasons, placing it close enough to the microphone to reverberate through the cavernous church.

Mary was mortified. She liked some rock-and-roll (thanks to her kids). But in church? What was Father Martino thinking? She quickly realized this was her son's idea, and turned to fix her wayward offspring with a withering glare. But he wasn't looking at her. He was engaged with everyone else in the church (including her husband and the priest) in clapping hands to the up-tempo song. Her anger and embarrassment vanished as she saw what her son had seen—that playing that song was a far more appropriate send-off for Patty than a morose hymn the girl would have hated.

As expected, the cemetery was heart-wrenching for everyone. As the group approached the burial site, struggling through a relentless late-July heat, the grimness of their mission hung over them. The finality of their goodbye was accentuated by the sight and smell of the mounds of freshly dug earth.

As Father Martino recited the burial prayers, Mary's eyes were wet, but also filled with concern for her husband, who was weeping so profusely she was afraid he might crumple. She discreetly slid her arm under his shoulder. Piza, standing on the other side of him, followed her lead. Mary thanked God they no longer lowered the casket into the ground with the family present.

After a traditional post-funeral repast at a local restaurant, attended by the seventeen people who were at the cemetery, Piza and his parents returned home. Removing his tie and jacket, Angelo announced he was going for a walk. His son said he'd join him, if he didn't mind the company. "Of course not," the man said. "You wanna come too, Mary?"

"No, it's okay. I'll stay here. But you two go."

"You sure you're gonna be all right, Ma?" Piza asked.

"Yes, positive. I'm pretty sure no one's gonna break in and kidnap me."

Her son smiled at her, then he and Angelo left.

Mary went upstairs to change. She hated wearing black. She stopped outside Patty's room and peeked in, surveying it to make sure nothing was out of place. Tilting her head in uncertainty, she entered, went over to the bed, and ran her hand along the bedspread, smoothing wrinkles that weren't there.

Patty's record player was in its usual spot on the floor. Mary picked it up and placed it on her lap as she sat at the edge of the bed. She removed some tissues stuffed up her sleeve and wiped a barely noticeable layer of dust off the top of the closed box. Opening it, she shook her head. As she suspected, Patty had left a record on the turntable, despite innumerable warnings to remove the last record played and put it back in its paper jacket. Mary picked up the turntable's arm, started to lift the disk, then stopped and let it fall back into place. She stared at the vinyl platter for almost a minute before closing the box and re-latching it.

Out of nowhere, her breathing accelerated so quickly it scared her. She wrapped her arms around the box, like it was a stanchion to cling to until this episode passed. But she felt control slipping away, and now she lifted the box, cradled it to her chest, and began rocking back and forth. Then, at last, she surrendered to the raw, terrifying sobs she'd somehow managed to fend off until she was able to bury her child.

CHAPTER 32

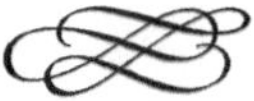

Theresa tried to shake off the haze of sleep as she fumbled to turn on her night-table lamp. "Who the heck is calling at"— focusing on her clock radio—"eleven-forty at night?" She picked up the phone and uttered an anxious, "Hello?"

"Theresa."

"Who— Anthony? What are— It's late."

"Is it? Oh. Hmm, maybe it is. Sorry about that."

"Are you all right? You sound— Have you been drinking?"

"I cannot tell a lie. I have. Juuust a smidge."

Both irked and apprehensive, she said, "Listen. Why don't you get some sleep, and if you want to talk you can—"

"My sister's dead."

Her breath caught—victimized by the tragic news, but more so by the startling detachment in his delivery. Jangled thoughts turned her mute.

"Still there, Theresa?"

"Uh, yes. I am. I'm so, so sorry. Had she been sick? Is— Is there anything I can do? For you? Your family?"

"She wasn't sick. Stroke. Out of nowhere. While she was

sleeping. Better that way, I guess. And actually, yes, you *can* do something. Not for my family really. But for me."

"Of course. Anything. If you need to talk in person, I can come up there. I can borrow Jasmine's car. Where are you?"

"At my parents'. Talkin' to you from my trusty old room actually. Always feel like a kid in this room. Nice sometimes. We buried her today."

Confusion set in. She instinctively knew how to comfort others. A gift she inherited from her mother. At this moment though, the mechanism that normally allowed for an effortless flow of empathy was jammed. How do you console someone whose grief manifests itself as a disjointed, dispassionate recitation of facts?

"Anthony—"

"No, not necessary for you to come up. But thanks for the offer. What I need, if it's okay with you, is to tap into your expertise. As a nun. Oops. *Former* nun."

"I don't understand."

"Well, what I— Oh, before I continue, it's important that I know if you're still on good terms with God. I mean, did you like royally piss him off when you ditched the habit and veil?"

Her concern for him was escalating. "If you mean do I still believe . . . still pray, the answer is yes. I trust that God understood why I did what I did."

"Ah, okay. Just checking. So, as you know, I took four years of philosophy and theology at Fordham. And I remember telling you at some point when we were outside at recess, waaay back in '74, about my catharsis. You know, my transcendental meltdown? When I came to the conclusion that when it comes to the concept of a caring God and an afterlife and blah, blah, blah"—he whispered 'if we're being honest with ourselves'—"none of us has an iota of certainty about what's real and what isn't. And then the bell rang and we had to get back inside and we never really discussed it anymore. Remember that?"

"I do" was her subdued reply.

"Okay. Good. And look, I realize we're talking about stuff here that's been analyzed and scrutinized and theorized and, hell, even pulverized . . . by those nasty atheists. But I'm kinda hoping that, since I can't even *find* the alleged ladder to heaven, and I'm assuming you firmly believe you're already on it . . . even if you slipped down a few rungs when you jumped ship seven years ago . . . that maybe you see something I don't, from your vantage point. Excuse me while I wet my whistle. Don't you love that expression?" There was a pause, then she heard him smack his lips. "Ahhh. Good stuff. Did you know Patty was twenty-nine, by the way? Did I mention that?"

Tears teetered on the precipice of her lower lashes. "No, I didn't. I just knew she was younger than you."

"Okie dokie. So, here's what I need to know. Can you explain to me why she's dead? Someone with the intellectual capacity of a *seven-year-old*? Who mostly all the time made people around her happy? Hmm? And ya know what? While you're at it, take a crack at kids with cancer, and some poor schmuck with five mouths to feed who gets wiped out by a truck driving home from work and, and feel free to throw in any other equally fucked up scenario you can think of. And I'm talking about an explanation that makes sense, Theresa, because if you tell me it was God's will, I'll be really, *really* disappointed in you."

"Anthony, talk to me."

"Huh? Whaddya think I've *been* doing? Don't tell me you missed everything I just said, 'cause honestly, I don't know if I can remember it all."

"Will you please just talk to me? You didn't call to get an answer to a question you know is unanswerable. So please."

She could hear him breathing—breaths that became more shallow by the second. And as he broke down, his words muddled by a shattering heart, all she could make out was "Peppermint Patty".

They were on the phone for three hours. She was able to comfort him once he lowered the firewall shielding his vulnerability. Her compassion was made more profound by the fact that when a heart attack took her father, she too had anguished over being deprived of the chance to say goodbye. She told that to Piza, and was moved by his earnest effort to comfort her in return.

Their conversation also managed to fill in, for each of them, some of the blank space of the other's life over the past twelve years. For Theresa, how she'd taken over the nursery school after working there when she left the order, financing the purchase with money her father had left her. How she'd named the school "Sonas" because that was Gaelic for "happiness"—a feeling she strove to instill in each of the children entrusted to her care, every day. How she'd rallied the diverse ethnic groups in her section of North Philly to petition the city for greater access to pre-school education. A battle they were still waging.

Piza, in turn, told her about working for a large law firm in Newark immediately after law school, leaving after six years because he was tired of the cut-throat environment, working till ten or later every night, and the pressure to bill clients for even so much as a passing thought about their case. He spoke about being worn down by divorce work, and his hope for a change by year's end or thereabouts. He asked her if the fact that he handled divorces bothered her. She assured him it didn't, and that it seemed pointless to her for two people to stay married if they were miserable.

As they talked, the conversation turned to their days of teaching together, recollections that gradually ushered in the revival of a familiar comfort; the effortless connection they'd shared before their world changed.

Despite the relaxed and pleasant course their discussion had taken, the initial reason for his call lingered in her thoughts, as it undoubtedly did for him. The death of a loved one generates a nebulous propriety. A decorum that, while difficult to delineate, leaves no doubt when it's been breached. She knew that was why neither of them had ventured into the territory of their feelings for each other. Although it was a topic in acute need of resolution after their last meeting, discussing it now would be an inherently selfish act, its substance and urgency diminishing the solemnity of Patty's passing.

Piza's muffled yawn led to a sheepish, "Sorry about that."

"You have to be exhausted," she said. "Why don't you try to get some sleep."

"I think I may take you up on that suggestion. I'm having trouble keeping my eyes open."

"I don't doubt it."

His light cough broke a momentary lull. "I— I want you to know how much I appreciate this. You helped me. A lot."

"I'm glad. And you don't have to thank me."

"No, I do. And I want to apologize for the way I talked to you in the beginning. Including my language."

"Again, no need." She gave a genial laugh. "And as for the language, trust me when I tell you it's nothing I haven't heard before . . . or said on occasion."

He returned the laugh. "Really. I might actually *pay* to hear that."

"I'll remember you said that. We can always use money for the children's snacks."

"Done."

Silence. It was like neither of them knew how to end the call.

"Well, okay," he finally said. "We'll talk again?"

"I'd like that. And, I don't know if your parents know about our . . . situation. But if you're comfortable with it, please extend my deepest condolences to them."

"They do, and I will. Thanks again for being there for me, Theresa."

"Of course."

"Okay. Bye."

"Bye."

He hung up. As she did the same, a rush of emotion inundated her. Eyes wet, and knowing sleep would never come, she made her way to the kitchen.

As she sat at the small, round table, hands wrapped around a mug of tea, she gave voice to the sentiment dominating her thoughts: "I'll always be here for you. If only I'd had the courage to tell you that twelve years ago."

CHAPTER 33

Seth Kaplowitz sat stoop-shouldered in the kitchen of his meager one-bedroom apartment, his posture the byproduct of an enervating effort to wade through five years of tax returns, credit card statements, and bank account records provided by Megan Sabatini. A tortoise-paced slog through a segment of the life of her and her husband.

It was 8 p.m., a time when the other associates at the firm undoubtedly were still at their desks. But he knew Bruzek didn't object to his leaving by six, as long as he brought work home with him. She'd told him so. She said she realized it was important to him to be there. He wasn't sure if her professed empathy for his situation was real. What he *was* sure of was that she knew his circumstances worked to her advantage. He needed money, and few local firms paid as well as she did.

His second yawn in a minute signaled it was time for a break. He got up and poured a cup of coffee, wincing at the bitter taste, the reheated black liquid having sat in the pot for hours. The aroma of kosher franks and scrambled eggs still dangled in the room, and he used his fingers to pick at the remnants that sat cold in a cast-iron skillet on the stove.

Cup in hand, he leaned against the jamb of the doorway that separated the kitchen and living room. A melancholy smile appeared as he watched his wife and three-year-old daughter asleep on the couch, looking like intertwining vines.

When he returned to the paper-strewn kitchen table, he decided to shift his focus to something that would qualify as billable time while minimizing his attention effort. At Bruzek's direction, he'd subpoenaed Joe Sabatini's employment records from the bank where he previously worked. The snowballing savings-and-loan fiasco was becoming common knowledge. So there was no reason to suspect anything questionable in the bank's letting him go. But the fact that his new job paid considerably less money gave Bruzek a plausible basis for requesting the information (in case her client questioned it), because sometimes people deliberately switched to lower-paying jobs in an attempt to reduce or even eliminate potential child support or alimony obligations. That really didn't seem likely with the Sabatinis, but Kaplowitz had seen his boss generate legal work for reasons much less tenable than this.

The employment file contained pretty standard fare: contact information; tax reporting forms; pension and health insurance documents; performance reviews; and, a stack of expense sheets. He tackled the performance reviews first, figuring that would be the only area where he might find something useful. He didn't. Sabatini's termination information was there, recorded on a single page, citing the need to let him go due to economic conditions.

Kaplowitz was inclined to riffle through the remaining material, which he surmised would be less substantive and, therefore, a greater waste of time. But he decided to at least glance at each piece of paper, so he could truthfully report to his boss that he'd reviewed the whole file.

He was glad he did.

Kaplowitz knocked on Bruzek's closed office door, opening it after a testy, "Yes, come in."

"Got a minute, Nadia?" He was trying to contain his excitement.

"What is it?"

"Well, you're not gonna believe this. I was going over the Sabatini file last night. Oh, how was the bar association dinner, by the way?"

"Fine. Get to the point."

"Okay. So I was reviewing Mr. Sabatini's employment file from the bank that laid him off. When I was looking through his expense reports, I found a memo marked 'confidential' that was totally unrelated to his expenses. I'm assuming whoever put this file together to send to us must have been sleepwalking through it, because there's no way the bank would want anyone to see this." He held up the document. "I can't believe they put this in writing to begin with."

Bruzek leaned forward and extended an arm. "Give it here." She took the piece of paper and sat back in her chair. As she read it, her eyes grew slightly larger, a rare display of something resembling emotion that had Kaplowitz congratulating himself. "My, my. This is interesting. Make sure this little jewel stays with us. Don't send a copy to the other attorney."

His boss's words snuffed out Kaplowitz's exhilaration. "How do we not send it to him? The 'notice for production of documents' he sent us specifically demands copies of any documentation we intend to use at trial. We have to give it to him. And I think when he gets it he'll cave immediately and give us anything we want. So I'm not sure—"

"Stop right there," she said, her unpainted fingernails tapping her desk in a staccato message of growing agitation. A long exhale preceded, "Listen to me, Seth. You're a smart kid. Good grasp of the law. Hard worker. I've told you before how much credit I give you for going to law school at night after putting in a full day's work. I told you that, right?"

"I'm sure you did," he lied.

"And, by all accounts, you can handle yourself in court better than some lawyers who've been at it a lot longer than you. And that's great. But that's not all there is to practicing law. If you're not willing to massage the rules, bend them to your advantage, ultimately you'll fail in this business. Mr. Sabatini's lawyer will get this. Eventually."

"How's that even possible?" the unnerved novice asked. "He's entitled to it upfront."

"How's it possible? Very easy. Because you didn't even know it existed until the last minute. One of our secretaries must have misplaced it when cataloging the piles of paperwork in the case. And that mistake will be discovered just in time for you to use it. Look, this case will go one of two ways. It will settle, or it will go to trial. You know it's my policy not to settle cases until right before trial. I believe that's usually best for our clients."—

You mean best for your bank account.

—"If that's where this goes, you push the negotiations as far as you can and then hit them with this information to seal the deal. But if it looks like this will go to trial, you save it for when you cross-examine Mr. Sabatini. This piece of paper will decimate his credibility." She handed the memo back to him. "And one final thing. I'm assuming our client isn't aware of this. I'm sure this isn't something her husband would have wanted her to find out about. Besides, she's a bit of a 'goody two shoes', so she likely would've said something about it already. Don't mention anything to her. I don't want her overreacting and mucking up the game plan."

Kaplowitz kept shifting his weight from one foot to the other, channeling his uneasiness. She must have picked up on it, because she transitioned to an almost maternal tone. "In many ways, this whole thing is a game, Seth. Everyone plays it. If you don't, no matter how knowledgeable or competent you are, you'll end up a loser."

His brain was under siege. He understood that in virtually every profession you might be asked to do things you weren't entirely comfortable with. He'd already experienced it in his few months with Bruzek. But what she was asking of him now extended beyond the borders of his already stretched-thin comfort zone. The question was: exactly how much of his integrity was he willing to compromise to keep this job?

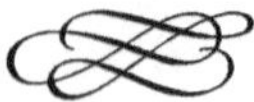

CHAPTER 34

The court scheduled the Sabatini mediation for Tuesday afternoon in the second week of August. Piza was pleased to learn that the mediator was Miriam Tannenbaum. Miriam was a lawyer who had opted to work for the county rather than in the private sector, and she was also a licensed social worker. That combination of expertise, together with her genial personality, made her perfectly suited to handle mediations in the combustive arena of family law. He was hoping she might be able to at least chip away at the bulwark separating the Sabatinis.

After apprising his client on Monday of what to expect at the following day's mediation session, Piza told him to call and update him when the session was over. The lawyer had barely settled in after returning from lunch that Tuesday, when his intercom screeched to life. "Tony, that Mr. Sabatini is here," Cecilia announced. "He said you wanted to see him after his mediation was over?"

"Why am I not shocked? Actually, I told him to *call* me. Do me a favor and ask him to get his hearing checked." She tittered. "As long as he's already here, might as well send him back."

"'Kay."

"You ready for *this*?" the red-faced Sabatini spat out as he roughly pulled out a chair from in front of Piza's desk, and dropped into it.

Already peeved, Piza launched into a one-man dialogue. "Hey, Strikes. Good to see you. Good to see you too, Tony. Sorry for showing up instead of calling. Oh, hey, no problem. You know my world revolves around you."

Appearing admonished, Sabatini said, "Sorry about that. How are you, Ton?"

"Harbor empty, Strikes. Ship sailed. So what is it I should be ready for?"

"The fuckin' mediation. The mediator, Miriam, gave us this talk about what's involved and all, pretty much exactly what you told me, and then she starts, and you know what Megan does? Not a goddamn thing. Shrugged off questions. Sat there like a goddamn bump on a log. So Miriam tells her the only way this is gonna work is if she participates. And ya know what Megan says? She says she doesn't think mediation's 'appropriate' for our situation because there's no way she could possibly agree to me keepin' the kids. And Miriam says it doesn't have to be an all or nothing. That if we could be open-minded, there's a lot of different arrangements that can be worked out that would let the kids spend . . . 'overnights' I think was the term she used, with each of us. And Megan says that in good conscience she doesn't see that happening, and tells Miriam again that she doesn't think mediation is appropriate here, and that she'd like to go home." He slowed to catch his breath.

"Shit. What'd Miriam do?"

"She said she was sorry Megan felt like that, because mediation can be very helpful. She really did her best to convince her, but Megan wouldn't budge. So finally Miriam said she couldn't force her to participate, so she'd let the judge know that the mediation was unsuccessful."

"Did you talk to Megan afterwards?"

"Yeah, I confronted her in the hall. Not threatening or anything like that but, you know, I needed to know what the hell was going on. She said her lawyer explained to her that mediation often ended up with people agreeing to things they regretted later on. Especially when it came to their kids."

Piza shook his head. "Did she say if it was Kaplowitz who told her that?"

"She kept saying 'she', so it had to be his boss, the Queen Bitch. And I'll bet the ranch that whenever Megan goes to see her, Candy's there too. So don't be surprised if she had a hand in convincing Megan this was a bad idea."

"Was Candy at the courthouse today?"

"No. Miracle of miracles. So what happens now?"

"Well, like Miriam said, she'll let the judge know what happened. He'll order a full-blown custody investigation, like we discussed a while back. I suggest you brace yourself. This is gonna get more expensive and a whole lot uglier. I'll let you know when I hear something."

"Crap. Nothing else we can do to force her to go along with mediation?"

"Afraid not."

"Okay. So I'll wait to hear from you. And sorry for just bursting in like this."

"Forget it."

Sabatini exited Piza's office, then immediately re-entered. "Oh my God, I'm such an asshole. My sister told me she read in the town paper . . . the obituary, that Patty passed away? She mentioned it a few days after the funeral. I'm so sorry. I got pissed she didn't tell me sooner. I'd have gone down there."

"Thanks. Yeah. She had a stroke."

"Oh, man. I'm really sorry to hear it. I remember how she'd dance at the drop of a hat. And shove her collection jar in our faces anytime one of us cursed on poker night. She was such a pisser. I miss those days. Will you give my condolences to your parents?"

"Sure."

"I wish you'd have called me, Ton."

"Yeah, well we kind of had a lot on our minds."

The lack of warmth in his eyes and tone evidently got his message across, as Sabatini blushed and said, "Well yeah. Of course. I understand." He stood there.

"Okay. Like I said, I'll keep you posted." Piza broke eye contact.

"Uh, right. Okay then," Sabatini said as he walked out.

———

Piza arrived at the courthouse a few minutes after four on the Thursday after the failed mediation. He'd received a message late Wednesday from Judge Williams's law clerk that the judge wanted to see him and Kaplowitz in his chambers. The message hadn't indicated why. Piza was perplexed, because if the judge wanted a status conference, that was usually done in open court, on the record.

When he got to the judge's courtroom, Kaplowitz was already there, sitting in the front row of the center gallery. No one else was around. Piza took a seat in the right gallery section. Neither of them acknowledged the other.

Within a minute, the law clerk poked her head out from a door at the side of the judge's bench. "Ah, you're both here. Great. Come on in."

Judge Williams, wearing a navy-blue pinstripe suit, was standing behind an ornate but scarred walnut desk. Piza had learned that it had been in the judge's family for generations. The man's sense of history was yet another reason to admire him.

"Grab a seat, gentlemen," he said. The two lawyers took their seats; the judge did likewise. "I asked to meet with you because I'm concerned about this Sabatini case. But I wanted our discussion to be informal. Off the record. Any objection to that?"

"Fine by me," Piza answered.

Kaplowitz looked less certain. "Um, I guess so, Judge."

"Okay. I received the mediator's report. She indicates that Ms. Sabatini refused to participate. That's troublesome. But what bothered me even more was Ms. Sabatini's statement that she didn't think this case was 'appropriate for mediation', according to Miriam's narrative. That language sounds a little formal for a layperson in those circumstances. So I guess what I'd like to know is whether her reluctance was induced by something other than her own misgivings." He looked at Kaplowitz.

The blushing young lawyer stammered, "I— I— I'm, uh, not exactly sure why you're looking at *me*, Judge."

"There's no accusation here, counsel. I'm looking at you because she's your client. And let me make it clear that I'm not attempting to pry into attorney-client privilege here, although I'm sure that's not even a relevant consideration, since I couldn't imagine that her obstinance was the result of instructions from you . . . or anyone else in your firm. I'm just trying to determine why this woman would be so set against mediation. And I also want to be sure we're all on the same page in trying to resolve this case with the least amount of damage to this family."

Piza was doing everything he could not to smile at the wily judge's circuitous route to warning Kaplowitz that he and his boss had better toe the line going forward.

"I can assure you, Your Honor, that um, *I* certainly would never tell a client not to participate in mediation. And I didn't speak with Ms. Sabatini before the mediation. Ms. Bruzek did. I mean, I wasn't in the room with them, so I can't swear to anything, but I don't think she would've instructed her not to participate." The drooping lawyer shifted in his seat.

Paging someone to extract Nadia Bruzek from under a bus. Way to cover your ass, kid.

Judge Williams said, "Okay then. So it appears the cause of Ms. Sabatini's intractable stance will remain a mystery. That said, I'm going to order a custody investigation. It's just a shame it's reached this point."

Kaplowitz came to life. "Judge, with all due respect, an investigation will be an expensive and punishing ordeal for my client and her children."

"Mr. Kaplowitz, it's pro forma."

"That may be, Judge, but I believe the court rule states that the court 'may' order the investigation. So I don't think it's mandatory."

"Your Honor," Piza said, "considering the issues with the older child refusing to see her father, and—"

Judge Williams waved him off. "Save your energy, Mr. Piza. Under the current circumstances, Mr. Kaplowitz, there's no way I'm not ordering this. I'd be beyond derelict in my duties if I didn't."

"Not necessarily, Judge," Kaplowitz said. "Mr. Sabatini isn't going to win this custody case. When Your Honor sees what we —" He turned crimson as he abruptly stopped.

"What we . . . 'what', counsel?" the judge asked with evident interest.

Piza was also acutely tuned in.

Beads of perspiration appeared on the young lawyer's forehead and upper lip. "Um, what I meant was that we firmly believe that Mr. Sabatini shouldn't have custody, and the evidence will bear that out."

With a bemused expression Judge Williams said, "So your position is that we should forgo an investigation because you're confident you're going to win this case. If I were to make a decision based on that, counsel, then we might as well dispense with a trial too."

The judge's tone had been good-natured, but Kaplowitz looked like the man had brutishly berated him. He delivered a defensive, "Then I may be forced to appeal your decision."

The judge's expression eased into a nonchalance Piza had seen before. "Counsel, you do whatever you feel you have to. But as a veteran jurist speaking to a new attorney, let me tell you that you'll be wasting your time and your client's money. Now, let's go into the courtroom and I'll put my decision on the record. And you can place your objections on the record as well."

When the two attorneys left the courtroom, Kaplowitz sat on a bench in the hall and started intensely arranging something in his briefcase. Piza looked around to make sure no one else was nearby, then approached him. "What the hell is wrong with you?"

Visibly startled, Kaplowitz quickly shook it off and came back with, "What's *your* problem? Not used to someone who can go toe-to-toe with you?"

"Jesus Christ, Seth. You're treating this like it's a criminal case. Are you channeling your boss, or are you this much of a jerk all the time?"

The word "jerk" elicited a single twitch of the right side of Kaplowitz's mouth. "Screw you, Piza. Don't tell me how to practice law."

"Well somebody has to, or you're gonna fuck up your career before it even starts. God knows, you're not gonna learn the right way to practice from Bruzek."

"Look, whatever you may think of Bruzek, I'm doing what I'm paid to do. If you don't like it, tough shit."

Piza was tempted to unload on him. But, for a reason he couldn't discern, he sensed he was missing something about Kaplowitz. What would cause someone so young to carry what appeared to be a deep-rooted, overarching animosity? He determined that finding the answer required a light touch. More scalpel than saber. "I'm not sure if this is just your nature, or you're toeing the company line, or both. But I get the feeling there's more going on here. Why are you so angry? What's got you so pissed off at the world?"

The comeback was a surly "Back off."

"I don't think so, Seth. I don't think I'm gonna back off. Because whatever bug you've got up your ass . . . about the law, or life, or whatever the hell else it is that's making you act like an asshole, you're making it *my* problem. And my client's. And, sooner or later, *your* client's. And I can tell you straight up, none of us needs this bullshit!"

Crap. So much for a light touch.

He figured Kaplowitz would tell him to stick it, then get up and storm out. Instead, he could see the young lawyer's bearing change; an apparent attempt at detachment. But if that was the image he intended to project, it was belied by eyes that couldn't conceal a simmering resentment.

"You have kids, Piza?"

"No."

"Oh, I see. So then you wouldn't know what it's like to have a sick child."

Caught off-guard, a flushed Piza said, "Look, I had no idea. I'm—"

Kaplowitz sprang from his seat, stunning Piza into silence. The pretense of control collapsed in the face of a torrent of raw anguish. "You wouldn't know what it's like to live every day of your life watching your child suffer. Knowing that despite all the doctors and all the treatments, you're— You're probably gonna be burying her when she's a teenager. A teenager! So don't stand there dissecting my anger and, and fucking passing judgment on me!" He wiped spittle from his lips with the back of his hand.

Piza's mind raced to process what he'd just witnessed. To

have this stranger reveal something so intensely personal. He was well aware that lawyers weren't immune from the strain of divorce. But his verbal joust with Kaplowitz hadn't seemed nearly fierce enough to explain what amounted to nothing short of a catharsis. Piza could only surmise that their exchange had been a catalyst that blew open an escape hatch for a pain the young father had lost the ability to contain.

"Seth. Do me a favor and sit down for a minute. Please." The depleted-looking man submitted. "How old is she?"

"Three."

"What does she have?"

"Cystic fibrosis." He looked numb.

"Look, I'm not gonna insult you by reeling off a string of platitudes. There's no way in hell I can begin to imagine what you're going through. But clearly you needed to get that out. And if you feel like talking about it. . . Do you wanna grab a coffee or something?"

Unsmiling, Kaplowitz said, "No. No thanks." He paused and took a breath. "You seem like a decent guy, and— Look, I'm sorry you had to hear that. It was unprofessional and it won't happen again."

"Screw professional or unprofessional, Seth. You seem to think there's some sort of . . . . I dunno, like this uncrossable dividing line between who you are as a person and who you are as a lawyer. There's not. There's always gonna be a fluidity between the two. I'm not saying you have to let your personal feelings influence every decision as a lawyer, but if you try to disassociate your humanity from how you practice law, you're gonna drive yourself nuts. Because it's impossible."

As Piza spoke, he noticed some of the tension slip away from the man. And he could tell he'd been listening.

"I understand what you're saying, Piza. But—"

"It's Tony."

"Okay. But we're hired to represent clients. To get them what they want. And that's the bottom line. If anything gets in the way of that, then we're not doing our job."

"You're parroting your boss. Lawyers aren't hit-men. And we have codified Rules of Ethics for a reason. We're supposed to do our best for our clients, sure. But there are boundaries. Sometimes what a client wants is just flat out wrong. If it's illegal, then it's a no-brainer. You say no. But you and I both know that legality and morality aren't necessarily interchangeable concepts. And when it comes to the morality of a decision, sometimes the lines can be blurry." He peered past Kaplowitz until he collected his thoughts. "All I'm saying is that every day we have to abide by a personal code of honor. Do what each of us believes in our heart is the right thing. At least if we want to be able to live with ourselves."

With a vapid smile Kaplowitz said, "That's easier in theory than in practice. What if it means losing a client? Or your job?"

"Then it wasn't a client worth representing." He locked eyes with the younger man. "Or a job worth keeping."

Kaplowitz held Piza's gaze, his expression noncommittal until it slipped into melancholy resignation. "Unfortunately, circumstances sometimes dictate the degree of righteousness we can afford."

Piza could have kicked himself for being so obtuse. *Who the hell am I to be preaching to this kid? Is there anything I wouldn't do to save my family?*

An awkward moment passed, then Kaplowitz stood up. "I've gotta get back to the office."

"Okay," Piza responded as he stood as well. "And I'm still hopeful we can work this out."

"We'll see where it goes, I guess." He picked up his briefcase and walked away.

Piza wasn't sure where—if anywhere—their conversation would lead. But he knew any impact on the case would probably be minimal, considering Bruzek's rumored iron-clad control of the decision making. He was as pessimistic as ever about how things would progress. And there was a lingering disquiet about whatever it was Kaplowitz had stopped short of revealing during their meeting with the judge, the attorney's attempt to deflect having been less than convincing.

If Piza knew what Kaplowitz had withheld, his uneasiness would have rocketed to outright panic.

CHAPTER 35

It took six weeks for the custody investigation to conclude—the fastest Piza could ever recollect. In the interim, not much happened with the Sabatini case. Both sides submitted answers to interrogatories and the production of documents. Lisa still refused to see her father, which weighed more heavily on the man with each passing week. On a positive note, Megan had completed the real estate course and obtained her license, and had started working for the same company as Candy. She hadn't sold any houses, but at least the seeds of a career had been planted.

A few weeks after Piza's phone call with Theresa on the day of Patty's funeral, she called one evening to check up on him, much to his shock. As he'd mentioned to Elizabeth not long after his Philadelphia trip, he was certain he wouldn't be able to engage in a phone conversation with Theresa without it being either a drivel of small-talk or a dramatic discourse on his love for her, neither of which was palatable to him. This call was the first test of that theory. (The call after Patty's death didn't count.)

He needn't have worried. After assuring her he was okay, they slipped into an easy colloquy. Two people talking about the substance of their daily lives, their discussion dotted with anecdotes. Another footstep in their narrative.

When Piza received the written custody evaluation, he had Gloria call Sabatini to set up a meeting. He'd only talked with his client twice while the investigation was proceeding. (Which isn't to say Sabatini hadn't pestered Gloria every couple of days in the recent weeks for any word on receipt of the report.)

The first time they spoke was to review his answers to interrogatories and the notice to produce documents, and have him sign the oath at the end, swearing to the truth of everything submitted. The second time was a phone call after the investigator met with Sabatini at his apartment, an interview the practically giddy banker told Piza he'd "absolutely nailed". "She loved the apartment, Ton. We really seemed to hit it off. I think she really felt for me with the situation with Lisa. I got a little upset when she mentioned the stuff Megan said in her complaint, about my depression and all. She asked for my doctor's info and I had to sign a release in case she needs to check with them. But I'm not worried about that. Oh, and she asked me about my concerns about Megan's drinking. So at least we know that issue's in the mix. I've gotta tell ya, I've got a really good feeling about my chances."

Having traveled this road before, Piza had attempted to temper Sabatini's enthusiasm. He didn't want to totally deflate his optimism, but felt he wouldn't be doing his job if he didn't reiterate the factors weighing against his being awarded sole custody. This was especially true because they still had no concrete proof of Megan's alleged alcohol abuse, or whether she was now drinking at all. And without that, Piza was certain there was no chance of Sabatini walking away with what he wanted.

The truth was, if Megan didn't have an alcohol problem, Piza wasn't convinced that what his client was requesting was necessarily in the children's best interest. He'd told Sabatini as much, but the man seemed to have developed tunnel vision, brought on by his daughter's refusal to see him. He assured Piza that if the court ordered the girls to live with him, he'd be able to "straighten things out" with Lisa. At that point, Piza determined it was best to stop talking and let the report deliver whatever its message might be.

When Sabatini arrived at Piza's office after work, he looked pasty and wilted, undoubtedly fallout from the runaway anxiety evident in his rapidly-blinking eyes. "Hey, Tony. So it's in, huh?" He glanced at Piza's desk. "That it, sitting there? Looks longer than I expected."

"Yeah, the psychologists who do this are very thorough."

"I'm, uh, kind of on pins and needles, so do me a favor and just bottom-line it for me, okay?"

"All right. Actually, it's hard to bottom-line. Some of the conclusions are contingent on other things happening, but—"

"I don't— Like what?"

"Well, let me finish. No matter where some of the other aspects of this go, the recommendation is that Megan maintain primary residential custody of the kids. Now that doesn't—"

Sabatini pounded the arm of the chair. "Dammit! I was so sure that. . ." He slumped in his seat as an obvious dejection wiped away signs of apprehension and anger.

"I warned you about this, Strikes. The investigator didn't find any evidence of alcohol abuse by Megan. She apparently was very candid about her father's alcoholism, and the fact that she'd started having a glass or two of wine in the evenings, which she said was out of character for her. But she said she realized that was a coping device for the stress of everything that was going on, and so she stopped."

"Yeah, but what if she was lying?"

"Well, she claimed she wasn't even keeping liquor in the house. And she's got no history. Frankly, considering the way she confronted you that Sunday morning, kind of staring you down and telling you your claims about her drinking were dead wrong? Honestly, I can't see Megan faking that kind of conviction. At least from what I know of her, including what I saw at the domestic violence hearing."

Sabatini's reply was limp. "I guess. I dunno. Was it my mental health issues? That what sunk me?"

"No. She found your depression and anxiety were under control, and you were functioning normally. But listen, nothing 'sunk' you. She feels that, ideally, the girls should be spending more time with you than they've been up till now. That's a big plus. And that—"

"So what're these other things . . . conclusions or whatever you were talking about." It was like Piza hadn't even been speaking.

"That's what I was getting to, if you'd let me continue. In order to facilitate increased time with the kids, it's obviously very important to get Lisa on track in repairing your relationship, because by Megan's account you and Lisa had a great relationship before. Apparently, Lisa wasn't particularly forthcoming in her interview." He picked up the report and thumbed through a few pages. "Here it is. The investigator used the word 'reluctant' in describing Lisa's reaction to discussing you. She ruled out anything involving abuse or—"

Sabatini's head jerked. "What? Did she suspect me of abusing Lisa? Like molesting her or something?"

"No! Absolutely not. Calm down. It's an issue she had to address, particularly in a situation like this, where a child wants nothing to do with a parent. It wasn't an accusation."

"Damn well better not be," Sabatini said as he loosened his tie.

"Trust me, it wasn't. Anyway, she feels that Lisa should be in therapy to get to the root of what's causing this, and to generally help her cope with the divorce. I'm hoping this will finally convince Megan to agree to it."

"Well, does this give us enough ammo to go back into court if she doesn't?"

"I think so. I mean this is basically what Judge Williams was looking for when we went in on the order to show cause. But here's the other thing. The investigator interviewed Candy too, apparently because she's over there so much she's almost like a member of the household. And let me tell ya, she was not impressed. Aside from the fact that Candy came across as really aggressive, she made no bones about how she feels about you. The report doesn't recommend she stay out of the house, but it indicates that her attitude could have negative implications if she voices her feelings about you in front of the kids. Of course, she claims she doesn't. And Megan said she doesn't ever recall her bad-mouthing you when the kids were around, or she would've done something about it."

Through a brooding shrug Sabatini said, "I guess that's true. Ya know, what Megan said about doing something if Candy tried that in front of the girls. I know she wants a good relationship between the kids and me." He straightened out of his slouch. "So, where do we go from here?"

"Well, that depends. First and foremost, will Megan finally agree to therapy for Lisa? If not, then we've gotta go back to court. But the other thing is— Let me ask you something. Do you know whether Candy's ever alone with the kids? You know, like babysitting and such?"

"Um, yeah. Amy mentioned that a while back. Like if Megan needs to run out for something. Why? You think maybe she's taking jabs at me when Megan isn't around?"

Piza sat back and tented his fingers. "I have no idea, but considering how obnoxious she is, who knows? I think the report left enough of an opening to justify following up on it. If we request a plenary hearing on the therapy issue, I can add this on. Get her on the stand and poke around a bit."

"Okay. Great. Uh, what's it called again? The hearing?"

"'Plenary hearing'. Think of it as a mini-trial. But if Megan agrees to counseling for Lisa, I don't know that it's worth asking for a hearing just on Candy. I mean, we have no proof anything's there. So I don't know that you wanna spend your money on a hearing that may amount to nothing."

"I understand, Ton. But I've gotta tell ya, the more I'm thinking about this, I'd like to know one way or the other. At this point, for my own peace of mind, it might be worth it."

Through a nod Piza said, "Okay. Let me touch base with Kaplowitz as far as the therapy for Lisa. But I'm pretty sure anything involving keeping Candy out of their lives is a nonstarter. I'll let you know."

"All right. I've gotta tell ya, I'm feeling a little better about this than I did a few minutes ago. I know I may not get everything I want, but at least it seems Megan's not drinking, which was kinda my main concern. Plus, it looks like I may be getting more time with the girls, once we get Lisa squared away of course. Maybe have them stay over and such. I still don't wanna give up on custody, but at least there are some positives here." He stood up. "By the way, will I have to testify at this hearing?"

"Yes. I'd like to put you on to talk about your relationship with Lisa before everything went south. Then maybe relate your interaction with Candy that Sunday morning when you said she came flying out of the house and started mouthing off. Kind of set the stage for my examination of her. You have qualms about testifying?"

"Are you kiddin'? Piece of cake."

There was a whiff of arrogance in Sabatini's answer. Piza wondered whether it was real or masked something else. Fear? Insecurity? He didn't know. Nor could he explain the ominous sensation that came and went so quickly he later wondered whether he'd only imagined it.

CHAPTER 36

Piza was elated. Megan had finally said yes to therapy for Lisa, after she and Sabatini met at a diner to discuss it. Sabatini said it was the first time the two of them had sat alone and had a civil conversation in as long as he could remember. He told Piza that the investigating psychologist's findings, aided by a recommendation from the children's pediatrician, had made the difference. Megan had indicated that Lisa wasn't eating very much and was losing weight. When she took her to the pediatrician, he couldn't find anything physically wrong, and—being aware of the divorce—had taken Megan aside and suggested that Lisa's condition might be stress-induced, and that she might want to consider therapy.

Sabatini mentioned to Piza that he was distressed Megan hadn't previously told him about Lisa's weight loss. But he decided not to push the issue in light of this breakthrough that he said had come about despite (as revealed by Megan) Candy's intense reiteration of her doomsday forecast.

Piza had called Kaplowitz to confirm the information, and to once again broach the possibility of distancing Candy from the family, setting up something almost like a visitation schedule. The young lawyer was more civil than in the past (although hardly exuding cordiality). He acknowledged Megan's consent to therapy and told Piza he'd discuss Candy with her again. The next day he called back. No deal.

With that, Piza had filed a motion seeking the plenary hearing. Judge Williams granted the request, over Kaplowitz's objection. The hearing was scheduled for Thursday afternoon, November 13, and would continue the following afternoon, if necessary. Piza planned to have Sabatini testify, and then would call Candy. He was certain the judge would allow him to treat her as a hostile witness, which would give him the right to question her as if it were cross-examination. Unsure she would appear voluntarily, he'd subpoenaed her.

He didn't anticipate any issues with Sabatini's testimony.

He was wrong.

Piza arrived at the courthouse five minutes late on the Thursday of the hearing. Sabatini was waiting for him on a bench in the rotunda. Kaplowitz was sitting with Megan and Candy on the other side of the room.

"Hey, Strikes. Sorry I'm late. Any idea if Kaplowitz checked in with the judge's staff yet?"

"I don't think so. I was here before they"—thrusting his chin toward the trio—"got here. He tried the courtroom door and couldn't get in. Since then, he hasn't moved."

"Oh, okay." He turned toward Kaplowitz and called out, "I'll let them know we're here, Seth."

Kaplowitz nodded. "Okay. Courtroom is locked, so—"

The courtroom door opened and the judge's law clerk stepped into the hall. "Everyone here on Sabatini?"

"We're all here, Connie," Piza answered.

"Great. Why don't you come in and set up. Judge Williams will be out in about ten minutes or so. He's on the phone with the Assignment Judge."

"You good?" Piza asked his client.

"Yeah. I'm ready." He gave a flimsy laugh. "I'd better be, after you prepped me for an hour and a half yesterday."

"Okay. Any last-minute questions?"

"Nope."

"All right, let's do this."

As both sides set up, Candy planted herself on a chair at the counsel table, next to Megan. Kaplowitz asked her to sit in the first row of the gallery, right behind them, then took a sterner tone when she balked the first time.

They sat there for an awkward fifteen minutes, nobody speaking, the silence quickly becoming the room's most conspicuous feature.

A door at the front of the courtroom opened, and the court clerk and court officer came out. Almost simultaneously, Judge Williams appeared from his door. The clerk, looking flustered at the judge's premature appearance, began his "All rise" proclamation before he even made it to his nook, but was waved off by the jurist.

"Not necessary, Mike. Please be seated, everyone. My deepest apologies for keeping you waiting, but there was some other court business that needed attending to." He shuffled some papers on his bench. "So, this is the plenary hearing on the Sabatini matter. Let's get your appearances on the record, counsel, and then Mr. Piza you can call your first witness."

Piza walked Sabatini through his testimony, replicating the questions he'd posed the day before, when the two of them sat in the conference room at Piza's office into the evening. The answers weaved a narrative of the relationship between Sabatini and Lisa—a warm, loving connection that had inexplicably deteriorated to its current state. Kaplowitz objected once, telling the judge that, in the interest of saving time, they would gladly concede that there had been a good relationship between the father and daughter. But Piza was having none of it, intent on providing a vivid portrait of the bond between them, arguing that the court should have a complete picture. Judge Williams overruled the objection.

The questioning then shifted to Candy. Sabatini related the incident that had occurred the Sunday morning when Lisa first refused to see him. How he'd been upset by Candy's influence on Megan, particularly about Lisa's possibly getting therapy. And how, when he confronted Megan about it that day, Candy flew out of the house and verbally attacked him. At that point he went off script, raising his voice and describing the realtor as "a raving lunatic". The judge sustained Kaplowitz's objection on that one, and cautioned Sabatini to refrain from "unnecessary characterization".

When Piza finished his direct examination, he was pleased with Sabatini's performance. He didn't mind his having wandered astray a bit. Sometimes a genuine display of emotion lent believability to testimony, helping it come across as less scripted.

Because the hearing was centered on Candy, and had nothing to do with custody, he figured Kaplowitz would avoid questions about Sabatini's relationship with Lisa. There'd been nothing to indicate he'd done anything to cause the downturn, and it was clear the connection between the two had been solid. Thus was Piza caught off-guard by the young lawyer's first question.

"I take it, Mr. Sabatini, you consider yourself to be a good father," he said, moving to within a few feet of the witness stand.

What the hell is he doing?

Sabatini responded with a brusque, "No. I consider myself to be a *great* father."

"*Great* father. Wow. That's really admirable."

Piza half stood up. "Your Honor."

"Mr. Kaplowitz," the judge said, "dispense with the gratuitous observations and move on please."

"Yes, Judge. So, Mr. Sabatini, as a 'great father' it's fair to say you wouldn't do anything to harm your daughters, correct?"

"Of course I wouldn't."

"Neither directly nor indirectly, right?"

Where's he going with this?

"Yes. I'd never do anything to jeopardize their well-being. In any way."

"So you don't think you jeopardized their well-being when you picked their mother up by her arms and moved her out of the way, right in front of them, resulting in—"

Piza was on his feet. "Objection! Mr. Kaplowitz is getting into an area that's totally irrelevant to this hearing, Judge."

The judge leaned forward and rested his forearms on the bench. "There's no jury here, Mr. Piza. So tell me what we're talking about?"

"There was a domestic violence complaint filed by Ms. Sabatini several months ago. It happened when my client went to pick up his kids for visitation and she wouldn't let him see them."

"They were sick," Megan meekly protested.

"Didn't look sick to me," from her husband.

Judge Williams gave a short rap of his gavel. "Let your attorneys do the talking right now, please."

Piza continued. "The complaint went to court down in Middlesex County, and the judge dismissed it after a hearing. And you know that's not something that happens all that often on DV complaints, Your Honor. At any rate, what happened back then has nothing to do with this hearing. We're here about Ms. Janicek's exposure to the children. Nothing more."

The judge looked at Kaplowitz. "Counsel? Your response?"

Kaplowitz, who had remained in place, replied, "Well, Judge, the witness went to great lengths on direct examination to describe his relationship with Lisa. And he said he wouldn't do anything to harm her or her sister. So if that *wasn't* the case, it—"

"It *was* the case," Sabatini testily interrupted. "It *is* the case."

"Mr. Sabatini, I won't tell you again," the judge said.

A somewhat contrite nod was the response.

"Anyway," Kaplowitz continued, "even discounting the domestic violence complaint, Mr. Sabatini's credibility is certainly relevant to this proceeding. Not only as to his relationship with his children, but also as to the status of Ms. Janicek, who's become almost like a member of this family." Megan nodded at the reference. "The motion that led to this hearing implies that Ms. Janicek is somehow responsible for the falling out between Lisa and her father. And I think we have a right to dig a little deeper to try to get a handle on where the problem lies, since that may very well determine how this hearing turns out."

"Judge," Piza said, "I don't see—"

The judge put up a hand. "I understand your position, Mr. Piza. But the witness's credibility is pertinent here." He turned toward Kaplowitz. "Continue with your questioning, counsel."

"Yes, Your Honor. Thank you. And we can move off the domestic violence issue. Mr. Sabatini, you testified earlier that for a few weeks before the day Lisa refused to see you, she'd been withdrawn during the time she spent with you, correct?"

"Yes. Quieter than usual."

"And when you asked her about it, she said nothing was wrong."

"Right."

"And you testified earlier that you 'chalked it up to moodiness'. I believe those were your words."

"That's what I said. Yes."

Kaplowitz stood in front of the counsel table, leaned back against it, and crossed his arms. "Well, it seems to me that if you were the great father you claim to be, you'd have pursued the issue, for your daughter's sake."

"Objection. Argumentative," Piza said, without standing.

"Sustained," Judge Williams said. "Keep your opinions to yourself, Mr. Kaplowitz."

"Sorry, Judge. Okay, Mr. Sabatini, let's turn to Ms. Janicek. Other than that one Sunday morning, when you and she argued in front of your house, had you ever interacted with her?"

"Well, I was with her when we were house-hunting. She was our realtor. But we didn't talk much. She was too fixated on Megan." He shot a glare at Candy.

"You don't like Ms. Janicek very much do you?"

"Objection."

"No, I'll allow it," the judge responded. "I think his feelings toward her are relevant. You can answer the question, Mr. Sabatini."

"No, I don't particularly care for her. Just like I wouldn't particularly care for anyone who implies that I don't take care of my family . . . the way she did that Sunday morning. And I resent her scaring Megan about therapy for Lisa, endangering our daughter's health all because *she* was a failure as a mother."

"I was a good mother," Candy shouted. "I'm not a failure, you're the failure."

A scowling Judge Williams responded with, "Madam, I won't tolerate outbursts like that in my courtroom. If you can't control yourself, you can wait outside."

"Well he was lying about me. I was just defending myself."

"I understand what you were doing. But this is a court proceeding, not a free-for-all. Is that clear?"

"Yes," she replied, her acknowledgment delivered through gritted teeth.

"Good. And Mr. Sabatini, I understand this is emotional. But if you lash out again I'm going to hold you in contempt of court. Consider yourself warned. Proceed, Mr. Kaplowitz."

"Well, Judge, seeing that we haven't heard a thing from this witness that would even remotely suggest Ms. Janicek had anything to do with Lisa's refusal to see him, I don't have any other questions."

Judge Williams looked at Piza. "Any re-direct?"

"No, Your Honor." *That was awfully quick.*

The judge nodded and turned to Sabatini. "All right, you can—"

"Judge, I'm sorry," Kaplowitz interrupted. "I almost forgot. I do have one more question."

"Go ahead, counsel."

"Mr. Sabatini, have you ever committed a crime?"

"What? Uh, no, of course not," a visibly startled Sabatini answered as Piza stood up.

"Objection. If Mr. Kaplowitz wants to engage in a fishing expedition, he should do it on a lake, not in a courtroom."

"It's hardly a fishing expedition, Judge," Kaplowitz responded, his tone even. "Evidence of commission of a crime is permitted for purposes of impeaching a witness's credibility."

Shaking his head, the judge said, "Actually, the rule references *conviction* of a crime."

Sabatini's words burst out. "I was never convicted of a crime, and I never committed one. Period."

"Okay, that's all I have, Your Honor," Kaplowitz said.

"Any other questions, Mr. Piza?"

"No, Judge," he answered, eyes squinted in wariness.

"You can step down now, Mr. Sabatini," the judge instructed.

Piza was off-center. Kaplowitz's cross-examination hadn't been anything like he'd expected. He'd gone after Sabatini on Lisa, which made no sense. And rather than attempting to intimidate and discredit the witness by launching an all-out attack on his turbulent relationship with Candy, the normally combative rookie had opted to ask a few questions, make a blanket statement, and let the subject drop. It demonstrated a restraint Piza hadn't seen in Kaplowitz before. A moderation that, in his opinion, was the wrong approach under the circumstances.

Something is off here. Sometimes less is more, sure, but. . . Still, he's new at this. Maybe I've been giving him too much credit.

Or maybe not enough.

CHAPTER 37

A pale Sabatini returned to the counsel table and took his seat. He leaned in toward Piza, but before he could say anything, Judge Williams said, "Call your next witness, Mr. Piza."

"I'd ask Candy Janicek to take the stand, Your Honor."

"Ms. Janicek, would you— Ah, you're already on your way up," the judge remarked as the realtor maneuvered between the counsel tables and up to the witness stand.

Mike swore her in.

"Your Honor," Piza said as he stood, "Ms. Janicek was subpoenaed to be here today and, as indicated in the custody evaluation, there's no doubt about where she stands relative to my client. I'd ask the Court's permission to treat her as a hostile witness."

Now Kaplowitz rose. "Judge, he hasn't even asked her one question. We haven't seen anything that would indicate she'd be a hostile witness."

"Mr. Kaplowitz, what's transpired in this room up to this point makes Ms. Janicek's feelings toward Mr. Sabatini abundantly clear," the judge answered. "Mr. Piza, you can question her as a hostile witness."

"Thank you, Your Honor." He sat. "So, how're you doing today, Ms. Janicek?"

"Just ducky. How do you think I'm doing? It's stupid having to be here for this stupid thing."

"Judge," Piza said, "I think Mr. Kaplowitz may have been correct. I'm not detecting any animosity whatsoever."

The court clerk and court officer laughed. Nothing from Kaplowitz. An amused-looking Judge Williams said, "Just move it along, counsel."

"Yes, Your Honor. Ms. Janicek, you spend a lot of time with Megan. Is that fair to say?"

"Yeah. She's like a daughter to me."

"You have a biological daughter, right? But you and she have been estranged for several years. More than twenty actually, correct?"

"Yes."

"Any other children?"

"No."

"What happened between you and your daughter? What caused your falling out?"

Kaplowitz stood. "Your Honor, I don't see what that has to do with this hearing. What happened between Ms. Janicek and her daughter is ancient history and has no bearing on what's happening now."

Now Piza stood. "On the contrary, Judge, I think you'd agree that our history shapes us. It's absurd to dismiss Ms. Janicek's relationship with her daughter as irrelevant, considering the circumstances of this case."

"Agreed, counsel." He looked down his nose at Piza. "Although 'absurd' may be a bit over-the-top. At any rate, her relationship with her estranged daughter is relevant."

Piza remained standing and moved toward the jury box,

about ten feet away from Candy. "So, again, Ms. Janicek, what caused your falling out with your daughter?"

With a sneer she responded, "Her father. My piece of— Piece of 'garbage' ex-husband. He took off on us when Nancy . . . that's my daughter . . . was fourteen. Really screwed the poor kid up. She was never the same after that."

"Never the same how?"

"Well, you know, she started rebelling. Answering back. Refusing to clean her room. Just— Just not following my rules."

"And how did you deal with that?"

Candy repositioned herself in her seat. "I dunno. You know, the usual ways. Took TV away for a while. Grounded her if she did something really bad. Like I said, the usual stuff."

"And did that work?"

Candy shrugged. "Sometimes." Her eyes hardened. "But her father had messed her up so bad . . . abandoning us and all, that she kept getting worse. So I talked to her guidance counselor at school, and that idiot said maybe we should try therapy for her."

"Idiot?"

"Yeah. Idiot. Because after a couple of months in therapy she ran away from home. Sixteen years old. And I haven't seen or heard from her since. I have no idea where she is. You happy now?"

It occurred to Piza that if Candy had shown even a trace of vulnerability, he might have felt sorry for her. Maybe not even vulnerability. Just a softness. Something other than the contempt that seemed to infiltrate every word she uttered.

"Did you do anything to try to find Nancy?"

"Of course I did. I hired a private investigator. But he wasn't getting anywhere, and I couldn't afford to keep paying him. I didn't have much money back then."

"Okay. So you blame therapy for your daughter running away. And is—"

"And her father. If it wasn't for him, she wouldn't have started acting up, and we never would've even had to think about therapy. But yeah, I think therapy messed up her brain. Put thoughts in her head."

"What kind of thoughts?"

Candy planted clenched fists on the front of the witness stand. "I dunno! Thoughts! Thoughts like she needed to get away, I guess. 'Cause that's what she did, isn't it? Ran away?"

"And because of what you believe therapy did to your daughter, you've been firmly opposed to Lisa's seeing a therapist, correct?"

"That's right. I don't wanna see the same thing happen to her that happened to my Nancy."

Piza nodded. "I understand." A brief pause. "Is it fair to say you're upset with Megan, now that she's agreed to therapy?"

A slouching Kaplowitz sat up straight. "Objection, Your Honor. That's irrelevant."

"No, I'll allow it," the judge ruled.

Piza continued. "You're upset with Megan, Ms. Janicek?"

"I guess. A little. She always followed my advice up till now." She looked at Megan like someone reprimanding a subordinate. The younger woman didn't break eye contact, but there was no sign of defiance, perhaps signaling a tolerant acceptance of the rebuke.

Piza masked his sarcasm with a velvet tone. "It makes no sense to you when people don't take your advice."

"Yeah, because I'm usually right. *More* than usually."

"Always?"

Candy hesitated. "No. Not always. But I'd say ninety-nine percent." Then, with conspicuously feigned humility, "I don't claim to be perfect, ya know."

Piza tossed her an overly generous smile. "Who is?" The smile disappeared as he paced in front of the jury box, seemingly gathering his thoughts. "So let me ask you something. If you see

Megan as another daughter, do you think of Lisa and Amy as your grandchildren?"

Candy answered with an irritated, "Well, I think I'm a little young to be a grandmother. But I guess that's as good a description as any."

Another smile from Piza. "Well, being a gentleman, I won't ask your age. But anyway, you're close with the girls?"

"Very."

"More so with one than the other?"

"I wouldn't say that. But Amy's kinda young, so there isn't as much to talk to her about. Lisa understands a little more."

"So you talk more with Lisa?"

"I guess," she answered with a throw-away shrug.

"Do you try to instill your values in the girls when you talk with them?"

"Your Honor," Kaplowitz said without standing.

"It's an appropriate question, Mr. Kaplowitz," the judge responded. "This hearing *is* about Ms. Janicek's relationship with the children. You can answer, Ms. Janicek."

"I never really thought about it, but I guess so." There was no mistaking the snark as she finished her thought. "Isn't that what a 'grandmother' would do?"

"Absolutely," Piza replied. "Even the very young ones."

"Your Honor," Kaplowitz said as he got to his feet, "could you please instruct my adversary not to goad the witness."

"Well, actually, Your Honor, I thought I was paying her a compliment," Piza said. He turned to Kaplowitz. "Sorry if it was misinterpreted."

"Yeah right," the young attorney muttered as he sat.

"Save the compliments for some other time, counsel," Judge Williams told Piza. "Let's move this along."

"Yes, Judge. So, Ms. Janicek, something's been perplexing me. My client testified . . . and, in fact, Megan actually acknowledged to him . . . that you told the girls that rules are no fun. And that sometimes it's good to be messy. What I'm having a problem with is that earlier in your testimony you said that after your husband left, Nancy started 'acting up'. And when I asked you how she was acting up you said she wouldn't clean her room. And that she refused to follow your rules. So I guess I'm trying to reconcile your attitude back then, about rules and cleanliness, with what you've been telling Lisa and Amy. Do you no longer believe in rules and cleanliness?"

Candy rolled her eyes and blew an exaggerated breath. "Of course I believe in them."

"So. . ."

"So . . . what?" She raised her arms chest-high then let them flop onto her lap. "Megan's kinda strict with the girls, so I try to lighten things up a little. That's all. Megan doesn't mind." She looked at her friend and received an acknowledging nod in return. "Sometimes people can overdo being strict. That's all I'm saying."

Piza moved a few feet closer to the witness stand. "Did *you* overdo it? With Nancy?"

Candy's discomfort came into full bloom. "What're you saying?"

"I'm not saying anything. It was simply a question."

"No, no. I get what you're doing. You're trying to get me to say I was a bad mother. Well, I wasn't!"

"Objection," from Kaplowitz. "He's badgering her."

"Overruled," Judge Williams responded.

"How can you possibly overrule it, Judge?" the bristling lawyer said. "He's clearly harassing her, plus he's probing into something that's completely off-topic."

The jurist glared at him. "Don't start, Mr. Kaplowitz. I gave you my ruling. You've conducted yourself well so far. Don't ruin it. Continue, Mr. Piza."

"Thank you, Judge. Ms. Janicek, I'm not implying you were a bad mother. I only asked if you were too strict. Nothing more."

It was evident from Candy's rigid body language that the brief interruption of the interrogation had done nothing to calm her. In fact, she seemed more agitated. "No way. I wasn't too strict. Absolutely not." She blinked hard a few times, and looked like she was unsure what to do next.

Piza sensed that she might be starting to falter. He held up on asking another question, choosing to wait a few moments to see whether she'd continue talking. She did.

Looking past Piza into the empty gallery, she said, "I— I was a *little* strict like . . . like any good mother should be." The defiance resurfaced and she resumed eye contact. "She had to learn to be tough. 'Cause let me tell ya something, you wanna get anywhere, you better be the one in control. 'Cause if you're not, you get stepped on. It was *my* job to teach her that. And that's what I did. And I'm not apologizing for it."

"No one's asking you to, Ms. Janicek," Piza replied. "Now, the last time you heard from your daughter was when she called a couple of days after she left, is that correct?"

"That's right."

"What did she say to you?"

She seemed taken aback by the question. "What's that gotta do with anything?"

Kaplowitz stood, but his slack posture telegraphed he knew it was a wasted effort. "Your Honor, is this really necessary?"

"It's a legitimate question, counsel. Take your seat."

"What did she say to you?" Piza asked again.

Candy huffed her displeasure. "She said she wanted me to know that she was alive, and that she wasn't coming home. And that I shouldn't look for her."

He moved slightly closer to the witness stand. "Considering how distressed she must've been to have done something as drastic as running away, you'd think she'd have said more than that."

"Judge, is there a question in there somewhere?" Kaplowitz said.

Judge Williams nodded. "Rephrase it, Mr. Piza, or move on."

"Let me ask you this, Ms. Janicek. How did Nancy sound in that last call? Sad? Angry? What?"

Her voice laced with frustration, she said, "I dunno! Angry, I guess."

Piza had noticed the woman's air of bravado visibly ebb, and her color fade, when he suggested her daughter may have said something more in their last phone call.

"She said something else in that call, didn't she, Ms. Janicek? Because she was so, so angry, she couldn't get off that phone without letting you know why she was destroying your life. What did she say?"

Kaplowitz sprang up. "Your Honor, this is—"

Candy talked over him as she blurted out, "She said 'First you drove Daddy away, and now me.'" A sob heaved her chest as tears surfaced. "She said 'Have a good life.'" She struck the witness stand with her fist, but it was a feeble effort. "She blamed me for her father leaving. And I'm sure it was because of that *damn* therapy. But she hung up on me. She didn't give me a chance to explain. To tell her it was his fault. Not mine. He left on his own. Because he didn't love us! Didn't love me and didn't love her. Any man who leaves his home . . . leaves his family unprotected . . . is a coward who doesn't love them. She didn't give me a chance to tell her that." She looked pitiful and hideous, her appearance victimized by hopelessness and the rivulets of mascara staining her cheeks down to her chin.

It was like the courtroom had been transformed into a theater. Figuratively darkened, with a spotlight illuminating the witness stand. The audience solemn and transfixed.

But not Piza, who felt like an electric current had shot through him. Calming himself, he spoke with as casual a tone as he could manage. "And that's why you told Lisa her father didn't love her."

Clearly caught flat-footed, Kaplowitz took a couple of seconds to recover. Enough time for his depleted client to nod and say, "Yes. She needed to know."

Simultaneous reactions from Sabatini and Megan caromed off each other. There was Sabatini's raging: "*What* the hell did you tell her?" And Megan's stunned: "How— How could you? Are you insane?"

Candy's listlessness turned to panic. Terror-filled eyes found Megan, and in a quavering voice that begged forgiveness she said, "It— It was just a couple of times. You know, to make sure she understood. So she wouldn't be confused like Nancy. I— I did it for all of you, sweetheart. You understand, right?"

Judge Williams's pounding gavel and stern "Quiet down, everyone" re-established order. (Albeit a tenuous one.) "That's better," he said. He gave a slight jut of his chin to Kaplowitz. "Counsel, you appeared on the verge of an objection?"

The ashen-faced lawyer said, "Uh, yes, Your Honor. I— I was going to say that the question . . . actually it was more of a statement . . . assumed a fact not in evidence. There's been no prior testimony that this witness ever said anything like that, so Mr. Piza had no legal basis for presenting it as a fact the way he did. What he should've done is ask her if she ever said it." He retook his seat.

The jurist nodded. "Agreed. The objection's sustained. Mr. Piza, you can rephrase."

Shaking his head, Piza said, "I'll let it go, Your Honor. And I have no further questions for this witness. We rest." There was no reason to pursue it. The disdain distorting Megan's face was irrefutable evidence that Candy's presence in her and her children's lives was over.

"Okay. Mr. Kaplowitz? Questions?"

In a subdued voice he said, "No, Judge."

Judge Williams instructed Candy to step down. Pleading eyes continued to home in on Megan as the realtor made her way back to the gallery. She didn't receive so much as a glance in return.

"All right then. Mr. Kaplowitz, you have one witness?"

"Um, may I have a minute to confer with my client?"

"Of course. Do you need a brief recess?"

"No. I can speak with her right here at the counsel table. Won't be long."

As he and Megan began a whispered conversation, Sabatini leaned in to Piza. "I don't know where to put myself. What kind of sick, twisted bastard could do that to a kid?"

"I know. But at least now we may have some insight into what's been eating at Lisa."

"Same thing I was thinking. How'd you know she said that to Lis?"

"I didn't. But when she said 'any man' who leaves his home, it struck me that she was talking about more than her ex-husband. So I took a shot. I figured the worst that happens is she denies it."

Sabatini put a hand on Piza's shoulder. "Well, thank God for your instincts. I don't—"

"Your Honor," Kaplowitz said as he stood, "my client has instructed me to withdraw our opposition to the motion."

Candy jumped up and gripped the wood railing that separated the counsel tables from the gallery. "What— What does that mean?"

A scowling Judge Williams pointed at her. "Madam, I've warned you. Now sit down."

She held her position. "No! I won't sit! I need to know what that means. Megan, honey, what does that mean?"

"It means you've gotta stay away from our kids," Sabatini spat out.

As the judge once again wielded his gavel, Candy stretched over the divider in a fruitless attempt to touch Megan, who recoiled at the sight of the frantic woman. "Please, Megan. Please let me explain. I did it for you and the girls. Please don't cut me out of your lives. It'll kill me, Megan. Please."

The court officer, who'd moved toward Candy as soon as she ignored the judge's instruction to sit, pulled her away from the divider. As she struggled, the judge ordered, "Remove her from the courtroom, Bill."

Sobbing while she continued to try to wriggle out of the officer's grip, Candy yelled, "Don't do it, Megan. Don't let him win. You'll regret this."

As the doors closed and a profanity-splattered tirade crumbled into indiscernible echoes, no one in the courtroom moved.

Piza couldn't remember ever seeing Judge Williams look like he did at that moment. He'd seen the man at the height of frustration, but this was different. He seemed shaken.

"In all my years on the bench, I've never. . . Is everyone okay?"

All of them answered yes, but Megan's glistening eyes and trembling hands said otherwise.

"Judge," Kaplowitz said, "I'm a little concerned by what Ms. Janicek said about my client 'regretting this'. I don't know that it was meant as a threat, but I'd be more comfortable if we could structure the proposed order submitted by Mr. Piza as a restraining order, barring Ms. Janicek from any contact. Ms. Sabatini has already indicated to me that she wants nothing more to do with her. And I'd rather be safe than sorry."

Piza stood. "I was going to suggest that myself, Judge. This woman appears to be unstable, and I think Ms. Sabatini and her children may need immediate protection."

"All right," the jurist said. "Ms. Sabatini. Mr. Sabatini. You're both okay with this?"

"Yes" was the concurrent response.

"Okay then. The law gives me a lot of leeway to do what's needed to protect people, especially children. Seeing what happened here today, I'm going to sign an order barring contact between Ms. Janicek and Ms. Sabatini and the children. Hopefully, this will put the issue to bed. If Ms. Janicek wants to fight it, we'll deal with it then. Mr. Piza, this was your motion, so you can see to it that Ms. Janicek is served with a copy of the order. We'll give Ms. Sabatini an extra copy to give to her local police department. And finally, Mr. and Ms. Sabatini, let me just say that it would be in everyone's best interest if you were to resolve this case. You both have able lawyers, so do yourselves a favor and try to settle this. We're adjourned." With that, he left the bench.

Elation in Sabatini's eyes and smile offset his pallor. "I can't believe we did it, Ton. Ha, listen to me . . . *we*. You. You did it. I don't know how to thank you."

"Well, I'm just happy it worked out. With Candy out of the picture, maybe now Lisa can start healing."

"God, I hope so. Hey, while we're waiting for the order, do I have time to hit the men's room?"

"Yeah, definitely."

As Sabatini left the courtroom, Kaplowitz came over to Piza. "You have a second?"

"Uh, sure. What's up?"

Kaplowitz motioned to an area of the courtroom away from the counsel tables. When they reached it he said, "Look, I just want you to know I had no idea what she was doing. Regardless of what I may think of your client, Janicek was totally out of line, and I never would've let her get away with it if I knew."

Piza shook his head. "It never crossed my mind for a second that you knew, so put that to rest. And I'm hoping therapy will help Lisa get past this. As for your feelings about my client, he's actually a pretty decent guy once you get to know him."

Kaplowitz's lack of response was irksome. Piza interpreted his flat expression as an uncalled for smugness, which led to a hard-edged, "You have reason to believe he's *not* a decent guy, Seth?"

The young lawyer looked uncomfortable. Through an awkward shrug he said, "Uh, not really. Just a sense, I guess."

Piza wasn't letting it drop. "Look, if you're judging him on the fact he's pushing for custody, let me assure you this isn't some baseless or vindictive position he's taken. I wouldn't be representing him if I thought it was. He believes he's doing the right thing. His world revolves around those kids, and there's nothing he wouldn't do for them." He paused. "I know you understand that mind-set better than anyone."

Kaplowitz drew a deep breath. "I'd better get back to my client."

"Of course. She's upset."

As Piza watched him walk away, he felt an obscure unease tugging at him.

With good reason, as he would soon discover.

CHAPTER 38

Candy wasn't waiting in the courthouse parking lot. Nor was she anywhere visibly near the family's house in Iselin. That's what Sabatini told Piza when he called the lawyer a couple of hours after the hearing. He'd driven Megan home. Two reasons. One, Candy had been her ride. (Not that she'd have gone home with her.) Two, they needed to discuss how to deal with the revelation of the woman's assault on their daughter's psyche.

Sabatini said he spent half the drive calming Megan and trying to ease her guilt, her distress so intense he'd held in check his craving for an "I told you so". When they segued into Lisa, his instinct was for both of them to immediately sit down with her and explain everything. But in light of how deeply ingrained in the child Candy's toxic fiction appeared to be, Megan felt it might be better if they talked privately with Lisa's therapist first, not only to determine the best approach to counteracting the lie, but also to figure out how to explain Candy's absence to both girls. As anxious as Sabatini was to heal the wounds and resume his relationship with his daughter, he realized his wife was right. This had to be done as cautiously as possible, to ensure Lisa's well-being. Megan said she'd call the therapist the next day to set up an appointment.

Picking up on his client's enduring stress from the day's trauma, Piza said, "With the Candy situation resolved, things should be relatively run-of-the-mill until the trial. So, you can breathe easy for a while."

Or at least until the next day.

The following morning, Piza got into the office about eleven thirty. He'd been serving as a panelist for the court's early settlement program, where family law attorneys volunteer their time to help litigants and their lawyers attempt to resolve their cases.

He'd barely gotten behind his desk when Gloria came in, her face a sober portrait of puzzlement as she held up a piece of paper. "So, this is very weird."

"Morning to you too."

"No, listen, this is really strange. This fax came in this morning. Hand printed. Sent from that stationery store on State Street." She handed it to him. "No indication who it's from."

He read it aloud: "To Anthony Piza. Ask Joseph Sabatini why he really got laid off from his last job. And do the right thing with this fax." He looked up at her.

"Told you it was weird," she said. "Any idea who it's from?"

With conspicuous annoyance he tossed the paper onto his desk. "Not a clue. Why is nothing easy with this damn case? I'll have to discuss it with Sabatini."

"No doubt. And what does 'do the right thing with this fax' mean?"

"Not sure. I'll give Sabatini a call later."

"Well, this whole thing is intriguing, I'll say that. Do you want me to put the fax in the Sabatini file?"

"Uh, no, that's okay." He gave her a half-smile. "Maybe if I stare at it long enough something'll come to me."

"All right. And don't forget, you have a new client coming in at one."

He nodded, and she left.

As soon as she was out of sight, he ripped the paper into small pieces and tossed them into the wastebasket. It was the right thing to do. He owed it to Kaplowitz.

What the fuck is this about?

Sabatini practically jumped out of his lounge chair, a reflex to the banging on his front door. He stormed the ten feet to the entrance, plastered his right eye to the peephole, and sucked in a gulp of air when he saw a grave-looking Piza on his porch, breath pluming in the nighttime cold.

"Tony," he said when the door was half-way open, a flaccid smile attempting to mask his concern. "Jesus, you scared the shit outta me. I thought someone was trying to break down the door. Were— Were we supposed to be meeting tonight?"

"Can I come in?" was the curt response.

"Yeah, of course. Come in. What's goin' on? Is everything okay?"

Piza did a cursory survey of the area, then removed his overcoat and sat on a small, faded tartan couch.

Sabatini felt his anxiety escalating at warp speed. "Ton, you're making me a little nervous here. Is there a problem with the case, 'cause if there is, then please just tell me, okay?"

Crossing his legs and leaning forward, Piza rested clasped hands on his knee. "I don't know, Strikes. Is there a problem? You tell me."

Sabatini's response held more entreaty than irritation.

"Christ, Tony, stop being so damn cryptic, will ya. I don't understand what's going on."

Piza locked eyes with his client. "Why did the last bank you were at let you go?"

Oh God. This isn't happening. "Whaddya mean? I told you, I got laid off. You know, because of the economy. The bank's financial problems. Where's this coming from?"

"Laid off . . . or fired?"

"What— What's with the semantics? Laid off. Fired. It's the same thing," he replied as a surge of heat assailed him.

"Tell me the truth now, or find yourself another lawyer."

A paralyzing apprehension overtook Sabatini. He stood there slack-jawed, unable to speak.

"Nothing to say?" No response. "Fine, I'm outta here." He grabbed his coat off the couch. "I'll be filing a motion with the court to be relieved as counsel. You'll get a copy in the mail." He started toward the door.

Sabatini shook off the fear and scrambled to position himself in front of Piza, lightly placing his hands on the lawyer's chest, a gesture that—together with his pleading eyes—conveyed submission. Piza glanced down at Sabatini's hands, and the man quickly backed off.

"I'm sorry. Please, don't go, okay? I'll tell you."

Piza glared at him for a few moments, then turned, tossed his coat back on the couch, and sat. "Okay, let's have it. Why did they let you go? And no more bullshit."

Sabatini slowly retreated to his lounge chair and eased himself down so deliberately you'd have thought he was three times his age. He lay his head back and rested his extended arms on the frayed arms of the chair. His eyes were cast toward the ceiling.

"I'm waiting."

"I embezzled some money," Sabatini said, still staring at the ceiling.

They sat in silence as the admission settled in: Piza looking shaken; Sabatini's lifelessness casting doubt on the expression "confession is good for the soul".

"Jesus Christ," the lawyer finally got out. "What the hell were you thinking?"

Sabatini momentarily turned his head toward Piza, then resumed looking into space. "When we met in your office that first time, I told you that, you know, that with Megan being a stay-at-home mom and all, money was a little tight. Well, it was more than a little. It got to the point where any unexpected expense became a crisis. Washing machine craps out; car needs brakes. Just one more hit to the credit cards. We had a pretty nice lifestyle before the kids, but . . . kids, man."

"How much did you take?"

"Ten grand? Little more, maybe. Over time."

"How?"

Through a cynical smile Sabatini said, "It's so damn easy. Find accounts with no activity. Ya know, dormant. Ones where someone's not likely to check the balance. Then siphon off some of the funds into your own account."

"How'd you get caught?"

"Elderly customer's daughter found his bankbook and decided to check on it. When she questioned the withdrawal, the bank traced it to me. It wasn't a ton of money. They told her it was an accounting error. They made up the shortfall."

"The bank picked it up? Did you reimburse them?"

"With what? I didn't have a pot to piss in. We made a deal. I told them the other accounts I'd tapped into, they made them whole, and I got 'laid off' instead of fired."

Discernibly perplexed, Piza said, "I'm lost here. Why the hell would they do that?"

"Because they wanted to avoid the possibility of an outside investigation that could open the floodgates. You've gotta understand something here. They were lending out money like it was candy. They'd sign off on shit with their fingers crossed behind their backs. Not to mention money laundering, kickbacks, all kinds of shit that was going on. And not just my bank."

"Did Megan know about this?"

"I never told her. But she's not an idiot. I mean, I took care of the checkbook, so she didn't specifically see what came in and went out. But she knew what my salary was. And she had to have at least a general idea of expenses. So on some level, she must've been aware that something wasn't right. But I guess it's like they say . . . if you don't wanna know the answer, don't ask the question, right? Although she'd never have suspected *this*." He shrugged. "I don't regret not telling her. Shielding her. But in hindsight, we should've discussed how bad the money situation was. Maybe she'd have gone back to work. Part-time, at least. Instead of just starting now. The realtor thing. I let my pride—" A sudden, chilling realization coursed through him. "How— How'd you find out about this?"

A scowling Piza said, "I got an anonymous tip that something was off about how you left. No details, but certainly enough to bring me here tonight. Do you—"

"But who could possibly know about this, other than the higher-ups in the bank? And *they* sure as shit wouldn't say anything. Makes no sense."

"I don't know. But obviously it's out there," Piza replied. He got up, paced a few steps, then stood behind the couch, his knuckles whitening as he gripped the top of the cushion. "Do you have any idea how badly you fucked up?"

"Look, I'm really sorry, Tony. I just figured that—"

"Save it! I don't give a rat's ass if you're sorry or not. The damage is done. To this case. Don't you get it? You committed perjury."

"What? What the hell are you—"

"The hearing yesterday! You testified that you'd never committed a crime. You lied under oath, for Christ's sake."

"Fuck" was Sabatini's faint, belated response. Desperation displaced shock as he battled to find his footing; something to save him from being sucked into the sinkhole opening beneath him. After a fifteen-second eternity, he delivered a sputtering, "Li — Listen, okay? Hold up a sec. Economics was the reason the bank gave for letting me go. Not embezzlement. So, so how's it a crime if that's their official position? See what I'm sayin'?"

Piza shook his head, looking at his client like he was a dolt. "Wake up. If I'm aware there's a problem, don't you think there's a chance Megan's lawyers are too? If Kaplowitz knows, he'd crucify you on cross-examination at trial. But never mind that. There's no way I could even put you on the stand if you're gonna get up there and lie. I have ethical obligations here. And if you think I'm gonna jeopardize my career for you, you're out of your mind."

Sabatini felt like he was being ripped apart in a feral tug-of-war between despair and terror. "Well, uh, what are— What're the odds of her lawyers having the information? Whoever tipped you off is probably on my side, right? Giving you a heads-up?"

"You don't know that. And did you not just hear what I said about ethics?"

Sabatini leaned forward, hands covering his face. He began pounding his temples with the fleshy part of his palms. "I feel like my fucking head's gonna explode. If this gets out it's gonna unleash a shitstorm." He turned wild eyes toward Piza. "I could lose my kids. My job. Christ Almighty, I could go to jail. Can't we just take a shot and not say anything? Pray that Megan's lawyers don't know about this? I'm begging you. Look the other way just this once."

Piza slowly returned to the front of the couch and sat, his demeanor stoical. "I can't look the other way. I won't. But even if I were willing to, it still wouldn't be worth the risk."

"Why, dammit? The odds of getting caught are—"

"I have reason to believe Megan's lawyers know the truth."

Sabatini's emotional frenzy skidded to a stop, like a staggering drunk being jolted into instant sobriety. "How? Based on what?"

Expelling a short, sharp sigh, Piza said, "Listen, when you first came to see me, you told me you wanted me to represent you because you felt I was the only lawyer you could trust. So I'm telling you . . . trust me on this."

Muscles tensed, Sabatini eyed him for a few moments. He wondered if this revelation was a ploy to end the argument. The possibility of finding another attorney darted into his thoughts; someone with more accommodating scruples. But intellect quickly displaced emotion. He knew Piza. He wouldn't have made the statement if it wasn't true. So even if he changed lawyers, it wouldn't make a difference. If the truth was already out there, he was finished.

"Did you hear what I said, Strikes?"

A terse laugh accompanied, "Yeah. My life is over." He freed a cigarette from the pack sitting on the scuffed serving table abutting his chair, and lit it. Leaning as far back as he could, he closed his eyes. A long draw and a languid exhale of smoke embodied his weariness. "So, since I'm already screwed, you might as well know."

Piza's eyes became slits. "Know what?"

"The embezzling. I'm still doing it."

I hope to hell she's in. Piza was counting on Nia Bradley's normal routine—being at her desk Saturday mornings. (He hadn't bothered to call; he was going in anyway.) He needed to discuss Sabatini with her, hoping she could help him figure out how to move forward, a subject that had been vexing him from the minute he stormed out of his client's apartment the night before.

The discourse after Sabatini's disclosure of his continuing theft had been brief. Piza (stunned): "What?" Sabatini: "Five Gs, give or take. But that's it. I'm stopping, if that makes a difference to you." Piza: "Fuck you, Strikes." With that, he'd picked up his coat and strode to the door. Sabatini, still splayed out on his lounge chair, hadn't tried to stop him.

Piza would have loved for that dramatic parting moment to have marked the end of his dealings with Sabatini. He saw the banker's deception as another betrayal. Not as painful as the one twelve years earlier, when they were adults more in age than temperament, and the collapse of a friendship destined to last forever was unimaginable. His "once-burned" wariness of Sabatini didn't allow for that level of intensity. But breach of trust was an upper-echelon entry in Piza's list of punishable misdeeds; one for which a second violation—regardless of degree—extinguished any chance of forgiveness.

Despite his personal feelings toward Sabatini, he had to contend with his obligations as a lawyer. And that's where he really needed Nia's input. The sight of her car in the parking lot produced an exhale of relief.

After acknowledging another associate who was a Saturday morning regular, he dropped off his coat and briefcase in his office and went straight to Nia's room. The only sign of her was a bright-red ski jacket draped over a client chair. *Conference room probably.* He saw her through the glass doors, sitting at the long, glass-topped table, piles of papers of assorted sizes neatly arranged in front of her.

"Hey there," he said as he strode into the room.

"Hey there back."

"You usually jump when I pop in without warning."

"I caught a glimpse of you pulling into the lot," she responded, jutting her chin toward the bank of windows to her right.

"Ah. I'll have to park on the street next time. So, you got a minute? Or twenty?"

"Twenty? You're lucky I like you," she said with a playful smirk. "Grab a chair."

He filled her in on the latest in the Sabatini saga. When he finished, her arched eyebrows and tightened lips confirmed his assessment of how bad his dilemma was. "Pretty damn messed up, right?" he said, affirming the obvious.

"Uh yeah. I would say so." A pause. "You look a little . . . I dunno. The way you related the story, it seems like you're letting this get to you more than it should. Emotionally."

"No, I'm okay," Piza said. "It's just— It's like I feel I should've known something wasn't right. I mean, he's been giving his wife a healthy amount of his paycheck. Against my advice, of course. But if he was having trouble making ends meet when he was living at home, there's no way he could make it work while living up here *and* making less money. Although I did ask him about it once, when I found out he was gonna rent a bigger apartment."

"And what did he say?"

"He said he could handle it. Made a joke about it. Something like he was living on cereal."

"Okay. We both know people stretch their money all the time. Pay this, don't pay that. So what were you supposed to do? Grill him? Slap him around until you were convinced he was telling the truth?"

With a grin Piza said, "You're right. But you know me. Inconsolable on those rare occasions I believe I've fallen short of perfection."

"And he's back. So, Your Worship, where are you on what to do about this?"

His turn for raised eyebrows, which accompanied a puffed breath. "Well, I'd love to just bail on this guy. This is the second time he's screwed me, so——"

"In this case?"

"No. No. First time was twelve years ago. A personal thing."

"I'm not following. Didn't you originally tell me he was an old friend?"

"I did, and he was. But I took this case more because of his kids. They're young and I was concerned for them. And he did apologize for the past. *Seemed* genuinely penitent."

She leaned back and folded her arms. "Well, I know you well enough to know you'll keep your personal feelings toward him out of any decision you make." A bemused expression materialized. "Funny though. As much as this guy painted you into a corner, I almost feel sorry for him. From everything you've said, he sounds like a desperate man who did the wrong thing for the right reason."

With a brusque headshake Piza said, "I don't buy that. I understand needing to support your family. But there are other things he could've done to make extra money. Hell, flip burgers on weekends if you have to. As far as I'm concerned, he's a casualty of his own arrogance."

Nia gave him a slight, understanding smile. "Point taken."

"Anyhow, as much as I'd like to get out of this case, I'm not sure it's feasible. Or even the right move. We're relatively far along and, since custody's still a genuine issue . . . despite being a longshot . . . we already have a trial date, so I'm not sure the judge would grant my motion. And—"

"Who's the judge?"

"Williams."

"Good judge. Smart. Considerate. If there's anyone who'd let you out, it's probably him. Although I agree he might be more reluctant with custody in the mix. But I think the way your client has tied your hands, you could have reasonable grounds."

"Which leads to another issue."

"I'm guessing you're concerned about how much you'd have to divulge to convince Williams to give you a pass?"

A nod from Piza. "Exactly. I took a look at the Rules of Professional Conduct and I don't think Sabatini's theft rises to a level where I have a duty to report it. And now, of course, he says he's stopped. So everything's past tense. If the law says I'm not required to report what he did, but I tell the judge anyway in order to get out, I think I may have an attorney-client privilege problem on my hands. And if I *don't* tell him, odds are he's gonna deny my request. I don't know that some generic excuse, like my client and I don't see eye-to-eye on how to proceed or some such thing, is gonna cut it at this point." He held out his hands, palms facing the ceiling. "Rock, meet hard place."

A clipped laugh from Nia. "Think of the irony here. You

want out because he betrayed you, but you likely can't *get* out because you're not allowed to betray *him*."

"Yeah. So much for fundamental fairness."

"Just out of curiosity, do you think Kaplowitz . . . and by extension, Bruzek . . . knows about the *current* embezzlement?"

"Not sure," Piza replied through a shrug. "But if he does, he probably would've alluded to it in the fax. I mean, he obviously was alerting me. Why hold anything back?"

"That's true. Any idea what possessed him to send the fax?"

"I've thought about that a lot. Clearly, they have something substantiating the embezzlement. And whatever it is, they didn't disclose it in discovery. Nothing in their answers to interrogatories or our request for docs."

"Ethics. So overrated."

He laughed. "My sense is that Kaplowitz is a decent guy. A little overzealous at times, but for the right reasons. He fights for his clients. And I don't remember him doing anything overtly deceitful in my dealings with him up to this point. So I'm assuming that not supplying us with whatever it is they have was Bruzek's call. Maybe the plan is to use it down the road. Maybe even save it for trial. Although that's a risky strategy. They'd have to give the judge a viable reason for not disclosing it sooner."

A sour-faced Nia said, "Yeah. Well, Bruzek's not above concocting some BS excuse, believe me. And I agree that this was probably her doing. She may not go to court, but she keeps a tight grip on major decisions in her office's cases. A sleaze *and* a control freak."

"That's the word on the street. So here's my take on this. Kaplowitz does a masterful job setting up Sabatini on cross-examination, and nails him with his last question, getting him to say he never committed a crime. Mission accomplished. Unbeknownst to me at the time, obviously. But I think Candy's testimony changed things. Kaplowitz was definitely shaken when he heard what she pulled with Lisa, and he made sure I knew he had no idea she'd done that. He has a sick child, which is probably why he went along with Bruzek on the discovery thing initially. He needs to keep his job."

"But his conscience got to him."

"Exactly. I think the potential impact of the embezzlement on Sabatini's kids hit him. Even if they weren't made aware of it directly, the fallout could be devastating. Giving me a heads-up doesn't make the situation any less grim. But at least he gave me a chance to avoid getting sandbagged."

"Took guts."

"Sure did. Not only doing it, but trusting me not to reveal what he did."

"Very true." Nia got up and stood behind her chair. "Need to stretch my legs a bit. When you mentioned before about not being sure you could get out of the case, you also said you weren't sure that would even be the right move. Meaning what?"

"The kids. Candy aside, the stress of the divorce has to be affecting them."

"Pretty much always does."

"And then factor in the number Candy did on Lisa's head. I mean, she's in therapy. Hopefully, she'll be okay. But my fear is that even if I *could* bow out, the delay it would cause . . . ya know, letting this thing drag on . . . could set this kid back. Maybe harm Amy as well. And it'd be even worse if some asshole took my place."

"No, I get it," Nia said. "It's a valid concern." She smiled. "Kind of sounds like you've already made up your mind about sticking with it."

He returned the smile. "I guess it does. I think maybe I just needed you to tell me I wasn't being a fool if I opted not to abandon ship."

"You're not a fool, Tony. You care. That's what makes you good at this." He nodded a thank you. "So, now that we've resolved that issue, the question becomes how to try to salvage this mess."

After discussing it for another fifteen minutes, they reached a conclusion.

There was only one way to avoid disaster.

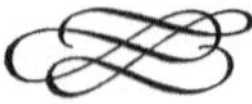

CHAPTER 40

"Wasn't sure I'd be hearing from you again." Sabatini's words accompanied his guarded navigation into a client chair in Piza's office Monday afternoon.

"I still have an obligation to represent you," Piza replied, his inflection flat.

"Okay. So, your secretary wasn't, ya know, doling out much information when she called this morning. What's going on?"

"I met with my boss Saturday to try to come up with a game plan to deal with the bind you put us in. And we—"

"Listen, Tony. I never meant to—"

"Save it. What you meant to do or didn't mean to do is irrelevant. It is what it is. So let's just address it and move on." His client's pained expression failed to register on Piza's sympathy meter. He'd disconnected that mechanism Friday evening, at least as to Sabatini. On the contrary, he was laboring not to savor the banker's distress, which he saw as a justified consequence of his deception.

A resigned sigh from Sabatini preceded, "Okay. I get that you're pissed. I probably would be too if I was you." If he was looking for a response, he was disappointed. "So, what'd you guys come up with? Is there a way out of this?"

Piza sat back and folded his hands in his lap. "It's our opinion that there's only one way this doesn't destroy you . . . and your family. This case can never get to trial. You have to settle it. If you work it out, there's no legitimate reason for the embezzlement, or your perjury, to surface."

Sabatini straightened in his seat. "And what happens if we don't settle it?"

Piza thought he detected some pushback in Sabatini's question. "What happens? In all probability, your crime gets into the official court record. That's what happens. And judges are supposed to report evidence of a crime in New Jersey. Not all of them do, but do you really wanna roll the dice on that? Bottom line is once it's in the record, it's in the record. Who knows who can pick up on it? You wanna take a chance on being prosecuted?"

"No, of course not. But you said 'in all probability' it gets into the record. So it's not definite?"

Piza's patience was hurtling toward its breaking point. But a momentary pause to calm himself pulled him back enough to realize the question was a valid one. "It's virtually a certainty. The only sliver of hope is that Megan's lawyers haven't provided us with whatever they have about the embezzlement. They had an obligation to let us know what it is by now. I'm surmising they're saving it for when it could do the most damage. But—"

"I don't mean to interrupt you, but if they're doing that, isn't that illegal?"

"It's certainly unethical. Based on that, we could ask the judge not to allow them to present any evidence on it. The problem is that what they'll probably do is give the judge some excuse as to why they didn't turn it over. 'Gosh, Judge, I could've sworn we sent it. Maybe it got misplaced in the mounds of other paperwork.' Some nonsense like that. And how do we prove it wasn't an honest mistake?"

"Yeah, I see your point."

"But look, even if the judge were wary of their explanation, it's unlikely he'd disallow the evidence. He'd be more apt to adjourn the trial for a while to allow us to investigate whatever they've got. Basically, all that does is delay the inevitable."

A visibly dispirited Sabatini sunk into his chair. "So, settling this thing. How do we go about doing that?" He suddenly looked puzzled, and he sat up again. "But didn't you tell me her lawyer doesn't settle cases?"

"No, she settles them. But usually not until she's convinced she's squeezed out as much in legal fees as she can. Typically, just before it gets to trial."

"But wait a sec. If she always settles right before trial, what are we worrying about? No trial, no mention of what I did, right? No theft. No perjury."

"I didn't say she 'always' settles, I said 'usually'. Her lawyers do take cases through to trial if need be. So right there that's not a risk worth taking."

"Shit," Sabatini said, resuming his slouch.

Piza leaned forward and rested clasped hands on his desk. "Look, truth be told—"

"But— Sorry to cut you off again. If we have to settle, where does that leave me regarding custody?"

Piza spat out a cold laugh. "Custody? Are you freakin' kidding me? I'm gonna assume that question was prompted by arrogance, because there's no way you're that stupid."

"Jesus. Could you ease up on the attitude? It was—"

"It was what? A legitimate question? I told you from day one that custody was iffy. And when the custody evaluation report came in it was pretty much game over. But now? What part of 'you committed a crime' don't you get? Custody? Holy crap."

Piza wasn't sure whether it was anger or embarrassment that

flushed Sabatini's cheeks. Nor did he care. "Getting back to your embezzlement. The reality is that even without a trial it could still be a factor. It won't become public knowledge, but Bruzek could wield it like a weapon. Use it to bludgeon you into a lopsided settlement."

Frantic eyes bore witness to the turmoil chewing up Sabatini. "So it— It sounds like you're saying I'm screwed either way. What the fuck kind of a plan is that?"

Piza stared at his client. Expressionless. Calm. "You done?"

The banker averted his eyes, but only for a moment, his state of fight-or-flight apparently generating a rickety courage. "Don't blame me for freaking out, Tony. Okay? My future's at stake here. So tell me straight up, is there something that can stop any of this shit from happening?"

"Not something," Piza said. "Someone."

Sabatini lay sprawled on his lounge chair. Tie loosened. Both hands balancing a tepid bottle of beer on his lap. A bowl of popcorn (tonight's dinner) sat untouched on the serving tray, its fading aroma rapidly losing the ability to lure him in. A living room lamp and the faintly buzzing fluorescent backlight on the kitchen stove provided the only illumination in the forlorn-looking apartment. Apt ambiance for his mood.

He'd spent the last hour mulling over his conversation with Piza from a few hours before. His initial focus was on coming up with an alternative to the lawyer's escape plan for him. Having failed that, he was now reviewing the instructions he'd been given to attempt to facilitate his salvation.

Attaining freedom is rarely a cloudless affair. And as far as Sabatini was concerned, it didn't get much murkier than when the key to your liberation is the woman you're divorcing. He was still smarting from the revelation; that moment when he asked

Piza who his redeemer was, and the word "Megan" kicked him in the head.

But he understood the logic in Piza's strategy, which was based on the assumption that Bruzek was probably withholding knowledge of the embezzlement from Megan. It was an assessment he agreed with, because if she knew, she undoubtedly would have confronted him already; the embodiment of rage and anguish.

As Piza had explained, the impact of his theft was an unknown, and at this juncture Bruzek would want to avoid anything that could impede her control of the case's progress—and the continuing flow of legal fees. So getting to Megan first and disclosing everything was their best hope for ending this now.

As much sense as that made to Sabatini, the thought of meeting with his wife—hat in hand and tail firmly planted between his legs—was demoralizing. A laying bare of his inadequacy as the family's designated provider; the income producer who couldn't deliver without also assuming the role of thief.

Another discomforting aspect of his mission (as he'd expressed to Piza) lay in Megan's potential response to his confession. What if she were too repelled by his sin to even consider the wisdom of his proposal? Or worse, what if she seized on what he did and instructed her attorney to grind him into dust, removing herself as a possible buffer between him and annihilation?

Piza had listened to his client's concerns, and said: "You're not thinking clearly. If she chooses to throw you to the sharks, so what? The sharks are already circling you. So you wouldn't be any more screwed than you are already."

And he was right.

Okay. I lay it out for her. Here's what I did. So, so sorry. I've stopped though. Did it out of desperation. Should I say I did it for her and the girls? Forgot to ask Tony about that. No. That looks like I'm laying some of the blame on them. Although if she'd gotten off her ass— Stop. Stick to the script. If this gets out, I could go to jail. I'd have no way to support you guys.

And think of the trauma to the kids. The last thing Lisa needs now. The only way to stop it is to settle the case. As soon as possible. And fairly. It's in everyone's best interest. Then I unleash the biggie—I'm giving up my request for custody. Should I say 'even though it's killing me'? Emphasize the sacrifice I'm making? Might be too over-the-top. And sounds kind of confrontational. Stick to the script!

Okay, once I've made my points, wrap it up. Tell her if she agrees with me, she has to get her lawyers to go along with settling. What else? There was something else. Oh, keep my mouth shut about her lawyers possibly knowing about this. Can't take a chance on her mentioning it and inadvertently tipping them off that there's a snitch out there somewhere . . . whoever the hell it is. Still don't understand why Tony's so concerned about that. Okay, pretty sure that's everything. I should probably write down exactly what I'm gonna say. Study it.

Christis, this better work.

***

"So, Megan. Seth tells me you're demanding we settle your case." Nadia Bruzek was sitting far back in her desk chair, arms tightly folded.

Megan was on the edge of her seat, bent slightly forward. "Well, I wouldn't say 'demanded' necessarily. It's just something, ya know, I feel we should do."

"Yeah," Kaplowitz piped in from his position on the couch, "I don't think I said 'demanded', Nadia. But she does feel strongly about it."

Bruzek's eyes shot a quick reprimand, then returned to their client. "I understand your husband is withdrawing his custody demand?"

"Yes. He's no longer insisting the girls live with him."

"Well, that's certainly a step in the right direction. But you have to realize there are many other elements of your case. Considering the fact you've been a stay-at-home mom with no income for many years, you're entitled to alimony. And, of course, child support. And then there's the matter of your mutual assets. The house and so on. All important issues to be discussed."

Megan nodded. "No, I know. Mr. Kaplowitz explained all that to me. And, after talking to Joey, I think we can work all that out."

"I'm sure, in time, we will. But may I ask why this sudden urge to settle? You've never mentioned it before today. And, frankly, I don't think the timing is right."

Don't let this woman intimidate you. Calm down and do this. Megan eased back in her seat. "Nothing specific. But with custody out of the way, it's just that with everything that's happened . . . you know, with Candy . . . and how it's affected Lisa and all, I just want to get this over with."

Bruzek's smile was acerbic. "Oh, yes. Ms. Janicek. Don't think I didn't get an earful from the attorney who referred you to me. Janicek threatened to take her real estate business away from his firm. She was that upset. He said she felt victimized."

Megan knitted her brow. "Are you aware of what she did? *She* feels victimized?"

Bruzek cleared her throat as she awkwardly adjusted herself in her chair. "Please understand that I'm in no way condoning what she did. Absolutely not. It's just interesting how people's perspectives differ. That's all. But let's not dwell on that. I have to tell you something that may change your outlook on rushing into settlement. Something I'm sure will shock you as much as it did Seth and me." She paused. "We have reason to believe your husband embezzled funds from the last bank he worked at. It was the real reason they let him go."

Bruzek's quizzical expression emerged within moments of her client's lack of reaction to the announcement. "Did you understand what—"

"Uh-huh. I completely understand. But I already know that."

Kaplowitz leaned forward. "You mean . . . you knew he was doing it?"

Eyes widened, Megan answered, "You mean when he was at the bank? No, of course not. I'd never have— No, he just told me. Two days ago."

Bruzek's poker face was not having its best day. "I— Why on earth would he admit that to you?"

Kaplowitz paled.

"He said he'd been feeling guilty for a long time."—

The color returned to the young lawyer's face.

—"You know, about not telling me. Living a lie. And he wanted to get everything out in the open between the two of us. He said that with everything that happened to Lisa, he'd been thinking a lot about— Wait a minute. How do *you* know about this? And how long have you known? Why didn't *you* tell me?"

Bruzek's response was so blustery and histrionic you'd think she'd been accused of skewering a baby bird. "I sincerely hope you're not implying that I"—looking at Kaplowitz—"that *we've* been withholding information from you."

Megan was momentarily taken aback. "Uh, no. I mean, I guess not. But when did you find out?"

Still a portrait of wounded honor, Bruzek answered, "Why it was— It was just a day or so ago, wasn't it, Seth?"

"Um, yes, yes. It was— What's today? Thursday? Yes, it was Tuesday. I found a memo about it among Mr. Sabatini's expense sheets. Must have been inadvertently placed in there at the bank."

"Yes. Tuesday, "Bruzek repeated. "In fact, I believe Seth was going to call you to come in to discuss it. But you called first. To make this appointment. We would never withhold something like this from you," she said, shaking her head.

"Oh, okay," Megan replied, not completely convinced.

"Good," from Bruzek as her rigidity returned. "So, now that that's straightened out, I'm sure you see how this information could provide us with enormous bargaining power in negotiations. And if we were to go to trial . . . well, there's no end to the damage we could inflict."—

Joey was right. He said this is what could happen if she ever got her hands on this information.

—"So, we'd like to keep this going until as close to the trial as we can. I *want* you to tell him we know. Let him twist in the wind as long as possible. The closer we get to trial, the more pliable he'll become. I guarantee it. In the meantime, we still have to take his deposition. Question him under oath here in my offices. We've been trying to schedule it for a while, but it had to be postponed a few times. The judge has extended the discovery period to allow us to get it done. Maybe we'll file a motion to keep discovery going even longer, if he says anything in the deposition that needs looking in to. Keep the pressure on him, as it were."

"But—"

"And if he doesn't agree to give us whatever we want in a settlement, we'll go to trial. I can assure you, when a judge hears this, you'll get everything you deserve for having put up with this man for as long as you did."

"I get all that, Nadia. I do. But I don't want to destroy him. I just want what's fair. For both of us. The kids too. And besides, if there's a trial won't what he did be out in the open? I mean he could possibly get in trouble, right? Criminally?"

Bruzek's lips compressed as she wiggled the fingers of her clasped hands. "I'm not sure you totally understand the significance of what I said, Megan. You're at a huge advantage here. You'd be a fool to let it slip through your fingers. As your attorneys, we'd be remiss if we let you do that."

Megan's peripheral vision caught Kaplowitz slightly rolling his eyes. She took a breath and sat up straight. "I completely understand, Nadia. And as much as I appreciate your concern, like I said, that's not what I want. And you didn't answer my question about whether Joey could get in trouble. So I'm assuming the answer is yes. What good would it do me or the kids if he went to jail?"

Bruzek's eyes went lifeless. "Just so you know, Megan, the trial isn't the only way your husband's transgressions could find their way into the public eye. So if *that's* your concern. . ."

Megan hoped her gulp hadn't registered with the stone-faced woman sitting across the desk. She was so unnerved by the comment, she was afraid her voice would sound puny and pathetic if she tried to speak. She knew she had to confront Bruzek. This was her life on the line. And her children's. And even her misguided husband's, a man she no longer loved, but also no longer hated. But this lawyer cowed her like no one she could remember.

She stole a glance at Kaplowitz, whom she was much more comfortable with. He always looked serious, but now she also detected concern. Possibly even anger. His obvious distaste for what he'd heard pushed her forward.

"I'm not quite sure what you're getting at, Nadia," she lied. "If it's not revealed in a trial, how else would it get out? Joey and I aren't going to say anything. Certainly not the people at the bank. Joey said he told his lawyer a couple of days ago, but other than that who else knows about it?"

Bruzek maintained her pose. "Just something to think about, Megan."

"But I think Megan makes a good point," Kaplowitz said, ending a tense interlude. He was speaking softly, but there was a noticeable pique in his tone. Looking at Megan, he continued. "No one you mentioned would benefit from this information leaking out. And *we* certainly wouldn't say anything. If this were to get out, it clearly wouldn't be in your best interest. And we have an obligation to protect that interest." He locked on to Bruzek. "Breaching that duty would be a serious ethical violation." Then, turning back to Megan, "So I tend to agree with you. If this doesn't go to trial, I doubt you have anything to worry about as far as what your husband did seeing the light of day. And we understand your desire to wrap this up as soon as possible." He met Bruzek's death stare head-on. "All things considered, Nadia, don't you agree?"

Bruzek's mouth looked misshapen as she tried to convert a scowl into a smile. "That, Megan, is why I pay Seth so generously. His keen insight. I'm comfortable that you're aware of what you're possibly giving up by settling this now. And knowing that I've done my job in that regard, by all means, let's try to get this resolved for you."

Megan felt the tension in her body dissolve. "That's great. And, I'll be working with Mr. Kaplowitz as far as the negotiations, right? We have such a good rapport and, to be honest, dealing with two attorneys gets to be a little confusing for me at times." *Get the message, you witch?*

The pretense of amiability gone, Bruzek replied, "That's fine. Good luck to you."

Kaplowitz escorted Megan to the door. "Let's go to my office. We can discuss a few preliminary things."

"Seth. A moment please." Bruzek's contrived smile was back.

"Um, sure. You go ahead, Megan. I'll be there in a minute."

"Okay," she replied with a nod.

As he reached Bruzek's desk he said, "Do I need to sit for this?"

She shook her head. "Not at all. I'll make this quick." After a pause that negated her last statement, she said, "You played that rather well. Frankly, I didn't think you had it in you."

"Look, I did—"

"I wasn't finished," she snapped. "We'll let this one slide. Chalk it up to you testing boundaries. But the next time you challenge me to a dick-measuring contest, you'll be filing for unemployment."

Kaplowitz stood there. Unblinking. "Can I go now?"

"Of course. We wouldn't want to keep Megan waiting."

CHAPTER 41

"I was thinkin' yesterday that maybe this was Patty's way of tellin' us that if she couldn't be here, nobody else should either." Angelo's comment—reflective and sober—came as he sat at the head of the dining room table. "But then I realized that was crazy. That's the last thing Patty would want."

"You're right, Pop," Piza responded. "Strange though, not having anyone else here. I don't ever remember that happening." He poured more brown gravy on his turkey.

"First of all," Mary said, "Patty's here. I can feel 'er. And as far as everybody else . . . hey, stuff happens. I'm sure Nunzio wasn't plannin' on gettin' the shingles."

"True," her son concurred. "And you can't fault Maria and Phil for taking the kids to Disney World, what with the package deal she got through the union." (Maria was Mary's cousin. A Sophia Loren look-alike, but with a mouth that spewed language so foul it wouldn't have been surprising to see a priest following her around, squirting holy water on everything within earshot.)

"Have you spoken to Aunt Rose, Pop?"

"I haven't in a while. But your mother talked to 'er last week."

Mary responded with a head-shake eye-roll combo. "Please, don't remind me. I mean, she's your sister, Angelo, and I love 'er but, Madonna mia, she don't shut up about the heat in Florida. And she's only been down there a month. And it's almost winter! How hot can it be? So I told 'er, why the hell did you agree to move there? Because your husband wanted to? Stupida."

With a nod Angelo said, "Yeah, that's true. She was never good with the heat. But the heat never bothered Filippo. Even when they were livin' up here, he used to wear a cardigan in the summer. Remember?"

"Well," Mary said, "God willin', everyone'll be here for Christmas."

A heartless dejection that must have been awaiting the right moment invaded the room and descended on them.

"Not everyone," Angelo said after a brief silence. His eyes pooled with tears. "I miss my little girl."

Mary reached over and placed a hand on her husband's.

Piza swallowed hard. He knew that if he didn't change the conversation's direction immediately, they'd *all* be weeping in a matter of seconds. "We all miss her, Pop. I'm especially gonna miss her bringing her record player down here and hijacking poor Phil to do the twist with her like a hundred times. It's a good thing he's such a good sport."

Angelo laughed as he dried his eyes. "I'll say. And he's as big a ham as Patty. I swear, the two of 'em shakin' up a storm. . ."

Anecdotes and laughter carried them through the rest of dinner.

"No coat for you, Frankie?" Mary asked as she accepted a hug from Frankie Falco. "And you too, Roger."

"Actually, Mrs. Piza, it's sixty-something out," Roger said.

"Really? I ain't even been outside today."

"Too warm for Thanksgiving," Angelo chimed in as he shook hands with both men.

"You got that right, Mr. P," Frankie said. "But watch. Tomorrow it'll probably be twenty."

Mary flung up her hands. "And they wonder why people get sick. Stupid weather. But I'm glad you boys stopped by." She gave Frankie a wistful look. "I miss the old days. Thanksgiving night. All'a you would come over, and I'd heat up food from the afternoon, and you all ate like you were starvin'. And then you'd clean out the desserts."

A grinning Frankie answered with, "Hey, if it means that much to you, Mrs. P, I can still eat like that. So I'm game if you are."

"Okay," Mary said with unbounded enthusiasm. "I'll heat stuff up for you right now. You want sweet potatoes with—"

Frankie extended his arms, palms out, as he laughed. "I was just kidding. But I actually wouldn't mind some dessert."

Not one to readily accept rejection when it came to food, Mary said, "You sure you don't want nothin' else? 'Cause it'll only take me a minute. C'mon. There's so much left over."

"I'm positive. Really. But thank you."

She cast a hopeful look at Roger.

"Same here, Mrs. Piza. I'm good. But I'm sure I could squeeze in a little dessert."

"Okay," Mary said through a shrug. "Pastries are in the fridge, and the cake's still out inside. And there's beer and wine in the fridge too."

They all talked for a while in the dining room, then Mary and Angelo got up to go into the living room to watch television.

"And you watched your football, Angelo, so now it's my turn."

"All right, all right. Did I say anythin'? Why you always gotta start in?"

With a laugh Frankie said, "Gotta love 'em." He took a sip of beer. "So, what's going on with Strikes? Anything you can talk about?"

That gave Piza an opening to run two issues by Roger. First, he wanted to get a definitive reason why Lisa—a precocious ten-year-old—would be taken in by Candy's lies; choose a virtual stranger over a caring father. Second, he was hoping for reassurance that the child was going to be okay.

He filled them in, mentioning nothing (of course) about the embezzlement.

"Wow," Roger said. "This Candy person is toxic." The way he said it led Piza to believe the psychologist hadn't mentioned anything to Frankie about meeting with him and Sabatini. "I feel horrible for that poor child."

"Tell me about it," Piza responded. "Ya know, something that intrigued me about this whole thing, Rog, was that Lisa believed Candy. I mean, considering how close she and her father had always been. And especially since, according to him, he told each of the girls he loved them every time he dropped them off after visitation. Although God only knows how often Candy was filling Lisa's head with that crap. So, I dunno, could it be it was just constant repetition getting the upper hand?"

"Well, I think that could be part of it," Roger said. "But consider the dynamic. Candy's telling her that her father doesn't love her because he abandoned the family. Yet, *he's* telling her he loves her every time he sees her. You'd think he would have the advantage. He's her father, and they have a loving history that goes far beyond her exposure to Candy. But every time he drops Lisa off, despite the fact he tells her he loves her, what does he do?"

A sad smile appeared as Piza replied, "He leaves."

"Exactly. To Lisa, he's constantly proving Candy's point."

Through a grimace Frankie said, "That's just awful. A kid should never have to go through that. You think she's gonna be all right, Rog?"

"Yeah, that was my next question," Piza said.

A nod from Roger. "I do. Children are remarkably resilient. And from what you've said, Tony, it doesn't sound like there were any underlying problems between father and daughter before Candy's appearance. Plus now that her parents . . . and her therapist . . . know what the problem is, they can tackle it head-on. So I'm optimistic. They'll have to be careful though, with a divorce seeming imminent."

"Yeah," Piza said. "Closes the door on any hope of her parents getting back together. Something *both* girls are gonna have to adjust to."

"Well, it seems like Strikes and Megan have their heads on straight," Frankie offered. "At least when it comes to their kids. And now that it looks like they're gonna resolve everything, there's likely to be less drama I would think. So all in all . . . I guess there's hope."

"Hear! Hear!" Piza said, hoisting his beer bottle. "Here's to hope. And Happy Thanksgiving, you guys."

"Happy Thanksgiving," Frankie and Roger responded in unison as they raised their bottles as well.

When the doorbell rang, Angelo was conked out on his lounge chair, and Mary and Piza were on the couch watching *Miracle on Thirty-Fourth Street*. It was their traditional holiday season kickoff event.

"You expecting anyone, Ma?" a wary Piza asked.

"At eight thirty? 'Course not."

"Okay. Stay here. Let me answer it."

He reached the front door and checked the peephole. A grin spread across his face as he opened the door. "Well this is a welcome surprise," he said. "Happy Thanksgiving, Lizzie."

"Same to you," she replied as they hugged.

"Ma," he yelled. "It's—"

"I can see who it is," Mary shouted back as she practically sprinted toward them.

Elizabeth moved to intercept her, enveloping her in a warm embrace which was immediately reciprocated. "Hi, Aunt Mary. Happy Thanksgiving."

"Oh, same to you, sweetheart."

"I hope you don't mind me showing up so late," the girl said. "But I can't remember not being here for Thanksgiving. And Dad was so uncomfortable and Cheryl looked exhausted. They were gonna lie down. So here I am."

"It's never too late for you to come over," Mary said. "You know that. How's Nunzio doin'? He in a lot'a pain?"

"Well, you know him. He could have a five-inch gash on his arm, and he'd try to convince you it was a paper cut."

"Well, hopefully this'll be gone soon. I feel terrible. But he better be here for Christmas or we're gonna disown 'im."

A chuckle from Elizabeth. "Believe me, we'd have to tie him down for him to miss Christmas."

"That's what I like to hear," Mary said. "So, you wanna eat somethin'?"

"No, no, Aunt Mary. I'm still stuffed from dinner. Cheryl went all out. But I could go for a cup of tea, if it's not too much trouble."

Mary waved her off. "Don't be silly. I'll put the water on. I was just about to make coffee for me and Anthony. Go in the livin' room and say hi to your uncle. It'll give us a break from his snorin'. Him and his sinuses. I swear."

When the movie was over, Angelo and Mary said good night

and headed up to bed. Elizabeth got off the other lounge chair and took Mary's seat on the couch. "So, how did everything go today? With Patty. Your parents handle it okay? You?"

Through a tepid shrug Piza said, "It was rough at first. It was so evident a piece was missing. This conspicuous void in the tableau. But we got through it. As much as I missed all you guys, in a way I'm almost glad no one else was here. Kind of forced us to accept the reality of it right off the bat."

"Well, I was upset thinking about her, and worrying how you guys were doing. I'm glad it wasn't debilitating."

"Thanks, Lizzie."

"So, at the risk of pushing you into the rabbit hole and ruining the day, what's going on with you and Theresa?"

Piza laughed. "Our relationship *is* a bit surreal, I admit. I called her this morning to wish her a Happy Thanksgiving."

"Oh! Great!"

"Yeah. We talked for about a half-hour. She was going to a homeless shelter to help serve food." He chuckled. "What a shock. Then she was heading to her assistant's family's house for dinner. Which I was happy about. I mean, the thought of her spending the day alone. . ."

"No, absolutely. That's great. This makes . . . the fifth time you've spoken since the end of July?"

"Good God, woman. You're keeping score?"

Elizabeth followed a melodramatic sigh with, "Anthony, Anthony, Anthony. Haven't you figured out by now that you two are the sole focus of my attention?"

He smirked. "What about work? And your personal happiness?"

Flicking her wrist, she said, "All secondary, my friend." A smile dawned then gradually dissolved. "So, seriously, are you ever gonna go back down there to see her? She calls you a couple of times. You call her a couple of times. According to you, the phone calls are great. Warm. Funny. And yet here you sit. At least *she* has an excuse. She doesn't own a car. But you?"

Piza's turn for an overdone exhale. "Elizabeth, Elizabeth, Elizabeth. It's a delicate process. You can't rush art."

"Art? If your relationship is art, it's a Jackson Pollock."

"Hmm. Perhaps. Unstructured . . . in a structured sort of way. Yet, still wondrous."

"Tony. . ."

"Fine. I don't know what's going on. Yes, our conversations are great. We discuss a million things. Some frivolous. Most substantive. But when it comes to 'the' issue, we talk over it, under it, and around it. And what's the purpose of my going down there if we're just gonna do the same thing in person. If anything, I think that'd make it more difficult. At least we can't look at each other through the phone." A brief silence. "I mean, who knows? Maybe this just wasn't meant to be."

Elizabeth pulled a face. "If one of you was abducted by aliens, then yeah, maybe you'd say it wasn't meant to be. But short of that I—"

"You seem to have a fixation with extraterrestrials, Lizzie. You might wanna get that looked into."

"Don't interrupt me when I'm about to say something deep. I don't think I've ever known two people who have such inexplicable misgivings about being happy. You love each other. I mean really, this shouldn't be that hard." She huffed her frustration. "Listen, circumstances being what they are, the ball's in your court. So unless you're an emotional masochist, do something for God's sake."

Piza didn't respond immediately. Then, "Wasn't really *that* deep." Silence from Elizabeth. "Okay, you're right. And you're not telling me anything I don't already know or think about every day. In point of fact, I hate letting our . . . *thing* just float around out there, like a balloon being buffeted by some fickle wind currents."

Elizabeth stared at him. "Now *that* was profound." She broke into a grin, eliciting a laugh. "Little contrived maybe, but still kind of poetic."

He laughed again. "Gimme a break. It's late." Drawing a deep breath, he said, "I know I have to do something. This is no way to live." A somber pause. "But hey, enough about me. What've you been up to?" A diabolical look surfaced and he said, "What have we here? Is that a blush I'm detecting? Is love in the air, my dear?" He maniacally rubbed his hands together and thrust himself to within a few inches of her face. "Tell Cousin Tony everything."

"First of all, I don't blush, coffee breath," she said as she pushed him away. "But . . . if you must know, I've been on a couple of dates with someone. From the hospital."

"Oh God. Please don't tell me it's another pediatric fence-sitter."

"No. A nurse."

If Piza straightened up any quicker he'd have popped a disk. "A nurse? Holy crap, Lizzie. I— How could I not have known this about you? That you were, um, open to that. I mean I'm thrilled for you, but. . ."

"He's a male nurse, you idiot."

"Oh! Okay. It's just that when I hear 'nurse' I think. . . Shit. Clearly I'm not as evolved as I thought. So, okay, this is great. What's his name?"

"Greg. Santucci. Works in the ICU."

"Unmarried? No kids? Please say yes."

"Yes."

"How old?"

"Thirty-one."

Piza puckered his lips and nodded. "Okay. Same as you. So far, so good. So, what drew you to him?"

"Well, let's see. He's compassionate. Funny. Bright. Big

reader. I knew you'd like that. In fact, he reminds me a lot of you."

"Oh my God! You must marry this man immediately. You've hit the jackpot. Made it to the top of Everest. Found the pot of gold at the end of the rainbow. Feel free to throw in as many additional 'ultimate success' metaphors as you'd like."

"So, so humble. Actually, wiseguy, he *is* different from you in one way."

"And what would that be?"

"He's a really good dancer."

Piza's pout wasn't entirely contrived. "What're you talking about? I'm a terrific dancer."

"Slow dances maybe. But fast dance? Uh, no. You may be a good athlete, but you're kinda stiff on the dance floor."

"Stiff? Are you nuts? I'm like silk. I'm the definition of 'smooth'."

"Smooth? Visualize a robot having a seizure." She got up and demonstrated.

When she flopped back onto the couch, Piza looked at his watch and said, "Gee. Look at the time. Shouldn't you be going?"

She gave him a "very-funny" look. "Anyway, I'd really like you to meet him. I dunno, Tony. I have a feeling about this. It's different."

He answered her with a smile and, "It makes me incredibly happy to hear that."

After a contented sigh she said, "Okay then. I really should be heading back north. I'm working tomorrow."

"You sure? Because—"

"No, it's late. But I'm really, really glad I stopped by. The thought of not seeing you guys on Thanksgiving. . ."

He walked her to the door and they exchanged a hug and kiss. Watching her drive away, he was thankful she was a part of his life.

As he sat on the couch, TV off, Elizabeth's words resurfaced.

About him and Theresa loving each other. "This shouldn't be that hard." And yet it was. He wasn't used to this. Being interminably trapped by doubt. He felt as if he needed some outside force to extricate him and shove him in the direction he needed to go—whether that path led to Theresa or not.

That catalyst was waiting in the wings.

CHAPTER 42

"What's today? The nineteenth?" Sabatini asked.

"All day," Piza said as they sat in the conference room.

"Okay. Okay. Little slow on the uptake this morning. End of the week fatigue. Plus I haven't had my coffee yet."

Piza thought about offering him a cup, but decided it would only give his client an excuse to linger. "Yeah, I know *that* feeling."

"Okay, do I have to sign anywhere else?"

"Nope. That's it," the lawyer said as he gathered and jogged the pages of the settlement agreement. "I'll have Gloria put your copy in an envelope for you. We'll hand-deliver two copies to Kaplowitz today. We'll put the divorce through on Monday. Eight thirty, at Judge Williams's. Take about fifteen minutes. In and out."

Sabatini's arms dropped to the sides of his chair. "I can't believe this is finally over. It's like after that hearing . . . this, this giant curtain lifted and the scene changed from night to day. Animosity. Anxiety. Gone. Mostly, anyway."

"Well, when people set their minds to actually resolving their issues. . ." Piza picked up the signed settlement agreement. "You're sure you understand everything in here, right? Everything we went over?"

"Yeah. It's great. Um, not to repeat myself, but you're positive this provision about the church annulment isn't gonna be a problem?"

Piza wore his waning patience. "Yes. For the third time. All it says is that you'll use reasonable efforts to cooperate with her when she applies for the annulment, 'reasonable' being the operative word. Look, I don't know what she's gonna try to base it on, considering how long you've been married. But a couple of the acceptable reasons are sufficiently vague, so I guess she's got a shot."

"Yeah, you're probably right. Anyway, I think it only makes a difference if she wants to get remarried in a church. Who knows if that's even gonna happen?"

"Got me. On another note, how are things with Lisa?"

"Getting better. Not all the way there yet, but we're definitely making progress."

"Well, that's good to hear." After a pause, Piza stood up. "Okay, so that about wraps—"

"Listen, I have some other news, Ton."

The lawyer slowly lowered himself back into his chair. "What's going on?"

"I met with my brother Saturday." An awkward laugh. "Desperate times call for desperate measures, I guess. Anyway, I asked him if I could borrow ten grand. Told him money was tight. That even though Megan got her realtor's license, she really wasn't able to go full tilt yet. Oh, she signed on with a new broker, by the way. Wouldn't stay at the one where Candy is, obviously. So anyway, I told my brother the house needs some work. Kids needed stuff. Did a real song and dance. And if you can believe it, he said yes. Without making me feel worthless, amazingly."

Piza lifted his fingers a few inches off the table. "Okay, well that's good. What're you really gonna use the money for?"

"Geez, Tony, whaddya think?"

"I have no idea, Strikes" was the peevish reply. "With your recent history of genius decisions, maybe you'll hit Atlantic City. Put it all on red. I don't feel like guessing, so if you wanna tell me, then tell me."

"Not sure I had that coming, but——"

"Really?"

"Look, I didn't come here to get into an argument. Okay?" He puffed out a breath. "I'm gonna use five thousand of it to make those accounts whole. The ones I took from up here. Some of it I'm gonna use to pay what I owe you. I know you've let me slide a little on that. The rest'll be for things for the girls. I can't believe Christmas is next Thursday already."

"Okay then."

"Wait, there's more. I'm not sure why my brother's changed. Mellowed. Maybe it was having a kid. Maybe that heart scare last year. Who knows? But get this . . . he's opening two new dry cleaning stores in May. Edison and Piscataway. And he asked me if I wanted to manage them. Twice the money I'm making now. Full benefits. 401(k). I almost fell off the couch."

Piza's eyebrows dipped. "Okay. Wasn't expecting *that*. What'd you say?"

"Whaddya think I said? How could I turn that down?"

"And if he reverts to being an asshole?"

"Well, honestly, I don't think that's gonna happen," Sabatini said. "Not after what I saw Saturday. But even if he does, I don't know that I really have a choice. Comes down to dollars, plain and simple. Plus both towns are a hop, skip, and a jump from Iselin. It means I can move back down near the kids."

"True. But you need to realize something. If your income goes up significantly, Megan has the right to go back to court for an increase in child support. Possibly alimony as well, depending on how well her real estate gig goes."

A pained expression accompanied, "Shit. But ya know what? If it's for the kids I don't have a problem with it. Alimony . . . that's a different story. But if it comes down to it, I think Megan and I can work it out. She's been solid during these negotiations." There was a grudging concession in his smile. "Listen to me. Singing her praises. Someone I detested a month ago."

"Well, granted it was in her best interest, but she did keep your secret. I mean if she'd been pissed enough to toss logic out the window, who knows? You could be facing a very different future right now." With a complacent smirk he said, "Considering she kind of holds your life in her hands, you don't really have a choice but to be nice to her."

Sabatini uttered a wimpish, "I guess. So anyway, I may need your services again, assuming this thing with my brother comes through. I might have to get out of my lease. I mean I'd only have three months left on it at that point, but I'm not really in a position to shell out money up here while I'm renting a place down there. Think we could do that?"

Piza stood up, and his client followed suit. "It's unlikely you could break it. But your landlord does have an obligation to mitigate her damages."

"Meaning?"

"Meaning she has to make a good faith effort to find another tenant. She can't just sit back and let the three months go by. So if she can find someone quickly, you could be off the hook."

Sabatini gave a satisfied nod. "Okay. And I guess if need be, I could just commute down there for the three months and avoid the hassle altogether. It's not *that* long a ride. But hey, something we can talk about again down the road."

"Well, you can talk to *somebody* about it. But it won't be me."

"Huh? Why not?"

"Because after this Monday, I don't want anything to do with you."

Piza eased through the rest of Friday. The office atmosphere was relaxed, as everyone looked ahead to the shortened workweek before Christmas. Plus, the office Christmas party was that evening, held each year in the wreath-and-garland-adorned conference room. It was an event Piza always looked forward to. A chance for the firm's lawyers and the office staff to mingle and chat about anything but the law—entertaining stories excepted. The generous array of food and drink played a healthy role (figuratively, at least) in bolstering spirits.

The lightened holiday mood notwithstanding, the morning's encounter still bothered him. Not because he'd expelled Sabatini from his life. Or the desolation in the man's eyes when he did it, his former friend's plea for them to try to get past the ugliness answered with an emotionless, "It's too late for that."

No, the confrontation irked him because it reminded him that he'd been duped; never an acceptable circumstance, but all the more untenable within the framework of his profession. He'd worn a wide smile the previous month, when he mentioned to Nia about being inconsolable on those rare occasions he believed he'd fallen short of perfection. A humorous delivery, but a troubling truth.

Shortly after five, Gloria poked her head into his office. "C'mon, you laggard. The festivities have already started. Time to kick off our shoes and party."

"Seriously, Gloria?"

"Okay, the kicking off the shoes thing may have been a bit much. But you love this shindig. So get off your duff and escort your decrepit old secretary down the hall."

"Decrepit?" he scoffed. "You're in better shape than me."

"I know that. But I was shooting for the pity incentive, as implausible as it was."

"Fine. I'll spare you from sacrificing any more of your dignity." He got up, went to the door, and offered his arm. "Shall we, my queen?"

When they reached the bustling room, Gloria peeled off in response to a wave from some of the other secretaries. "Behave," she told Piza.

"Yes, Mother."

Cecilia, the receptionist—dressed in red leggings, a Christmas-plaid skirt, fir green blouse, and elf cap—flitted across the room to greet him. "Hi, Tony. I'm kind of the unofficial hostess for the party. Do you want anything?"

"No, not right now. But thank you. Might I say you're a Christmas vision in that outfit. The elf cap's a nice touch."

"Thanks. I wasn't sure if I should wear it. But my boyfriend said I look sexy with it on."

Piza gave her an earnest nod. "Well, there you go. What better reason for wearing it to a Christmas party? Is your boyfriend also an elf?"

Her eyes crinkled as she covered her mouth to hide a titter, as if he'd said something she was bashful about laughing at. Maintaining her apparent commitment to concealment, she leaned in and whispered, "Don't tell anyone, but I think you're the funniest lawyer in this place."

With genuine warmth he said, "Is there any doubt that you're my favorite receptionist of all time?"

"Well that was really sweet," she answered. "Thanks, Tony."

"You're very welcome."

Nia joined them. "Nice party, huh?"

"It's great!" Cecilia said. "So much food and . . . everything."

"Well I'm glad you're enjoying it. Do you mind if I borrow Tony for a sec?"

"No, 'course not. I have to go see if anybody wants anything anyway. Bye."

"Sweet kid," Piza said as she waltzed away.

"She is. Although her intercom routine takes a bit of getting used to."

Piza laughed. "This is true. So, what's cookin'?"

"How're you making out with your friend's case?"

"Good. We're settled. Gonna put the divorce through on Monday."

"Good for you. Guess the skids got greased once his . . . 'indiscretions' came to light. And I'm sure it didn't hurt to have that bizarre realtor person out of the picture. Did the wife ever hear from her again?"

"She did. When we had our first sit-down to discuss settlement terms, she mentioned that Candy called her the evening of the hearing. Weeping. Begging forgiveness. Megan . . . that's the wife . . . told her the judge had signed a restraining order, and that she'd call the cops if she ever contacted her again. I had our process server hand-deliver a copy of the order to her the morning after the hearing. But two days later, Megan saw her driving by the house, at a crawl. Then again a few minutes later. Like she was circling the block. So she called the cops. One of them came over and parked outside the house. Sure enough, Candy passes by again. But this time she cruises by at normal speed. Obviously, she saw the cop car and got spooked. That was the end of that."

Nia's expression unveiled her skepticism. "I'm kind of surprised she backed off, considering how obsessed she was."

"I was too. Maybe she realized it was hopeless. Or she could've just been scared of getting arrested. Plus, that could jeopardize her realtor's license, depending on what they charged her with."

"Good point." Motioning with her head, she said, "Come out in the hall with me for a minute."

"Um, okay. This sounds ominous."

"Only if you consider getting fired 'ominous'," Nia said as they exited the room. "No one here can stand you, so we figured it would have maximum punitive impact if we canned you at the Christmas party."

"Makes sense," he replied. "God knows I deserve it. You should announce it when we go back in."

"Oh, I plan to, ace."

They walked several feet down the hall. "Okay," she said when they stopped. "In all seriousness. We had our end-of-year meeting with the accountant this morning. Bottom line is income for the year wasn't what we'd hoped for. So, unfortunately, we're not gonna be able to hire someone new to take over for you in matrimonial. I know how much you wanted to transition to litigation, but we just can't do it right now. I'm really sorry, Tony. I debated holding off telling you, because I didn't want to put a damper on your Christmas. But I promised I'd tell you what was going on as soon as I knew, and I felt I owed you that. I'd have told you this afternoon, but I was out at a meeting."

He'd known this was a possibility. Yet, for some reason, he hadn't prepared himself for it. (An intellectual lapse to be analyzed at some point.) But for now, he had to concentrate on fighting through the instant emptiness and tell his boss . . . his friend . . . that he appreciated her respect for him.

And lie to her that everything was fine.

CHAPTER 43

When he told her, she said she wasn't completely shocked. Not by the decision anyway. The speed, she admitted, was unexpected. A life-changing choice in the space of a weekend.

As Piza sat in his car, accompanied by the scant, pleasant aroma of gasoline, he was replaying his meeting with Nia Bradley from Monday of the prior week. The attendant's light rap on his window jogged him into the present. He paid the man, heaved a purposeful breath, and eased onto the highway.

Nia had been gracious. (He'd expected nothing less.) And she was open about being saddened at the thought of him leaving. A sentiment he returned. She asked if he'd consider working through January, to give them time to find someone to replace him. He said he'd certainly stay the month, although he doubted anyone could truly fill his shoes. That had garnered a laugh and a promise to have a portrait of him prominently displayed in the waiting room. He took the opportunity to tell her something he'd given thought to over the weekend.

"Can I make a suggestion, Nia?"

"Of course."

"Seth Kaplowitz. The kid on the other side of the Sabatini case. He's a little rough around the edges, and kind of serious. I mentioned to you about the situation with his daughter. But he's smart, quick, and thorough. You're one of the few firms that pay as much as Bruzek. I think he's miserable there, and clearly he's uncomfortable with her methods. If he were here, in this environment, with you mentoring him, I think he'd flourish. Might be worth putting out a feeler."

"Interesting. Definitely something to think about."

After meeting with Nia, he'd taken Gloria to lunch to let her know. It broke his heart when the no-nonsense woman he'd come to care so much about teared up. But she rebounded quickly, telling him that if he didn't keep in touch she'd track him down and do things that would make the Spanish Inquisition look like a prance around the Maypole.

He'd asked Gloria not to say anything, and trusted Nia to break the news to everyone else (other than the other partners, of course) as she saw fit.

As far as the two women knew, he was leaving because he needed a change. A different area of the law to pursue. Which was true enough. What he hadn't revealed was that he didn't believe this recent turn of events was simply happenstance.

***

Twenty-two minutes. That's how long it had taken Piza to drive from Cherry Hill, New Jersey to Philadelphia. *Not that bad, really, for four-twenty on a Tuesday.*

As he drove down Kensington Avenue and approached Theresa's building he felt chilly and turned up the heat, readily acknowledging that nerves were the likely cause. *Perfectly normal, buddy. This is a big deal.* The lights in the nursery school were off. Not unexpected for the week after Christmas.

"What's with the parking around here?" he muttered as he

scoured the street for an opening. He ended up parking around the corner, about a block from Shorty's. As he walked past the restaurant he sneaked a peek through the window, targeting Theresa's corner table (empty), then quickly averted his eyes for fear of Jasmine spotting him and giving chase with a utensil of death in hand.

When he entered the building, he saw that each apartment had a buzzer. But there was no intercom. *What building doesn't have an intercom, for God's sake? This could be dicey. No breezy, vestibule repartee to ease the transition to face-to-face. Assuming she's home.* Adjusting his tie knot, he pressed the button for 3B. A ten-second lag, then a return buzz. With a "Here goes nothing" he opened the door.

The landing area was brighter than he'd expected, at least in terms of lighting. But he soon realized that was because two of the three lamps suspended from the ceiling were missing a covering. And there was nothing cheery about the worn-out etched marble floors, the chipped-paint tan walls that bore the vestiges of insufficiently scrubbed graffiti, or the narrow, dull mahogany staircase that was probably elegant once.

Yet, he was smiling. The sad state of the structure had succumbed to the pleasurable convergence of cooking smells that reminded him of the South Bronx building his family lived in for the first few years of his life. A hive of relatives of varying degree, some of whom still lived there, unwilling to abandon the old neighborhood.

The smile dissolved as his mission shoved nostalgia aside. He closed his eyes and slowed his breathing, to little avail. *This is crazy. What's gonna happen is gonna happen. Just start climbing.*

By the time he reached the third floor, he was breathing hard. *Must be my overcoat. Weighing me down. I know I'm in better shape than this. Theresa does this a few times a day? She must have lungs like Secretariat.* He paused a few moments to settle down and catch his breath. *Okay. 3B. Ah, there you are. Seriously? No peephole? I sincerely hope you don't open the door without asking who's there, my dear.*

He knocked twice. More tentatively than he'd intended.

"Yes, who is it?"

Good. At least she asked. "Well hello there. Santa here. Just checking to make sure I didn't miss your"—

The door swung open.

—"house on Christmas."

"Anthony?" It was more an exclamation than a question as her eyes widened.

"In the flesh. Is, uh, this a bad time, because I—"

"No, no. Not at all," she said as an uncertain smile turned into a grin. "Just caught me off-guard is all. You didn't say anything about coming down, when we talked Christmas night. Come in."

"You sure I'm not interrupting anything?" he asked as he crossed the threshold into the invigorating scent of lemon furniture polish and pine needles. "I kind of wanted to surprise you."

"No, absolutely not. I was just reading. Come. Sit. Would you like something to drink?"

"No, thanks. Not right now anyway." *Sure. Invite yourself for a leisurely stay. I'm such an asshole.* "Looks very festive in here. And a real tree. My kinda girl. Although how you got it up three flights is beyond me."

"Oh, it was a community effort, believe me. Here. Sit on the couch," she said as she grabbed a strewn afghan and tossed it onto a sturdy-looking wooden rocking chair. "And let me have your coat." She took it and lay it on top of the afghan. "Excuse the mess," she added as she lightly tugged at the bottom of the light-blue denim shirt hanging loose over her jeans. "I wasn't expecting company."

"Mess? Are you kidding? The place looks spotless . . . yet lived in. Isn't that what a home's supposed to look like? It's a nice apartment."

"Thanks. 'Lived in'. There's a nifty little euphemism I'll have to remember." Had she not followed it with a laugh, he might have been embarrassed. "Actually, I think it's probably a little spartan for most people's taste."

"Well, first of all, knowing you I'm not surprised. But hey, a couch, a very cool rocker. Tasteful throw rug to add some warmth and still showcase the wood floor. Nice little coffee table. Good size bookcase. I remember you were a reader. Hmm. Gotta get you a bigger TV though. This one looks like an exhibit from the 1939 World's Fair. Ha! Just kidding." *Oh my God, what are you taking inventory? Shut up already.* He stood and walked to a wall—anything to stop the gush of gobbledygook he seemed unable to control. "Did you take these photos?"

"Uh-huh. Lot of history around this area. Tried to capture it as best I could."

"Lot of sorrow too, I see. The homeless. The starkness of the black-and-white is really powerful." He wandered the room. "Oh my God, tell me that's not the same guitar from twelve years ago?" he said, gesturing to the instrument propped up in a corner.

Another laugh. "One and the same. Hey, if it ain't broke. . ."

"True, true." He made his way back to the couch and sat at one end. She sat at the other end, toward the front edge of the cushion.

"So, you look nice," she said. "Double-breasted gray pinstripe. Pretty snazzy. Although you certainly didn't have to get all dressed up for *me*."

"Well, in the interest of full disclosure, I didn't. I was in Cherry Hill before I came here."

"Oh. Work-related?"

"Um, in a manner of speaking. Job interview."

Concern swept across her face. "Oh. What happened with your other job?"

"Nothing nefarious. I mean, they didn't fire me or anything like that. But you remember I was looking to move from family law into litigation, right?"

"Yes. You said you weren't happy doing divorce work anymore."

"Well, turns out the firm wasn't in a financial position to allow me to do that. So I decided to move on. But they were great about it. In fact, one of the partners set up the interview for me. Old law school buddy of his manages the Cherry Hill firm, and he knew they were looking to expand. They made me a nice offer, by the way. So I grabbed it."

"Well, that's great. Congratulations. When did all this happen?"

"Um, I told my boss last Monday. I didn't say anything to you Christmas night because I didn't wanna, ya know, dampen the holiday spirit with shop talk." *Or risk tipping my hand.*

"Oh. Well, I wouldn't have minded." The quizzical look she'd been wearing found its voice. "But Cherry Hill's a long way from Hackensack. There weren't any jobs available up around there?"

He clasped his hands to prevent them from betraying him as his anxiety surged. "I imagine there were. But it's a heck of a lot easier to commute from Philly to Cherry Hill than it is to north Jersey."

Her expression said she'd heard his words but couldn't grasp the meaning. "I'm— I'm confused. Commute from Philly?"

If he clenched his hands any tighter they'd have melded into a single appendage. "So, here's the thing. Even if I didn't have the interview, I was coming to talk to you." He thought she might tense up, but there was no sign of it. "I'm hopelessly in love with you, Theresa. And if I didn't do everything I could to try to make this work, I'd be second-guessing myself for the rest of my life. Wondering every day if. . . Well, you get what I'm saying."

She radiated the deepest blush he could ever remember seeing. She said nothing, but still didn't seem panicked.

Somewhat relieved, he continued. "And I don't mean to be presumptuous, but I can't help thinking it would be the same for you. Listen, I know how much this place means to you. And that's the thing, see? Just from the stories you've told me, I believe you're the glue that holds this neighborhood together." She shook her head. "Well, you may not wanna believe it. But the people around here, the ones whose children you take care of every day? They need you. And they trust you." He freed his hands and allowed his body to relax as best he could. "This is my really wordy way of saying that I'd never ask or expect you to stop doing this. Leave this place. So I'm coming to *you*."

She sat there staring at him. As if she were frozen in the moment. As much as he would have done anything to get her to respond, he knew he couldn't. This was her move, and he had to let the scene play out.

After a light sigh she said, "Now would you like something to drink?"

Oh man, this is the same thing she did in the restaurant that time. The 'more tea and lemonade' thing. And look at how that went.

Squelching his fear, he answered, "Okay. What've you got?"

"Let's see. Grape juice, hot tea, beer, or water, obviously. No lemonade or coffee, I'm afraid."

"Um, will you have a beer if I have one?"

"Sure." She got up and went to the kitchen, a small room he'd caught a glimpse of on his living room tour. "You want a glass?" she called out.

"Only if it would impress you."

"It wouldn't," she said with a smile as she re-entered the room, holding two bottles. She handed him one and sat again.

He raised his. "Well, here's to the continuation of an awkward conversation."

She raised her bottle a few inches in return. "So, let me——"

"Oh, can I just say something before you go on? I want you to know that this isn't like some conditional thing for me. One way or the other, I'm committed to moving here. Unless, of course, you tell me straight up you don't love me anymore. I just wanted to make that clear."

She puffed out the slightest of breaths. "Well, I can't say I don't love you, because that would be a lie. But you already knew that or I don't think you'd have put it up for discussion." Donning a mischievous look, she said, "I do feel obligated, however, to let you know that one of my four-year-olds proposed to me last week."

His face clouded. "Dammit. Another suitor. I may be forced to engage him in combat. Perhaps an arm-wrestling contest."

"He's big for his age."

"In that case, I'll have to give it more thought."

She flashed a grin, then adjusted herself in her seat. "So, despite the fact you dropped this bombshell on me, I'm feeling remarkably clearheaded right now. I didn't know whether this moment, or something like it, would ever come. But I've thought about it. Pretty much every day. And the thing is, I'm afraid. I have no compunction about saying that to you. We've opened up to each other about so many other things in our phone conversations, it wouldn't be right to sidestep my concern."

"Good," he said, although unsure what was coming.

She took a sip. "Before you left the restaurant in June, I told you we lived in different worlds that were, in my opinion, intractably at odds. And that because I knew I couldn't bring myself to leave my world, you and I being together would mean you'd have to conform to my way of life. And I didn't think you'd be able to do that."

"I see I'm not the only one who had that conversation etched in their brain." His expression conveyed nothing, because he still wasn't sure where this was going.

"Well, it was important. Anyway, you told me you should be the one to determine whether you could make that move. But I could tell you weren't sure you could do it. Now you've suddenly committed yourself to being here. Which I appreciate more than you could imagine. But I don't think that alters the underlying problem."

He set his beer bottle on the table and answered with a restrained, "Meaning?"

"Meaning being able to make this work would involve more than you getting an apartment down here. I think it would mean fundamentally changing who you are. And I truly believe that when people reach a certain age . . . younger than both of us . . . they simply can't change anymore. And—"

"But that's—"

Her raised hand cut him off. "Just hear me out. When we hit that mark, no matter how much it looks like we're reshaping ourselves, it's all just presentation. The chocolate squiggle on the dessert plate. Despite our efforts, we already are who we are. Characteristics. Habits. Social expectations. Permanently ingrained."

There was a pause as they stared at each other. She—anticipative. He—circumspect. Then he said, "I won't get into your theory about the ability to change. Let's just say we'll agree to disagree on that. But you know what's interesting? As much as you and I know about each other, it's amazing how little that actually is. Just the fact that you think I'm incapable of adjusting to how you live. That I'd have to 'change' for that to happen."

"It's just how I feel," she said.

"Okay, let me level with you. You're right about June. Back then, in that restaurant, I wasn't positive I could do this . . . as desperately as I wanted to believe I could. You picked up on that, and your change theory kicked in and *instantly* led you to conclude that you and I . . . the concept of 'us' . . . couldn't happen. But I've been analyzing what 'us' would mean." His brow furrowed. "'Analyzing' probably isn't the greatest word. I don't mean some cold, ya know, scrutiny. Just the logic of things. It's how my brain works. So please don't take it the wrong way."

There was comfort in her tone. "I didn't."

A relieved nod. "So, a couple of things came out of my . . . 'introspection'. First, it confirmed what I already knew. That if

I wanted to reach the highest level of happiness available to me, I needed to be with you. The second thing was more of a revelation. And it goes directly to your concerns. As far as habits and characteristics, every couple lives with those. That's not an issue. The only thing that could realistically be an impediment would be social needs . . . or 'expectations' as you put it. But what I realized is that mine aren't all that different from yours."

"That's hard to believe."

"Well, it's hard to believe if you have a preconceived notion of my lifestyle. I think you're making assumptions based on my profession." He became more animated. Apprehension gone or at least sufficiently suppressed. Excited to share his conclusions and open her eyes to the truth he'd discovered. He stood up and started pacing. "Granted, on its face my way of life might not seem quite as uncluttered as yours. But in terms of what matters to me? Like I said before, we're not all that different."

Her skepticism hadn't appeared to diminish. She hadn't said anything, or conveyed it with facial cues, but he could sense it.

"Okay. You want the reality of my life, Theresa? I wear nice suits because I have to. But I'm much more comfortable in jeans. Wanna know how I spend my weekend mornings? In front of the television in a tee shirt and boxer shorts, eating cereal. No silk pajamas. And in the evening? No smoking jacket while sitting in front of the hearth, sipping brandy."

He hadn't been sure what her reaction might be, but he certainly wasn't expecting laughter.

"What's so funny?" he asked, his attempt at indignation falling apart as he watched her struggle to regain her composure.

"I'm so sorry," she finally got out. "It's just that I don't know what's more disturbing . . . visualizing you in boxer shorts slurping a bowl of cereal, or the thought of you sitting down to breakfast in silk pajamas. Breakfast is served, m'lord."

He'd started laughing as well. "For your information, I look absolutely fetching in my boxers. And I could pull off silk jammies no problem."

She replied with a grin and, "I don't doubt it."

Heaving a sigh, he said, "Listen. I rent an apartment in Jersey. I could've bought a house, but I didn't. Because it really wasn't important to me. I hate big parties and anything that involves wearing a tux. Except maybe a wedding. I'm infinitely more meat-and-potatoes than foie gras. The only luxury I really allow myself is my car, for no reason other than it's fun." He sat back down, locking eyes with her. "I don't care about prestige, Theresa. I care about you."

She nestled into her corner of the couch, saying nothing. Then, "You must be one hell of a lawyer."

"I have my moments," he said. "Speaking honestly helps."

She picked up her beer, took another sip, and placed it back on the table. Bringing her knees up to her chest, she hugged her legs. "So, what if we do this? Try to make a go of it. And you discover at some point that it was a mistake. That as sincere as your beliefs and intentions are today, you just can't hack it. The lifestyle or whatever. And you're stuck. And your resentment of me grows and grows because I'm not great at making concessions, and things deteriorate until the relationship is poisoned beyond repair."

"Holy crap. I always thought that whole thing about Irish melancholy was a myth."

"I'm serious, Anthony."

"Okay. I get your skepticism. But you need to understand that I'm really good at self-analysis. So what I told you before about what I need to be happy, that's who I am. And as far as making concessions, obviously that's something we'll both have to do to a degree. There's no way around that in a relationship. But I'd never ask you to do something that would impinge on your values. Or what you see as your mission in life." He paused. "You've been blessed with a gift, Theresa. Your enormous capacity to love. And you use it every day, in how you help people. But what about yourself? You say you love me, and I believe you. But to have that stirring inside you, and not follow through on it? Especially knowing that my love for you matches yours for me in every way possible? If that's not wasting a gift, I don't know what is."

She breached the ensuing stillness by resting her chin on a raised knee. "Feel like getting something to eat?"

Piza flung his arms up. "Oh my God! You just did it again."

Her head snapped back. "Did what again?"

"Do you realize that when a crucial juncture arrives in a conversation . . . something that demands you take a stand or whatever . . . you deflect by talking about things food-related? You did it in Jasmine's place in June. And this is the second time you've done it since I got here."

Resignation in her voice, she said, "I know. Tends to give me time to collect my thoughts."

"And is that what you're doing now?"

She delivered a playful, "Right now, I'm just really hungry."

Shaking his head, Piza said, "Sure, let's get something to eat. Shorty's I presume?"

"Only if you want to."

"Okay by me. My only fear is that when Jasmine sees me she might try to hurt me."

"Nah. I'm pretty sure she likes you."

His eyes widened. "Really? She said that?"

"No. But I have a feeling."

"Hmm. Okay. But I'm not sitting with my back to her."

"Fair enough. Let me grab my peacoat."

As they stepped outside, she started buttoning her jacket. "Yikes."

"Yeah. Temperature dropped." After a few steps, he stopped short. "Oh my God."

She spun around toward him. "What? What's wrong?"

Tapping his right temple, he said, "I can't believe I forgot to ask you?"

"Ask me what? What is it?"

"Do you like Chinese food?"

"What? Are you— Yes, I love Chinese food. Was that important enough to scare me half to death?"

He leaned in toward her. "Important? Are you joking?"

Eyes narrowed, she said, "So you're telling me the future of our relationship hinged on moo shu pork?"

"Well, I'd have gone with chicken in black bean sauce, but . . . yes."

They resumed walking.

"You're a strange man."

"You have no idea."

Her laugh dispelled the evening chill as she slipped her hand in his.

THE END

THANK YOU AND FREE STORIES

Thanks so much for reading "The Expiration of Joey and Megan". I sincerely hope you enjoyed it. (I mean seriously, how could you not have?)

With a zillion books floating around these days, reviews are critical to an author's success. So if you have a moment, I'd really appreciate it if you'd leave a short review on the site where you purchased the book, or anywhere else you think it would be appropriate. (I have mixed feelings about bathroom walls but . . . whatever.)

Be sure to visit my website at www.jfpandolfi.com to get FREE short stories.

Thanks again, and be well.

J.F. Pandolfi

ACKNOWLEDGMENTS

Heartfelt thanks to all those who supported me through this second foray into the joyous, yet at times maddening, world of novel-writing.

AJ, you remain the ultimate second set of eyes. Laura and Cheryl, thank you for beta reading the book, and for your insight and continuing encouragement. And a tip of the hat to my fellow writers group members. Despite our meetings being cut off at the book's midpoint by the pandemic, your input was as invaluable as ever.

www.ingramcontent.com/pod-product-compliance
Lightning Source LLC
Chambersburg PA
CBHW051215190726
48288CB00006B/1970